TIME AND TIME AGAIN

Albert Plank

Courtney/Mike —
From Albert —
Hope you enjoy at least
Some of this! Albert Plank
A.K.A.
Mike Wall

PublishAmerica
Baltimore

First printing

ISBN: 1-4137-1027-1
PUBLISHED BY PUBLISHAMERICA, LLLP
www.publishamerica.com
Baltimore

Printed in the United States of America

*This book is dedicated to
all the teachers of chemistry and physics
I've had through the years.*

TIME
ONE

ONE

I don't recall anything about my birth and very few things about the first years of my life. I suppose this is true for most of us who have not had the experience of being regressed under hypnosis in order to be born again. Not that I think this is actually possible, this revisiting of times past with conscious comprehension of the events. I think what is possible is that humans are capable of creating awareness of possible events that are later indistinguishable from real memory.

So even my own memories of the past are called into question. Not just the early traumas that I think I lived through, but even the accuracy of what I witnessed yesterday. What I do recall from childhood involves fear, like the fear of falling. There is a vague recollection of being on a narrow wall several feet above a concrete patio. This memory, if real, could only have come from when I was three or four years old and living in an apartment house on an Air Force base in Germany.

Another memory involves the fear of being left. My family was moving from Germany back to the U.S. and I was in a crib in order to keep me out of the way of the hustle and bustle of packing and loading. I didn't know it, but my crib and myself were to be the last items put into the car. I just recall everyone leaving and the vast emptiness of the room, the quiet, and the sense that my family had gone, and left me behind.

Whether these events actually occurred or whether they are subconscious constructs of basic human fears—a sort of embodiment in thought of nightmares we all share, even as adults—I can't be sure. They could be invisible instincts made into vaguely recallable episodes to give these sometimes irrational fears subtle substance.

There was one event at age six or so that may or may not have occurred. You see it doesn't really matter if the event was real, all that matters was that it seemed like a memory, a recollection of a real event. Even that doesn't amount to much, but what it led to was a feeling, an emotional response that had the impact of a life-changing alteration in perspective.

It was really very minor. It was at night. My house in Orlando, Florida, had a large dark basement that could be entered only through a fairly massive (for a six-year-old) metal-covered hatch at the side of the house. I had to hold this heavy wood and sheet steel doorway up with one hand while starting down the cement stairs and avoiding a trip. It was also important to avoid dropping the door, which would, I was quite sure at the time, produce a head injury severe enough to result in my parents finding my body intact but my brains spread across the floor. Another problem was the darkness.

The light for the basement was a bulb hanging near a wooden support beam that was at the center of the relatively vast open space. I would have to cross this huge expanse of floor, probably littered with snakes, scorpions and a variety of hungry life forms heretofore unknown to man, but known to every child because of their nutritional preference for small boys and girls. The actual distance was probably six to ten feet. The key to success was to memorize the position of the post by the dim and fading light of the closing door and then dash to the location of that held mental image, reach above your head, feel for the otherwise invisible string that hung from the bare bulb and pull it.

Pulling that string resulted in salvation. In the instant flood of photons the real or imagined (what's the difference?) basement horrors were swept away. God forbid that the bulb would be burned out!

I had just lowered the door behind me, I had made it into the dank room without falling or receiving a massive head injury. Now all I had to do to dispel the encroaching monsters was to make it to the light and pull that string.

Contemplating this move was as far as I got.

My eyes were open and staring in the general direction of the beam which was my goal. Not that having my eyes open helped, but it did allow me to see the little light, the little light near where I hoped the post was. Two, three, maybe four inches in diameter, dim, wavering, altering its shape and luminosity as it seemed to ooze along the floor. It had no recognizable form.

As an example of the fallacy of memory, I don't really remember going up the basement stairs, pushing the hatch up ahead of me. I don't recall rushing up the landing to the back door and into the house to get one of my older brothers to venture back into that twilight zone of a basement with me, to determine the exact nature of this phenomenon. I do remember going back into the basement where my brother, with an impressive lack of fear, walked across the floor and turned on the light. Of course I was holding the door open so he could see a little. If it had been pitch black I'm sure he would have been just as tremulous as I.

But there was nothing on the floor but dust. No undiscovered biologic entity, no footprints, no slime trail of deadly poison left behind by the phosphorescent alien.

My brother's mirth did nothing to improve my mood.

So it was probably a phantom and the whole episode may have been constructed in my mind at a later time, a dream perhaps, that when called up from the depths of wherever memories live, was mistaken for something that really happened. As I said, whether it was real was of little import, what mattered was that it induced in me a sense of Uh-Oh. Like 'Uh-Oh, things aren't quite as cut and dry or black and white as I thought.' There may really be some otherness out there that I couldn't see, a place or a reality that can be glimpsed only in rare moments of darkness, with the senses unprepared for input.

It left me wondering. And I've been wondering ever since. What more is there beyond what I see, feel, hear, taste and smell each day? Is there more, and had I stumbled upon a little bit of it in my basement? I still don't know, but it is of no consequence. It was the start.

TWO

I tripped through life just as any other child. My share of triumphs, although I can't recall many, I'm sure there were some, and my share of tragedies and mischief, all of which stand out in my memory like lasers burning into my tender self-esteem. But I at least avoided imprisonment and managed to do well enough in school to induce the school bureaucracy to let me advance and eventually graduate.

Through childhood and most of high school there were no great mysteries, no enlightening spiritual experiences. I didn't solve quadratic equations in my head at age ten, no signs of genius unfortunately. Also no signs of prodigy in the creative arts, and in terms of physical prowess and coordination, I learned early that I was notably deficient in these areas. Not only was I always chosen last in the humiliating team-picking process, but I was usually picked last even for the girl's teams. The boys already knew of my excellence at dropping balls of various types so I was ignominiously banished to the female side of the playing field. This actually suited me because my life was mostly in my head anyway and I really had no desire to be athletic. Besides, it was at a very young age that I learned that girls were much more interesting than boys, anatomically for sure, but I thought mentally as well.

This notably unnotable existence went on for about 17 years when something did actually happen. Well, once again I'm stuck with saying that I recall an event that profoundly changed my life, but whether it really happened, I'll never know. These confusing apologies over my confused memories may make more sense to you when you reach the end of this story. Then again....

I had gone to bed. I had not taken or smoked any substances that would otherwise have altered my mental state. I had certainly done so in the past, I was no slacker in this regard. I was a product of my time, a proud long-haired hippie peace freak, against the establishment and all. I had not yet however

10

ventured into hallucinogens. Marijuana was about the extent of my rebellious experimentation, maybe some beer. At any rate, what happened I could not attribute to drugs or flashbacks. That was my conclusion at the time anyway and it made me take what happened seriously. If I had been under the influence of some neurologically active chemical, I would have dismissed it, but I surely would have sought out and taken that chemical again!

I think I recall all of the events of that night. What occurred was indescribable and by describing it, it becomes somewhat concrete, less mystic, less spiritual if you will. It's one of those explaining-color-to-a-blind-man kind of things. I can't really put it into words, but when I try, I inevitably limit the experience, narrow it, confine it, demean it even.

For example, take that unbelievably complex and beautiful interaction between photons and retinal cells that produces an explosion of visual cortex activity which is interpreted as an awe-inspiring sunset or an incomprehensibly large hole in the ground like the Grand Canyon. Trying to describe such visions with words is never adequate. Thus by attempting to clothe this otherworldly experience in language for you to read, I diminish the memory of the experience. Not only do you get a mere verbose interpretation of an uninterpretable event, but even within myself, the event becomes more of a sequence of descriptive rhetoric rather than an experience. And the more I tell this story the less like an experience it becomes and the more like something I made up using vague descriptive terminology.

I say all this in prelude because I wish you to know at what cost I reveal these matters. Putting this experience into words becomes like remembering a Mozart violin concerto by saying: "It starts out with a frequency of 440 hertz then goes up two full tones for a brief time then it drops down three and a half tones and stays there for a while before dropping the additional half tone to settle at a harmonic frequency to the first tone." What was beautiful music to me becomes more of a story of little consequence or interest. I myself lose the beauty of it while you receive at best a mere shadow of what really transpired. All of us lose.

I was positioned in a comfortable way, which I don't think has anything to do with anything except that in being comfortable I was able to accomplish being immobile for a prolonged period of time. I remember a train of thought that began with a typically naïve adolescent sort of philosophic inquiry. "What are the logical consequences of making the assumption that a God exists?" In other words, if you assume there is a God, then what purely logical conclusions about our reality can be derived from this assumption? I suppose

11

I thought I would later pursue the logical consequences of the opposite assumption....what if God does not exist?

That night however was devoted to thoughts of the implications of divinity. I remember the sequential steps in my mental exploration; their content is not important and revealing them would probably result in you thinking me more a fool than you already do. The net effect however was a deeper and deeper meditation into the nature of a universe with a God.

A deeper meditation—there is the key. All of you in search of enlightenment, all you need do is learn to meditate. It's easy, you simply keep motionless in whatever position suits you and contemplate one thing until you get there. From this you will assume that on the evening I've been discussing, I became enlightened. Well, perhaps. Unfortunately, enlightenment is not a permanent state and actually may not be able to exist in our material reality. Therefore, even if I were "enlightened" I certainly am not now, nor can I with any hope of clarity describe it.

There was a process however. From thoughts to deep unknowing, possibly even sleep. Then from deep unknowing to a sense of awareness of myself as a living body, but one that could not move. Initially, I sensed that it was there, but I had no control over it and a fear developed that I was paralyzed. This fear made me want to wake or move, and with enough will I could have, I guess, and thus been freed from this experience, but I suppressed the fear and remained still.

My whole being seemed to travel up and center in my head. Now I felt as if I had actually lost contact with my body even though I had a sense that I was still in it. Everything that was "me" was concentrated near the top of my head and "me" was no longer in the rest of my body.

Again came a wave of fear, I suppressed it and moved on. There was this vibration, this static charge, this sound, this sense of motion. It was almost painful, as if my teeth would rattle from my head. From here the fear almost overcame me, but the motion had begun.

The movement out. Was it through a tunnel? Toward a light? Perhaps it can be described as such, but no description from this point on can accurately relay this other reality into our everyday experience. All the mystic writings of all time, seemingly dissimilar, are simply attempts to describe this state to no avail. The great prophetic writings of the world's religions might as well be, and probably should be, considered nonsense, because all the wisdom they seem to contain, and the world they attempt to describe, is nothing compared to what really happens when you leave your body.

In a universe trapped by time, I cannot describe timelessness. The air was both light and dark. Matter was both solid yet translucent and penetrable. There were no hands upon the clock. There was no distance I couldn't see. All that I wished to know was known, every question I even began to contemplate was answered. The very reason behind all existence was obvious and the humor of it was apparent and laughter continued what seemed to be movement toward a loving.

Cares fell away, reality fell away, nothing mattered more than the total immersion in that sense of being. But there was also some sense of the material world. Everything seemed to be pastels, or was it? If there was light then there might be colors, but if it was dark, the colors should disappeared. If there were both light and dark or neither, then there was only what could be described in this world as shimmering pastels, hovering between reds and greens and blues and the ubiquitous gray that nighttime brings.

In the distance, through the walls that I thought were solid, were others, other humans sleeping in the house, bright patterns in the near distance seen through the ephemeral dry wall and studs. My parents. Then there was myself. Yes, turning I saw what I interpreted as my body in what I perceived as a bed and I looked to be dead. Now there was fear, fear I couldn't seem to override. Even with the lure of all-loving-all-knowing hovering within reach, the fear pulled me back.

Very quickly, the sound, the rushing, the motion, and with a jolt, as if my spirit was solid and had fallen into the container of my body with abrupt deceleration, I was in my room. My body had not moved. My breath was rapid and my heart was racing. I had perspired enough that I felt the moisture in the sheets. I should have gotten up, splashed my face with cool water, stretched, laughed about my utterly realistic nightmare and gone back to sleep. But I stayed still. Inside myself I knew that if I stayed perfectly still and returned to my contemplation, I would return to the place from which I had just come.

Indeed, in a few moments, as the physiology of calm reclaimed control over my heart and lungs, I again found myself entirely in my head. Then the vibration, the sound, the movement, the sense of passing out through the top of my skull, and there I hovered.

The same place, the same timelessness, the same all-encompassing sense of well-being, as in "all is right with the world" and "all you need is love" sort of wrapped up together. I seemed to rise higher, out of my house and into the air, toward distant stars and that infinite Thing that was out there that I could be a part of or one with if I could just break free. But there, down through the roof of my house, there was a body on a twin-sized bed and the body was mine.

Even as far as I had come I could feel the fear. And the fear drew me back again. Like air rushing into a vacuum, I felt like I was being sucked back into my body, once again panting, sweaty and tachycardic. Still I refused to move. Again I went through the paralysis, the cephalic confinement, the rush into the other world. Even further toward that place of oneness I rose, almost into the stars, all my desires and questions satisfied.

No joy, the fear again was there to trap me. It hunted me down, netted me, bound me and carried me back to my breathless body and deposited me back into that corpse that resembled me so closely.

What time was it? How long had this been going on? Was I ill toward death? Was I having nightmares the likes of which I had never experienced before? Why was I exhausted?

I was exhausted. As if this mental journey had been a physical marathon, my body felt the fatigue as did my mind and perhaps my spirit. But I still had no control over my physical being. This then became my focus. Not to stay still and leave again, I had no energy left for that. The focus was to move, to regain control, to be unequivocally alive again. All of the mental energy I had left was put to one task. If I could just wiggle my right big toe, I knew I would be OK. And move it I did, although the effort seemed Herculean.

Instantly I was awake in my room. I sat up, stretched, looked around in wonder at how solid everything was, how the clock had hands, how the walls had substance which prevented me from seeing my sleeping parents in their room across the hall. Now all the things had colors and textures that were once again a fixed reflection of their chemical composition. I looked back at my moist sheets and did not see myself still lying on them. That was most reassuring. Perhaps I was still alive. Perhaps.

THREE

Aftermath. I told my closest friend about this amazing experience. I knew he would understand. He and I shared the deepest insights, the same birthday (whatever that might mean), and he was and is still, the only person with whom I ever communicated ideas without the need for words.

He laughed at me. Made fun of my experience, belittled it, thought I had gotten into "some pretty good stuff" and wanted some! Thus started the isolation. I knew I would never fit in with anyone because as soon as I began telling them of this great life-changing, life-enhancing event and realization, I would be rejected as a fool, a dreamer or even insane. So I kept it to myself for the most part and went on about my business; that is, growing up and becoming a responsible adult. I finished high school, took an extra quarter off before starting college, worked as an upholsterer's apprentice and saved enough money to buy a killer stereo system and then went off to the University of Florida.

The dorm was 100 years old, a tower, a central stairway with two, two-person rooms and a collective bathroom on each of four floors. I was on the second with a window overlooking a courtyard with crisscrossing walks. One walkway led directly from my dorm to the Rathskeller on the opposite side of the plaza. This was the on-campus beer and movie house, a place much frequented but of poor repute. At that time in Florida the legal drinking age was 18 and drinking was not barred from campus, so this stale-smelling place was an accepted part of the university life and indeed I even remember going into the building at least once.

I didn't really want any part of that scene, although I must confess, I found it entertaining when large numbers of males and females would exit the beer hall and run around the plaza below my window completely nude. The females were of particular interest, for at that time I had still not explored their most intriguing physical characteristics to any depth. This was at the

15

peak of the "streaking" phase of the mid-seventies. I did a lot of watching but no participating, and my love affair with alcohol was in the future, but by this time I had burned out on pot.

I got to where smoking would simply make me cough, provide me not with a high, but with a headache and in addition rob me of all motivation. I felt that "reality," whatever it was, needed my full attention for some reason that none of us are allowed to fully grasp. I was still a hippie. Long hair kept in a ponytail, and was by now very anti-sports and decried the fact that a significant portion of my tuition went to finance the lavish dorms and huge high-protein meals of the football team. (A little sour grapes perhaps? I didn't think so then.)

I was a biochemistry major, and this was at a time when people weren't really sure what biochemistry was. I was academically oriented but my primary pursuit was the study of religion and philosophy. I was not doing the classic "finding myself" thing. I somehow ended up with a good sense of myself as a worthwhile human being, but I wouldn't let on to others about this. I was driven to find the meaning behind the experience I had and described ad nauseam in the previous chapter. I learned a great deal, I think.

For one thing, I learned that my experience was far from unique. I'm not sure in which order I went, probably none, but I read everything I could find having to do with religion, philosophy and spirituality. I read about Edgar Casey and the concept of a universal consciousness. Obviously this was an oversimplification and his claims to contact this consciousness for the benefit of himself and others were laughable. In an historical context I learned that his teachings were in line with the vast number of religious and spiritual charlatans and pseudo-scientific cults of that time.

One of these, centered in a small town in Florida had "proven," to their own satisfaction anyway, that the Earth was not round but that it actually curved in the opposite direction of the accepted view. Their "science" taught that the world was a hollow sphere, that we lived on the inner surface of this sphere and that the sun was at its center. Fortunately this cult also believed in strict sexual abstinence, so they have since ceased to exist.

Besides religious cults there were also communal experiments underfoot in America, communism before Karl Marx. Many American communes were started; at least one of which is still in evidence today as the Oneida Silverware Company. This corporation was an outgrowth of the Oneida Community.

The Mormons with their claims that the Americas were settled by a lost tribe of Israelites and that the American Indians were their descendants played into the popular belief at the time that new archeological finds in South and Central America had supposed Egyptian influence. This has now been disproved but the extraordinary luck of an extraordinary con-artist established a religion that is growing, wealthy and influential today. Fortunately their efforts to establish the Kingdom of Deseret failed. They did the next best thing though. They abandoned their prophet's teachings of God-decreed polygamy in order to become the state of Utah, still enigmatic to this day.

The Jehovah's Witnesses also got their start in these tumultuous times. Times where many feared the end, the apocalypse, the coming Armageddon and were looking for answers. Times when most men's knowledge of the world around them was so limited that any explanation of their mysterious reality could be proposed and believed regardless of how bizarre. Since there were so few established facts, nothing could be disproved and anything could be proved. The era can best be seen as a remarkable illustration of human gullibility.

Just like our current time. I don't really mean to pick on the culture of the mid- and late-1800s or the Mormons or Jehovah's Witnesses per say, but one thing my studies revealed was that there was, and still is, no shortage of charismatic humans without morals. Unfortunately there was, and also still is, no shortage of humans who believed in these con-artists and follow them even unto death.

Over millennia really, these prophets, cults and religions came and went along with their followers. Millions died or were killed for their beliefs. On every continent, in every time, none of them accomplished anything other than divisiveness and murder.

And I came to see gullibility as one of the most basic defining characteristics of man.

I thus began rejecting almost everything I read about religion and philosophy in relation to divinity or in relation to a path to follow in life, a path to supposed Godhead. I began looking for some underlying message, the essence of what all these enlightened or unenlightened/unscrupulous people taught through time.

I could not accept any one dogma, although at times I called myself Hindu and joined the Self Realization Fellowship, led and inspired by Paramahansa Yogananda. From that group I learned meditation techniques that led me to the conclusion that meditation is simple but that it was made purposefully and immensely obscure by Hindu and Buddhist teachers so that Americans would keep having to pay more and more to learn more, on an endless trek toward an essentially unobtainable enlightenment. Meditation, and the enlightenment it promised, became unfathomable and virtually unobtainable goals for the average American.

To me it became an almost daily event. It got to the point where if I assumed a supine position at any time of the day, I would slip out of my body, never to the degree of that first time but out none the less. Sometimes I would get stuck in one phase or the other, paralysis, in my head, stuck with one part in and one part out, stuck in that vibrational state where it felt like my head would shake apart.

Sometimes there would be peace out there, other times there would be "bad vibes." Sometimes I would feel a presence that came across as evil to me and sometimes I felt it close by when I was partway in and partway out of my body. Sometimes I'd felt this presence on my "back." I would then have to "wrestle" this being for possession of my body. An empty body was apparently a vessel that could be filled by any consciousness that happened by in that timeless world.

I became afraid, I began to fight the experience. It became a damn nuisance to try to take a nap and be transported to this alien place where I got the distinct feeling I didn't belong. I came up with an analogy.

We are land-dwelling, air-breathing animals, perfectly adapted for our environment, as are thousands of other land-dwelling, air-breathing life forms. Under the oceans are thousands of oxygen-extracting, aquatic animals perfectly adapted to their environment. Leaving your body prior to the, in some way, appropriate time was like suddenly being transported several hundred feet under water. You weren't meant to be there. There were certainly things of immense beauty there and you might be able to survive for a brief time, but you could not stay. And there were sharks…beings perfectly adapted to the underwater world that you were alien to, an alien that looked like lunch.

So I learned to stop meditating, a practice that is tempting but deceptively dangerous. I'm sure there are some who think they can go "out there" and maintain control, but I don't believe it. My belief? The original inhabitant of such a person's body drowned and was eaten by the sharks and the entity that now produced locomotion in that collection of muscle and bone was from another world. That being could exist here because our reality was and is a subset of theirs. We cannot travel for long beyond the parentheses that define our limited set.

In spite of the sometimes weird mysticism and the seemingly real potential of demonic possession, I continued to study religion and began to feel that all of these belief systems held a kernel of truth, even those that were obviously corrupt. It appeared that there must be some partial or partially hidden truth present in order to attract followers. This "truth" was recognized on an unconscious level I think, and then twisted into any form, even evil. Aside from cults, obscure philosophies and spiritualists, I also delved into mainstream religions.

In the Bhagavad-Gita and other ancient Hindu texts I found descriptions of my out-of-body experiences, but in a cultural context that was foreign to me. In the Koran I found descriptions of travel outside the body. In the Tibetan Book of the Dead, as well as the Egyptian, I found descriptions of my "religious" experience but again so heavily clothed in past and alien cultures and inadequate translations that it could hardly be seen.

I was for a time a born-again Christian and spoke in tongues. I found in the Bible, descriptions of out-of-body experiences I could recognize but that were once again obscured by culture and interpretation. In Isaiah, in Ezekiel and in Revelations. The now seemingly universal message was there also, particularly in the teachings of Jesus.

In the Tao te Ching I saw the message, clothed in beauty and clear in the contradictions. It was getting easier to spot the small portion of what may be truth contained in all these writings. In the sayings of Confucius, in the religion of the Navajo, in the writings of Carlos Castanedas and everywhere I looked I began to see the same basic concepts.

All these things so sacred, so mystical, men could hardly speak of them. Mere men had to resort to words so twisted to try to convey the perfect and perfectly obvious that wars were fought and millions were killed because people perceived differences when there were none.

I came to believe that I had a pretty good grasp of the underlying message in all this and that I had learned all I was going to from the study of the most sacred of man's literature. It would be a while before I could express this truth to my satisfaction, but at least I was aware of what it might be. I eventually got the basic messages down to four words but even that wasn't of sufficient clarity. Here's a clue though—if you are reading about religion and philosophy, the more words there are in the text that supposedly answers all the questions, the less likely you are to find those answers. Brevity is next to Godliness.

But what of science? I was becoming a scientist. Logical, rational, able to separate the reality wheat from the obscuring chaff of unreality, to see through the Maya.

Bullshit.

I had decided however that one way to better myself was to help others. I threw my huge library of religious and philosophic texts into the trash, which took many trips over several days, and changed my major to nursing.

I finished my bachelor's degree in nursing, married my first wife and worked for six years as an RN before giving in to the growing fear that I wasn't doing what I was supposed to be. Throwing caution to the wind, I returned to college and finally did get a degree in chemistry. This was however only a stepping stone to my real goal of getting into medical school. I accomplished this feat also and graduated but it was not until I started the year-long torture referred to as internship that I really hit my stride.

I had an advantage. I was older, more mature (?) and due to my nursing background, more experienced than my fellow interns. I worked hard, read everything and became outstanding. I hit a grand slam in fact. I was unanimously elected intern of the year and I won the award for best medical record keeping and otherwise made a clean sweep of all the honors that were afforded the interns that year. It was kind of embarrassing. I had to go up to the podium so many times I began to feel kind of ridiculous. This sense of the ridiculous was made even stronger by the fact that my wife was expressing her extreme pride in me.

You see, it was just prior to this that I contracted a venereal disease from my spouse and mother of my three perfect children. I, of course, being monogamous and an astute diagnostician, realized that if I caught it from her, then she must have gotten it from someone else. Her pride in me was not sufficient, it seemed, to keep her with me. Thus this marriage ended. I have never yet reached a level of competence or achievement that compares to that year. It introduced me to loneliness, to alcohol as an escape, to coasting through life, at least until the events of the rest of this book unfolded.

My study of medicine also brought me into close contact with death, or more particularly, near death. I actually spent some years as the head of a resuscitation team. If any patient in the hospital died, it was my job to try to bring them back. Sometimes it worked, and sometimes I would hang around to find out where the patient had been while they were pulseless, breathless and lifeless. Some recalled events with many similarities and not unlike my own mystical experiences of years past. I began reading again, everything I could find about near-death experiences and found them to be the same as the descriptions of the enlightened place, the breathless state, samadhi, the out-of-body experience.

All of these sources of information were attempting to grapple with a reality beyond our own, one that won't fit into ours, as in the way a three-dimensional object cannot exist in a two-dimensional world. (I read the book *Flatland* by Edwin Abbott.) Thus the confusion. If what exists beyond cannot be expressed in words then attempting to do so will only lead to frustration, misunderstanding, the elaboration of belief systems that can only hope to be partially true and will appear to be different even though they are from the same source. This apparent difference and each group's belief that they and only they have the real truth accounts for most of the suffering and death on our planet in the past and that which is ongoing in the present is a damn shame.

As my medical career progressed I did accomplish a few things in spite of drinking nightly. I finished my residency in internal medicine and after only three lackadaisical failed attempts equally lackadaisically passed my internal medicine board exams. Interestingly, on the strength of past accomplishments I think, I became a vice-chairman of the department of medicine in my somewhat prestigious teaching hospital and was given the title of clinical associate professor of medicine. A friend of mine liked me well enough to add my name to his book as a co-author, so I became published, lectured and was sought after for TV and radio spots. I was a participant in a preventive medicine program where an internationally known businessman came for an exam and by serendipity I found this great man's prostate cancer, thus supposedly saving his life. The notoriety added to my relative fame.

But being a famous physician was not my fate. Throughout this time I felt at a loss. There was something missing. The alcohol was always there. The isolation was there. The knowledge that I had experienced nirvana and couldn't talk about it was always there. I had actually communicated my experience to a few people along the way. I did have a small circle of friends and a reasonable relationship with my neighbors. The people I talked philosophy with were of a similar bent, philosophical, and it was either entertaining to discuss these issues or a relief. It was amazing how after more than 20 years, discussing my experience on that night when I was 17 still made me anxious, sweaty and with fluttering heart.

The feeling that I should be doing more to help others was still there. This sense of wanting to help other people led to my next great downfall. You see, medicine had by then been taken over by businessmen with a very malignant attitude, one that put profit on a pedestal far above concerns for the welfare of mere people. The only way to enhance profit was to make physicians—essentially owned by the now vertically integrated, monopolizing, health maintenance organizations—see more and more patients per day.

My belief was that it took time to really get to know a person, to approach them as unique individuals and work, not just to cure or treat their various ills, but to prevent future health problems. Work to keep them as healthy as possible rather than waiting for them to show up in the midst of a medical crisis that I may or may not be able to help them survive.

Thus I ran into conflict with the money mongers that hired and fired. My contract to supply medical services for my particular organization was not renewed. I was then not only alone, but was unemployed.

It was idealism that kept me going. I thought I could start my own health care company and provide excellent and prevention-oriented medical care to my fellow humans. I did this, but even with the influx of a relative fortune from a remarkably good friend, the business failed financially. The insurance companies upon which all people depended to cover all their health care needs did not pay for prevention. They would not pay for prevention, but they would pay without objection for the astronomically expensive interventions required to treat the diseases that I could have prevented in the first place and for a relative pittance.

Thus I became not only alone and unemployed but bankrupt also!

It was about this time that I burned out on alcohol. Drinking no longer offered me refuge from my pitiful existence. It made me sweat, made it impossible to sleep and my hangovers would start within an hour or so of the onset of a drinking binge. It would no longer make me giddy and forgetful of how far down I had come. It simply added to the misery. So I quit.

What was left? Time, I had plenty of time. And I made more and more of it. I became addicted to time, time to myself, time alone, time without the ever-present obligations to creditors and past patients who still sought me out for advice, free advice at that. I put a trashcan on my front porch and all my mail went directly into it. I disconnected my phones for long periods to rediscover the bliss of peace and quiet, of privacy. I had a little money stashed away so I could survive for a time without working but I had to be extremely careful.

I became a vegetarian, not because of any deep philosophic feelings, but because it was cheap. I subsisted on mixtures of beans and grains. There was a time in my life when I thought about accumulating wealth as a way of life but money had lost its charm for me. What little I had was spent on necessities only. I thought of being a monk also, but I could not disconnect myself from my family, particularly my children, enough to accomplish this. I also contemplated pursuing pure science, but I couldn't believe that true understanding was achievable through the religion of the scientific method.

I also rediscovered the bliss of reading for pleasure again. Mysteries, science fiction, technothrillers. And I rediscovered my love of the basic sciences and my love of learning. Now the tragedies of my past didn't seem so bad. Without them I would not have found the time to surf the Web, constantly viewing and reviewing the latest findings in chemistry, physics, math, archeology, astronomy, biology and medicine.

In isolation for a period of years I studied, and as with the study of religion, in all these sciences there was a Truth, but it was hidden. Hidden by the specialization of scientists, none of whom looked at the big picture. Each was stuck in his or her obscure and esoteric universe, a universe that was just a small lab on a campus at a university somewhere on Earth. Each found little pieces of the puzzle. It was as if there existed a complete jigsaw puzzle to be seen, but all of the pieces were jealously and separately guarded so that no one could actually look at the whole beautiful illustration.

And there were many misconceptions and incorrect assumptions. Each of these led many scientists down dead-end paths. Theories with beauty and symmetry both in content and in their mathematics were twisted by newly discovered but misinterpreted phenomenon. To explain these problems the concepts became difficult to grasp, blurred, distorted and the math became tortured, esoteric, beyond the comprehension of but a few, no beauty, no symmetry and in fact, ugly.

A good rule of thumb, if you are trying to explain some new scientific finding based on existing theories and your math becomes ugly, then either the theories are wrong or you have misinterpreted the findings. Look in a different place.

In spending days and weeks and months in isolation, learning and integrating seemingly divergent and unrelated facts, I stumbled upon beauty. I found symmetry. I found the one scientific Truth that unified all physical phenomena into a whole. Wholly comprehensible, glorious, beyond imagination and in fact infinite. So grand that the infinite became possible, even simple.

I could see the equation of the universe from Big Bang to the end of existence and I could see in this relatively simple math that infinite amounts of energy were attainable, yes infinite. Not just attainable but usable! It all had to do with time and a basic misconception about time that all men made simply because we perceived time as ticks of a clock, as a movement from birth through aging to death, as the predictable rotation of the Earth that makes the sun seem to rise and set each day.

Who could have guessed that time was the missing element, an actual vector force, another form of matter and energy that can be harnessed and studied and even converted to matter, converted to energy, even infinite amounts of energy. The trick was that if you wanted to use an infinite amount of energy, you had to use it in an infinitely small amount of time. Simple.

FOUR

In instantaneous transformations of matter, an infinite amount of energy is required, but as long as the event is in fact instantaneous, it has no impact on the physical universe! I could see the balance.

Astronomers could find only half of the material of the universe and theorized that the rest was "cold dark matter," invisible cosmic dust or anti-matter tucked off somewhere in the universe where it could do no harm. They tortured themselves over explanations that could not make sense because they were all held prisoner by misconceptions about the nature of time.

They looked with interest at the fact that half of all that could be found in the universe could be measured as energy, essentially photons, and that half could be found in matter; molecules, atoms and subatomic particles. They even thought it was a temporary state of which we happened to be witness. And even though this measurable matter and energy only totaled to one half of what could explain the structure of the universe, they continued to bang their heads against a wall trying to explain a whole universe while only contemplating half of it.

The missing element was time. Finally someone did an experiment with a particle accelerator that seemed to indicate that time had directionality, but they still didn't grasp the implications. I did. Time is a vector force, a form of energy that results in seeming directionality in the movement of matter. In other words, the moon was over there ten minutes ago, now it is over here. This is how we discern time, but it is only motion, motion controlled by an innate property of matter called gravitation. Gravitation controls the motion of matter and that motion we perceive as time. Gravitation and time are the same thing, the same property of the universe called by different names, like solid water is called ice and gaseous water steam. Because it is in another state does not alter the fact that it is H_2O.

Time/gravity is instantaneous. The sun produces photons that travel at the mere speed of light. If the sun blinked out it would take about eight minutes before we learned that there were no more photons coming from the place where our sun used to shine. If the sun rekindled its fire, it would take eight minutes for the light to once again warm our planet and sustain all life. But what of gravity? How long does it take for the gravitational effects of the moon to reach Earth? If another moon suddenly appeared next to the original, the photons reflected from it would take a moment to arrive, but how long would it be before that mass of matter impacted our tides?

The answer is no time. Gravity is time. It is an innate property of matter that exerts its effects in all directions, throughout the universe, instantaneously, simply because it exists. The speed of light may be a limiting velocity as far as the movement of matter as we know it goes, but instantaneous travel, travel at infinite speed, moving any distance in no time, was possible. It requires only an infinite amount of energy, which according to my calculations was readily available.

Time can be converted into matter, as can energy. These three states of being are interchangeable. It's part of what happens at a source of massive gravitational or time energy, that is to say, a black hole. If you take all of the known matter in the universe, add to it all energy detectable in the universe after it has been converted to matter and then add all the matter that could be produced from time/gravity, you will come up with the amount of substance that explains our universe. It's not all that difficult. A simple diagram suffices:

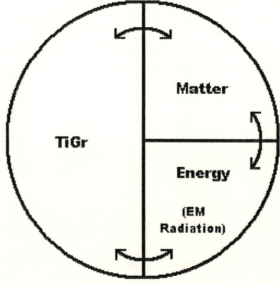

This concept explains all the forces at work in the universe, it unifies the mathematical model of the universe into one beautiful and symmetric equation that explains black holes, time travel, where all the antimatter is, where all the missing material in the universe is, the shape of the universe and even what is beyond the universe!

This power is harnessable. Just as Einstein's equations led us to the harnessing of nuclear power, this model can lead us to unlimited power, to the control of time, to travel anywhere in the universe and perhaps beyond the universe. Beyond the universe to that place we go when we leave our bodies. The place without time, the place beyond time, the place where God may live. (It sounds good but it didn't turn out to be true, but I'm getting ahead of myself, something that starts to happen quite frequently in what I still mistakenly call the near future.)

It took many years and much hard work to bring the theory of relativity to a practical (or perhaps immensely impractical) application. Thus it will take time and effort to reach the point where the practical application of harnessing the energy of gravity/time will become possible. It is this application, the construction of a device that would allow for it, that came to consume me.

I had three related problems however.

The first was financial. Some of the materials I would need to build this device were expensive beyond what I could currently afford. I would have to be very creative to assemble the needed components.

The second problem concerned some theoretical aspects of the project that I had not yet clarified. I assumed or hoped that these problems would be resolved as the project moved forward. As it was, there were several mathematical expressions that needed work. They did not yet combine to form a unity. I could sense the answers but lacked the knowledge to solve these equations and proceed. This did not need to inhibit me from starting, but at some point, if I did not find solutions, it would limit the completion of construction of the time/gravity power supply or its implementation in a useful form.

I would not be able to construct the device or power supply I had envisioned in my head that would transform time/gravity into matter and/or energy. This in turn would prevent me from building a vehicle, powered by this device that would be capable of travel to any point in the universe instantaneously. A vehicle that would give me infinite power.

This was the third dilemma. What would I do with such power if I did indeed succeed? I would like to think that I would use it in ways that would benefit mankind. I would like to think that I would share it with the world. But what would the world do with infinite power?

If the past were any indication, mankind would use it as a destructive force. I had come to believe that another of the very basic characteristics of mankind was and is self-directed violence. Genocide, ethnic cleansing and the use of weapons of any kind to destroy perceived enemies even if it meant our own destruction as well. How could I trust mankind with such power?

How could I trust myself with such power? I had no illusions about being altruistic. I was as capable of being corrupted as any man. An excellent example of this comes from my own profession. The well-educated, dedicated and esteemed physicians in pre-World War II Germany joined the Nazi party in greater numbers than any other professional group and it was these physicians who were placed in charge of the camps where mass murder would evolve into a process of such efficiency as to be nearly an art form.

Doctors would listen to Mozart in the evenings while reading the finest literature, sipping the finest wines and occasionally looking up to appreciate the fine stolen art on their walls. In the day they would don their white coats and see how many men, women and children they could kill by forcing needles directly into their hearts and pumping phenol into that pumping chamber. There were rewards for higher numbers, honor and respect for those who could murder more. (Read *The Nazi Doctors* by Robert Lifton.)

Was I really different from these men that if given such power I would not become corrupted? Infinite power corrupts infinitely, a frightening extension of the cliché.

One additional small problem. I had to come up with a name for this new substance—time/gravity. I tried many combinations and permutations and finally settled on Tigr. That's correct, it's pronounced Tee Eye double Guh Er. You see there is humor in all things. If you choose to pronounce it as Tiger, it then embodies the grace, beauty and power of the animal. Either way it fits. I preferred the comedic form.

In laughter there is insight, a connection to the world of joy beyond. I remember laughing while out of my body when I saw how simple and beautiful the reason for the existence of the universe was. I can't of course recall that reason now, but it was humorous at the time. This connection between humor and the beyond is what I believe Herman Hesse was implying when he wrote that all that was needed to enter the magic theater was a hearty laugh (*Steppenwolf*).

With the minor problem of what to call gravity/time solved, I was ready to begin my project. I could at least get a good start and hope the other problems would resolve themselves over time.

FIVE

I began by digging. I made a sub-basement beneath my house where I could experiment without being observed. I felt like the classic mad scientist. I explained to my neighbors that I was finishing and enlarging my existing basement as a cover for all of the dirt I was removing. My neighbors were never around during the day, since unlike me, they had to work, so no one was really aware of the volume of dirt I removed. If they had kept track they would have been able to calculate that I added a space about as large as the entire previously existing structure, about 2,000 square feet of useable space hidden behind a secret door in the basement that was already present. Not huge, but a place I could go to be alone and work. Of course I did expand and enlarge my existing basement. I had to. I knew there would be a time when my neighbors would want to see the results of my remodeling, so I also ended up with a pretty nice "public" basement also; overall not a bad little project.

I needed energy. I could draw some from existing electrical circuits, but I had a feeling that eventually I might be drawing enough current to make the little wheel in my electric meter go ballistic and launch itself into orbit. This turned out to be untrue, but I thought I might need vast quantities of electrical energy to achieve my goal. I turned to methane-powered fuel cells. There was no easily detectable exhaust, the fuel was easily compressed and transported to my lab and they were not noisy. I bought a small one, tore it apart and figured out how to build them and then built a few more myself. I was able to generate enough electricity to power the basic equipment I would need. A computer, some power tools, lighting, a few appliances of convenience and hopefully, eventually a device that would align itself to the gravitational center of the planet and then resonate with the Tigr of Earth and allow it to be channeled into useful work.

My mathematical model indicated that I needed a super-cooled, super-conducting mass of Bose-Einstein Condensate (BEC) contained within, and whose electrical current was aligned with a strong magnetic field. This field would further more have to be contained within an electrically charged metallic structure in the shape of a parabolic reflector. Seemed simple enough!

The magnetic field could, I think, be generated by a super-cooled, super-conducting coil of wire similar to those used in magnetic resonance imagers in most large hospitals, only it would be a long thin coil or narrow ellipse rather than a torus. I would obviously be in need of some extremely cold liquid nitrogen (easy to get) to encase some even more extraordinarily cold liquid helium (not so easy to get) and would need to generate a significant vacuum (pretty tough).

This vacuum would have to be essentially the absolute absence of matter, other than the BEC, and would be needed to surround the near absolute zero soup of this material. It would have to be encased within a field that would suspend the condensate within an area that other matter could not penetrate. You see, in a space where there is no matter surrounded by matter, even a steel, platinum or ceramic container would evaporate a few molecules into that space if there weren't some means of totally isolating it. In this space I would need about 10 grams of BEC present for about 10 to 15 seconds. Thus far, scientists had only been able to produce unimaginably small amounts of this stuff and it only existed for a few nanoseconds to a few milliseconds at best.

The low temperature provided by the liquid helium would need to be enhanced by pulses from a laser directed at the condensate in such a way as to knock off the last few remaining energetic particles removing what minuscule amount of energy was left at a degree or two above absolute zero. This is where I needed some real energy. My own little nuclear reactor would be nice but the price was a bit above my budget. The laser would bring the temperature of the BEC to within a few billionths of a degree above absolute zero. Theoretically.

I had my work cut out for me.

Lasers would also be used to contain and compartmentalize the mixture of free-flowing subatomic particles. By creating a grid of laser beams of the same frequency I could produce standing waves that would form little pockets, sort of like an egg carton made from photons. In these little wells of light, the BEC would pool and organize.

In spite of all the precision and theoretic absolutes required by the mathematics, reality is not likely to be so demanding. I had a feeling that even if the condensate was not completely isolated and a few stray atoms or molecules entered the containment area, these compounds would simply degenerate into their subatomic components also and add to the mix. This goes along with my theory that things work when they're supposed to simply because that's the way things work.

It's like genetic engineering. It's not like you have to physically go into the nucleus of a cell and with some kind of microscopic scalpel (a carbon nano-tube perhaps), cut the DNA at the appropriate spot and "suture" the new DNA in place. If this were the case it would be impossible. You would have to perform this surgery on every cell in the lungs of a patient with cystic fibrosis, for example, to correct that genetic abnormality. Not only would the procedure be impossibly small, but it would have to be repeated about a billion times in each patient. The surgeon and the patient would die of other causes long before the patient could be cured.

Fortunately, all you had to do was take the correct sequence of nucleic acids, the DNA coding for the normal gene that resulted in the production of surfactant in the lungs, and clone it in vast numbers. This was simple to do and fully mechanized. You then had to insert the strands of DNA into a viral protein coat that was designed by evolution to take up and then inject genetic material into eucaryotic cells, the kinds of cells of which our bodies are made up. By inhaling a few million of these viral particles, you introduced the DNA into millions of lung cells simultaneously. Once the DNA is in a cell, the cell just sort of knows what to do with it, not because it has some innate intelligence, but because, fortunately for the sufferers of genetic diseases, that's just what cells do.

The DNA is transported to and into the nucleus, where such substances belong. The chemical systems within the nucleus are able to recognize the DNA, identify the sequence of nucleotides, determine where in the vast human genome this particular sequence belonged and put it there. Once in place, the new DNA is transcribed and translated into the correct enzymes that then accurately produce the missing component, surfactant, and violà, the patient is cured.

I was counting on this "nature of things to work simply because that's the way things are supposed to work" concept to help me out where the calculations got vague or where the exacting limits of the theoretical physics were beyond my technical ability. Everything was sort of approximated to the ideal and then I hoped that when everything was in position it would sort of jiggle itself into just the right orientation and simply do the right thing because that's how the universe was.

I got to where I had a grid of copper electroplated with platinum shaped into as perfect a parabolic form as possible. Don't ask me how many catalytic converters I had to salvage from wrecked cars to get enough platinum to plate the copper. Platinum wasn't the kind of stuff I could go down to Sears and buy a couple pounds. For my purposes I needed a relatively small amount to cover the copper and prevent corrosion. It was enough that I couldn't afford to go out and buy it. I was living off of beans as it was, and didn't have much to spend on precious metals. So I spent many a night in junkyards and I'm afraid to say, used car lots, collecting converters. I did take a couple from cars just parked on the street (I'm so bad for an enlightened person) but these belonged to my ex-wife and her despicable new husband so it was OK.

I also got a fairly good-sized coil wound that I could send current through to produce a magnetic field the strength of which I calculated I would need. I was able to encase this within a container of sufficient strength and durability to hold liquid helium. This thermos-like, tube-shaped vessel was then held within another that would be filled with liquid nitrogen. This I insulated as well as I could, given the size limitations. Both containers required pressure valves to bleed off the gas that would form in spite of the tremendous pressure and cold. Both containers would also therefore have to have a means of replenishment.

My calculations indicated that this might not be so. Once the device was functioning it would power itself even without super cooling. That is, it would become a source of power in and of itself. The fields required to align and capture the Earth's, and in effect, the entire universe's Tigr energy, would not be needed once the device was operative. This was similar to a fusion reactor supplying more energy than it took to start and maintain its subatomic reaction, or like a superconductor, once it was charged, you could unplug it and the electrons would just keep spinning around.

It looked like the BEC would likewise be temporary. Its existence was required only for the time needed to charge the grid, charge the super-conducting electromagnet and fire the lasers. Once this was done the physics of the device would allow it to operate without the need for these exotic temperatures and materials. At least I hoped so.

I then built concentric spherical containers similar to the cylindrical ones that surrounded the electromagnet. This set of spheres not only needed the gas vents and a means of refilling that I hoped I wouldn't have to use, but it also needed 200 small holes that would be filled with minuscule fiberoptic cords that would transmit laser emissions. These had to be placed in symmetric quadrants on each hemisphere in groups of 25. A wire mesh, super-conducting current would have to be aligned within the inner sphere in such a way as to allow the laser beams to pass through, but it would also have to produce an electromagnetic field of sufficient force to contain the condensate and keep out stray molecules.

The condensate itself would have to initially be a gas that could be injected into the center of this field even as it turned ultra cold and formed a coherent mass of protons, neutrons and electrons arranged in a soup rather than as groups of discrete nuclei with electrons orbiting. The properties of this free-flowing matter would resonate with and be able to focus or channel Tigr energy, which would then be directed by the magnetic field into the charged parabolic reflector.

Once this energy was focused on the super-conducting coil at the focal point of the parabola, it would induce its own current within that coil and in fact would become self sustaining and would increase in strength to match the demands placed upon it. If I wanted to toast bread, it would provide a few hundred watts; if I wanted to supply the entire planet with electrical power, it made no difference to the device, it would simply supply it. If I needed an infinite amount of energy to make an instantaneous trip to another galaxy, it would likewise comply.

The power supply would then have to be placed into a Vehicle of some kind that could use the power and convert it into useful work or movement.

The design for the Vehicle was already complete within my mind and deserved to be referred to with capitalization. I'm not talking theoretic possibilities or science fiction here. This was as real as men on the moon, and must seem as unreal to you as men on the moon did to the people of the 1800s.

The Vehicle was two metallic grids shaped again, as parabolas, whose lengths were pi times the length of their focal point from their apex. When the two halves were placed together, wide ends attached, connected to the power source and charged with current, everything within this space could then be moved in relation to fixed gravitational fields, moved at any velocity or instantaneously without any internal sense of acceleration or deceleration. The control of Tigr would allow a passenger in such a Vehicle to feel one G, or any other pull, in a direction straight down into their seat regardless of their orientation to any outside gravitational field.

Because the power supply would be connected directly to the grid housing the Vehicle and because current would be constantly moving through this grid, the Vehicle would literally have a sort of sense of self, that through which it could conduct a current shaped as a pair of symmetric end-to-end parabolas, and the space contained within them would be self. That which was outside this semi-egg shaped contraption would be not-self.

This meant that the Vehicle would act and move as a single entity. No one molecule within this structure could be moved without moving every molecule of the structure. Since the power supply would be locked in place to a fixed gravitational point, the ultimate point being the exact gravitational and time center of our universe, it could not be moved in relation to that point by any force. That is, if I parked my flimsy wire mesh Vehicle in front of your house, you could push on it, smash it with a sledge and finally try to move it by pushing it with your car, but it would not budge.

No molecule within this structure could be moved without the power supply being moved and the only way to move the power supply would be to reorient the Vehicle in relation to its source of Tigr energy. So, if the Vehicle were drawing power from the Earth's gravitational center, then you would not be able to move the Vehicle from its current coordinates in space without moving the whole planet. If the Vehicle was drawing power from the gravitational center of the universe, then you could not move the Vehicle without moving the whole universe.

You could detonate a hydrogen bomb adjacent to the vehicle and it would not move from its coordinates. Furthermore, not one molecule of its structure and the space it contained would be moved or altered. I could be sitting in my little quantum car and watch your bomb go off and feel nothing. What would I see though?

The image of photons and particles from the explosion could be perceptible if desired. They would actually dematerialize at the surface of the vehicle and rematerialize on the opposite side traveling in the same direction with the same energy. The degree to which this happened could be controlled.

You see, the power at my disposal would be such that I could program the skin of my vehicle to allow only a certain intensity of photon bombardment. This would allow me to see the outside world, but it would not allow in a sufficient number or intensity of photons to cause harm. Because the power supply was a means of converting Tigr into energy, it would also convert energy into gravity/time. It would simply take all of the energy thrown at it (except in wavelengths and intensities that it had been programmed to allow), convert it into gravity/time, conduct it around its surface and then reconvert it back into energy and re-emit it exactly as if the photons involved had passed through.

I shouldn't really use the term "conduct" here. What would really happen could be described as quantum tunneling. A photon would strike one spot with a certain direction and wavelength. That energy would be absorbed and simultaneously a photon would be produced with the exact properties of the original and continue onward. This was not unheard of—already a group of scientists had done the same thing with a single photon in a lab. The result was that the photon had been essentially "transported" to a new location. This was reported as kind of a prelude to a *Star Trek*-like transporter but it was a far sight from moving matter around.

In relation to photons, you must realize that this would confer on the Vehicle the ability to be invisible. If it were between you and a tree, the photons reflected off the tree would strike the surface of the Vehicle, be converted to Tigr and be re-emitted on the opposite side of the Vehicle exactly as if the Vehicle had not been there. Those photons would the strike your retina and you would see the tree. This would occur in all directions and to any observers regardless of their angle of view. Utter and complete transparency, the equivalent of invisibility.

So much for energy, what about matter? Well, the power source would also be capable of converting matter into gravity/time and back. So theoretically it could absorb the matter in a rock thrown at it, convert it instantaneously into gravity/time as each molecule in the rock came in contact with the surface. (I keep calling it a surface, when it is really the equivalent of an event horizon near a black hole.) It could then reconstruct those molecules with the exact relationship to each other that they had and moving in the exact linear and rotational vectors that they would have had if the Vehicle had not been present and the rock would appear to pass through.

This would actually give away the position of the Vehicle because the rock would cease to exist in that space encompassed by the Vehicle's invisible walls. The rock could simply be allowed to bounce off the surface, but this would also give away the Vehicle's position also. Ideally the rock would be absorbed and re-emitted on the opposite side of the vehicle while the power source also created and emitted photons that would perfectly mimic the rock passing through it to any outside observers. This would take programming that was beyond my capability and the capability of the fastest computer now known. And if several people threw several handfuls of rocks, the calculations to mimic all those photons in their various wavelengths, intensities and directions would be unimaginable. So for now the Vehicle would be invisible but detectable.

Then you must realize the implication of this photon and matter production capability. The Vehicle could be programmed to emit photons in phase at any wavelength and any energy level. In other words, it could produce indescribably powerful lasers. The destructive power of the Vehicle would be essentially infinite. Small delicate beams to cut through fine materials on a microscopic scale or beams the diameter of the whole Vehicle with enough energy to bore through the planet.

And what about the reproduction of matter process? The rock seeming to disappear at one event horizon and reappear on the opposite side as described above? What would keep me from programming the power supply to produce matter made up of atoms with 79 protons, 118 neutrons and 79 electrons in an orderly crystalline structure? That would be gold. It could be induced to produce platinum or carbon in the form of perfect diamonds. Not only that, but with an infinite source of energy, I could have it produce tons of gold or 10,000 carat diamonds.

What does all this add up to?

A Vehicle that would be immovable, indestructible from without and with infinitely powerful weaponry. A Vehicle that would be essentially invisible and that could move at any velocity, even instantaneously. And it would have a driver that could program it to provide essentially limitless wealth. If this thing worked, it would be the biggest kick ever! (You can now see more accurately the moral dilemma of being in control of such a device.)

It would also be wrought with danger.

The sphere containing the BEC had to be located with its center at the apex of the parabola. The center of the magnetic field had to be at the focal point of the parabola. If these were not accurately placed, the whole thing could simply open a vent into the space outside of our physical universe. This could result in a release of energy that could potentially destroy our galaxy and produce a large black hole, one that would absorb the small black hole already at the center of our galaxy.

I was fairly certain that this degree of accuracy would not be needed. Once the device started functioning, all of these components would be pulled into alignment, as long as they were reasonably close to where they were supposed to be. This would be sort of like iron filings aligning themselves in a magnetic field, at least I hoped so. Otherwise I'd have to have the destruction of our galaxy on my conscience, if such a thing as conscience exists! Again I was relying on the principle of "things will work simply because that's the way things work" described previously.

I also had to be certain that the Earth's gravitational field had a fixed center. Since the planet itself rotated and precessed, it was entirely possible that the gravitational center actually moved or wobbled. If this were true, and I constructed a device that was locked into coordinates based on that center, then as soon as it was activated it would begin following that motion. Since the device would be indestructible, it would move through anything that got in the way of its motion. This could result in the destruction of myself, my lab and if the motion was significant enough, my neighborhood or even the whole city.

You see, an indestructible object in motion cannot be impeded by mere matter. If the Vehicle was on Venus and I wanted to move it to Mars, I could do it instantly and it would seem to pass through the Earth without harming anything. (This assumes the planets are aligned.) If I decided to travel to Mars at some finite velocity, the Vehicle would pass through the Earth as easily as it had passed through the relative vacuum of space. The Vehicle would be unharmed but the Earth would probably be severely damaged due to the ten-foot diameter hole made through it by the passage of the Vehicle.

In this case I was counting on the liquidity of the core of the Earth. The center was probably solid, in spite of high temperature, due to extreme pressure. Fortunately this solid core was floating within liquid strata and my theory was that the solid center wobbled within its liquid layer allowing the gravitational center to remain in one place in relation to local space/time. Thus, once activated, the device would remain motionless in relation to its surroundings. I hoped.

Another problem could occur when I charged the electromagnet and parabolic grid. A single parabolic device aligned with the Earth's center of gravity could only move in alignment with that gravitational field. In other words, straight up or down. This motion could be controlled by the strength of the charge applied to the device. I had calculated this, but if my calculations weren't exact, then the device would move upward if the charge was too great, or straight downward if too weak. I planned to deal with this by adding power to the device at exactly the amount calculated *plus or minus* an amount I felt would provide a 95 percent confidence limit of being correct. The charger would vary the voltage up or down within these limits if upward or downward motion were detected.

From this information you can see that if a power supply for my so far theoretic Vehicle only had one parabolic device, it would only be able to move in two directions, toward or away from its gravitational reference point.

My calculations indicated that a Vehicle capable of travel in any direction at any velocity would ideally have six parabolas fixed at right angles to each other forming a three dimensional X, Y and Z coordinate system. The model I was building in my secret basement was simply a test device to see if all this would work; it wouldn't really be useful. Oh sure, I could supply the entire Earth's energy requirements, but that would give its existence away.

I was well on my way to finishing the trial version of my power supply. I had a little work left to do. Some of the physics I had still not quite worked out and I continued to struggle with the problem of the potential for destroying the world. I was also running out of money.

And so it was, I was sitting in my overstuffed recliner in the corner of my living room, contemplating these weighty matters when I felt the out-of-body process beginning within me. It had been years since I experienced this phenomenon and I didn't appreciate the intrusion into my contemplation. I realized that I was holding very still in my chair and it was true that I was concentrating on a single problem. I did not expect it to produce the usual meditation result, although I guess I should have. Over the next few months, as I grappled with various problems related to the science and ethics of my project, these near out-of-body experiences became more frequent.

I eventually hit a solid technological and financial roadblock to my hidden basement project. It seemed I just didn't have the financial, mental or even the spiritual resources to solve these problems. I had believed that things would work themselves out in due course, but it was apparently not to be.

One afternoon, I was again in my recliner contemplating the consequences of my actions when I felt the vibration, not of my soul attempting to pass out of my body, but of the knock upon my door at 1582 D Street.

TIME
TWO

SIX

I remember my birth. It almost seemed like I was present and watching from a point just above my mother. Even stranger than that, I seemed to continue to observe myself growing from a location just behind and to the left of my physical head for some time. Most of what went on were only vague recollections, probably figments of my imagination, that I eventually forced from my consciousness and ignored.

At some point I guess I was integrated into what I perceived as my body and lost this outside observer perspective. The birth itself though remains quite clear. It seems the bleeding was a bit excessive and my mother needed a transfusion, something about blood type incompatibility.

At any rate, I rejected these visions as a product of my dreams or propensity for reading science-fiction books and went on with my life.

I do have a few recollections from my early years, mostly centered on traumatic events like nearly falling off a narrow wall or ledge when I was three, or being left behind when my family was making a move from Germany to the United States. Otherwise my life as a child was pretty ordinary.

There was one event that stood out for some reason. I was about six or so and was going down into the basement of our big old rundown house in Orlando, Florida. I spent a lot of my time down there because it was where I built or rebuilt stuff to sell. I had the place pretty well memorized and wasn't afraid to traverse the basement floor in the dark to the spot where I could reach up and turn on the lights.

This time however, just as I was about to move from the large hatch-like door, I noticed a blob of light. I don't know what else to call it. It seemed formless and moving in a sort of amoebic way. I figured it was a little white mouse, just barely perceivable in the dim light. Because of this I leapt across the floor and flattened whatever it was under my foot. I then reached up,

43

turned on the light and looked under my shoe, but there was nothing where I expected to see blood and guts. There were no tracks, no evidence that anything had been there at all, except my imagination. It made me feel weird though to have "seen" something that turned out not to be there or not to be real. A bit of a shiver ran through me.

I shrugged the event off as best I could and picked up the rebuilt sting ray bike I had made from found spare parts and took it upstairs. A friend of mine was going to buy it from me for $20 the next day and I was relishing the idea of that money, and the power it represented, being in my hand.

In retrospect, that little event in the basement may never have actually happened. Memories are such fleeting things and prone to variation over time even though we would swear in court that our memory was accurate. It's like several witnesses to the same crime, one swearing in court that the perpetrator was white, one swearing he was black, one swearing he had a beard, one swearing he was clean shaven and one swearing he was a she.

I was a scrawny kid who was not popular with others and didn't have the coordination to play sports, so I didn't waste time playing Little League or football. I spent my time scheming about ways to make money. I learned at a very early age that money controlled everything. I was in a fight with Tommy Bliston over the love of my life Gena Freemont. He was bigger, he was well built and well coordinated and he was a pitcher for a Little League team and thus a kiddy sports hero. Already the girls swooned over him, including my Gena. It would come to blows. Or would it? Tommy and I met on a dirt road near Gena's house. One look at him and I knew he was going to knock my block off. I had originally planned on fighting, but since I had no experience and no particular gross motor skills, it suddenly seemed like a pretty poor plan. The grin on Tommy's face didn't help, he knew he was going to beat the crap out of me and not even break into a sweat. Gena appeared on the sidewalk nearby, the challenge was issued, the prize was at hand. I faced utter humiliation and the loss of my heart's desire.

I changed plans. I reached into my pocket and withdrew a wad of bills, one of which was a twenty, at that time a lot of money. I held it out to Tommy and said something like, "Disappear, don't tell anybody and it's yours." He hesitated for a moment, his smile changed, and as he reached for the bill he said, "You're all right, you know that?"

As he turned and walked away I saw Gena eyeing the rest of the bills in my hand. She walked up to me with such a sweet smile and asked me if I would buy her a Cherry Coke at the Rexall down the street. This was at a time when there were such places and Cherry Cokes were made by a guy behind a counter rather than mass produced and canned. In fact it was a time before soft drinks were canned at all.

I bought her the Cherry Coke and later she let me feel around under her dress.

What an incredible developmental episode. I of course lost interest in Gena and realized that real gratification, even beyond the satisfaction of feeling the funny little bumps that seemed to have a moist indentation between them through a little girl's panties, was in accumulating wealth. I knew then that I could buy off any threat, and pay for any woman I wanted.

I did fairly well in school, especially in math. Math was one of the keys to understanding economics, and understanding economics was one important step in the path to vast wealth and power. I craved these. Even as a kid I made a fair amount of money buying and selling. I would take apart every piece of junk and discarded rubbish I could find, figure out how it worked and either fix it or use the parts to construct other things that could be sold.

Most of the discarded treasures that people thought were broken were simply malfunctioning due to a loose wire or a stuck gear. Half the time it seemed like the problem was caused by someone who spilled into the machinery something like Cherry Coke, which would then dry into a thick caramel that prevented movement. If people would simply take things apart and look at them instead of assuming that the internal workings of most devices were technically beyond their abilities or worked by some sort of magic, they would throw out a lot less stuff. I guess they figured that the guts of a vacuum cleaner were too complicated to figure out, or that once the "magic" that ran the machine ran out, they had to buy a new one.

Along the way I fixed and sold a lot of junk and figured out how just about everything worked. Everything was just a combination of the basic machines we learned about in school. Levers, inclines, screws and gears, pistons and drive shafts very large or minutely small, all put in motion by the application of force to one area that was translated, transformed, amplified or de-amplified to do something that was too hard or too delicate to do by hand. Sewing machines, in my mind, best exemplified this process. Electricity combined with these simple machines produced even more variations and potential, but it was all the same. Nothing remained mysterious to me, and as I aged my "junk" became more sophisticated.

I began torturing radios and amplifiers, televisions and other electrical devices to learn their secrets. Then one day my father brought home a device that changed my life.

My father was a pretty smart guy. He had taught calculus in the Air Force (which accounts for my birth in Japan and my early residence in Germany) and upon retirement became an engineer and technical writer for the aerospace industry in Florida. This was when the space race was really heating up and the company he worked for, Martin-Marietta, was thick into it. He would bring papers home from work and read through them, edit them and apparently memorize them, because he would later burn them in the barbecue grill and carefully stir the ashes. Needless to say he had a pretty high security clearance and access to some pretty cool stuff, stuff I'd like to get my hands on!

On the day I remember so well he brought home a little device. It was the color of gold, and looking back it was probably at least gold plated. It was a circular disk about three-eighths of an inch in diameter and about one-eighth of an inch thick. From one flat side extended three relatively thick wires, about an inch and a half long. They were like a little tripod the thing could stand on. In fact he stood it on the dining room table on its three little legs and I gazed upon it at what was about eye level for me at the time.

He was almost mystic in his reverence for this little brass-colored thing. His awe and wonder at it was contagious. I wanted to know what it was, what it did and I wanted to take it apart to see how it worked. My father told me proudly that this tiny device was a "transistor" and that it could do the same job as a much larger vacuum tube and use much less energy in the process. This seemed to be almost miraculous to him. I thought it was kind of cool and I could see where it could be used to make smaller radios, amplifiers and TVs, but I wasn't awestruck. I knew that if I pulled it apart I would find the same basic machines and devices that were the inner workings of all things, only on a smaller scale.

When I later stole this little treasure from my father's dresser and pried it apart, I was amazed to find only little wires leading to a very small chip of glass or plastic-like material. Nothing moved! I couldn't place the parts in an orderly fashion on a workbench, figure out how the thing operated and put it back together! This was something very new alright, mysterious and a little frightening, because I couldn't understand it. Even when I smashed up the little disc in the middle of the thing, I couldn't make it make sense.

It was a few weeks before I asked my dad about the transistor again. He immediately asked me if I had seen it. It seems it had disappeared from his dresser several weeks ago. The suspicion in his eyes told me that he had a pretty good idea about what had happened to it. Most of the things in the house disappeared from time to time only to reappear at a later date with signs of tampering. Fortunately all of these things continued to work as well or, more often than not, better than they had originally, so no one got too upset. The transistor was an exception. I had brushed the crumbs of this device into the trash, feeling pretty humbled that I wouldn't be able to return it to my father's dresser seemingly undisturbed and hopefully operational.

I gazed innocently into his eyes and told him I hadn't seen it and in the same breath asked him how the thing worked. My father could be easily distracted if you asked him to teach you something about math or technology. Even though he might have been about to accuse me of taking his little prize, he now had an opportunity to expound upon the wonders of microelectronics, and this overwhelmed his desire to accuse, convict and punish me for my crime. In addition to the power of money, I had also already mastered the ability to manipulate people through identifying and appealing to their passions.

He described in great detail the entire process and theory behind what he called "solid state" electronic devices and how they would revolutionize the world. He led me into a world where hundreds or even thousands of transistors could fit in a space the size of a quarter. He explained how many transistors, being in a state of on/off, or zero/one as he called it, would be able to perform calculations at the speed of light. He said they would one day be used in huge devices called computers that could store and manipulate information as ones and zeros and solve math problems in days that would take an engineer with a slide rule weeks to work through.

About two-thirds of the way through his discussion, most of which was irrelevant, I saw the big picture. Using binary code and variably charged solid state, or basically molecular or chemical "machines," one could store as well as manipulate theoretically unlimited amounts of data. Now this was interesting, because one other truth I had learned was that controlling data, or information, was even more valuable than controlling materials.

For example, if you had a bunch of silver, sold it high and then spread the word that the silver market was going to drop, prompting others to sell, then the bottom would indeed drop out of the silver market. You could then re-buy your silver and a whole lot more and then leak information out about how silver was going to be a great investment and bingo, you made a fortune, not off silver, but off controlling the information about silver.

I learned that lesson through collecting stamps and coins. I could buy a coin from one dealer, polish it up and sell it to another telling him that it was in much better condition than it actually was. By changing the data relative to the coin, it became more valuable. It was still the same coin. I once purchased an 1882 Columbus commemorative half-dollar from a dealer at the opposite end of the little shopping center from the above-mentioned Cherry-Coke-serving Rexall store. It had a black stain running over the reverse side, so I got it for a reasonable price. I fiddled around with a few chemicals and eventually removed the stain. The beautiful coin looked about mint by the time I was finished. About a year later I took it back to the same dealer and sold it to him for three times what I had paid for it. He was impressed by its excellent condition and fortunately did not recognize the coin or me. A minor triumph.

It was during this time that I also developed a fascination with the very small. My fantasy life was full of unclothed women most of the time, don't get me wrong, but I also spent a fair amount of time thinking about extremely small-scale devices. Microscopic things with tremendous power. The interplay of increasing power with ever-decreasing size. Was the limit really infinitely small and infinitely powerful?

So I went through my childhood being somewhat isolated and kind of a nerd. I took a lot of science classes and planned to be a chemistry major in college. I felt that understanding chemicals and learning to work with them on a molecular or atomic scale would result in the ability to make molecular- or atomic-sized machines. This was interesting to me, so I chose to major in it, or maybe math, or maybe physics. They all sort of overlapped and I didn't want to limit myself to one narrow view. Besides, I had plenty of time to decide.

Also during this time the fruits of the transistor revolution began to ripen. The first portable four-function, non-mechanical calculators hit the market. My dad of course bought one for about $300. Soon they became hand held! My dad bought one for about $300. Then they came out with some that would do squares and square roots, and my dad bought one for about $300. This continued with smaller and smaller calculators coming out with more and more functions, each new model irresistible to my father and always costing about $300. Because of this interest in calculating devices, by the time my father died he had a complete collection chronicling the evolution of calculating technology from base 18 abacuses to spiraled circular slide rules with 33-foot-long scales to relatively massive four-function calculators to some of the early high-tech programmable scientific calculators made by TI and Hewlett-Packard.

Unfortunately my father died before the advent of the first true user-friendly "computers." The Sinclair, the Radio Shack, the Apple and finally the IBM PC. If he were alive today, he would be in heaven. (An interesting phrase.) If he could see the string tie I made from an old 486 processor, the first with over one million transistors in a single chip. He'd be proud and amazed at how far his little golden three-legged solid-state device had come. It had evolved much more quickly than anyone suspected. Anyone but me, but I'm getting ahead of myself.

Toward the end of my high school years I did get a little weird. I started smoking pot a fair amount and began thinking of things philosophic and even spiritual. This was not helpful in terms of my plans to amass a fortune, which could basically only be done at the expense of others. It was as if I were developing morals, which would paralyze any efforts to take advantage of my fellow man in order to obtain information and thus money and thus power.

Finally one night while I was about 17 years old I decided to give some serious thought to this God problem. What if some kind of God did exist? What implications did this have? Did it imply that there was some sort of universal morality that I had to abide by? If there was, and I chose to believe it, then it would put a real crimp in my future plans. I held the firm belief, and still do, that there is no such thing as an honest rich man.

So I stayed quite still in my bed and contemplated this dilemma.

I don't really recall the thought process, all I know was that after awhile I started to feel strange, as if paralyzed, and then I seemed to rush out of my body through the top of my head to hover nearby. There was this sense of knowing everything and understanding the nature of the universe and there was this sense of being drawn toward some bright spot or source of this knowledge. There was also the sense that my body was lying in my bed but that I wasn't. This gave every appearance of death to me and I hadn't even made my first million yet.

Fortunately this fear, combined with my lust for cash and power, somehow propelled me back into my body and I woke sweating, panting and with a racing heart. I figured I had somehow just about died and was lucky enough to spontaneously recover from whatever had caused my premature potential demise. I also figured that this experience meant that thinking too deeply about things like God and universal moralities could really get weird and immediately resolved to ignore this aspect of…of…"reality?" for now.

I had to concentrate all my willpower on producing some kind of movement. It seemed I had to actually force myself to re-exert control over my body after having been gone for a moment. Finally I wiggled the big toe of my right foot and everything returned to normal. I opened my eyes, rolled over, stretched and sat up on the side of my bed.

I had to get away. Perhaps the moral influence of my born-again Christian parents was repelling me. Perhaps it was the experience I had just had and the fear that if I stayed at home it would happen again. Whatever it was that drove me, I knew that to achieve my goal of excessive financial success I had to go somewhere else, follow a different path than my current environment would allow.

I got out of bed and went to the deepest drawer in my dresser where I had built a false bottom and had squirreled away the earnings from my childhood selling and scamming. No one in my family knew anything about the $2,340 I had stashed. I took it all and some clothes and sneaked into the bathroom to change. For some reason I didn't even look back at my bed as I left. I was actually a little apprehensive about looking at the bed, afraid that I might still see the too still body of myself lying there. The bathroom had an exit onto a back patio and I had used this route to get out of the house in the middle of the night many times.

I went out into that particular night to literally seek my fortune.

In later years I would look back on this time and hear the guitar of Tom Petty ringing like a bell, his course voice accompanying:

"And she made a vow to have it all

It became her new religion.

Oh, down in her soul,

It was an act of treason."

Although Tom was singing about a she, it applied to me as well.

It took time but it was easy to get to Los Angeles by bus. No one took notice of this long-haired kid and I used whatever name came to mind while buying tickets or talking to people. On the way to LA the bus stopped in a place I'd heard about in disrespectful terms. Las Vegas. I spent several days there sneaking into casinos. If they suspected that I was under 21 they quickly

51

...ed it when I pulled out a thick folded stack of $100s. I didn't gamble ... I played the slots long enough to determine that, statistically, they were a losing proposition. This was also true of the poker machines and the roulette table. It seemed like there was a fair chance of winning at craps but what really attracted me was blackjack. It seemed with time and experience that a person might actually be able to consistently win at this game, particularly if that person didn't set unrealistic goals like turning $300 into a fortune.

I actually left Las Vegas about $50 richer than I was when I arrived. I knew I'd be back; it was my kind of town. I would read and study everything I could find about blackjack and practice on my own until I felt confident to go back and play for some real money. The key seemed to be knowing when to quit and being satisfied with a small profit.

I learned that card counting actually wasn't that helpful. Even in my short stay I got to where I could accurately count two decks in less than 60 seconds but realized that when the count favored high cards, the dealer was as statistically likely to get the good cards as any of the players. Not only that, but if the casinos caught on that you were doing the traditional card-counting thing, they'd throw you out. It was nice to keep track of the count just in case you needed to know the relative likelihood of getting a particular card when making decisions to hit or stand, split or double, but in general, forget about counting exactly and just keep a vague idea about what cards have been dealt and what cards are still in the deck.

I'll tell you what, and I'm getting ahead of myself again, something that's hard to avoid, I'll fill you in on my blackjack strategy that guarantees the perceptive person profit.

First, don't be greedy. If you play five hands starting with say $500 and you're ahead by $50, quit. Realize that you just made a 10% profit in about a half-hour. If you turned a 10% profit per half-hour in the stock market, you'd own the whole world within a short time. Be happy with your relatively immense success, take a break, stash your winnings and go to another table again with your same $500 and start over. Likewise, be willing to lose $500 and make sure it is money you can afford to lose.

Let's say you've been playing for four hours, you've lost as much as $400 and have finally gotten back up to $501. Quit. You're ahead. Rest, go for a walk, eat something, come back and start fresh later. If you are worried that you'll win and then stay on and lose your winnings and your stake too, then do the following. Bring with you several self-addressed stamped envelopes. Every time you get ahead by more than $50, fold it into a piece of paper or two, stuff it in one of your envelopes and drop it in a mailbox. This way you'll never lose more than your stake, and if you do lose your stake eventually, in a couple of days you'll get some of your money back in the mail.

Also, while at the table, keep only a few hundred dollars out on it. Whenever you start accumulating chips, discretely slip a few into a pocket. You don't want the dealer or pit boss figuring out how much you're winning. They probably know, but it's nice to make it a little hard on them.

I was playing in Las Vegas once, early in my career. I had $300, which was my minimum stake to ply the $5 minimum tables. I played for almost six hours straight, even had a beer or two while I played. The dealer of course had changed numerous times over the course of the game. Finally, when my butt could no longer tolerate the stool I was on, I told the dealer I was going to leave. I had about $500 in chips on the table and the dealer volunteered to convert my chips to $100 denominations to minimize my load when I went to the cashier. I said sure and stood up.

I took over $2,000 out of my pants pockets, the pockets on the outside of my jacket, the breast pocket of my jacket and even from my shirt pocket. Most of the chips in this eye-popping pile were $25s. The people at the table and the dealer were speechless as she and the pit boss traded me 22 $100 chips and some change for my 1s, 5s and 25s. I traded all this for currency at the cashier, mailed $1500 to myself in three separate envelopes, ate a great complimentary meal and retired to my complimentary room to sleep and win again tomorrow. Since I had a little over $700 left, I'd play at a higher minimum table and hopefully fill my pockets with even higher denomination chips.

Although I drank some beer during that marathon, in general it's very important that you DO NOT DRINK, at least not alcohol-containing beverages. It is useful to act like you've been drinking alcohol so that you seem like an easy mark for the dealers and they won't scrutinize your playing too closely. Drink coffee whenever you can, it will keep you sharp. Take frequent breaks and change tables frequently unless you're in the midst of a pocket-straining winning streak. It's also helpful to get over the feeling that you're playing with real money.

You are of course, and it better not be your rent money, but in general, it's better to think about chips as points. The amount you're betting doesn't alter the odds of winning. If you are pretty sure you're going to win, you'll win whether you have a $2 bet on the table or a $2,000 bet. Also realize that the more you bet on a particular hand doesn't increase your winnings in terms of percentages. If you win $4 on your $2 bet, you've doubled your money, 100% profit. If you put up $2,000 and win $4,000 it's exactly the same. The problem with big bets is that when you lose, it seems to hurt a lot more than if you lose $2! If you view the chips as points instead of dollars then you won't get so emotionally involved. You could be betting with $1 chips or $1,000 chips. It's all the same—a chip is a chip, you win it or you lose it.

Another helpful bit of advice, buy 16 decks of cards and make a deck (you'll be able to make four actually) that has four of each denomination, two through nine all in the same suit, four aces in the same suit and then sixteen tens in the same suit. You see, there are functionally only ten cards in a blackjack deck. Suits don't really matter so there are the cards two through nine (eight types of cards with different values), an ace (one type of card with two different values), and four cards valued at ten that might as well all be tens of a single suit. Think of the deck as having four twos of spades, four threes of spades, etc., four aces of spades and sixteen tens of spades for example. This will tremendously simplify the work of learning all the ins and outs of the game.

Realize that the real opportunities for profit are in doubling and splitting and use these opportunities whenever they present themselves, particularly when you feel the cards are in your favor. This will sometimes result in you doing things that others at your table will think are dumb, but as long as you walk away ahead, they can think whatever they want.

I was in the midst of a winning micro-trend and split a pair of queens. What a dope, right? But I knew the dealer was going to bust. He did and I quadrupled my original bet. The biggest winnings however come from varying the amount you bet. Learn the game completely. Know all the traditional advice about when to hit and when to stand in relation to all the card combinations in your hand and the dealer's up card. You do have to play skillfully most of the time when the cards are just idling.

What do I mean by cards idling and cards being for or against you? This is where you have to get into chaos theory. You see, most people think that the order in which the cards come out of a deck or shoe is random. This is not strictly true. Remember, there are really only ten different cards in each deck of 52. The fact that these cards repeat themselves introduces some regularity. For true randomness, there would have to be 52 entirely different cards in the deck, like a 23 of hearts or a 46 of spades.

Chaos theory tells us that seemingly random events are not. They simply involve too many variables for our poor little brains to keep track. The leaf growth on a tree may seem random, until you find out that the branching pattern follows a rule that mathematically resembles the equation for the spiral shape of a snail's shell. Add to this the occasional loss of a branch or leaf from wind and what you see appears chaotic. There is no perfect tree.

In blackjack, you have the perfect tree. All of the functionally ten cards will always be there (or better be!) so there will always be some regularity to what happens. By looking at the decks as having only ten cards you have suddenly reduced the number of variables to keep track of and you can start to pick out some of the regularities in the sequence of cards coming out of the deck.

What you look for is not the complete predictability of every card dealt. What you look for are micro-trends within the seeming chaos.

Card counting always starts at zero and ends at zero. If it doesn't, it means you screwed up the count. Thus the chaotic events of the deal have to stop and start at about the same place. It's not exact because of the cut and the fact that in some places the first card in the deck is discarded, but it is a good approximation. The deal can then vary between two extremes. The high and low cards come out in exactly the right proportions to keep the count at minus one, zero or plus one, or all of the high cards come out first with the count ever rising until they run out and then the low cards are dealt and the count moves back to or close to zero. The neutral cards—sevens, eights and nines—don't matter. These extremes can be illustrated graphically:

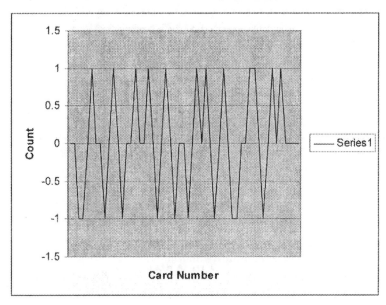

This shows the cards coming out in a random way but where the count never goes above one or below minus one. When a game goes like this I call it coasting.

And:

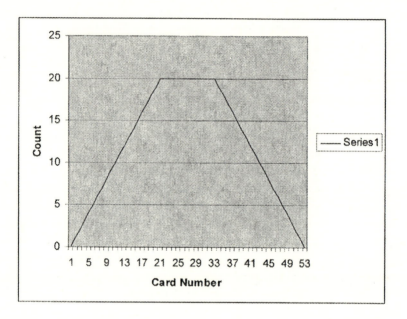

In this case all the high cards came out first and the count went up and up, then the neutral cards came out and finally all the small cards came out. This would obviously be a fixed deck, but there is a slight probability that this could happen.

What really happens of course is somewhere in between, where the count rises above and falls below zero in a seemingly random way.

This same set of graphs can be used to illustrate winning and losing. The extremes would be breaking even, with you and the dealer alternating wins, to the dealer winning all the hands followed eventually by you winning all the hands. This assumes you can play the game with adequate skill to keep the odds about even, something that is close to possible.

What really happens of course is somewhere in between, where you win some and lose some in a seemingly random way.

But the count and the winning and losing aren't really random. There are small trends that occur, micro-trends that you can watch for and of which you should be sensitive. For example:

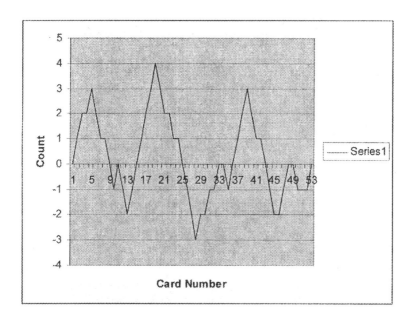

As you can see there can be only 20 ups (cards ten through ace), 20 downs (cards two through six) and 12 evens (cards seven, eight and nine).

You may play for a while just going back and forth, winning a little, losing a little, but if you're sort of keeping track of the count and the win/loss trends you'll suddenly realize that you're in the middle of a good or bad trend. You'll start to see these trends and even anticipate them. While running even and in the midst of a bad trend you keep your bets at the table minimum. But if you sense a good trend, that's when you get aggressive. Bet ten or more times the minimum, double and split if you can, play two or three hands at once. Since you're not following traditional card-counting strategies your betting pattern will look random and the people at the table, including the dealer, will just think you're a little crazy. You will lose just enough to convince them of this but over all you will be winning more than losing.

It won't always work but it can work often enough that when you combine it with a lack of greed and knowing when to quit, you can almost always come out ahead. Practicing with your special all-one-suit deck of only ten different cards will help you filter out the noise and concentrate on micro-trends within the wins and losses.

There, now you have the secret to making a living as a gambler. If you see me at the table with you, go to a different table because I've given you enough to beat the house, but not enough to beat me!

Back to the story. Shortly after reaching LA, I got my hair cut and shaved, stayed a few nights in a low-end motel until I found a little place to rent. Where I lived and how well didn't matter, what did matter was security. A dump in a bad neighborhood was fine as long as I could make it relatively impregnable.

I ended up with a decent small furnished place in a slightly less than decent neighborhood where I could reinforce the front door, install some major locks and add iron bars over the windows, even though I was on the third floor. The landlord may have felt I was a little paranoid but since I paid him six months' rent in advance and promised to pay for the modifications, he really didn't seem to care much about what I did with his 700-square-foot, two-bedroom place.

The building was seven stories, brick, and had a west-facing entrance leading to stairs, no elevator. Each floor had seven apartments arranged in a U around the central staircase. My apartment was in the middle of the north side with two windows from the living-dining-kitchen area and one window from the "master" bedroom, all overlooking the blank brick wall of the apartment building next door. The wall facing my windows was windowless, five stories tall and about seven feet across a little used alley.

There was just enough light in this alley to support the growth of a thorny hedge along the side of my building. There was a narrow paved path covering the rest of the ground between the apartment houses. The front of the alley opened onto the street where the building entrance also stood and there was a street light at that point which illuminated the alley to a degree. The back of the alley opened onto a narrow one-way street used mostly by residents and a few service vehicles. From this point there were a variety of escape routes away from the neighborhood.

Once in, I began constructing hidden places for storing cash and weapons, places that would be tough for anyone else to find but easy for me to get to. I then did a little remodeling that I wasn't going to tell the landlord about. I removed the entire bedroom window with its frame and bars, hollowed out some of the concrete and brick wall around the window and then reinstalled it with hidden hinges so that it could open like a door in the wall. The latch kept it secure and immovable until the appropriate brick was moved and a lever was pulled. The whole window would then swing in or out as a unit allowing access or egress from my residence. I could leave clandestinely if I wanted to, or rapidly in case of an emergency.

So I had a little fortress where I could keep large amounts of cash safely and get into and out of efficiently without having to use the front door. If someone were breaking through the front door somehow, I would have the time to grab my stash of cash and a weapon or two, zip out the window and make it to the ground by way of a rope. If someone were watching the front of the building I could get into my apartment by pulling a string hidden among the shrubs beneath the window. This would cause a coiled rope on the windowsill, not visible from the ground, to drop down to me. Then I could climb up, push on the disguised hinged brick, pull the hidden lever in the wall, push the whole window inward and slip inside.

I tried it a few times at night and it actually worked. Between the shrubs and the fact that I made sure the streetlight near the alley that ran between my building and the next was always out, I could use my secret passage without being seen. I planned to use it only at night. In the case of an emergent departure in daylight I'd take my assets and disappear. It wouldn't matter if someone saw me because I wouldn't be back.

From the ground you couldn't see the fine cracks in the wall around the window and as an added cool escape route, I had an equally invisible wire running across the alley to the adjacent brick building. Pulling this wire would allow a rope hidden on the roof of the five-story neighboring place to drop down. On this I could swing to the wall of the next building and climb to the roof, hopefully to freedom and further wealth.

With my average build, my average haircut and my average to slightly below average wardrobe, I was virtually invisible myself. This became my world headquarters, the first residence of what I hoped would become an empire.

EIGHT

The first thing I needed was information. Enough time had passed since my father's relatively large transistor had been a breakthrough development that it was clear computers based on transistor technology were going to be a key part of our future culture. I needed information about computer development or more particularly, companies that were developing computers or the programs that ran them. The best place to get this data was from nerds.

I went to UCLA and started hanging around the classes where subjects like BASIC and FORTRAN were discussed. Sure enough there were enough nerds around to hold a *Star Trek* convention.

One thing about nerds is they love to talk about the esoteric knowledge that makes them nerds in the first place. In fact, as nerds, there's very little else they can talk about. I doubt if some of them knew what the President's name was.

Another thing about nerds is they are deep into science fiction and thus love to speculate about the future, love rumors about developing technologies no matter how farfetched and once in a while one of them even knows about someone who might actually be doing something meaningful in the field of computers and programming. I'm not talking about Bill Hewlett or other established giants. I'm talking about people on a cutting edge, the little guys in basements and garages developing things that would revolutionize the industry. The big companies were too entrenched in the technology of the status quo, too full of over-educated idiots who never questioned their professors when they were told that some things were impossible. My favorite example of this phenomenon was William Lear. He never got a Ph.D. or even a BA, so he hadn't learned that the general consensus among scientists was that it was technologically or scientifically impossible to build a radio that would fit in a car. So Lear did it. Had he been better educated, he would have known better than to have tried. The same goes for the eight-track tape player and a small jet engine that came to be known as a Lear jet.

So I was looking for people outside of the mainstream who had the creativity to do new things, usually because they didn't realize that what they were trying to do was thought to be impossible by the "experts" in the field of endeavor involved.

From these sources I found out about a guy named Jobs who had recently started up a company to mass produce a computer for home use that he and a friend had built in their garage. I also heard about several companies that were getting into the business of making microprocessors for such machines and I heard about a couple of guys, one named Gates, who had written some programs to control the basic operations of microprocessors and the computers in which they were installed. I heard a great deal about many other things, most of which didn't pan out, but I was to become ecstatic about investing in Apple, Intel and Microsoft. What little I lost in other start-ups was more than made up for in the hundreds of millions I eventually made off these three companies alone.

I kept my investments well disguised with dummy off-shore companies and pseudonyms, but it was mine, all MINE.

Of course it took many years to build this fortune and to start off I didn't have much of my original $2,400 left. So I started collecting useful junk, rebuilding it and selling it, began buying things of value that through one scam or another I could later sell for a much higher price. I never got greedy enough to really piss anybody off and I rarely got caught in a con anyway, but if I did, it was usually settled with cash rather than violence.

Overall I slowly did quite well and was able to make larger and larger purchases and bigger sales. I contemplated getting into drug importation, but again, I didn't want to get too greedy, and getting caught shipping a few tons of marijuana into the U.S. was not the way to financial success.

I finally had enough to start investing in the stock market seriously, again focusing on start-up technology and then pharmaceutical companies. It's odd how I seemed to have a feel for what companies were going to make it big.

I was also able to start buying real estate, some of which made me untold millions, none of which I actually lost on. A good example of this was a near ghost town close to Salt Lake City in Utah. It was called Park City and had once been a thriving mining town. I saw the potential of this place, particularly for winter sports, so I started buying buildings on the almost deserted main street and quite a bit of surrounding acreage.

This seemed foolish to some at the time, but in more recent years the city has become an arts and skiing mecca. I was finally and ultimately rewarded and vindicated for my investment when, through bribery, threats and blackmail, my little city was selected for the 2002 Winter Olympics.

I also eventually had enough money to do some serious gambling, so much so that I kept a penthouse apartment in one of the Las Vegas casinos. I certainly didn't limit myself to Las Vegas. I gambled all over Nevada and eventually Atlantic City, Monaco, Macao, and many other exotic gambling havens. When overseas I would use false documents and Swiss bank accounts to deposit winnings. The fact that I had several excellently documented identities helped me stay lost in America too.

My family did try to find me. In the early years I stayed pretty well hidden in my fortified apartment in LA. When I had too much stuff to keep there safely, I rented other secure facilities to keep large sums of cash and valuables, and I also started wiring money to banks in the Caymans, the Bahamas, Monaco and Switzerland. The false identities, the low profile, it kept my mom and dad from getting close to me. My father eventually died of lung cancer before he could even retire and enjoy life. My mother lived to a fairly ripe old age but was a 90-pound diabetic for the last two decades of her life and a little too frail to do much. After a few years I didn't hear much over the grapevine to suggest they were still looking so I guessed I was in the clear.

With my family no longer looking for me, I settled in to make some serious money, without having to look over my shoulder too much. I did eventually have to move out of my little hideout overlooking the alley and the move did turn out to be a little rushed. I was doing a lot of looking over my shoulder that day.

It all started while in Europe posing as a technology maven from a large and growing company from North Carolina, one of the technology triangle companies with Duke University as its apex. I came across a stamp dealer who had about 13 of the original two-penny black postage stamps from England. These were genuine samples of the first postage stamp ever printed in the world. They weren't all that rare but these were in good shape and I got a good price for buying them all. Back in the States, I of course fiddled with them to remove stains and in particular cancellation marks of various types, some quite indelible. I ended up with three pretty good stamps and ten that looked in mint condition. These I sold one at a time to American collectors, usually at philatelic meetings.

At these meetings I would meet relatively inexperienced collectors who were lured by the stamps' high quality and the aura of owning one of the world's first stamps in unused condition. I would get a pretty high price, usually even more than book value. I was a pretty good sales (read con) man.

One of the shows was in Los Angeles. One of the buyers there learned he got ripped off from an expert in the field who could tell that the stamp had been tampered with and was therefore actually pretty worthless. Unfortunately the guy had enough connections to find out where I lived. Being high up in the West Coast organized crime syndicate helped. It also meant that he had the means to wipe me out and make me disappear for real, and that he probably had no scruples about doing so.

From what I heard on the street, people who crossed him were usually picked up by members of his "family" and roughed up a bit to make them relatively harmless. They were then taken to this stamp collector/crime boss where he would finish the poor slob off in very creative, slow and usually quite messy ways. Not very appealing to me. When I sold him the stamp, I didn't know who he was, but since I continued to deal in rare stamps and coins I did hear from a source that the guy had tried to have the stamp authenticated and got pretty upset when it was not. The source also let me know in no uncertain terms exactly what this guy's other hobbies were, hobbies involving razor blades and slow blood loss through small lacerations too numerous to count.

I didn't even like to nick myself shaving. So I got a little edgy when I saw a couple of guys I didn't know hanging around the neighborhood. I didn't know who they were but it was pretty easy to see what they were. They always had that genuine I've-killed-people-for-less look about them that made people give them plenty of room on the sidewalk. Close scrutiny would also usually reveal a large weighty bulge under the left side of the expensive Italian sports coats that they always wore even in the sweltering LA summers.

Then you'd see some really slimy character slither up to them and whisper a few words, accept the almost imperceptibly passed bills and ooze off into the crowd again. I kept an eye out for this kind of activity because I assumed that one of these days I'd see someone distantly related to the Mafioso stamp collector or one of the many other people I had scammed, looking for me, dead or alive, but mostly dead. Once, while watching this happen from a half a block away and on the other side of the street, I noticed that the slime ball informant was pointing at my building and sort of motioning around to the north side. When he held up three fingers in conjunction with his words and other gestures I had a pretty strong feeling that it was my apartment he was telling the weight, the heat, the hit men, the shooters, the enforcers, about. I went through a couple dozen synonyms for these guys but I couldn't find one that didn't make me worry about losing bladder control.

Fortunately I was sporting a goatee at that time and had been cleanly shaved when I had sold the godfather the stamp. I was also wearing a pretty cool custom-made rabbit fur felt hat and wrap-around shades. I sort of blended back into the crowd and sauntered in a direction generally away from home. I had a few other places I could stay in by then but there was about a quarter of a million dollars in my apartment and my favorite Glock. There were also several other fine weapons that I didn't really want to lose but the Glock was a custom-made select-fire 19C with a longer 6.02 inch barrel from the model 17L and several 31 round magazines for its 9mm ammunition. The fact that it could be selected to fire in full automatic made it desirable but also extremely illegal. The slim competition composite frame made it easier to carry concealed and it was several ounces lighter than its larger cousins. With the high-capacity magazine it weighed in at about two pounds four ounces but without the rapidly insertable clip, it came in at only 20 ounces. The long barrel made it remarkably accurate and I had practiced with it enough to be just that myself, at least with targets. I don't know how accurate I'd be against two thugs while sprinting semi-backwards in a narrow alley, and I didn't want to find out.

It was only 3:00 in the afternoon and I didn't want to go to my place for about 12 hours. I made it to one of my cars parked in a long-term lot and drove to a safe little condo I kept primarily for sexual activities. I could be alone here and plan. The problem was I didn't have a plan. Basically I was all nerves and thought I had to have a detailed and ingenious plan for outsmarting the two gorillas outside my apartment house. All I could think of was sneak up the alley from behind, climb to the secret window/door, grab everything I could carry and climb back down. I would then nonchalantly walk back to the rear of the building (there was no back entrance so they wouldn't have a guy back there, supposedly), hop over a small wall and walk between a gutted paint factory, where street people slept, and a storehouse for auto parts. There I would find my 1974 Chevelle, brown and nearly invisible, where I would leave it in a dark spot by one of the auto-part loading docks.

I should say a bit about the car. It had the fattest Eagle GT + 4s made on it. The traction was needed to keep the wheels from spinning under the load of the 270 horsepower 350 V-8 that I had had custom built. The Z-28 high-rise intake manifold with a pair of Holley four barrels on top made sure plenty of fuel and air could get into the engine, then the Headman headers efficiently exhausted the products of combustion into the cross-ventilated dual pipes fitted with Cadillac reverse-flow mufflers. The four-speed transmission with the Hurst shifter made for a pretty quick getaway when needed.

The car was geared for acceleration, not a high top end. It's a rare road that you can actually drive over a hundred miles an hour on, and when you do you attract too much attention. To me the ability to get from zero to about eighty in a number of seconds you could count on significantly less than two hands was more important. Also being able to down shift into third at about 50 MPH, stomp the gas and have the car practically explode out from under you was useful in close situations. Many a young lady had squealed at that maneuver and gotten a little wetter between the legs for me too.

I dozed fitfully, had about two fingers of my beloved, oh-so-smooth and gentle Glenfiddich, at a time when I knew the effects would be worn off before I had to be putting myself in harm's way. I paced, I thought about razor blades, I rubbed black goo from the underside of the stovetop on my face. I changed into black Levi's a size too large with pockets I had made even larger, for flexibility and the ability to hide stuff; a black long-sleeved turtleneck that no con-artist should be without; black socks and black sneakers. A black denim backpack that I had sewn myself on a 1964 Bernina 530-2 Record sewing machine, which I had found in someone's trash and fixed up, completed the outfit.

The backpack had been designed to carry large sums of money. It covered almost my entire back from the lower buttocks to the upper back, curved a little from side to side and laid fairly flat to keep the center of gravity close to the body. This design allowed for a maximum number of stacked $100 bills, stacks that could be about five inches thick each. One hundred bills could be compressed to a minimum of three-eighths of an inch. Believe me I know. I compress my stacks of bills with a C clamp and a couple of chunks of three-quarter-inch oak before I wrap them tightly in plastic. This would give me 13 bundles of 100 bills per five inches and since the pack was exactly five times the length and seven times the width of the typical six-and-one-eighth inch by two-and-19/32nds inch US dollar, it would hold 35 such five-inch stacks. So we're talking 35 stacks of 1300, 100-dollar bills, or $4,550,000 as a maximum capacity. I had about half this much in the apartment ($2,200,000 give or take) so I could pack the bag to two and a half inches thick and carry it closer to my body. It would also be more flexible but would still weigh a good 52 to 53 pounds. I wouldn't exactly be light on my feet.

This and any guns and ammo I wanted to add to the load.

These are the kinds of stupid calculations I did while waiting for my appointment with the dealers of death. Like I'm sure I'm going to have a couple of hours to neatly sort and pack the money!

Finally the time came to get in my 1974 Saab Sonett III with my black leather driving gloves on and drive to where I kept the Chevelle. If I never got back to pick up the little Saab, it would be a big loss. That sporty little car had been responsible for a lot of girlie pick-ups, especially since I took the Saab identification marks off and replaced them with Lamborghini name plates and symbols. The car was rare enough and exotic looking enough that people, and for my purposes, women, were usually fooled.

The two-door Chevelle, a classic sleeper, roared to life. Each of its two doors weighed about as much as my fiberglass Sonett! And when I say roar, I mean loud. It then idled down and sat in its stall making a low slightly irregular rumble as it rocked from side to side from the torque. I let it warm up for several minutes and noticed I was warming up a bit myself. Not that I was all that hot you understand, I was sweating as if I was though. OK, so I used the car warm up as an excuse to procrastinate. I finally pulled out of the garage and into the street, being very careful not to attract attention, not accelerating hard or making too much noise.

I really had no idea what to expect when I got to my apartment house, but I could see the back of it coming into view as I entered my neighborhood.

NINE

I parked the car as quietly as possible in the shadows of the auto parts warehouse. I gathered up the backpack and put it on. It would be easier to carry on my back and it would keep my hands free for the 50-caliber Israeli Arms Desert Commando that I had selected for this trip. It was the logical choice since accuracy would be difficult. Basically, if a slug from this massive handgun hit you anywhere it would knock you into the next block. The destructive force was sufficient that even an arm or leg wound would be fatal because the extremity would essentially be blown off and the limbless one would quickly exsanguinate.

The semi-automatic, with the silencer I had made from some small tin cans and cooper wool, fit into the specially enlarged right front pocket of my extra baggy jeans. I had learned the hard way that steel wool can catch fire when used in a homemade silencer, but that's another story! I couldn't exactly quick draw the gun but I figured if I kept my hand on it in my pocket then I could just bring my whole leg up and fire through the pants. I'd have to remember to keep my knee bent to avoid shooting my foot off and fortunately the gun did not have as much of a recoil as you might think for one so large. I could probably fire it while standing on one foot and not be blown over. Probably.

I sat in the quiet car and reconnoitered (read procrastinated), allowing my eyes to get used to the relative dark. After disabling the interior lights, I not quite but quietly closed the car door and walked to the pathway between the two old buildings across the one-lane, one-way street behind my building. The first unpredictable event—a couple of street people, both males, humping in the bushes near a glassless window into the abandoned paint factory.

They caught sight of me and stopped wiggling for a moment, somehow sensed that I wasn't really dangerous but were aware that I was probably up to no good in my black outfit and black face at three in the morning. But being used to the seamier side of life, they went back to squirming and grunting, wanting nothing to do with whatever mayhem I had planned.

The real problem was whom I might run into on the way back past this same spot when I was carrying a bag stuffed with millions. It hadn't occurred to me that I might run into some disreputable types on my way back to my getaway muscle-car. I hoped I would have enough firepower to scare anybody off without having to actually fire the power. I decided I would carry the Commando out in the open on the way back. I'd take the silencer off so that the definitive shape and shine of the chromed handgun would be obvious. Also, if I had to fire it, the sound would let people know that I was carrying a virtual cannon.

I came to the low wall that separated the properties behind my complex from the narrow road. Here I had some cover as I crouched in the weeds behind the wall. Looking over it I could see most of the length of the alley that ran beneath my secret window/door. In fact I could see it too clearly because someone had fixed the damn streetlight I always sabotaged to prevent this very visibility problem. Who in the hell would have had that lamp fixed? I guess I really knew the answer to that. A regular citizen could call the city works people every day for months and nothing would happen to a broken light. My stamp-collecting mafia buddy probably made one brief call and within an hour the street lamp was not only fixed but restored to pristine condition.

I figured that blowing the light out with a 50-caliber slug from my silenced gun would still attract a little too much attention. They might not hear the shot but when the light blew up like it had been hit by a bazooka, they'd probably know something was up.

In truth I didn't even know if anyone was out there waiting for me. I just wasn't willing to bet my life on it. A good gambler knows when the odds are against him. It was time to walk away. I kept low as I retraced my steps between the buildings. The two guys making what they might call love were still there. I think they had traded places but I really didn't study them closely to confirm this. I did hear some snickering as I went past. Maybe my knees were visibly shaking. It wouldn't have surprised me.

Back at the car I eased into the driver's seat and cranked the engine as quietly as possible. I then made a little hastier escape than I should have although no one seemed to notice the squealing tires. I had a brief image of the two guys in the weeds suddenly choking on the pungent odor of burnt rubber.

I smiled in spite of the fact that I was about to puke from fear.

I went back to my other place, parked the Chevelle where the Saab used to be—it took up about twice as much room—and went up to the condo. I poured about four fingers of my soft, sweet, oh-so-smooth Glenfiddich and gulped it like it was a cheap white zinfandel. When consumed in this fashion it was neither soft nor sweet and definitely not "oh so smooth."

My gums and lips went temporarily numb which allowed me to focus more clearly on the seething pain in my throat and esophagus. My mind moved from this soon-to-seem-insignificant mild discomfort to a pain in my stomach that made me wonder if I had somehow shot myself with my silenced monster handgun while withdrawing it from my pants. Through the tears and squinting lids I could not see any blood so I had to assume that the several ounces of single malt Scotch had gone right through my stomach wall and were now in the process of dissolving the remaining organs in my abdominal cavity. It's a good thing I hadn't reached for the Bookers bourbon. At 161 proof, it would have poured right through me and dribbled onto the floor, eating its way into the apartment below mine like the acidic blood of the alien from *Alien*.

Slowly the cramped muscles of my stomach relaxed. The seven fruit-flavored Tums I chewed and swallowed may have helped some but the ethanol was also being rapidly absorbed, probably overwhelming my liver's ability to detoxify it, and rising to such a level in my blood and brain that I almost forgot that I had left over two million dollars in cash in my old apartment. Almost.

I wasn't about to give up, but I sure as hell was going to soak in the Jacuzzi and then pass out in the womb-like waterbed I kept at this location. Fortunately there was no one sharing it with me. The thought of the rocking and rolling of sex in the waterbed just about made me lose my lunch just before I lost my consciousness.

I woke up feeling only moderately bad. I hadn't had that much to drink really. It was the speed with which I drank it and the empty stomach it went into that caused the problems. It was 2:00 PM. I watched TV. I ate four poached eggs on toast with melted mild cheddar on top. A little salt and some fresh ground pepper and it was a stomach-warming meal that brought back wonderful memories of my mother, who cooked this, my favorite breakfast, for me frequently.

I wondered what old Mom was up to, and I suddenly had an urge to be with her but realized that this was the equivalent of just crying "Mama!" in a time of need. My time of need was at hand. I was actually planning on going back to get my money again tonight. I looked at the Scotch, then I looked at the bourbon. Maybe it would be better to guzzle a bit of each of these and forget about the cash. I had many times that amount in other places, but it was the principle. I had scammed long and hard for that money.

First I had a little chore to do.

I walked to a less than reputable area of town where I was known of course, being a bit disreputable myself. I found a kid who needed a bit of cash and liked adventure. We went to a used car lot and bought a piece of junk. I paid cash, put the title in the kid's name and went to a State Farm insurance office where I got the car insured for everything. The date of purchase and the active date of the insurance happened to match and had occurred about three weeks ago. This slight alteration in a minor detail on the forms did add a bit to the price of the car and to the insurance premium, but it was worth it. I'd spent about $1,900 and if everything worked out, I'd get my millions back in exchange.

It was dusk when the beat-up old car driven by the inexperienced and probably high teenager came barreling down the street in front of my apartment house. The car was swerving from side to side as it moved south on the fortunately not too busy street. It seemed, to the two men standing in front of the produce shop across the street from my building, that the crazy kid was going to lose control at any minute. Sure enough, the car swerved to the wrong side of the street, the kid then over corrected, panicked, hit the gas instead of the brakes and just about flew into the air as the two-ton Detroit land yacht jumped the curb and literally took out the light post at the entrance to the alley that ran beneath my apartment windows.

It was a real stroke of luck that the kid was uncharacteristically wearing a seat belt. He was a bit stunned to be sure, but he had the presence of mind to hang around and tell the cops about how the steering had gone out. When they got around to checking, they found out that the steering had indeed been faulty and they learned that the kid wasn't drunk or stoned. The case was closed and the kid was able to collect a hefty chunk of insurance change, a lot more than the car was worth.

Sometimes you have to make your own luck. Making the steering look out of whack on the car was a little tricky because after all it still had to work well enough to allow the kid to accurately hit the telephone pole. And the kid had to be pretty motivated to risk injury just for the thrill and insurance money he would get. Of course that assumed he survived the crash. But that pole, and the light on it, was out of there. I mean, the splinters from the stump reached only about four inches into the air; that sucker was cut right off at the ground and it had been mangled to complete unusability beneath the massive chrome-plated steel bumper of the car/battering ram. Why, I bet even one of the most influential men in LA, using threats of violence, couldn't get that light repaired before morning. Yes, it was my lucky day.

Same scenario, different night. Cloudy, less light overall and a hell of a lot less light in my alley! There weren't any horny guys out tonight. I didn't see or hear anyone as I made my way to the wall where I had aborted my last attempt at rescuing my fortune and my favorite gun.

Here's what I had planned. I get in and start opening the hidden panels in the wall along the floor of my bedroom. This wall was shared with the bathroom and the built-in tub was just on the other side of it. By opening the disguised doors I had access to the space beneath and around the tub, plenty of room for cash and a few weapons like the pump-action pistol-grip shotgun and the Uzi that were there. Behind a spring-loaded and magnetically secured panel in the headboard was the Glock, a 15-round magazine installed with one already in the chamber. A touch of its secret panel door would spring it open, the gun could be grabbed and, since it had no external safety, all 16 rounds could be fired in a second or two just by pulling back the half-inch travel of the trigger with 3.2 pounds of force. (I had it reduced from the stock 5.5 pounds.) Man, you got to love that kind of home security!

I would carefully pack the money and the guns into the backpack. Getting the pack snuggly battened down to prevent shifting and rattling would be important for the stealthy moves I would need to make as I climbed back out the window. With the weaponry, I'd be carrying close to 75 pounds and I wasn't really in that good of shape. The only aerobic exercise I got was when I was on top, and I tended to avoid that position unless the woman was on her knees and begging for it from behind. There were a few times when I think I got a little heart-related chest pain during those sexual stress tests, but it was worth it. There just aren't too many things more beautiful than a woman's ass being offered up to you. Holding those smooth round cheeks while you bumped up against them was one of the greatest experiences in life.

I was easily distracted by these thoughts. They kept me from thinking about the terror that could occur in the next few minutes. I could be holding my own not-so-smooth hairy buttocks in my hands since there was a good chance that I'd get my ass blown off!

Everything looked perfectly quiet and adequately dark. I made it over the wall and across the narrow lane and crouched at the back entrance of the alley, covered a bit by the anemic-looking bushes that grew there. Getting a good look of the entire length of the walkway confirmed that there was no one present in the alley or in a location across the street that would allow them to see into the alley. Things were going my way. Some of the wooden wreckage from the unfortunate accident involving the lamppost could be seen, but just barely. It was pretty dark without the light. I chuckled to myself and almost started laughing out loud, probably more due to hysteria than any actual humor.

I kept low and near the bushes as I made my way near the midpoint of the alley. Here I worked my way between a couple of sickly shrubs and found a thin wire tucked into the cracks between the bricks of the wall. Pulling this wire caused the rope on my windowsill to fall with the end just reaching the tops of the bushes. The knots in the rope made getting up it a lot easier. I wanted to actually use the knots with hands and feet to keep as close to the wall as possible rather than "walking" up the wall using only my hands on the rope.

I slowly lifted myself onto the rope and, carefully calculating each move, made my way quietly up the wall. I had to move along the wall laterally a little bit to go around the windows of the two apartments below mine. This was done by holding the rope and literally rolling on the wall to one side of the windows then continuing up at a slight angle. The friction of my clothing against the wall was enough to keep me from swinging back and forth in front of the neighbor's windows like some incompetent second-story man on a TV comedy. I actually envisioned this as I was making my way past the fortunately small widows and again I almost lost control to mirth.

Finally at my window, three bricks to the right of the sill, I pressed on an ordinary-looking block and it swivelled inward. The opening allowed me to reach into a hollow space in the wall and gently turn a metal lever that pulled the wedge-shaped bolts that firmly held the window/door in place. The window, bars and all, then quietly opened inward on its well-designed hinges. No loud noises, no squeaking, just a little faint scraping sound. I made a little more noise as I grunted my way over the wall and into the bedroom. Not a particularly graceful entrance I'm afraid and one that removed a little skin from my stomach, sort of like a road burn injury, as I came over the ledge. When I stood up and felt the stinging and then felt the blood soaking through my sweater—not a lot, just a enough to make the material moist—I issued a faint explicative.

I had swung the window closed and moved to the side to go around my bed to the opposite wall and it was a damn good thing I did. Otherwise the silhouette against a back-lit portal would have been mine and I would have been an easy target. As it turned out I was pretty invisible against the wall and the silhouette was of someone else standing in the door of my bedroom, back lit by the faint light coming through the living room windows. This made the other guy an easy target. Well, it would have if I hadn't fumbled it.

I guess I was a little spooked. I never imagined that there might be someone in the apartment waiting for me. I always thought they would wait for me to come home and then come up the stairs after me, break down my door and pulverize me. Anyway, I forgot all about lifting my leg and firing my silenced Desert Commando through my pants. Instead I clumsily tried to pull the gun out of my pocket. The tin can silencer caught on an internal fold and I had to tug pretty hard, in the meantime managing to make a little commotion. The other guy was apparently a little spooked also. He didn't expect anyone to walk through a third-floor wall but the whispered cuss word used to express my dismay over my flesh wound must have caught his attention and brought him to the door. Mother always told me cussing was a bad thing. Shit, I should have listened to her.

The barrel of my gun pulled out of the silencer and thus rather suddenly out of my pocket. By this time the guy in the door had recovered enough from his dazed amazement to start raising the gun he already had in his hand up toward some of my vital organs. My gun had so suddenly popped out of my pocket, sans silencer, that it was practically pointed at the ceiling when the first round went off. The sound was impressive and a little disorienting to the guy in the doorway. His first shot went a little wide to my right and shattered the glass in the dual function window. My slug had hit the door frame above my visitor's head and sent splinters of wood, paint and plaster showering down on him, a momentary distraction.

A moment was all I needed. The barrel of my gun was now down to the level of his chest and as near as I could tell, dead centered. The hole in the barrel of this gun is about the size of the tip of an average index finger. I could get the first inch or so of my little finger into the thing! I wondered how big it looked when it was pointed right at you and you could see the finger on the trigger moving slowly back. I never wanted to find out and the guy in my doorway was very sorry he had.

My second round exploded from the end of my gun before my company could get off a second. The hefty hunk of lead hit him in the mid-chest just

73

like I planned and lifted him off his feet and halfway across the living room. He spun halfway around as he sprawled over the couch. His body rotated so that his back was toward me as he actually spilled over the furniture. I use the term spilled because it's exactly what he was doing. The exit wound in his back could have been pretty neatly plugged with a basketball. The contents of his chest were literally spilling out over the couch as he spun and fell. I thought of things like "Come on, buddy, spill your guts" or "I hated that guy's guts anyway" or I wondered if *Hints from Heloise* would advise me on how to remove heart tissue stains from my sofa, especially since some of it was still rhythmically contracting, sort of trying to dig itself into the fabric.

Anyway, the guy was dead. I had moved and was now in the doorway to my bedroom looking out on the offal of a fellow human. I started to move a lot more when I heard the heavy footsteps on my stairs. Ha, I thought, it will take them at least five minutes to get through my door. Wait a minute, they had all day yesterday to get through my door, that's why there was a guy already in my apartment when I arrived. I was in trouble.

I ran to the wall opposite my bedroom window and kicked the hell out of my carefully constructed secret doors. I then reached in and started cramming plastic-wrapped packs of bills into my baggy pants. There was no way I was going to be able to take the backpack off and load it up. I was in the process of stashing wads of hundreds in my clothing when my front door opened smoothly on its hinges as if the assassins had not only broken through my locks but had then taken the time to oil up the hinges.

I stood partway up and did a back roll with a half twist over my bed so that I would end up standing on the other side facing my blown-out window. This actually worked, much to my amazement. I reached over with my left hand and pushed on a spot on the headboard of the bed, just inside the bedpost. A little door popped open and I grabbed my Glock and one of the 31-round magazines. In about the same motion I put the Israeli Arms behemoth back into my pocket where it clunked against my useless silencer and a few thousand dollars. I reached for the rope on the sill and was preparing to grab it and leap out the window, letting myself crash back against the outside wall of the building while still somehow managing to hold onto the rope and my Glock. I never found out if this would have worked. The rope was not there. It had been cut away by the stray bullet or the flying glass. I almost threw myself out of the window without the rope!

I caught myself in time to do two things: 1) feel for the wire just outside the right side of my window; and 2) hear the guys in the living room making noises of disgust as they walked around the couch to enter through the bedroom door. I pulled the wire and the rope on the roof of the building next door dropped down. I had to then pull in all the slack wire and bring the rope over to me. I grabbed it, turned my back to the window and brought the Glock to bear on the bedroom door with my left hand while I threw myself butt first backwards out the window. (See, I always do things ass backwards.) The bad guys came in as I went out but they didn't have time to set their sights on me. I, on the other hand, didn't care about aim. I simply let loose 15 rounds of 9mm hollow points into the room. The effect was that I was literally propelled out the window by the kick of the Glock as it spit all 15 rounds in less than a second.

I had a chance to feel a little freefall, a little cool air, then I had the unique opportunity to feel myself slam into the wall of the neighboring building. How I managed to hold onto the rope with my right hand and my gun with my left I'll never know but the next thing I remember I was hanging with my back to the wall looking into my shattered bedroom window. The would-be killers seemed to have been delayed by my 15 sudden random acts of violence. I had time to drop the empty magazine out of my 9mm and then had to figure out how to reload. I was holding the larger magazine in my left hand also, gripping it and the grip of my gun in my sweaty fist. I brought the pair up to my mouth and clutched the magazine as hard as I dared with my teeth and lips. I then put the business end of the magazine into the end of the butt of my custom grip and by keeping a tight hold with my teeth and moving the gun rapidly toward my mouth, I was able to lock the clip home. My teeth just about shattered but I wasn't finished with them yet. Meanwhile my right hand was getting into some serious hurt. I shuffled my heels against the rough surface of the wall and got a little purchase. It was enough. I then bit into the top of the barrel of my gun and slid the gun across my face like some sort of very malignant harmonica.

That popped the first of 31 rounds into the chamber and that was just enough. It was also just in time. The two guys trying to kill me, one looking a bit wounded, came tentatively to the window. Luck was with me. They naturally were looking down to see if my body had splattered against the pavement resulting in good fortune for them. My body wasn't there and as they looked up due to my maniacal laughter, I pulled the trigger on my trusty automatic and probably tore those two guys to shreds with about 12 bullets each before they even had a chance to realize what was so funny.

What was so funny was, I knew as I went out the window that I was going to make it. It's the same feeling I'd get at the blackjack table when I knew for sure that I was going to win the next hand and slid a few thousand bucks into the golden circle on the green felt of the table in front of me. A calm and certain excitement. Now what? There were lights coming on all over the place and sirens drawing near.

TEN

I hate to be redundant at the start of a chapter but...I had to get away. I dropped the long magazine out of the Glock and then dropped the gun into my left pocket. Not all that smart. The damn thing was hot enough to burn my leg and if it had slipped a little toward the mid-line, it would have burned some even more important parts of my anatomy. The pain took my mind off the cramped-to-the-point-of-numbness-and-paralysis muscles in my right hand. Finally I was able to grasp the rope with my left hand and turn to face the wall. I then walked my feet up until my legs were perpendicular to the wall and practically sprinted up the two stories of brick to the roof with my hands moving over each other on the rope as fast as I could make them go. I had a picture of myself as a cartoon character running straight up a wall in an attempt to flee from my burning rear end. It wouldn't have surprised me much if I had left a trail of smoke like a sky writer behind me as I went.

Once on the roof I stowed the rope, took off the backpack and put all the cash, the cold gun with the silencer and the hot gun still smoking, into it. I then put the far-lighter-than-I-had-planned pack back on and ran quietly across the roof to the fire escape on the opposite side. Once on the ground I headed back toward the one-way street only to be met by a chain link fence. Hell, after what I'd just been through, a fence was a piece of cake. I was up and over that sucker before I realized it was really there. It's amazing what adrenaline can do.

I ran along the opposite side of the old paint factory and almost tripped over two guys doing "it" in the weeds. I guess they had moved to the north side of the building because of the traffic last night on the south side. I blew past them so fast I couldn't even tell if they were the same two guys, much less which one was on top now.

I made it to my car no further scathed and apparently undetected, except by the gay lovers in the grass. I got in my car and drove of at a surprisingly genteel pace, no eau de burning rubber tonight. I took back roads away from the scene of numerous crimes and in a roundabout way made my way back to my condo. Another night, another crash, only this time without the whiskey. I didn't even wait to count the money. I didn't want to be that disappointed just before bed. I wanted to bask in the joy of still being alive for about two-tenths of a second and then pass out for ten hours. I did just that.

The next afternoon I got out of bed, took a long shower and thought about the men I had so dramatically killed. It didn't seem to bother me. Sure, seeing the anatomic details of their internal workings grossed me out a bit, but the fact that I had taken life didn't result in any guilt. As far as I was concerned, they deserved it and therefore I had done society a service. I was actually kind of proud of the way I had handled myself.

Out of the shower I poured enough Scotch into a glass to make three ice cubes float. This time I was able to savor the liquor. It was indeed gentle, sweet and smooth. After an hour of getting my thoughts together and feeling the alcohol-induced fatigue, I went back to bed. It was like I had a bad case of jet lag and had to get myself back in tune with local time. It was late enough in the day that I couldn't get much accomplished anyway so I figured I'd get up early the next morning and start working through the contingency plans I had for disappearing from the City of Angels.

At 4:30 AM I couldn't sleep anymore, so I took another shower and made coffee. I wanted to just sit, relax and read the paper. I wanted to daydream about Hawaii or maybe that 17-year-old blonde I had picked up last week, hard to say which was more appealing.

Instead of indulging in fantasies I put the phone in front of me and began calling. First a few calls to banks in the Caribbean and Europe, where the day was well underway. Then calls to contacts on the East Coast where the business day, Friday as it turns out, at least I was pretty sure, was getting started. I then made calls to people and businesses farther west, marching through the time zones at about the same rate as the sun crossed the sky, finding each contact just after they had arrived at their offices.

By then local time was 9:23 AM and I could start making calls around California to complete the task of making the man I was here vanish. I had to do a lot of shuffling of assets. Emptying accounts that were in my LA pseudonym and transferring the money through several off-shore banks to numbered accounts I had under different names. I also had to liquidate some real estate assets, including, as it turns out, the building I had lived in and recently bloodied. The landlord I rented from had no idea that the quiet guy in 3B had become the building owner and he would never find out.

He did find out that I was not as quiet as he thought. I saw a short piece on the news about a shoot out in my old apartment building that the police felt was a drug-related massacre leaving three dead (good!) and at least two assailants missing. From the amount of expended ammunition they estimated that as many as three other people might have been involved in spraying the interior of the apartment with lead (good!). I had left behind two different calibers of slugs so maybe that would mislead them into thinking a small army had visited havoc upon my peaceful neighborhood instead of just one scared shitless guy trying to reclaim what was rightfully his.

Speaking of which, I had only managed to salvage 17 packs of 100 hundreds or $170,000. The cops were going to have to figure out what to do with the over $2,000,000 that was left, like high-priced insulation, around my tub. I hoped that they would not find prints. So far I had managed to stay out of trouble and not get my fingerprints onto any police database. I was meticulously careful about this when handling the plastic-wrapped bundles of bills in particular. That plastic took a print so clear that it might as well be a picture of you with your aliases, addresses and phone numbers.

I also kept the rest of the apartment clean and had been wearing gloves on that last visit. I did leave a little blood and a few too many skin cells on my windowsill. The dry cracking skin on my belly was a reminder of that, but this was well before the time when DNA analysis could be done on a fragment of tissue and identify you with an eight billion to one probability of accuracy. Not good enough odds to convict you of anything as it would turn out, but a hell of a lot better than anything I could get in Vegas.

So I "sold" properties to myself in another guise, disguised by layers of corporate names with fictitious CEOs. The only things I lost were in my old apartment and I would lose a few cars I kept stashed around in various locations in case I needed them. I emptied my scattered rental storage units of liquid assets, packed everything into my trusty Chevelle and headed east, toward the city of lost wages. From the City of Angels to the city where flesh and blood angels could be bought and sold like fast food.

The guy who recently had his apartment shot up in Los Angeles had vanished, hopefully without a trace, and a new persona in an old car with new Nevada plates was the secret executor of that missing person's private and large estate.

I got into Las Vegas and dropped my car at a paint and body shop where I asked them to repaint the car red and convert it into a convertible instead of a vinyl-covered hard top. They were a little reluctant but the appearance of a large cash-in-advance payment and the carefully orchestrated yet seemingly accidental revelation of my shoulder-holstered weapon got them motivated in short order.

I took a cab to my casino hideaway. The cab driver helped load all my suitcases, bags and brief cases into his venerable Checker. My Chevelle had been so loaded down with this stuff that I was afraid I'd get pulled over on my trip, either for suspicion of transporting a huge load of drugs or for the public nuisance of leaving a trail of sparks along the highway from bottoming out on every minor crack and bump in the road. I envisioned my car as a traveling Fourth of July fireworks display bouncing over the blacktop.

Actually the trip went smoothly and I arrived on Saturday afternoon a little ahead of schedule. A little (a) head was just what I was thinking about too, that would really hit the spot, or at least slide up and down on the spot. It had been a week or eight days since I'd had lurid sex with a well-paid skilled female and this was too long. Finding a clean professional was near the top of my priorities.

The day of the week and the time of the day didn't make much difference in Las Vegas, everything was basically available all the time and it was easy to lose track of what day of the week it was. The concierge at the casino always knew though and he also knew, for the right tip, just what woman of loose morals was available to be sent to my pleasant penthouse.

After satisfying numerous of my lusts and fantasies, and a fair number of the stunning brunette's with the pale blue eyes also, I was ready for some food and a relaxing game of blackjack.

What a life. The game of twenty-one that I could hardly seem to lose, the comped meals from all-you-can-eat buffets. I took up smoking even though it killed my dad. It made the gaming more fun somehow and I figured that I was inhaling so much stale second-hand smoke that I might as well inspire some fresh vapors from burning tobacco leaves now and then.

The women were plentiful and compliant. I was not a violent man and got off as much on satisfying the women I was with as on satisfying myself. I sometimes spent so long with my face tucked between a pair of beautiful thighs that my tongue would hurt for days. Other times I would use the fingers on my right hand until they would cramp up and go numb like they had when I was gripping the rope on the night I escaped from LA. It was worth it to see a gorgeous female writhing in pleasure on my bed. Watching them have an orgasm was so dramatic and sexually arousing that I'd sometimes ejaculate spontaneously without even touching myself.

These women weren't faking it either. They were experienced, as they knew I was, and they appreciated a man who would take the time to satisfy them, a rare event in their line of work. Because of their experience they had learned to have incredibly intense orgasms when they did have them; the screams, the passing out, it was real alright. So real that a few would come by from time to time for freebies.

Like I said, what a life.

I took care of business over the phone mostly, occasionally traveling. I'd take one of my beautiful playmates with me and would use the trip as an excuse to have sex in new surroundings as well as to take care of a little business. I was moving out of scams and moving into legitimate investments in a big way. I could make more money in a usually sort of legal way by working the world's stock markets and buying and selling currency than I could through the more traditional forms of illegal cons and legal gambling. It was all like a blackjack table though. You had to see the order in the chaos, watch for the trends and move in a big way when things were going your way. I wanted to get to the point that through my various corporate shells I could start making sure that the stock trends would move my way with a little more frequency and predictability.

This was the great thing about the stock market. Not only was it an enjoyable and usually profitable game of chance, but you could actually walk behind the table, so to speak, and mess around with the deck and the dealer's hand without getting thrown out of the game! At least if you were careful.

It required information management on a level that even my seemingly well-above-average brain could not handle. That's when I got my first computer. It was an incredibly powerful machine with twin five-and-one-quarter-inch floppy drives, loaded to the max with 540 thousand bytes of random access memory and an 8088 processor that blew the socks of anything previously available. I loaded in several floppy disks that contained a "disk operating system" or DOS that was being produced by one of the companies in which I was heavily invested.

I was proud to see the little greater than sign, called a prompt, eventually show up on my screen indicating the computer was ready for action. I had gone all out and bought a device called a modulator/demodulator, or modem for short, that could transmit data over a phone line at a blistering 300 bits per second. I learned that this was called a baud rate. I then began exploring DOS and learned how to write little programs called batch files to run everything almost automatically. I was hooked on this machine and even ignored my genitals' demands for attention and my favorite dealers on the casino floor.

Locked away in my room with a view, I unlocked the mysteries of my computer and found out about a fledgling network of computers at various university and government offices that were trying to link up via modem and share information. Now that had potential. Not only for the ability to access and control that information, but also for the investment potential in the companies that would evolve to manage the network they were calling the web, when it actually got up and running. With this tool I could be in touch with nerds all over the country, who due to their egos and my beguiling ways, would spill in great detail the contents of their current projects and their rumors of upcoming developments.

The problem was I was becoming a nerd too, just like the guys I used to get information from and make fun of at UCLA. I even mastered BASIC and began writing my own programs and applications. I had to, because I was beginning to put a huge amount of very confidential information on these floppy disks. Information that could get me into trouble if it got out, information that I used to have to keep in the RAM of my brain to the point of pushing even my capacity beyond its limits. In order to grow, I had to have an alternative place to keep important information and these little black-coated, magnetizable disks were just the things. Soon I had dozens and then hundreds of them stashed in safe places, so many that I had to write an indexing program that I kept on a floppy to help me keep track of all my other floppies!

Meanwhile there was my health. Since my gymnastic escape from my apartment in LA that would have gotten 10s, even from the Russian judges, I had done very little. I had access to the never-ending buffet of free fatty food and got little or no exercise. Even sex was becoming slowly less aerobic for me and slowly more aerobic for my partners. It wasn't a problem though because the svelte beauties I was having sex with were athletic and into exercise anyway. Plus they made a good living off me, or I guess it would be more literally accurate to say on me.

The net result of my change in location and lifestyle was obesity; I was growing fat. Sitting for hours staring at the blurry green symbols on my computer screen didn't help. But that was where the money was.

My next step to financial freedom, or more like financial dominance, was to become an active participant in the management of some of my companies. Most of my organizations were just names with lists of other names that made up a board or group of controlling executives. Very few of these people existed and if any were sought out, the message eventually ended up in front of me and I occasionally had to make calls while pretending to be one of the key leaders of one fraudulent company or another. Dodging the FTC, the IRS and a few other groups of initials became a big part of my daily activities.

I legitimately wanted to start an investment company, an insurance company and a technology consulting company. The investment company would actually help me manage the funds in my more legitimate companies and investments and would allow me to invest further using other people's money. What a concept. I loved America. With the kind of leverage obtainable with legitimate funds from numerous wealthy investors I could really start to manipulate things. Combine this with my illegitimate contacts and the surreptitious control over a whole raft of other publicly traded companies and I might actually be able to manipulate markets for my personal gain.

Spreading what seemed to be reliable good or bad information about the companies over which I did not have direct or indirect control was another useful tool. It allowed me to manipulate my competitors into positions where I could make money off of their losses or make money off of their profits or in some cases obtain control of them, at which point I could drive them out of existence while funneling their assets into another of my companies. I could also make them hugely successful, at least on paper, and mop up with my majority ownership of their stocks, with its artificially inflated prices. I had to love it.

There were really just two things I had to track. Net worth, which was meaningless ink on paper that could be made to vary by many decimal points depending on the situation, and real assets, that is property and cash on hand. It was important for me to keep a balance between these two. I may want to look cash heavy but worth little more than the cash I had, which would make me look like a good investor in a get rich scheme. Or I may want a minimal of liquid assets and a huge net worth to apply for credit with which to further build my empire or destroy somebody else's. So under different situations, some legal and some not so legal, and under different names, both personally and corporately, I made my fortune grow.

It was about then that I got my first hard drive. There was a ten-megabyte disk available first but I held out for the massive 20-megabyte drive that came along fairly soon after the ten. Can you imagine twenty million bytes of information? I could load most of my key financial information onto the disk and have almost instant access to it. No more flipping floppies in and out and waiting while they made that funny humming and sort of grinding noise while I sat there waiting for the data to be written to the screen. In addition I upgraded my modem to one that transmitted at up to 1200 baud! Most sources of data on line couldn't transmit that fast yet but I was convinced it would eventually become the standard.

I wanted to start an insurance company because it was the biggest legal scam going and the industry was growing fast. It was gambling in reverse. Now I was the dealer with the endless supply of chips who took small numbers of chips from a large number of people who were willing to risk a seemingly small amount of money on a regular basis to avoid a one-time major loss. Fortunately the odds of the big loss were so low that being in the insurance business was like owning your own casino where the games were all fixed. It was hard to lose, especially if you didn't let ethics get in your way.

The technology consulting company would simply be fun, but it would also allow me access to technologic insider information that could be useful. And so I embarked on my career as several presidents and CEOs of these new companies.

By the time I got these companies organized and had enticed the cream of the crop of the not-always-completely-ethical business people to work for me, by offering large signing bonuses and compensation packages both above and below the table, a year had passed and I had put on another 50 pounds. The below-the-table stuff was important because it gave me a lever to control those executives who did not respect me or did not feel any loyalty to me. (The majority it seemed.) Many just wanted the money and prestige and would put up with me. They would work hard to make the company financially successful because that was the key to their financial success.

A few would be like me, trying to build an empire at everyone else's expense. They would covet my job and some might actually get it. If they succeeded me it would be due to the fact that I let them because their "promotion" allowed me to make even more money in one way or another. None of my employees knew of even a fraction of my real holdings. When they attempted to manipulate me, they saw themselves as slightly smaller dogs going up against a slightly bigger opponent in this dog-eat-dog world. They usually believed that they could make up for their smaller stature because they inevitably thought they were smarter than I was. In fact, any one of them trying to push me around was like a housefly trying to push an elephant out of the way of a particularly succulent fresh dung pile. Not only that but I had yet to come across anybody that was as smart as I was. Just a statement of fact. It was true and if you ignore the truth, it will eventually hurt you. You just have to accept it. I did.

ELEVEN

I was pretty close to first in line when the IBM PC XTs came out. The muscular 286 processor in a machine with dual floppy drives, one of them the new three-and-one-quarter inch, high-capacity model, and a 40 meg hard drive! It was fleshed out with the full 640 kilos of RAM that the operating system was capable of handling. My chip company, Intel, and my software company, Microsoft, were doing well. I call them my companies. I'm proud of them like a parent. I don't have a controlling interest in either company but I control a lot more stock than most, it's just that no one knows it. In Microsoft, for example, when they do a mailing to shareholders, I eventually end up with 34 copies mailed to locations throughout the world to people and businesses seemingly unconnected. Each of those entities own hundreds to hundreds of thousands of Microsoft shares, mostly purchased before the boom of Microsoft domination of the world of operating systems. I hadn't met Bill Gates, but I thought he might be as intelligent and crafty as I was. His only flaw was a sense of morals he seemed to have that kept him from really competing with me. He eventually became the recognized richest man on Earth, but I was to be the first man with a net worth of over 100 billion dollars and I was destined to be the world's first trillionaire. But to get back to my story.

It was from the seat of power at the head of the table in the boardroom in my investment management company that I first caused the death of a man in a way other than through self-defense. By this time my company had been in business for about a year and had made quite a name for itself. The companies it invested in always seemed to do well, which was easy to understand when you knew that most of those companies were under my control. I could shift money in and out of them in ways that were not visible and make them look like heavenly investments, or ripe for takeover by another of my companies that didn't even know it was one of my companies. It was a huge game of chess and I felt like I was the only guy playing who could see the whole board.

Speaking of the board, in the boardroom, we were discussing a particularly bothersome competitor with one of our smaller (less than a billion a year) companies. The competition was owned as a legitimate enterprise by the head of a Chicago-based crime family. The company looked legit but I knew what was really going on. These organized crime types had even fewer scruples than I did, at least up to that point in time. I mentioned casually and with humorous intent that it would be a whole lot easier to make our company profitable if a couple of key players in the other company would suddenly disappear.

Within two weeks, they did. Accidents, like when that car hit the light post by my apartment building in LA. I didn't know who did it or how. I didn't even know who on the board had the connections to pull off these high-level hits and I didn't want to know. Once I saw what the untimely death of key players in a competing business could do to the surviving business' stock, I was sold. I didn't do it often, but whenever I had a particularly sticky opponent in a business endeavor, all I had to do was make a joke about them disappearing and, just like magic, they did.

Two or three each year didn't make enough of a splash to start people thinking about connections. Even when I arranged for the mid-air explosion of a chartered jet with practically the whole executive team of an international distribution company on board, no one talked about conspiracy in relation to that tragic "accident." I guess in a way I was responsible for the policies that were put in place after that. Only one key executive per flight. No company would ever lose its entire management team in a single airline crash again. It's nice to have contributed to a worthwhile development.

The 386s were out. I now had on my desktop more computing power than NASA had for the Apollo missions. If they could get to where astronauts were playing golf on the moon, just think where I might go. I started having daydreams about interstellar flight and became a *Star Trek* fan of huge proportions. This was both figurative and, in terms of my figure, literal. I continued to expand, smoke, drink and play with "girls" every chance I got. My Scotch had changed to a blend in a ceramic jug call Usquebach. It was a lot more expensive than Glenfidich and I was drinking a lot more of it. The cost of my habits had risen from negligible to microscopic so I didn't sweat it much.

The 486s came out. I had several and always kept them upgraded to the highest level of performance possible. But I started needing more computing power. I eventually bought a Cray super computer, not personally, but one of my technology research companies did, and I used it a fair amount. Everybody who used the thing did so by appointment only and had to wait for their allotted time to try to complete as many calculations as possible. I kept an eye on the schedule and was signed up under various guises for about half of the available time.

It gave me some real power to manipulate financial markets and delve into chaos theory in relation to the Earth's supply of wealth. It actually seemed that I would soon be able to set up some programs that would make my control of the world economy inevitable. I had to reach a certain critical mass in terms of net worth, leverage on world markets and control of key industries before I could put the whole plan on autopilot and watch the world literally become my oyster.

I got into energy technologies. Like a linear accelerator whose circular track was so large it crossed more than one state line, and like my favorite project, fusion.

This drew me like a magnet and for the first time I had to start learning a little more math and science than I ever really wanted to know. But I had to know. A device that would power itself and generate even more power than it consumed. A limitless supply of power from water with a device that generated waste materials that were utterly non-toxic and non-radioactive. It kept me awake nights thinking about it, unlimited power. That's all I really wanted.

The Pentium processors came out. Working with them is what gave me the idea to build my own computers with multiple parallel Pentium processors and huge amounts of RAM instead of large-scale storage devices. Designs based on my ideas were built by some of my companies and set new records in the mips, then bips and eventually the tips range. (Millions, Billions and Trillions of Instructions Per Second, respectively.) I eventually settled on a design for personal use with 120 Pentium II processors and 450 giga-bytes of RAM. Every program I needed was loaded into RAM and ran from there with no delays for disk access. The tasks were also handled at a rate of 120 per clock tick, with each processor handling its designated load at its top speed. Every time a faster processor came out, I'd have to buy 120 of them and sometimes redesign my giant "mother" board to handle faster clock speeds. I developed a system of tiny tubes that allowed me to cool each individual processor with its own little ethylene glycol refrigeration unit. What a blast. Designing and building those little coolers got me interested in micro-miniaturization. I kept thinking about smaller and smaller things becoming more and more powerful and started struggling with concepts like limitless smallness with limitless power or instantaneous power of infinite magnitude.

I don't know why, but my brain would end each day drifting into thoughts about my fusion reactor project and end up thinking about small but powerful machines and their ability to harness energy beyond fusion and maybe even beyond time. I was into some really deep water here and couldn't see clearly through it besides. It's not that I knew what I was thinking about, it was just images and stray thoughts that seemed to be important but that I couldn't quite grasp.

Several interesting trends were occurring at this time. The fusion project was growing. It started with a modest doughnut-shaped reaction chamber, called a torus, where super-heated fast-moving deuterium nuclei could be contained at such high temperature and pressure that when two streams moving in opposite directions at just under the speed of light met head on, the nuclei would fuse forming heavier but non-toxic elements and releasing more energy than the device consumed getting it started and keeping it going. The reaction could theoretically be self-sustaining like the fusion reaction occurring in our sun. All we had to do was set up the same environmental factors as were present near the center of the sun and then jump-start the reaction, sort of like starting a 100,000-square-mile forest fire with a single match. Simple.

The size of the project kept expanding. The lasers that were needed had to be more powerful, the torus had to be larger, the magnetic fields had to be stronger, the whole shape of the containment field would have to be changed, etc.

Meanwhile my waistline, which had pushed out to a point where I was carrying around 312 pounds, began to shrink. I didn't know why. I really didn't change my habits. It's just that my belt kept having to be snugged up. It was a good thing, right? Anyway, the more the fusion-related devices grew, the more I shrank.

Another trend was occurring at night. Again my brain would get looped into thinking about things on a smaller and smaller scale, things with more and more power, including the power to build elements similar to the way the fusion reactor did only in a programmed way that would allow for the production of any substance desired.

The last trend was the old out-of-body sensations that I hadn't felt since my teen years. They started up again. I could see the parallels. I was lying still in bed thinking deep thoughts on very focused topics that were really beyond my grasp and suddenly I'd be in that all-in-your-head kind of place where you were afraid you'd become paralyzed. Some times you'd swear you were moving and suddenly pop back into wakefulness to realize that you hadn't been moving at all. It was a damn nuisance and left me tired in the morning like having too many wet dreams in a row. You wake up in the morning as exhausted as if you had actually had sex with 20 or 30 women. (You can do this in your dreams if you learn to consciously control them, but it can be addicting and as I said, a little exhausting.)

Over the next year my weight continued a relentless lowering. It began to worry other people. It began to worry me. The fatigue was also taking a toll and I gave up drinking and smoking in order to make time for drinking more coffee. Don't worry, I'd never give up sex, but it was getting to be a strain.

By the time I hit 150 pounds again, for the first time since high school, I had noticed the blood in my bowel movements. The fusion project had grown to a stature that could only be described as colossal and was threatening to drain even my vast financial reserves. My nights continued to be sweating restless periods where I would intermittently go from thinking clearly about miniaturizing the fusion torus to suddenly wrestling some Thing for possession of my wasting body.

I went to a doctor for the first time in my life. He worked for a large HMO that one of my insurance companies controlled and the organization was in the process of squeezing every drop of profit from the health care system, even if it meant taking it out of the doctors' pockets and at the expense of the lives of our subscribers. A dead patient didn't cost the company anything. No care was cheap care and no care resulted in the early demise of those potentially costly clients. That left behind only the younger and healthier clients who would pay the steep premiums and yet not use any benefits. What a scam, and it was legal!

To get the attention of this doctor I didn't have to pull any corporate strings and as far as anyone at the HMO knew, I didn't have any strings at corporate headquarters to pull. In reality I could pull a whole rope if I wanted to, but I usually kept the bundle of fibers in anonymous hands. So to them I was just another retched uninsured person trying to rip off the system by getting free medical care.

It was hardly free. The attention getter I used for the MD was 10,000 in cash to interrupt his busy schedule and do a colonoscopy on me in the privacy of my own home. The outcome was a pretty sure bet. Several large pink and red cauliflower-looking masses were found within my colon, all of which were pretty well-advanced cancers.

The doc took color photos of each through the amazing miniature video camera on the end of his long slender scope. He left me copies to ponder, a little collection of pictures of my gut gone bad. I could frame them and set them on a mantle and show people my little growing mutant clones. Colon cells having been taken over by evil spirits and growing into monstrosities that were literally eating the fat off my body, eating me alive, and they would continue eating until I was no longer alive.

The growths would die also, consuming their own host the way the HMOs were consuming doctors who in reality were the only source of income for the companies. The growth of the HMOs would eventually kill its host and the whole body of medicine would become a rotting corpse for lawyers to argue over for decades.

I was a goner. I asked the doc about time. For the first time he made eye contact and looked at me. He looked sad and defeated. He said he could tell that the whites of my eyes were a little yellow, what he called icteric. This meant that the cancer was already in my liver and well on the way to destroying it. People only live a few days without a liver. I had those few days plus a couple of months while the cancer finished off every last liver cell I had.

I lost interest in most of my projects. My latest super computer modeling showed that I was within six months of hitting the critical mass that predicted inevitable financial domination of the world. I wouldn't be around to see it. If I had made it to that point it would have been so much fun to slowly reveal myself to the public as the real source of power behind things like the stock markets of most of the developed countries and most of the multi-national corporations that had been going through merger madness and growing global.

I had planned the ultimate merger where every financial entity on Earth would be merged into my fold. Almost every paycheck in the world would have my signature on it. Political institutions like the comparatively powerless government of the last remaining super-power, America, would bow to me. I could buy and sell Presidents and Senators the way I used to buy and sell whores. There really wasn't much difference. It's just that I wouldn't have sex with the politicians unless one happened to be a gorgeous female. Speaking of sex, the doctor who looked at my colon had drawn some blood at the time. I was HIV positive. It figures.

All that planning, all that power, all that pleasure sucked up by a kilogram or so of cells growing faster than my body could supply them with energy.

I kept obsessing about power, the kind that a fusion reactor could produce. I kept thinking about miniaturization. I would dream about three-dimensional snow flakes with their six points pointing in mutually perpendicular directions, each shaped like a little cone or bell maybe.

Mostly I surfed the Net and liquefied assets. It was terrible to put the breaks on the huge financial powerhouse I had built. My net worth began shrinking by billions per day instead of growing by billions as it had in the past. These were trivial losses however. I just wanted to get everything I could into four numbered accounts in the names of my three genetic brothers and my one genetic sister who I had kept track of through the years.

They however had never heard anything about their little brother since the night he left home before even finishing high school. I'd fantasize about these guys in black suits I would arrange to have hired after I was gone. They would go to each sibling's house, and with frighteningly serious faces, reveal the fact that each of them was tied for first place in the competition for amassing the largest fortune in the world. I wish I could see their faces as it slowly sank in that each of them would be worth over a hundred billion dollars!

The funds would be utterly impossible to trace. Between my control of the banks involved and my ability to alter computerized transactions in any part of the world, I could arrange it. The money would be there, legal, secure and untouchable by anyone but my siblings and there would not be one damn thing that they or anyone on Earth could do about it.

I was on the Net checking in with some of my techno-nerd friends. I had started up a chat room where we were discussing power sources, the nature of the universe and similar heady matters. One of my online buddies had heard through a friend that there was some guy in Salt Lake City who claimed to be working in his basement on a machine that would harness gravitational energy and would be in control of what could theoretically be an infinite source of power. It was offered as a joke, but…

It got my attention. I felt electrified and as if I had energy for the first time in about a year. I got my friends to start tracking this guy down and told them to get back to me as soon as possible with his location. They probably thought I was even crazier than they already thought I was. Of course they had no idea who I was in reality. I was just an anonymous online name who shared some of their bizarre interests.

My skin was an odd shade of light brown with a little yellow orange thrown in. It sagged around me like slowly tanning leather dyed a color that even nature couldn't like. It didn't keep me from going to Salt Lake City though. I had gotten this mad scientist's name from the Web heads I had set on his trail. It hadn't taken long. Everything on Earth was available on the net if you knew how and where to look and these dorks knew that much.

I walked up to the front door of the house at 1582 D Street and knocked.

TIME THREE

TWELVE

I actually believe that I can recall my birth as if I had been a witness to the amazing event. As I would doze off later in life I would oftentimes see my mother and myself in a delivery room. My body had just flopped out, released from the confines of the birth canal, and what I perceived was that I moved toward my little, wet, squirming body and seemed to hover near its head. I think I stayed in this somewhat disconnected state for some unremembered amount of time but eventually my perspective became as it is now and as it should be, through my eyes. The bleeding from the Rh incompatibility, that was a problem in those distant days, led to the need for my mother to receive a transfusion. For some reason these events stuck with me through the years. Whether they were real or induced memories from psychological mind games I wasn't sure.

What I was sure about was my ability to learn. My mother told me that I was a very quiet and observant baby and that by six months of age I had suddenly started speaking pretty clearly. Words and phrases led to sentences by nine months. They discovered that I could read quite by accident. I was a month into my third year when I corrected my mother's reading of a new book she had purchased for me. I explained that I had been reading along with her for as long as I could remember and that reading seemed very natural to me, something I was just supposed to be doing not struggling to learn. After I pointed out the sentence she had slightly rearranged, she asked me to read the rest of the book to her. I did so.

From that point on I was pretty much on my own. I would read or try to read everything I could get my hands on. Many things were simply incomprehensible to me, as if they were in a language I didn't know. This was true to a degree. My father's math and engineering texts were in a technical language that I did not have the capacity to grasp. Even I had to crawl before I could walk and walk before I could run. I didn't understand that concept at the time so I was just frustrated by the books with titles like *Differential Equations* and *The Physics of Flight*.

Eventually my father sat me down and started in with some organizational starting materials. Using blocks, paper, pencils and crayons he started in on addition, subtraction, multiplication, division and how all of these things could be related to a logarithmic scale on a device called a slide rule. There was addition and subtraction of real numbers, and multiplication and division were simply the addition and subtraction of the logs of those numbers based on an arbitrary value like 10 or e. He discussed properties like positive and negative, rules that determined the logic of how numbers could be manipulated like how A+B = B+A. He did this using simple graphs of what I learned were x and y axes and with symbols for numbers to make the explanations more universally applicable. These lessons would occur each evening after he returned from someplace called "work."

He also got out a large colorful chart with an initially intimidating array of symbols, letters and numbers on it. He said that this one chart could teach me more about the nature of the world around me than any other single source of information. He then began telling me about protons, neutrons and electrons and how the relative numbers of these so-called subatomic particles determined the characteristics of each element. Furthermore, the properties of these elements determined how and in what combinations they would interact and that these various combinations made up every bit of sense-able matter in the world. It was all so simple.

He then told me that there were combinations of these elements that formed huge molecules called DNA that determined every characteristic of every life form known, including me. At the time I thought he had gone off the deep end on that one, until he showed me the genetic code and I saw what intuitive sense and beauty it had. Even the human body was reduced to a comprehensible mass of chemical reactions controlled by and based upon the basic chemical properties of simple elements in a large repetitive spiraling molecule that folded itself into what were called chromosomes. Amazing. I was intensely interested in this submicroscopic world for some reason, a preoccupation that sort of plagued me throughout my life.

The next lessons involved the Laws of Newton. These were basic rules that determined how relatively large chunks of matter interacted with each other and with their environment. He couldn't explain how some of these things worked but he had names for them like gravity and magnetism. He then enlarged upon this by explaining how these laws of motion, when combined with a set of basic tools or machines like the inclined plane or the pulley, could help us make these laws work for us to accomplish things that we couldn't do with our bare hands. It would be a few years before I learned that magnetism was the result of the unbalanced spin of an unpaired electron in the highest energy orbit around a nucleus. There were only a handful of elements that would exhibit this property, iron being the most prominent. It would be a few decades before I uncovered the nature of gravitational energy and that feat would first require that I throw out almost everything I had learned in the past.

By the time I was ready to enter public school he finally revealed to me the secret of an area of study called calculus, which dramatically demonstrated the relationships between equations related to motion and many other properties. Here I had been memorizing these equations and their iterations and all along he had a simple and elegant way to derive them one from another. It was so wondrous that I wondered why I hadn't thought of it myself and I was a bit peeved at my dad for withholding this key information. It was like giving me the blocks needed to build an arch but leaving out the keystone. Calculus was like the keystone that made everything else stand up, be in balance and endure.

The world made sense to me. I began taking everything I could get my hands on apart and putting it back together. In this way the things around me became just familiar examples of the basic and repetitive machines and forces of nature.

I was still just a kid though and I remember being scared about almost falling off a wall in the backyard of our big yellow apartment complex on the Air Force base in Frankfurt, Germany. I remember my illogical fear of being left behind when my family was going to make the move from Germany back to the States too.

The only thing I couldn't understand, and still don't really, was the nature of a globular glowing object that I found moving along the floor of the dark basement of our house in Orlando, Florida. I had closed the hatch to the basement behind me and was preparing to walk over to the wooden support beam that was beside the string I had to pull to illuminate the room. I had done this a million times and had long since lost my irrational fear of something as insignificant as the mere absence of light. I walked over to the glowing spot and tried to look at it more closely but it seemed the closer I got the more nebulous and murky the phenomenon became. It was like looking out the window on a very foggy day. There was no depth, or maybe there was infinite depth, you couldn't tell because there were no reference points. Trying to stare at and focus on the object was like that. It seemed intangible, simultaneously solid, liquid and gas. I thought I could see the floor through it and yet when I really tried to focus on the floor I couldn't. My gaze would seem to carry into eternity like looking up into a relatively starless portion of the night sky. I stood up and turned on the light.

There was nothing there. Not only that but there were no detectable traces that anything had been there, and what was even worse, when I turned the light back off, there was still nothing there. Whatever it had been, it had evaporated in the cascade of photons from the naked bulb that hung from a rafter above my head.

That was the first thing I had encountered in life that I couldn't explain. What was it? Where did it come from and where did it go? More importantly, why did it seem to have characteristics that could not be explained by the laws that I knew governed matter and energy, the only forms of "stuff" there was in the universe?

That's when I started to get into relativity. I always started at the source. When it came to Newton I read the *Principia*. When it came to big Al, I read his own impressive tome on relativity. What a book. Turned my whole world upside down. Everything I thought was solid was not and everything I thought was easily explained was not. There were concepts of time and energy here of which I couldn't have dreamt. And the fact that matter and energy were simply different forms of the same thing and could be converted back and forth was a real eye opener for me.

It was at this time that my father introduced me to a newly developed device called a transistor. I had sort of figured out how vacuum tubes worked in radio receivers, amplification devices and TVs. He then showed me a relatively small gold-colored disk standing on three little wire legs. This dinky thing could do as much as a much larger vacuum tube, consume less power doing it and generate less heat. It could also be easily mass-produced with far less trouble than the glass and metallic tubes. A tremendous revolutionary step. I later took the little thing apart, none too elegantly I'm afraid. It was crimped together by a machine, no screws. It took a pair of vice grips and a hammer to get to the guts of the thing out and then they were a little disappointing, a bit of silicon with no discernable features other than the three tiny wires that were attached to it.

I began studying "solid-state" electronics and learned about semi conductors, integrated circuits and large-scale integrated circuits. Suddenly the world started spinning around me. Enough of these little things, made ever smaller and smaller, could be arranged to accomplish extremely complex calculations, calculations that would take weeks to perform by hand. I felt like I was falling down a never-ending spiral toward ever more complicated and powerful devices that were ever more powerful in spite of their declining size. I ended up seeing molecules with special properties, moles[1] of them, arrayed on a surface that could manipulate and store vast quantities of information, a source of analytical power of extreme, almost infinite magnitude. I wondered if pressing this process to its limit, as was done in mathematical equations, and approaching an infinitely small size, if you would achieve infinite power, a mind-blowing concept.

The road ahead was clear to me now. I would study the field of physics until I could understand and integrate the whole universe into one grand unified theory that would show with clarity and grandeur how everything was interrelated and how nothing in our world could not be analyzed and understood.

I just about did it too, but I'm getting ahead of myself.

First I had to "grow up."

I once wrote a poem with a line in it that went something like…"growing up is the gradual process of compromising the ideals of our youth." I was determined to stick with my ideals though. Knowledge for the sake of knowledge. Knowledge as a source of power. Knowledge as a means of understanding and thus controlling the world around me. I did my best. And I was well on my way until the age of 17.

I had been taking some classes at Rollins College and working in a little upscale upholstery shop right across the street in a wealthy district of the area called Winter Park. I was also finishing up what classes I needed to get an official high school diploma, although the University of Florida had already let me know that I could go there with a full academic scholarship. My parents had only let me skip one grade in school and wouldn't let me advance any faster for fear that I would not develop the proper social skills and would not have any peers in my age group with which to interact. As far as I was concerned, I had no peers and was already a social outcast.

I was a long-haired hippie freak with a 4.0 average taking all independent study classes so that I could get in a third year of chemistry, a second year of

---

[1] A mole is defined as one Avagadro's number of anything, 6.02 times 10 raised to the 23rd power. More easily conceived of as a whole bunch.

physics and a third year of biology while still in high school. Since all the science classes were in a single pod I spent almost all of my time there. There were two major benefits to this arrangement. I was able to study at my own pace and I had access to the labs, which were fairly sophisticated for a high school.

Consequently I finished the two-year curriculum in biology in one year, took the exams and finals when I was ready and made the second highest grade on the second-year biology final in relation to the kids who had been taking the subject for two full years. I thought this was an adequate performance since biology was not my primary interest. I did better in chemistry and physics and of course excelled in math. I would usually complete the assigned text in a math class in about two months, take the final, ace it and then become the teacher's aide to help grade papers and teach some classes.

The math department also had a small programmable device that used cards with holes punched in them for data input and output. It was called a computer but by today's standards it was like a steam-powered car from the early 1900s compared to a world-land-speed-setting rocket car.

My high school was pretty special. I went to public schools but starting in the second grade I was segregated into a special group of kids who were in "Phase 5." Each subject was taught on five levels, the fifth being the highest and most challenging (not to me, but to my "peers"). The phase level was calculated into the grade point average so an A in a phase one class would be a $(4.0 + 1)/2$ or a 2.5. My grades were usually As in phase 5 so my GPA was usually $(4.0 + 5)/2$ or 4.5. I actually maintained a higher than 4.0 GPA.

This system was in place because there were an unusually large number of very bright kids in this geographic location. Believe it or not I didn't actually stand out all that much. This was due to NASA. The Apollo program was running full blast and the same companies involved in space launch technology were also developing missiles for defense and offense in a nuclear-powered arms race called the Cold War, exemplified by the Mutual Assured Destruction philosophy. The acronym should have given these guys a clue but they pushed ever onward.

This rocket- and weapons-based economy attracted more Ph.D.s than the Los Alamos project and the companies like Martin, TRW and Harris would compete to see how many Nobel Prize winners they each employed. Because of this concentration of brainpower, of which my father was a part, the offspring of these "geniuses" were in need of an education a cut above the average, at least that was what their parents felt. The local public schools therefore got public funding to provide for these "wonder kids" and this evolved into the Phase system mentioned above.

The schools were able to set up fairly sophisticated labs and buy exotic things like computers. It was in this system that I grew up. When the Apollo program shut down and funding dropped, the number of exceptionally bright kids also declined and the Phase system was phased out. I was lucky to have been in the Cape Canaveral area during those boom years.

I had a lot of problems with non-science classes. English in particular. I just couldn't stand to do the assignments. They were just inane mental masturbation in which the As went to the students who most nearly emulated the teacher's own views about whatever literary work we were studying. There was no room for real creativity or independent thought and if you did display these characteristics you got a lower grade because the teacher disagreed with your analysis. All the "experts'" opinions in these matters differed and were utterly arbitrary but each was staunchly defended as Truth. I couldn't stand it. I'd rather work with quantum mechanics, solving Heisenberg's or Shrodinger's equations where there were some real answers. As a result of all this I was making an F in English and the English teacher was threatening to block my graduation. To solve this problem I spent a free afternoon writing poetry, about 45 different poems taking up about 60 pages. These blew the English teacher away, some even got published, so he gave me a C and decided he would let me graduate.

During this time I was, like most adolescents, struggling with spiritual concepts relating to "Why am I here?" I was also struggling with females. I could not relate to them at all. I had my share of crushes and had even almost gotten into a fight over one young lady named Gena something. When I approached my competitor for this vision of loveliness' affections I realized that if I fought I would get badly hurt and probably inflict no discomfort on my opponent other than the bruises he would have on his knuckles from striking them against my head. It was my head I was worried about. I didn't want to take any chances with my brain. The thought of a concussion or worse stopped me in my tracks on my way to meeting with this Tommy guy who wanted the love of my life and wanted to beat the life of my life out of me.

I went on a verbal offensive instead of a physical one and, of course, completely outwitted the fool, whose primary goal in life seemed to be throwing a baseball over home plate without it being hit by a bat. We didn't fight and he was utterly humiliated, but he didn't even know it. He walked away thinking he had won somehow. And when I turned to see the admiration in my Gena's eyes, I learned he had. She was walking away with him!

Females were worthless illogical distractions in my pursuit of knowledge.

In my teen years the desire to investigate female anatomy was there, but I suppressed it. I learned all I needed to know from anatomy texts at the Rollins College library.

The spiritual dilemmas I faced led in quite a different direction. I knew a great deal about the physical universe around me and if I had had a geeky haircut I would have been classified as a first-order nerd, but I had this rebelliousness against authority. This was probably due to the fact that the authority figures always thought they knew more or were smarter than me. That is why I started experimenting with drugs. I was lured by the concept of "expanding your mind" as put forth by Ken Kesey and his pranksters. You see, I didn't just read science books, I read everything. It would only take a few hours to get through the average 400-page novel so I was able to consume quite a bit of literature on a variety of subjects. Books were to me what television was to most kids.

The drug experiences got me interested in the world outside of the physical universe, if such a thing existed, and brought back to me the feeling I had when I encountered the seemingly non-existent white blob in the basement when I was a kid. I therefore began applying my considerable brainpower to thoughts about the divine, the ephemeral, the spiritual. On one particular night something quite extraordinary occurred.

THIRTEEN

I was lying quite still in my bed thinking about the implications of divinity, if such a thing existed. Somehow by focusing all of my mental energy on this single topic and letting my body remain inert until my consciousness lost interest in it, I was able to experience the sensation that I had left my body.

There was a sequence of events that preceded the departure that were interesting but not germane to the story. The net result was that I found myself hovering above my bed in a state that seemed timeless. Now this was of intense interest because I had already begun to rethink my ideas about time and what time might be outside the physical universe. My theory indicated that time did not exist beyond the boundaries of our universe. This would lead to an unbelievable condition where everything that occurred within the universe would be simultaneously observable and there would be instantaneous comprehension of all of these events. It would be as if you were looking at a photograph of a sunset on Earth, you take the data in as a whole, not as a sequence of photons reflected from the surface of the picture. Looking at our universe would be like seeing the entire history of the universe, from Big Bang to collapse, as a single image rather than as a sequence of temporal events.

This was the state I seemed to be in. And if I could be there then it may actually support my theory. I began to explore this place. I turned my perspective around and saw a body lying on my bed, and it was my body. This was disconcerting enough that the power of my intellect could not override the sense of panic I felt that I might have just died. In an instant I was back in my body.

I was in a very adrenergic state. Pulse rapid, respirations rapid, diaphoretic. But rather than try to move and calm myself I had the distinct sense that if I remained motionless, I would return to that place beyond time.

I did. This time I was able to gather more data. It actually seemed as if all knowledge was available instantaneously. I found and understood answers to questions both mundane and mathematically esoteric but I didn't have to ask the questions; the answers were simply apparent. The entire universe unfolded before me. Two parabolic solids, apex to apex, extending from a singularity and expanding in opposite directions. The entire universe and all the events that had ever occurred within it were visible at a glance. I knew the answers! I even knew what the nature and material of the realm beyond the boundaries of our universe was, and I could see how and where these two places of being intersected and interacted.

But again, I sensed my body on the bed below me and was again overcome by the irrational fear of death and was sucked back into my body against my will. This time I put my energy into regaining movement, accomplished this and sat up panting on the side of the bed.

I had seen it. I had seen the universe and the universe beyond. I knew everything, EVERYTHING! And everything was almost trivial in its simplicity, as if it could all be taken for granted. I had the sense that this knowledge was so obvious that if I shared it with someone, they would say, "Yea, so that's the way it is, so what?" It would be as if I ran up to a friend and proclaimed, "Look, I can breathe, I can actually breathe!" It was so beautiful!

But I couldn't remember any of the details. As I realized that I had grasped all this but that now in my waking state the "facts" were losing coherence and all I was left with was the sense that I had known all, but couldn't actually recall it. The solutions to some very difficult equations I had been struggling with were obvious to me in that altered state, but now I could not remember the proofs. All I was left with was the knowledge that the solutions were possible and that they made sense.

This was intolerably frustrating. Why had I seen all this only to have it pulled from my mental grasp? Why didn't I retain the precise information I needed and wanted so badly? It was as if knowledge and understanding from that other place could not be dragged back into this time-burdened reality. The two could not coexist just like a sphere could not exist in a two-dimensional world. I would have to work through the physics I had seen myself. It would not be handed to me on a silver platter for some reason.

But why had I had this experience? I concluded that it had happened because I was indeed destined to unlock these mysteries of the universe. I would be the one to derive the GUT or the TOE (The Grand Unification Theory or the Theory Of Everything). I later learned that my experience was not uncommon and was easily explained by psychologists as "sleep paralysis" and "hypnagogic hallucinations." Nevertheless, at the time my future was clear.

I couldn't accomplish my goal to derive the GUT in my current circumstances. I had to get out of there. The rules of my parents and my school were preventing me from moving forward. I gathered up some clothes, a few valued possessions and what money I could find in the house and disappeared quietly into the night.

I ended up at MIT, the Massachusetts Institute of Technology, where there were labs and brains of the highest order with which to work. By faking a few records I was able to get admitted and enrolled in a few basic science classes, not because I needed the information but because it would give me legitimate access to the labs and other resources.

I initially sought out some of the wizards of cosmology of that time to discuss my theories but their minds were closed. They had accepted the dogma of Einsteinian relativity and couldn't see beyond it. I was looked upon as a misguided kook. I was getting nowhere fast and was running out of money.

I got a job as a waiter at a local vegetarian restaurant frequented by mystical madmen who were supposedly enlightened. I got the feeling that they were all just a little schizophrenic rather than in Nirvana. I made a little money, enough for tuition and books as well as a room in a house near campus. I even managed to save a little.

For several years I worked and studied and wrote equations on blackboards. Some made sense, some didn't. The little restaurant went out of business as mysticism and vegetarianism gave way to capitalism and meat- and martini-containing power lunches. I was unemployed, not making any progress with my theories and would be broke again soon if I couldn't find another way to make some money. I was depressed.

For the first time in my life I went to a bar and started drinking. I wanted to sit at the bar and I wanted to be left alone. I didn't even know what to drink so I just ordered whiskey. Of course the barkeep, as I heard him called by others, brought me a little glass of their most expensive Scotch. They knew a sucker when they saw one. So I sat there slowly sipping several glasses of something called Glenfiddich and trying to figure out what my next step was.

Soon I was feeling pretty looped, but as long as I sat very still and concentrated on ways of finding funds or something like how the knots in my shoes looked like little pretzels, I avoided the vertigo and the nausea. I was not thinking clearly, that's for sure, so I wasn't really accomplishing anything. Eventually I noticed that a man had taken the stool beside mine. He looked over at me and asked what the problem was. I initially didn't want to say anything. What could this guy in a bar know about quantum mechanics?

Something about him seemed caring and in my inebriated state I couldn't resist trying to tell him all about it. I tolerated the disequilibrium and turned toward him and spilled my guts about my frustrating search for knowledge and how the lack of financing was going to prevent me from continuing.

I figured he had no idea what I was talking about, but listened sympathetically and then summed up my dilemma for me.

"So if you had some money, you could keep doing this math thing you're talking about, right?"

I said, "Yes, if I had some money I would get my own place and work on my theories until I found solutions or died." My speech was not all that clear. It's no wonder he couldn't understand any of the physics I discussed. If I had heard a recording of myself I probably wouldn't have understood it either. But he had narrowed it down to the simplest common denominator: money.

He went on to inform me, "If you need money you should just go to Las Vegas and win some at blackjack. I know a bunch of guys who make a pretty good living doing that."

I gave him a look that I hoped would convey my scorn at this absurd idea and said something unintelligible along the lines of "what a bunch of bullshit."

He persisted, "No really, it can be done. How much money do you have left?"

I had sold my stamp and coin collection after I had left home and had managed to save a little from my job so I had a stash of about $2,100. I stupidly told him I had this much, but let him know it wasn't on me.

"That's plenty," he said with renewed enthusiasm. "It can get us to Las Vegas by bus and leave plenty to build a small fortune out of."

Suddenly he and I were "us." I wasn't really liking the sound of this but I think numerous of my neurons had ceased functioning due to ethanol toxicity. This process always started with the higher order neurons that control things like logic and common sense so drunk people often did things that were neither logical nor made sense. I was certainly a drunk people.

I gulped the remainder of my Scotch and said, "OK, shlurrr, wha not?"

He helped me out of the bar and to my crummy car. He drove me to my sleazy room and stayed in the car while I went in and got my cash stash. I wove my way back to the car on the walkway in front of the rundown house, a paved path that I would have sworn was straight in the past. I climbed into the passenger seat of my used Vega, handed him the money, threw up and passed out. What an idiot I was, especially when you consider the IQ I have!

Surprisingly I woke up in the car rather than on the side of the road somewhere. The car was moving and so was my stomach. My head however was not moving. It was stuck in some kind of thick glue that made it impossible to turn my head or turn my thoughts. I was being bombarded by horrendous road and car sounds seemingly amplified to potentially life-threatening decibel levels. The waves of nausea dulled this input and gave me some respite from the noise to the point where I looked forward to them so I could have a little peace and quiet. I was hoping I would pass out again but then I opened my eyes.

Mistake. Bright. Stabbing into my head like I could feel the photons burning the backs of my retinas and then feel the far too powerful nerve impulses traveling through my brain to my occipital lobe where the visual cortex transformed these inputs into images. It actually felt like these lightning intensity neural signals were going to pass right through the back of my skull and blow the back of my head off. I think I actually reached up to make sure my head had not exploded.

The pain from the visual input caused me to close my eyes tightly but the pain persisted, now resonating and building to the rhythm of my heartbeat, which I noticed with some concern was occasionally irregular.

I had to open my eyes though. I had to figure out what was going on. I opened one partway. Everything was overexposed. Too bright to make out details. It took a while for my eye to adjust and I was able to make out the interior of the Vega and finally the guy behind the wheel. He was actually smiling at me. Almost laughing, I didn't know why.

"Welcome back to reality," he quipped.

I found that I could not respond because my tongue was apparently paralyzed. No, that's not quite accurate. It was glued tightly to the floor of my mouth and to the roof of my mouth so that I couldn't move it or open my mouth without some serious effort. My initial response to his statement was therefore, "Gd inmp ba plaahh!" The "plaahh" accomplished the feat of getting my mouth open.

Another mistake. The influx of air into this scorched cavity stimulated salivation and this moisture in turn stimulated my taste buds. The flavor was the extreme opposite of good. And as I gasped, the flavor was also translated into smell. Whoa, and I thought the taste was bad!

My driving companion handed me a cola of some kind which helped considerably and I was soon able to put a few words together that made sense.

"What in the hell is going on?" was the first thing I managed.

My driver asked me how much I remembered from last night. I replied that I remembered the bar, meeting him, going to my house and some absurd plan about Las Vegas. I told him that I couldn't remember his name.

"Bob, Bob Gennis, and we are on our way to making you a fortune in Las Vegas," he said, as if this was a great idea and really what I wanted to do.

"Wait, wait," I said trying not to panic. "We can't really do this. I mean, it's one thing to fantasize about it at a bar but I can't believe you'd seriously think I would disappear to Vegas with a complete stranger! Where's my money? I remember going in and getting my money."

Now I was really getting into panic mode and began sort of pawing at myself and at Bob to see if I could uncover the location of my cash.

"Don't worry, don't worry, your money is safe, except what I spent on gas and food. Stop, stop patting me all over the place, you're going to make me wreck this already wreck of a car."

I stopped groping the poor guy and asked him again where my money was. He told me it was in the back under the spare, which was flat by the way.

"OK." I tried to calm myself by taking a few deep breaths. This was also helpful in relation to preventing me from vomiting, or I should say vomiting again. I could smell the puke of yesterday although it appeared that Bob had tried to clean up. I had an uncomfortable squishiness in my left shoe however, but I wasn't about to investigate it now. "Where are we?" I demanded as I finally got my other eye open.

Bob replied, "We've made great time, we're on I-90 heading into Ohio."

I was staring at my watch trying to figure out what day it was as well as what time. "Ohio, I've never been to Ohio," I mumbled while I stared at my watch like it was a timepiece from a different planet. I noticed that we were coming up on an exit with a truck stop. "Stop, you've got to stop here, I've got to pee so bad I can't stand it," I pleaded. I did actually need to go but not all that badly. I really just wanted to get off the road and figure out what was going on.

Bob obediently pulled off the highway and into the truck stop parking lot. A truck driver about the size of the average NFL center gave me a look like I was an opposing lineman as I passed him to use the bathroom. I found out why when I saw myself. I looked like I had just been through an NFL game but had forgotten to wear my pads and helmet. I peed, I washed my face, I wet my hair and kind of patted it into place, I brushed my teeth with a paper towel and powdered soap (not recommended…it took fourteen rinses to get the flavor out) and straightened out my clothes as best I could. I then took my suspicious left shoe off. Suspicions confirmed!

I ran my shoe under the water for a while and scrubbed it down in much the same manner as I had my teeth. I then washed my sock thoroughly and realized that I'd have to wash the other shoe and sock too or the pairs wouldn't match. This took about a half-hour and about 20 apologies, verbal and non-verbal, to the truckers that came and went. Some took an interest and asked if they could help, but when they found out I wasn't gay they left. (Fair weather friends!)

I finally looked and felt only about half as bad as I had when I entered and I figured this was going to be about as good as it was going to get, so I left. I had to find Bob, find out more about this stupid trip and then convince him to go back to Boston. But mostly, I wanted to salvage what money I had left.

Bob was waiting by the car. I told him I needed some food or at least some coffee and that we should go into the restaurant and talk about our escapade. He agreed.

"So, Bob, let me get this straight. You picked me up in a bar, stole my car and my money and then kidnapped me in order to use me and/or my money in some way to generate a fortune playing blackjack in Las Vegas. Does that about sum it up?" I didn't think he could miss the sarcasm or the threat in my voice. He did, or pretended he did.

"That's right," he said with enthusiasm. "I figure we can make it in three days if we share the driving and take speed. I scored some here from a long-haul driver."

"And I suppose you 'scored' this using a little more of my money?"

"Well, sure, just a little, but we'll still have plenty to gamble with when we get to Vegas."

I was not reassured and said so, but my head was throbbing and it was hard to argue. The coffee came and I added real cream in order to cool it to gulping temperature and gulped it. I poured another cup from the carafe generously provided, added cream and gulped again. A little too much gulping, now my stomach and my head were in competition for my attention. I sat back and went into deep breathing mode again. It was hard to concentrate on Bob. He was talking about blackjack and how he had won in the past and he was talking to the waitress ordering the steak and egg breakfast that I figured was on me. The thought of the grease forced me back to the deep breathing exercises.

I had to get a hold of myself. This was a seriously disastrous situation and I didn't even know who this Bob guy was. He may pick up guys in bars, take their money and kill them somewhere as far as I knew. I forced myself to concentrate and ate some crackers.

"Bob, we've got to go back and you've got to give me what's left of my money back. I'm not leaving this truck stop until we agree on this and I will call the authorities if you don't agree, so you might as well agree right now." I sort of spit this rambling sentence out in a single breath hoping it would pass as resolve.

"Oh come on," Bob said. "Where is your sense of adventure? We'll be meeting a guy here who will convince you to continue on to Las Vegas. He's a professional and is willing to help us win big if we stake him."

"If we stake him!" I expired with exclamation. "You mean if *I* stake him. Who the hell do you think 'we' are? Where's your money in this little deal?"

Bob admitted that he was a little short right now but that we would win back more than we could imagine if we stuck together and worked with this guy we were supposed to meet here. I realized that Bob had not pulled into this truck stop because I needed to pee and asked him about this.

"Yea, I called the guy from a phone booth while you were sleeping and told him to meet us here. You'll like him. He's an amazing man," Bob explained as if this was supposed to make me feel much better about things.

"I don't want to meet him. I want my car keys, my car and my money and I want to be heading east instead of west when we leave this place." I was trying to be firm while my stomach and head felt anything but solid.

I was thinking he was getting the message when a darkness fell over the table. The darkness was caused by the bulk of a man who had just walked up to our booth and was preparing to sit next to me thus trapping me in my bench-like seat, which suddenly seemed to small to accommodate two adults.

Bob of course was enthusiastic. "Martin," he said, "this is the guy I called you about who has some money and wants to turn it into significantly more money in Nevada!"

Martin held out a beefy hand and said hello. His voice was like the rest of him, gruff, but surprisingly soft. I guess when you are as physically intimidating as this guy, you don't need to talk loud.

I hadn't really felt trapped before because I felt like I could take Bob out if I had to, but Martin was a whole 'nother matter. I had purchased a very large semi-automatic handgun about four months ago for protection at home. I was now sorry I hadn't thought to pick it up as I helped rob my own apartment. That 50-caliber monstrosity was about the only thing that could probably stop Martin.

I gingerly shook his hand, and thankfully, he didn't crush mine. He had a firm handshake but it didn't cause permanent injury. He also didn't have the hard calluses that I expected to accompany his massive paw so apparently he hadn't been doing any heavy physical labor recently. I kidded myself that maybe he was out of shape and I could overpower him. I had a picture in my throbbing brain of a flea jumping around on the head of a rottweiler, trying to knock it out. I would have laughed if it didn't hurt so much to do so.

Martin reached into his jacket with his right hand as I stiffened expecting to see the glint of gunmetal soon and up close and personal. Instead he withdrew a small book. He handed it to me and I read the title: *Winning at 21!* by Martin Wertmeyer, Ph.D. It also had a picture of a smiling Martin on the cover looking very well to do. He took the book back from me suddenly, took a pen out of his pocket, signed the inside cover and handed it back to me with a half smile. *Good luck at the tables*, followed by a scrawled autograph now defaced or I should say graced the book.

Bob said, "Martin really is an expert blackjack player, so good that he is barred from gambling at most casinos. Since he's cut off from his only source of income, he's a little down on his luck so he's agreed to help us become winners!" He said this with a level of excitement that made me think that he thought I was going to jump up and down and thank the stars for my good fortune. What I really thought was that he was an idiot, only slightly less so than myself.

I was hesitant but tried to say as nicely and fearlessly as possible, "Um, I'm really not too much in favor of this…a…plan. I'd rather just sort of get my money back and head back to Boston, if that's OK with you guys." I even managed to smile a little as if we were all good friends and they were going to smile back, hand over my cash, my car keys and rise to let me out with handshakes and heartfelt good-byes all around.

Instead Martin said, "Well, we'll just have to convince you to 'favor' the plan. Won't we, Bob?" His voice was a little harder now and there was an unusual emphasis on the word convince that made me think we weren't going to be holding a debate on the pros and cons of the plan. I was going to hear and possibly 'feel' the pros and they were going to be the cons.

FOURTEEN

I was sure I was in for a little bruising but to my surprise Martin grabbed his book instead of me, opened it to chapter one and told me to start reading. I of course started reading, although at first I was not really comprehending. I was just sort of scanning lines of blurred text on the page, a little too scared and hungover to focus. Martin grabbed the book from me again and started reading.

"The game of twenty-one or blackjack is deceptively complicated. If you want to win you will have to be intelligent, calm and well versed in the math of probabilities and chaos. You will also have to restrain your greed and most of all, stay sober." I felt like a little kid again being read a bedtime story by a massive adult, and to tell you the truth, Martin's voice was actually kind of soothing. I needed all the soothing I could get.

I asked, "Chaos, chaos, what does chaos have to do with gambling other than what it does to people and families of gambling addicts?" That word had struck a chord because I was acutely interested in chaos in relationship to cosmology, not that I thought these guys would understand this.

Martin handed the book to me again and told me to keep reading. I took the book and instead of reading I flipped through the pages. The pages soon became filled with equations describing the probabilities of various cards being dealt under different circumstances. The math was basic, at least to me, but was pretty sophisticated for a book aimed at a bunch of boozing gamblers who probably never finished high school. Another chapter started into chaos theory and I began to see equations with the elongated "S"s of integration and subscripts like "lim" and "0 ." I took a second look at Martin.

"Um, Martin, what is your Ph.D. in?"

"Mathematics, particularly the mathematics of estimating probabilities in seemingly random events," he said with complete seriousness. I had figured that his title on the cover of the book was a joke, but now I was wondering.

114

I wondered out loud, "So how many of these books did you sell, Martin?"

He looked a little hurt and said he hadn't really sold very many, mostly he gave them away after having paid to have about a thousand printed. He explained, "I'm a bit chagrined because I overestimated the intelligence level of my audience a little. All of this seemed pretty obvious to me but no one else could figure out what in the hell I was talking about." He managed a chuckle and went on, "You see, I did my thesis on random events and used blackjack as a system to study and illustrate my concepts. It actually went over pretty well with my thesis committee and I got my doctorate. I taught for a while but became intrigued by gambling and found out that I could make a lot more money in casinos than in the hollowed university hallways."

I looked back to the book, flipped it to chapter one again and began reading. I'm a fast reader, so it only took me about 30 minutes to get through the slender volume. The math didn't slow me down much. It was well delineated and clear. It went a step or two further than I had previously gone in the direction of chaos and I was actually excited to review some of the equations. In the meanwhile Martin and Bob sat in the booth silently, sipping water and waving the waitress away occasionally. She looked a bit peeved.

"So, Martin," I asked with a bit more respect in my voice, "some of this would apply to the non-random distribution of matter in the universe which is not explained by the Big Bang theory because it holds that the universe was once a singularity and therefore uniform. This means it should have exploded into a completely symmetric sphere with the matter and energy…"

"I know," he interrupted. "It's also exactly like the application of the Heisenberg uncertainty principle to the behavior of electrons in a two-dimensional mesh at near absolute zero." There was some real excitement in his voice.

I was sitting with my mouth open when the waitress came by again, but rather than signal her to leave us alone, I asked her to bring me some more coffee, a couple of aspirin and a BLT. My head and stomach were feeling considerably better and Martin and Bob had suddenly become more intriguing and less frightening. They took the hint from me and ordered some food, which returned a smile to the face of the nonetheless not too attractive waitress.

I made a bit of an intuitive leap. "So what am I really doing here?"

Bob and Martin looked at each other but it was Bob who spoke next.

"Look, we're both pretty broke. It's not like jobs for mathematicians and physicists grow on trees. We have been looking for someone like you to work with us on getting back into the casinos and getting out some money. We had to have someone who could understand the theories in Marty's book and was a bit down on their luck. I spotted you in the labs at MIT and thought you'd be a good choice, but it wasn't until I ran into you in the bar that I finally made up my mind. I didn't really mean to 'kidnap' you, it's just the way things worked out. By the way, if you're going to drink Scotch, you may want to slowly build up a tolerance to alcohol first or the next guy that picks you up in a bar might not be as nice as I am."

Martin was snickering next to me. He wasn't making any noise but I could feel the whole booth shaking as he tried to contain his amusement.

"So, I'm supposed to believe that you're the physicist, Bob?" I asked.

"Well, I've gotten a master's and was going to get my doctorate but ran out of money. That's another reason for this scheme. Martin wants to help me get back into a graduate program and continue my studies," he replied.

"And what exactly were you studying?" I was actually expecting to be surprised now.

"Oh I was looking into the use of lasers to set up standing waves in a grid that would then trap the particles from a BEC and then use additional lasers to knock off the more energetic particle to further cool the condensate to near -273.15 degrees. My calculations indicated that this method would achieve temperatures only a few billionths of a degree above zero Kelvin." He said this as if it were just the usual thing that people everywhere did in their spare time and went on to explain, "You see, that's how Marty and I met. We were both interested in particle behavior at extremely low temperatures. He wanted to see the absolute regularity of the material and then observe the behavior of the matter as it warmed. See, it's another case where an almost fixed geometric lattice yields to seemingly random particle distribution and movement."

"What happened to your research?" I asked hoping to hear more.

Martin took over the story, "Well, Bob and I were sort of outcasts, me because of my gambling hang-up and weird theories about randomnicity, Bob because of his odd beliefs about the relation of time to gravitation which he felt he could demonstrate at extremely cold temperatures."

I waited silently, all my senses on edge. These guys were talking my language! Rather than open my mouth I wanted to encourage them to keep talking, and Martin did.

"Bob actually built a model of a device that would detect and possibly conduct gravitational energy and…well, it blew up. We still don't know what happened, but when he charged the thing up, it took out the whole lab. Fortunately Bob was working by remote some distance away. The weird thing was, there was nothing in the room that was explosive. There was a big hole in the ceiling, through the second floor and through the roof however. We never did find any evidence of the contraption Bob had built. It was like the thing had disappeared. The college not so politely asked Bob to disappear also."

Bob looked embarrassed but for the next hour we were submerged in an ephemeral realm where protons, neutrons and electrons flitted about like birds fighting for space on a power line. The universe on an extremely small scale and as a vast cosmos drifted around us like a beautiful part of the atmosphere in the otherwise dismal diner.

We finally sat back and looked at our pretty much untouched food. The cold grease oozing from the French fries reminded me that my stomach was still a bit sensitive. It was time to leave and much to my amazement I was going to go with these two guys and head west toward Nevada. What a bizarre turn of events. I went from fearing for my life to feeling in my element.

Back in the Vega the smell just about made me spew what little lunch I had onto the back of the front seat. I held it in and with all the windows open it wasn't too bad. I was in the back because Martin probably would not fit in the back and I wasn't going to argue with him about it, he just barely fit in the front. Once we were outside his bulk could be more accurately assessed. He was massive, but not fat. He just happened to be about six-five with shoulders just about as wide. He moved with grace however and even through his clothes you got the impression that he was well muscled. Nope, if he wanted the front seat, it was his. The old 800-pound gorilla joke went through my mind.

While we drove toward Cleveland, the sun shining acutely into the windshield, we maintained an animated and esoteric conversation about physics, time and gravity. I was steering the conversation in that direction trying to see if I could glean more new information from the unusual pair of scientists. Bob was steering the car in an occasionally erratic way due to his enthusiasm for the topic and his desire to gesticulate when describing equations, sort of like writing them on an imaginary blackboard hovering in the air between the wheel and the windshield.

Night fell, but with the help of the speed Bob had he was able to make it just past Chicago as the eastern sky began to lighten up. I figured Bob and Martin had taken turns driving although I don't recall them switching. As the conversation had waned, so had my brain and I drifted in and out of sleep during the night. They wouldn't let me drive because they were afraid I would puke on the dash and crash. I think they were also still a little worried that I might try to split somehow.

I woke with the sun just as we pulled of the road to find a motel in the western outskirts of Chicago. We'd driven a long way. It had been about 30 hours since I walked into that bar in Boston and we were almost halfway to Las Vegas. My muscles, and in particular my butt, were sore. I didn't find out about my butt until I got out of the car and started to walk. That's when the numbness wore off and the pain started. It was manageable but it was a really odd sensation to have your scrotum and penis "wake up" from pressure-induced anesthesia.

We checked into a decent motel and got two adjoining rooms. Bob was talking about making it all the way to Vegas in one push while Martin argued that one more stop for rest would be better and safer. I agreed with Martin but I didn't say so. I figured any argument between Martin and his diminutive friend would end in Martin's favor.

I went into my room looking forward to a real shower but I couldn't decide what to do after the shower. I didn't want to put my old clothes back on; in fact, I wanted to throw my clothes into an incinerator. Unfortunately, there wasn't one handy. I took the shower anyway and sat in a chair with a towel wrapped around me, looking out the second-floor window. I felt like most of me was made out of wood but at least it was clean wood. Martin and Bob came through the door between the rooms all excited and just about made me fly out of my chair and lose my towel. They laughed at me. I wasn't laughing. I was a bit embarrassed to be almost bare-assed in front of them.

They were excited about the clothes they had purchased for me, undoubtedly with my own money.

"Look at this great stuff we got you," Bob said. "We found a great men's store in a mall not too far from here and we knew you were going to need some new clothes, even if the stuff you were wearing weren't barfed on beyond usability and was just out of style." He was obviously still a little high on the "white cross" he had taken.

They held out the clothes. Three cotton shirts made by Hathaway, beautiful yet subtle vertical stripes in a variety of colors. A pair of black wool pants from Italy with a thin black leather belt. Some dark socks, some pretty standard briefs and a cashmere jacket that probably cost as much as everything else combined. The shoes were black leather and made in Italy by a company whose name I couldn't pronounce, but by the attitude of the two costumiers, I got the feeling they were in competition with the jacket for most expensive single item of clothing on Earth.

I looked at them like they were crazy but they said I'd have to look good to gamble and the last thing they wanted was to get back in the Vega with my reeking old clothes. The smelly items in question were placed in the trash bag on the maid's cart as Martin and Bob left. Martin looked back at me as he was closing the door to my room.

"Looking a bit flabby there, man. You better get into some exercise."

This embarrassed the hell out of me too, not only because it was true but because he was being serious. So what if he was built like a giant sequoia stump and barely fit through my door! The guy had some gall.

The two of them were apparently on their way to do a few more chores. I was going to try on the clothes but figured I'd probably fall asleep in them. They would then be a wrinkled mess when I woke up and Bob and Martin would have to spend more of my money replacing them. I closed all the curtains to block out the early morning sun as much as possible, let go of my towel and crawled into bed. I swallowed three aspirin with a gulp of water and dropped my head onto the pillow. That's the last thing I remember for quite a few hours.

It was well after noon when I woke up. I heard noises from the room next door so I guessed Martin and Bob were back. I stretched under the covers and it felt marvelous. For the first time in a while I felt good. My headache had cleared up and my stomach felt like it was ready for a double beef cheeseburger with bacon. In fact, that sounded great so I got out of bed to pee and get dressed.

While I was standing in the bathroom wondering why they didn't put urinals for men in hotels and private homes as well, the noise from Bob and Martin's room got my attention. I sounded as if they were fighting about something. I could hear muffled exclamations and something thumped against the wall. I hoped it wasn't Bob. I knew for sure it wasn't Martin.

I finished my "business" in the bathroom and put on my fresh new underwear, socks and pants. Not only did they fit, they also looked great. I wondered with a silly grin if Bob had taken my measurements while I was unconscious! While I put on one of the shirts, which fit well also, I kept an ear out for sounds of a struggle next door. I heard what I thought was Bob groaning in agony and moved to the door between our rooms to enter and investigate. Just before doing so I heard Martin, I'm pretty sure, hiss a low "yesssss." I stopped with my hand on the doorknob. I hoped the two of them had found a couple of women to bring back to their room, but I didn't really believe that.

Instead of opening the door between our rooms, I went to the window and opened the drapes. I then went to the front door of my room, opened it and almost tripped over a newspaper. Rather than venture out as I had planned, I settled into my chair to read the paper, frequently looking out the window at the non-distinctive landscape of flat and dingy suburbs. I tried not to think about Martin and Bob.

About an hour later they knocked on my door. I had finished the paper and as usual had found that the comics were the most useful and interesting section. I didn't even bother to look at the sports section. Professional sports, what a waste of time, energy and money.

I took a breath and opened my door, trying not to look like I suspected anything about their sexual orientation. In retrospect Bob seemed a little effeminate, but Martin looked like a man's man. Well, I guess he was.

"Wow, you look great," Bob said this as the two of them walked into my room. "Did you get some sleep?"

I replied in the affirmative.

"Good," he continued, "we have some serious driving to do. Marty and I got a few hours also so we're ready to go. We thought we'd get some dinner, a bucket of coffee, some snacks and head out of here."

We checked out on the same calendar day as we had arrived, which got us a weird look from the clerk, but we were soon on the road again. Apparently one of the chores that Martin and Bob had taken care of was the Vega. I asked them about it.

"Yea, we had it detailed. It almost smells good now, but I don't think any amount of detailing would make a Vega look good. What it really needs is more power." Bob was explaining this while he took two tablets of speed with a cup of strong coffee, kind of redundant I thought.

We drove west as the western sky grew dark, not from sunset, which was an hour or two away, but from clouds that were rolling in. It rained pretty much from Chicago to Omaha, which slowed us down some. At one point we stopped under an overpass because the hail was getting as big as marbles and was moving horizontally in the strong wind. As we sat there I was pretty sure a tornado passed pretty close to the car. My ears popped from the sudden drop in atmospheric pressure.

Before we stopped the little car had been buffeted around to the point that

Bob had to concentrate on driving so hard, that he couldn't participate in the conversation. Martin and I discussed blackjack and the strategy we would use in Las Vegas. While parked under the underpass Martin took over driving so I would be stuck talking to Bob for a while.

After Martin wrestled the seat into a position that would accommodate his frame we started off. For a while I thought he was just going to rip the front seat out and drive from the back seat. He would probably have been more comfortable. I never saw him take any speed, but he seemed to keep alert and was a better driver than Bob. My guess was that the car was so intimidated by its driver that it wouldn't dare blow out of its lane.

Bob seemed to come down hard, sort of deflated into the front seat and slept. I was still confined to the back and since Martin wasn't in a talkative mood anymore, I dozed off also.

When I woke up from this somewhat restless rest the sky was clear, the sun was coming up and we were west of Omaha. Martin was still driving but he wasn't enjoying it. Bob was still out of it so I offered to drive. Martin pulled over and managed to pry himself out of the car. I also had to struggle a bit to get out of the back seat. We were both stiff. I stretched while Martin did some kind of exercise routine that reminded be of slow ballet. I didn't really want to watch, but it was extremely powerful, graceful and I had to admit, somehow beautiful to see this man move. I wasn't turned on, just sort of awed at his physical control. I almost fell down just stretching onto my toes.

He eyed the back seat of the car like it was a sardine can and he was the last sardine to be packed in. He managed but he didn't look any more comfortable than he had when he was driving. He sort of accordioned himself into the back with his feet up on the seat and his shoulders against the driver's side of the car. He could watch the passing countryside this way but I soon learned there wasn't any countryside to see.

Bob had stirred and mumbled incoherently as we made the switch but I don't think he really regained consciousness. He shifted a little as I shifted into gear and he and the car made similar snoring noises while we got underway again. Martin told me to just follow the signs to Denver and seemed to pass into a somnolent state.

So here I was driving my dilapidated but finely detailed Vega, across the United States with two fags, one of whom was big enough to break me in half, and with a harebrained scheme to make money gambling. I must be losing my mind but Martin's work on the mathematics of blackjack, combined with the strategies he outlined for me, actually made it seem like we could pull it off.

I needed the money. I just hope there was enough left when we got to Las Vegas to make a wager.

I drove and daydreamed about gravity waves moving across the universe like huge curling threads merging toward black holes where they disappeared into some other place that could not be imagined. This vision drifted through my mind and I noticed that there were also black holes where strings were appearing into our universe from somewhere else as if there was some kind of equilibrium involved between our universe and some place outside that involved gravity and time. My brain was just entertaining itself with these images I assumed, but it kept my mind off the otherwise mind-numbing scenery. Flat, flat, flat. Oh wait there's an oil well to break up the horizon! I feigned excitement, as if the well were worth driving hours to see.

The oil well did get me thinking about energy again, and again I was drawn to the strings of gravity moving in and out of the universe. They were continuous and ever-present, exerting their influence over matter instantaneously across space and actually seemed to be a source of energy themselves.

Bob, sitting bolt upright in the seat next to mine, broke me out of this reverie. He blinked and rubbed his eyes. He looked over at me with a bit of surprise showing in his face, twisted to look at Martin and then twisted his wrist to look at his watch.

"I'll drive," was all he said.

I pulled over while he punched Martin into a waking state. This time we all got out of the car and stretched and walked around for a bit. I think we all peed also. I know I did but I didn't look around to confirm that the other two had relieved themselves. I didn't want them to see me looking. I also didn't want to, but did anyway, have an image of them standing side by side urinating into the dry grass, Martin hung like a stallion. I erased the image from my mind and continue walking around until I was sure that if they were going to pee, they had done so.

I walked back toward the car. Bob was stretched out flat on his back in the grass while Martin was going through his dance routine some distance away. I took up position next to Bob and nodded in the direction of Martin.

Bob explained, "Marty is a kung fu master. Those exercises are his way of loosening up and remaining toned. You should see the guy compete. It's like watching some Greek god doing hand to hand with some inferior mortal. He loses once in a while in spite of his size but he generally just wipes his opponents out in the first few seconds. I'm not sure I've ever seen him actually sweat during a match."

Bob thought this was pretty funny and started to yell at Martin, asking him about breaking into a sweat when fighting. Martin stopped his routine and walked toward us. He was amused also and said in an overly masculine voice, "Only when I'm fighting with you, little man!"

They both got a laugh out of this and I laughed along not quite sure what else to do.

We got back in the car. Bob driving, Martin in the front, me in the back again. Martin poured Bob a cup full of coffee, which he used to wash down a couple of his little white pills.

"Denver or bust," he said as he pulled onto the interstate.

FIFTEEN

We made it across the unbelievably dull landscape of eastern Colorado, saw the Rockies rising in the west and made it into Denver before stopping for some real sleep. It was late afternoon and nobody was interested in being in the car anymore. Any thoughts that Bob had about pushing on were pushed aside. If we hadn't gone through the storm west of Chicago we might have made it, but....

The hotel was just like the one we had been in before. Even the view seemed the same from my east-facing windows. Flat dingy suburbs again with an airport in the distance to add a bit of excitement. I was extremely fatigued. This was not just from being cramped in the car. It was also because of the mental work I'd been doing in relation to gravity and blackjack. Then there was the weariness of wondering what in the hell I was doing going to Las Vegas. I actually liked Bob and Martin, but it still seemed ridiculous to be participating in this escapade. We ate something nondescript in the motel restaurant and went to bed. At least it was dark outside and I slept soundly enough that I didn't hear any noises from the room next door, if there were any.

Breakfast was great. A Denver omelet of course. I almost felt like a normal human being again. It was just that I was on this very abnormal trip. Bob and Martin seemed to be well rested and in good spirits.

Once we had satisfied our appetites, we piled into our awful car and drove toward the beckoning mountains. Being back in the car sort of put a damper on our moods but at least we knew that our next stop would be our last for a while. The charged-up Bob was at the controls. His comment about the lack of power in the Vega became apparent as soon as we headed up the grade into the Rockies. Some of the semis were passing us! When we finally made it to the pass and to the other side of the Eisenhower tunnel, we made up for time on the steep downhill run. The scenery was incredible to me. I had never been out west and I wanted to stop and see everything. We passed places like

Breckenridge, Copper Mountain and Vail. I wanted to stop at them all, but the others objected. I really didn't have much choice.

Through Glenwood Springs (food and bathroom stop) through Grand Junction (bathroom stop, coffee bucket refill) and into the state of Utah. The terrain was getting less spectacular but just as interesting. The desert. Grand mesas and cliffs. Signs pointing to places like Arches National Park, Canyonlands National Park, Capital Reef, Bryce Canyon, and finally Zion's National Park gave the impression that all of southern Utah was one big park with a few Indian reservations thrown in.

We finally got off I-70 and turned south onto I-15, which would take us into Las Vegas. During this part of the over 700-mile drive the sun set and the desert darkness closed in. This made the drive between St. George (bathroom, snacks) and Mesquite (didn't even bother to stop) eerie. The narrow canyon was meandering at best but was illuminated with reflected head, star and moon light that gave the rock walls almost a purple fluorescence. It was majestic.

The world turned flat and desert after this but it wasn't long before a bright spot appeared on the horizon and steadily grew. One of the best-lit cities in the world slowly came into view. We had arrived.

Now came the tricky part.

We had to check into a hotel/casino. Martin and Bob were well known in Vegas and didn't want anyone to know that I was affiliated with them. We stopped the car a couple of blocks away from the hotel/casino Martin had picked out. Bob handed me some of my own money and told me to check in. The plan was for the two of them to check in later after I had called them at a nearby pay phone with my room number. They wanted to get a room at least on the same floor as mine if possible. We would meet at a predetermined time at the elevator and act like strangers until we were out of the hotel and in a diner two blocks away, where we could talk freely. It seemed a bit paranoid to me.

I checked in, called the pay phone and gave Bob my room number. Exactly one half hour later I stepped into the hall and joined the two at the elevator. They were looking fairly sharp and I again had to wonder if any of my money would be left with which to gamble. We exited the elevator at the noisy lobby level. Some fairly hefty guys in dark suits immediately stopped Bob and Martin. I was surprised but concealed it and moved away as if I didn't know either of them. I went out of the hotel and to the right looking for the little restaurant we had agreed to meet in. A few minutes later Bob and Martin showed up and we were again sitting in a booth together.

"What in the hell was that all about?" I asked.

Martin looked a little miffed so Bob did the talking. "The hotel security people were just making sure we were satisfied with our accommodations, welcomed us to Las Vegas but let us know politely that we would not be welcome on the floor of the casino."

We discussed the plans for tomorrow. Tonight we were supposed to get a good night's sleep then meet in this same restaurant to plan our assault on the first casino. We were planning to hit every major gambling attraction in town except for the one we were in, that was deemed too risky. We were going to Caesar's Palace first. I was to go to a two-dollar minimum table and start betting the minimum while I got the feel of the game. About every half-hour Bob was supposed to walk through where I could see him. He wouldn't be able to stop or even look at me because he would probably be followed closely by security, but as long as I saw Bob on this schedule, I could keep playing. If I saw Martin walk through at anytime it meant I was supposed to cash in, leave and meet them at the usual greasy spoon. I asked about what was left of the money.

"Don't worry, we still have plenty and there are people in town who will give us more when they hear that we have a guy on the inside playing Martin's game at the twenty-one tables," Bob explained.

I didn't like the sound of it but I had committed to giving this plan a try. We returned to the hotel separately. I went to my room, took a mini bottle of Scotch out of my mini-bar and sipped it gingerly. I was at first a little repulsed by even the smell, but I stuck with it and began to settle down. Martin had instructed me to give my clothes to the valet for cleaning and pressing. He also told me to polish my shoes.

He said, "If you're going to be playing me in absencia, you better look as good as I do," in a way that let me know that this would not really be possible regardless of my wardrobe, but at least he said it with a humorous glint in his eye. I felt like giving him the finger but I thought I might need it later.

I was watching TV and had gotten adventurous enough to open a second mini bottle of Scotch, but I didn't finish it before the valet, or more precisely a pimple-faced kid that worked for the valet service, came to the door and gathered up my new clothes, including my shoes. As I made my way back to the bed I realized that I had no clothing with which to sneak out with and try to escape back to reality. I couldn't help but wonder if this was why Martin had insisted I send everything to be cleaned. This idea depressed me. I sipped at the Scotch, decided it wasn't worth the trouble and went to bed with a little left in the glass.

There was a knock at the door. I got up and put on the complimentary robe that had come with the room. Bob came in quickly when I opened the door. He scanned the room, went over to the glass I had left on the bedside table and gulped down the remaining Scotch. As he rinsed the glass he said, "Don't let Martin catch you drinking. He's very serious about gambling. Besides, I figured you'd be allergic to this stuff."

As he said this, the door again made a light tapping noise. This time Bob opened it and let Martin in. As the big guy entered, Bob checked the hall and then closed and locked the door.

Martin directed me to the small table and after Bob had dragged over a third chair, we all sat down. Martin then produced a deck of cards. I mean he produced it. His empty-appearing hands were in plain sight but with a quick movement from the wrist he was suddenly holding a deck of cards splayed neatly, face up, before my eyes.

"What do you see?" Martin asked.

"A deck of cards...wait, wait there's something wrong. There are no face cards and they are all the same suit. There are also way too many tens in the deck." I knew if I had just said "a deck of cards" Martin would have probably shoved the whole deck up my ass one at a time. He had that kind of look on his face.

"Correct," he said, but not in a congratulatory way, "this is a real blackjack deck pared down to the basics. Nothing else matters but these fifty-two cards and the standard deck just confuses people because they are concentrating on fifty-two separate cards when really there are only ten..."

He dealt and he talked. I played and made stupid decisions about what to do with each hand. He let me know just exactly how stupid each decision was but in a fairly short time I was getting good enough at his strategies that I didn't feel like I would be killed at any moment. I kept looking over at the mini-bar.

"Don't even think about drinking," he said. "Even if you could hold your liquor, which you can't, it dulls your concentration and you need to be sharp."

I was hoping to dull my senses a bit, just in case Martin reached over and slapped me upside the head for not paying attention. I would have hated to be in one of his classes. I was imagining several students leaving his classroom bruised and bleeding because they had screwed up a proof or forgotten their homework.

We played blackjack with his funny deck for about an hour, then Bob pulled out some rolls of dollar coins. He peeled open the paper and stacked 50 of the shiny disks in front of me.

"OK, there are your chips. It's time to start betting," he explained.

Up to that point I realized we had been concentrating only on whether to hit, stand, split or double and had not been putting any money on the table.

First Martin tried to teach me to palm the coins, which were about the size of real chips. When he realized how clumsy I was he sat back shaking his head.

He said, "Look, just try to get some of the coins from the table to your pocket as discretely as possible."

After ten or twelve tries I thought I was doing pretty well. Martin reached over and put ten or twelve chips in front of him. He glanced suddenly toward the door. I looked quickly in that direction fearing the worst. When I looked back, there were only five coins in front of Martin. His hands were exactly where I had seen them before and I swear I didn't see any movement out of the corner of my eye as he pulled the old non-verbal "hey, look over there!" gag on me. I felt a little impressed and stupid, so of course I insulted him to pretend that I wasn't.

"Show off."

That was about as insulting as I could get though. He and Bob laughed pretty heartily and the atmosphere became more comfortable. Martin was an excellent slight of hand artist, probably had to do to some extent with his kung fu training as well as his gambling. The guy had more fine motor control in each hand than I had in my whole body.

We played and practiced card combinations and betting strategies for another hour. There were a lot of gives and takes, verbal abuse and snide remarks but it was fun. Then Martin told us to be quiet. He told me to remember the micro-trends in seemingly random events. He was going to deal hands to Bob and I in silence and I was supposed to "feel" the patterns and alter my bets accordingly.

After about five minutes I wasn't feeling anything but decided I better do something so I put 20 bucks out. Up until then I had been betting one or two dollars per hand and trying to get the "feel." Martin stopped dealing and looked at me like I was an idiot.

"If you're not going to take this seriously," he said, slow and low, "then we're going to have to go back to our investors empty handed."

I swallowed. He dealt. I lost.

I started paying attention. After about another 20 minutes I actually did sense some kind of a rhythm or pattern. I suddenly became certain that probabilities supported my winning the next hand or two. I put out five dollars. Martin dealt. I won. I put out ten dollars. Martin dealt me a pair of sevens. I split them, got a ten and a six but didn't feel bad about it. Martin had a six showing, uncovered a ten and dealt himself a nine. Busted. He didn't say a word. I put out a dollar, quite sure I was going to lose. Martin dealt himself a blackjack to my 20. I put out one again and busted drawing on a 14. I put out seven bucks and won.

I sat back and let out a breath. I think I had been holding it the whole time.

Martin sat back and smiled. "See, you really can get a sense of the short periods of non-random movement in the cards," Martin said this as Bob nodded in agreement. "Now you have to do the same thing with all kinds of noise around you, people blowing smoke in your face, waitresses wearing next to nothing trying to shove drinks in your hand and a dealer who may not want you to win."

"No sweat," I said and shrugged my shoulders.

Needless to say we practiced for about two more hours while Bob and Martin kept up a continuous distracting dialogue and Bob blew smoke in my face from time to time. They said they were sorry they couldn't emulate a scantily clad female for me. We had quite a few laughs except when I did something dumb. This was getting less frequent though. Even when I was down to only 22 bucks, they reassured me that everything was going OK, that I should expect times when the trends would be favoring the dealer and to ride them out calmly. I got back to where I was ahead by about seven dollars and suddenly knew it was time to quit, don't know why, wasn't tired, but I knew. I picked up the few chips I was keeping on the table and added them to those I had "secretly" placed in various pockets and stood up.

Martin looked up at me with some mild and uncharacteristic admiration in his face. "Excellent," he said. "You quit after a long stretch when you got up to fifty-eight dollars. Always quit while you're ahead even if it takes you hours to get there or even if you get there in five or six hands."

"Fifty-seven," I said.

He made me dump the 58 coins on the table. The guy didn't miss a thing.

"Now," he went on, "I want you to think about each of those coins as meaningless pieces of plastic. They have no value, they are simply points. Some chips are one point, some will be five points, some twenty-five, et cetera. Ignore the actual value of the chips. You'll get freaked out when you put out a ten thousand dollar bet and think of it as anything but a few chips. If you think about it as ten thousand bucks, you'll pee your pants." He said this as if he knew for a fact that I would lose bladder control under these circumstances, and I wasn't so sure he wasn't right.

Bob and Martin gathered up the cards and coins and left one at a time. I rushed to the mini-bar and wolfed down a bourbon. Ouch.

I was amazed at what had happened. For the first time I was excited about being here and gambling for real money. I had dollar signs swimming in front of my eyes. I knew I needed to sleep though. I took off my robe and got in bed.

I tossed and turned for a bit but finally drifted off. I think I dreamed about men the size of Martin very forcibly removing me from a casino.

We met at the restaurant at eight-thirty. Bob had a newspaper and slid it over to me. I picked it up and unfolded it thinking I would see an article of interest he wanted me to read. Instead about 50 $100 bills fell out of it onto my lap and almost onto the floor. Fortunately they were held together with a rubber band.

"Holy shit!" Bob blurted while Martin rolled his eyes. I tried to pick up the cash and conceal it back in the paper but was fumbling it onto the middle of the table instead. A large hand moving with incredible speed passed over the bills and they disappeared into that hand as if they had never existed. Martin had his hands folded on the table in front of him but he was looking right at me as I juggled the paper. Bob grabbed the paper from me, crumpled it quickly into a ball and stuffed it in the space between his leg and the wall. Martin drew my attention.

"Look, dip shit, I'm going to reach over and hand you the money. You will take it in the palm of your hand and nonchalantly place it into your inner coat pocket. You will do this while continuing to look me in the eye or I'll shove this wad down your scrawny throat."

I did exactly what he said, exactly.

Once I started breathing again I nonchalantly quivered a question. "Where did you get the, um, resources and, you know, about how much is there?"

"You've got five Gs," Martin stated quietly. "There will be more if we win but that five will do for now. Bob and I have some 'investors' who are willing to put up some capital on the assurance that they will enjoy a substantial return."

"And if they don't enjoy this return?" I asked a bit hesitantly.

"Then you won't enjoy your first and last visit to Las Vegas," Martin said with a sinister smile.

I suddenly lost my appetite and wanted to raid the mini-bar in my room. I settled for coffee instead.

Bob tried to calm me down. "Look, you've read the book and what's more you understood it. You've also practiced and did pretty well in spite of what Martin thinks."

I looked at Martin, who was disdainful. "What do you mean, 'what Martin thinks?'" I asked a little rebelliously.

Martin chose to answer this little challenge himself. "He means that if I had been playing last night and you had been dealing, I would have left the room with about one hundred and forty dollars instead of your pitiful fifty-eight."

Somehow I believed this and was appropriately humbled. Besides, I had now lost my taste for rebelling against Martin along with my appetite.

Fear does that to a man.

SIXTEEN

I walked to Caesar's with Bob and Martin somewhere behind me. I was dressed in my fine clothing and could feel the hundreds bumping against my chest and my legs. I had split the cash into three smaller bundles and put one in each front pocket and one in the breast pocket of my coat. My wallet was in my back right pocket but Martin had removed everything from it including identification. He had then stuffed a few extra hundreds into my left shoe "just in case," he said.

"Just in case what?" I inquired.

"Never mind," was his response.

I didn't feel never mindful about this but left it alone.

I went in the front door to be greeted by the usual noise and smoke. I moved to the left and followed a crowd of women who must have been there as part of a fat butt convention. It had to be something like that because they were all displaying their relatively monumental buttocks, dimples, cellulite and all, in tightly stretched polyester of various colors never intended by nature.

I made it to the blackjack tables and walked around as if inspecting the place. Sort of sniffing around for a dealer on a losing streak. Really I was just trying to find a table with a good view of the entranceway from the lobby so I could see Bob walk by on his semi-hourly schedule. I had to wait for a seat to open up and it was at a five-dollar minimum table instead of a two-dollar minimum.

Oh well, I thought. *Close enough.*

I thought this just before I thought that with Martin, there was no such thing as "close enough." I almost moved but instead I decided I felt like living dangerously. Bob walked by as I put out $500 which the dealer spread on the table, announced to her pit boss, shoved into a slot in the table and slid sixteen $25 chips and twenty $5 dollar chips over to me. She spread these out in neat little piles before letting me have them so that the overhead cameras could confirm the count. I tried not to glance up.

I bet five. She dealt.

A half-hour later I was down about 50 bucks. Bob walked by the arched entry. I kept playing. The next time he came by I was up about 40 dollars, but had only about $250 on the table. The rest was "discretely" tucked into my pockets, although I was pretty sure the dealer knew exactly how much I had even though the dealer had changed a few times.

The next time Bob walked by I missed him because I was in the midst of a streak. I was playing two hands and had about a $120 bet with one hand doubled down. I won. I was up about $400 and some of my pockets were getting full. I kept playing, but more conservatively, and hoped that it was Bob I had missed and not Martin. I caught Bob on his next round and was about even where I had been.

Just as I thought my rear end was going to be permanently shaped to the stool and my bladder was stretched even farther than my pockets, Martin walked by. I noticed he was being escorted by a couple of guys that weren't exactly friendly. I finished the hand, lost and got up from the table. I was so excited about turning $500 into around $900 that I forgot to go to the cashier's window and cash in my chips. I walked out into the lobby with my pockets bulging. Just before I went into the street, Bob came in, glanced at me without interest and then looked back at me with interest and grimaced while pointing to his pocket. I looked down and saw the irregular contour of my own pockets and realized what I had done.

I did an about-face without looking up and cashed in. I then walked quickly to the restaurant/meeting place and sat down. Bob came in first followed by Martin a few moments later. Bob had just enough time to tell me that Martin didn't know about my almost leaving the casino with my pockets full of chips, the clear indication being, don't let him know or else.

"Well?" was all Martin said as he sat down.

"Oh, I about doubled my money," I said as if this were as common an event as taking a breath.

"Shit, you were in there long enough you should have done better than that. Bob said you never changed tables the whole time. Did you get up to stretch or pee? Did you order some coffee?" he asked.

I couldn't think of any appropriate elaboration so I stuck with, "No."

He shook his head while the waitress took Bob's order, then mine and then the order for a dozen eggs scrambled, with ham, from Martin.

I looked at him with my mouth open.

"That's his usual brunch," Bob said. "Lots of protein."

"Puts muscle on you," Martin stated emphatically. "You could certainly use a little more muscle and a little less flab," he said as my mouth snapped shut. "Tell me all about the game," he added as if I weren't supposed to take offense.

I didn't actually. Martin was an extremely dangerous man, but I knew he was not really a danger to me.

I went into as much detail as I could recall about each hand. He listened quietly but interrupted now and then with comments and suggestions about how he might have done things. Overall he seemed satisfied.

When we had finished eating and Martin had made me drink an extra cup of coffee, he said, "OK, little gambling guy, take your money to the next casino down and play some more. This time I want you to get up every now and then, at least once per hour, and walk vigorously around the casino, just taking in the sights. Go to one of the bars and order coffee, take a leak, eat a little something. Go back to a different table each time. Stick to tables with ten dollar or less minimums and try to play two or three hands at a time if you can and don't forget to watch for Bob."

This was more words than I had ever heard from Martin at one time. A virtual encyclopedia of instructions. I nodded my agreement with them and left.

The next casino was not quite as loud but made up for it by being more dingy, dimmer and smokier. I made the rounds of the 21 areas and picked a likely looking seat at a ten-dollar minimum table. I felt like betting big. Then I felt overconfident and worried that I should go to another table. Then I thought, what the hell, they're just points, it doesn't make any difference. Then why I didn't get up and go to one of the empty $100-minimum tables? It made a difference. Besides, I figured I better follow Martin's instructions to the letter.

I played and pretty much broke even. Bob walked through quickly. It didn't look like he was being followed. I got up and walked around, drank about a half a cup of coffee and went back to the tables, picked one with a five-dollar minimum and played for an hour. Just after Bob walked by for the third time I got up and relieved myself. I also went to the cashier's window and relieved myself of about $700 of excess chips. I had been doing pretty well at that last table and still had about a thousand in chips stashed around my person.

On my way back to the tables I felt around my various pockets and found one empty. The back right hand pocket. The empty wallet. Someone was in for a bit of a disappointment. Just as I was about to sit down again a thin sleazy fellow stopped me and handed me my wallet. He nodded, winked at me as if we were fellow cons and walked away. I almost felt a sense of brotherhood and belonging! This "professional" had acknowledged me as a colleague somehow, just because I carried around a completely empty wallet. I had to remember to ask Bob about this.

I sat at a table and was immediately impressed by the cleavage of the dealer. Not only was it delightful to see, but there wasn't much that couldn't be seen in her low-cut blouse. I got up and moved to another table. Damn, I was proud of my control!

I lost a few hundred and got up discouraged and with a headache. I went to the little convenience store in the lobby and bought some aspirin. I then went into one of the restaurants and ate a fair amount of fair food. I noticed a guy that actually resembled me at a booth nearby, only he was about 200 pounds bigger and had a couple of over-made-up bimbos with him. I shook my head and went out onto the floor.

The next table went well. I broke the rules and went to a $25-minimum table. It was perfectly located and because the minimum was so high, it was not crowded. I could therefore play two or three hands at a time. The only drawback to this was that you had to bet twice the table minimum to play two hands and three times the table minimum to play three. I was laying out as much as $225 per hand now. My head felt better, my stomach was full, my bladder was empty, I knuckled down.

I didn't realize how much time had passed. I was immersed. I was getting these patterns in my head of mini-trends in the cards dealt to each hand. I was keeping pretty good track of the cards pretending they were all the same suit and that all the face cards were just tens. I looked for every opportunity to double and split and I got to where I could sense the different rhythms for each of the three hands I was playing. I'd bet low on one and high on the other two, then low on all three, then high on just the second. Around and around the cards went. I didn't really notice that I had become the only player at the table, and I didn't notice that there was a little crowd formed around me. What I did finally notice was some loud explicatives from the direction of the lobby. I looked up to see Martin walking by with two bouncers, one in each hand, in some kind of paralyzingly painful hold. He looked my way as he allowed the security team to "escort" him out of the building.

Oh shit. I wonder how many times he had walked by before he had to raise a ruckus to get my attention. I looked at the huge pile of chips, mostly hundreds, on the table, realized that my pockets were stuffed, saw the pit boss staring at me with suspicion and then noticed my admirers.

Oh shit! I wondered how much trouble I was in, not only from the casino, but from Martin too.

"Well, I think I've had enough for a while." I said this trying to be cool about the small fortune that I had won. I stood and stretched. The pit boss came over and asked if I'd like to exchange my chips for larger denominations to make it easier to carry them to the cashier. I agreed and watched as the dealer carefully stacked 100s and 25s, knocking over each little stack so the cameras and the pit boss could confirm the accuracy of the count. I was sort of mesmerized by this activity when I remembered the chips in my pockets. I began unloading them and the dealer began making more little piles. Even her mouth dropped open a bit when I dumped the "hidden" chips on the table.

The pit boss got pretty friendly about then, smiled and started joking about the casino going broke and kibitzing with the crowd. I just wanted to get out of there. He invited me back enthusiastically and started writing on a little pad of paper. He tore off pages as he wrote and handed them to me. As the dealer finished up I read the notes. Free dinner, free room, free bottle of champagne. This winning stuff was pretty cool!

I picked up six $1000 chips, four $100 chips, two $25 and a one. I gave one of the 25s to the dealer and headed for the cages behind which the real money was kept. I noticed that a bigger than average guy stayed close to me on the way there and on the way to the front entrance where he politely smiled, held the door and told me to be sure to come back so that the casino could have a chance to win back some of its money.

I walked down the street in sort of a daze. Over $6,400. I remembered the pickpocket and became suddenly paranoid and looked around. I sighed with relief when I saw Martin shadowing me discretely. If anyone messed with me, he'd mess with them in a big way.

I got to the restaurant and sat down next to an agitated Bob. Martin walked past and didn't come in until about 15 minutes later. In that time Bob explained to me how much trouble I was in. The more he talked, the more I sank down in my seat, the more I wanted to disappear before Martin showed up.

Martin showed up. I could have just slid under the table and hugged the centrally located table leg and whimpered. Maybe then he would have mercy on me.

I smiled instead.

"Wipe that stupid grin of your face before I wipe it off for you," was the response I got for my trouble. The smile dropped like lead.

Martin continued, "Don't get greedy, I told you that a million times. Those assholes in the casino are pouring over the videos of every hand you played right now trying to figure out how you did that. They can circulate a picture of you to every casino in town and you'd be made to feel very unwelcome in all of them. You just about screwed the pooch."

I wasn't familiar with the last phrase but I countered with another canine quip, "I thought I was making out like a tall dog!"

Martin looked at me like I was tall dog shit. "Look, I made some inquiries and I don't think you did any damage. You sure as hell won't be able to go into that casino again and we should probably shave you and buy you a new jacket," he said.

I came back with, "Well. At least we have enough money to buy one or two."

He returned with, "Don't be a smart ass, I hate smart asses." His teeth were a little clenched.

I suddenly wanted to be anything but a smart ass. But I couldn't help myself. "How about if I'm just an ass then," was my not too considered response.

Martin's eyes widened and he rose a bit off his seat. Bob was just about to bust a gut trying not to laugh and when Martin perceived this, he turned on Bob instead of me. "Don't you encourage him!" he almost yelled at Bob while rising to a crouch. But seeing Bob in his epic struggle to control his mirth got to Martin who started to chuckle even while he continued to grimace.

He fell back into his seat, nearly breaking the back off the booth and let lose some pretty amazing laughter. Bob gave it up at that point and laughed along. I sort of smiled uneasily.

Bob tried to explain how Martin had kept walking back and forth outside the passage from the lobby to the casino. Each time he had move a little faster and grunted or coughed or sneezed. Finally he practically skipped by while singing an old Bob Dylan tune, but even that didn't work. What it did was attract the attention of the two security men I had seen who made the mistake of trying to eject the obviously deranged Martin from the building. Before they knew what was happening it was Martin who was escorting them and it was their screams of pain and streams of obscenities that had finally gotten my attention.

Bob had tears going down his face and Martin's eyes were pretty moist. My sides were starting to ache a bit and it had taken Bob a few minutes to get the story out between the laughs.

We all settled down a bit, and ordered some food from the waitress who had been waiting for us to compose ourselves before she bothered to come over.

I told Martin that I wasn't being greedy.

He said, "I know. It's the dance of the cards, isn't it? You can get hypnotized by them and play as if in a trance. Bet the minimum, bet the minimum, wait, wait I see a pattern, bet the house!" He clearly understood the process and shook his head. "I should have warned you about it. It is actually dangerous to win too much. It attracts attention that we don't need. If you want to win more, you'll need to go to the high minimum tables and play in short bursts."

I proudly showed him my slips of paper for free stuff. He tore them up and dropped the pieces into my half-empty coffee cup. So much for my pride.

"You aren't ever going back in that casino again," was all he said.

SEVENTEEN

We hit two more casinos that day, but I didn't have any spectacular winning games like I had before; in fact, I made sure I didn't. Maybe I didn't because I was too nervous now to allow myself to fall into the trance-like state I had been in at the other casino.

I stuck to $25-minimum tables except for one brief period when I sat down at one of the empty $100 tables. Another man with a much younger woman glued to him like a remora on a shark sat at the table just after I did. We started playing. The dealer didn't talk; the man with the female appendage didn't talk. This game was serious and I didn't like the feel of it so I left after only a few hands. I said thanks as I got up which got me a nod from the dealer and a grunt from the other player. I didn't think I was quite ready for that game yet.

By the time I quit for the night I had the $5,000 that Martin and Bob had originally given me plus about $6,400 more. Not a bad day's work, but I was worn out. I returned to my room and soon after was joined by my co-conspirators.

I put all the money on the bed and Bob counted it. He seemed pretty happy about things and even Martin seemed in good spirits. Speaking of spirits, I glanced over to the mini-bar and Martin nodded. I got the two restocked minis of Scotch and poured them into a glass with a little ice. This time it was simply delightful to sip.

Martin talked about tomorrow's strategies. I had to establish myself as a serious player in the next casinos. I had to show them the color of my money so to speak, sit at the highest minimum table, play seriously but not win too much. Martin said I could then ask about any private tables with higher stakes.

Bob had bundled up the cash and took some more out of a paper bag he had brought in with him. He passed stacks of bills over to Martin who slid them over to me.

"Twenty thousand dollars is what you'll need to convince them you're serious," he said.

I looked at the pile and felt a little uneasy. Apparently they had been back to one of their "investors."

It was late so they left. I finished off the Scotch and hit the sack. Tomorrow was going to be an interesting day. I hadn't realized that there might be private tables where the betting had higher minimums and potentially non-existent maximums. I wondered how much money these guys wanted to take away from Las Vegas as I drifted off to sleep.

The next morning at breakfast Martin showed up with a briefcase. He slid it under the table to me and told me to put the money in it.

"I didn't bring it with me," I said. "There was too much to carry so I hid it in the room." I thought Martin would be pissed but he said it was OK.

He just said, "You'll have to go back to your room and pack the money into the case. It's probably a good thing you didn't bring it. You'd probably drop it all over the table and floor trying to transfer it into the attaché."

Bob and he shared a little chuckle at that but I tried to keep a straight and insulted face.

Martin went on, "When you get to the casino, take the briefcase to the cage and ask them to put it on an account and issue you a credit voucher to give to the pit boss where you play. Go to the hundred-dollar-minimum table, get five thousand dollars in chips and play hard for about an hour. Then I want you to lose some back and start looking a little frustrated. That's when you ask the boss about a private table with higher stakes. Hopefully they'll escort you to a back room. You'll be on your own. Bob and I won't be able to get any signals to you so play for two to three hours and leave. Go back to the hotel and call our room. Let the phone ring twice and hang up. We'll meet you twenty minutes later at the fried chicken place three blacks east of here."

Bob continued the lesson. "We're all going to check out of the hotel today and move to the Hilton by the airport. I'm going to buy tickets for us in case we need to get out of town quickly."

I was starting to feel a little more uncomfortable now and said so.

Bob tried to calm me, "Don't worry, we're just being careful. Nothing will happen…probably."

"I feel much better now," I quipped.

"Look," Martin said, "we're playing with the big boys here and we're playing for big bucks. When a little money is involved they'll let you get away with a few things, but with the kind of money we're talking about taking out of this town, well, it's a sum many people in Vegas would consider much higher than the worth of a human being."

"Oh, I'm really reassured now." I said this a little loud and started twisting in my seat as if to find an escape route. "Just how much money are we talking about?" I asked in a whisper now.

Martin looked at Bob and Bob said, "We'd like to raise about a quarter of a million before we leave."

I couldn't believe it! "You expect me to believe that I'm supposed to come here with a lousy twenty-one hundred dollars and leave with over one hundred times that?"

"It's been done," Martin said matter-of-factly.

"Not by me it hasn't," I responded.

"Look, Bob and I know this town. We're being overly cautious because there is always some danger involved in trying to rip off casinos. But we've got every angle covered. Pretty soon we'll have enough to pay back our investors and still have plenty left to make a small fortune with before we quit." He explained this as if I were a child.

Bob jumped in. "You're going to be making much larger bets now so the money will grow pretty fast. When we get to our goal you'll leave a thousand-dollar chip at your place at the table, say you need to use the bathroom and leave. No one will expect you to leave behind the thousand dollars so it will be a while before they realize you've taken off. That way if there is anyone tagging us, we'll get a head start."

Bob pulled out a map of the city and continued. "Here is where we are now and…here's that really cool fountain I was telling you about." The waitress had come by to see if everything was satisfactory. We all smiled like a bunch of tourists and said yes. I wanted to order a fifth of Scotch, but I restrained myself.

Back to Bob in a conspiratorial voice, "Here's where we are, here's the hotel we're at now. From now on you'll take cabs wherever you go. We're going to leave the Vega parked on this side street with the key under the mat in case one or all of us need to get out fast. Memorize the layout of the streets around this area so you can find your way around even at night if you had to."

My hands were a little sweaty as I took the map and memorized the pattern of streets. It was easy. I had an almost photographic memory for patterns. I didn't do as well with lists of things but it only took me a minute to commit the map to a place in memory where I knew I'd be able to pull it up and view it again just as if I were looking at the real thing.

141

Patterns. Very important.

We finished our food and I left with the briefcase to gather the money up and head for our new target. I also packed my minimal belongings into a nylon duffel bag and checked out of the hotel on my way out. I hailed a cab and told the driver where I wanted to go.

I took a breather in the back of the cab. This scene was getting pretty heavy. I thought we'd come to Vegas, gamble, have a little fun and leave with a little more money. I had no idea what I was getting myself into. I felt like whatever "it" was, I was already in "it" over my head.

I carried the two bags into the casino. I checked my duffel with the bell desk and went into the casino with the briefcase. Everything went as planned. I sat at a $100-minimum table and turned my five grand into about eight. I then started losing and got back down to around four. I kept rubbing my face as I lost and shaking my head. To add to my act I actually ordered a Scotch on the rocks, which I really felt like I needed anyway.

After sitting out a couple of hands and finishing the watered-down drink, I waved the pit boss over and asked about the possibility of getting into a higher stakes game. The boss man looked at my credit and at my chips, made some kind of meaningful eye contact with the dealer and said, "Come with me."

I followed him around the table to an unmarked door. He knocked, someone looked out through a small opening and then let us in. He led me down a hall with several doors along its walls. He stopped at one, tapped and entered.

The quiet was the first thing I noticed. As the door closed behind us, the obnoxious noise of the casino stopped abruptly. The room must have been well sound-proofed. It also smelled of tobacco, but of a much finer grade than out on the floor. Here a couple of the players were smoking cigars that probably cost more by the box than tuition at MIT.

There were six places, four players. I took the seat in the middle to avoid taking the one at "third base" as it was called, the last seat before the dealer as the cards went around. It didn't really matter but I didn't want the people at the table to think I was overconfident and take up this place of supposed responsibility.

No one introduced themselves and I didn't give out my name. When the current hand was completed the pit boss handed the dealer my credit slip, put my chips on the table in front of me and again made some kind of message containing eye contact with the dealer before leaving. I think the non-verbal message was "this one's a sucker."

"Thousand-dollar minimum, no limit," the dealer said as he began dealing from the six-deck shoe.

Shit, I thought, I only had about $19,000 with which to play. I started out very conservatively but still lost down to about $6,000 over the next 45 minutes. I was pretty sure I was getting an ulcer and that it was going to finish its job of drilling all the way through my stomach just as my money ran out. This was OK with me because I would rather die from gastric bleeding than face Martin and Bob with only an empty briefcase in my hand.

I had $2,000 out. Blackjack. I put $2,000 out. The dealer got an eight up and dealt me a pair of tens. I split them. The play stopped. The cigar in the player's mouth next to me almost fell out onto the table. The dealer stared at me like I was crazy, but after all, the pit boss had marked me for a sucker. He had that questioning, "Are you sure?" look on his face and I nodded. A jack and a king came my way. I tried to look like I knew this was going to happen and that this was no big deal. Others kind of groaned or let out a louder than normal breath. Everyone else had either busted trying to beat 18 or held at 18 or better.

The dealer flipped over a king. 18. I won both hands.

One of the players left, opening up a seat next to me. I put two grand out on each of two circles on the green felt. Lost one, won one. I wasn't into my pattern so much as the dealer's. The guy was due for a downward trend. I could just see it on the little graph I kept in my head of each player's wins and losses and the dealer's performance. I played the two hands. I played well. I was getting into the zone. It wasn't until I slid $50,000 onto the first circle and $2,000 out onto the second that I realized what was happening. The $50,000 suddenly broke through my concentration and I saw it there as money instead of meaningless plastic and metal chips.

"Damn," I said out loud.

The dealer and the other players looked at me like I had interrupted a deep conversation. The spell was broken. I mumbled an apology for some reason and the dealer dealt.

The dealer dealt me a jack of spades on the first and larger bet and a six on the other. The cards came around again. I looked at the second hand first. An eight, a sure loser. I picked up the other hand and saw that an ace of spades had joined my jack. I dropped them onto the table face up and everyone issued an explicative or two, including the dealer. I lost the second hand as I expected but took pleasure in pulling the $125,000 pile of chips toward the rail in front of me. Another gentleman entered through a back door.

He smiled and held out his hand. I took it as he said, "Congratulations, sir, you seem to be having a pretty good day. I think the casino would like to reward your patronage with a comped suite near the top of our hotel so that you can rest as comfortably as possible and return refreshed to play tomorrow."

I was being asked to leave.

"Ah, sure," I said, "thanks, I'll do that."

I got up from the table and was escorted to the cashier. The dollars pretty much filled my briefcase and it had a nice hefty feel to it as I took it from the young lady across the counter. Somehow it didn't make me feel better. The next stop on my personalized tour of the hotel was the front desk. I saw Martin looking a bit nervous on the other side of the lobby. I had never seen anything more frightening in my life. I almost felt my urinary sphincter relax. If Martin was nervous, that meant something really shitty had happened. I'm sure I was pale as a ghost as the gentleman who had escorted me from the blackjack game arranged for my fabulous room with free room service and an open bar. I signed a piece of paper and tried not to think about Martin. It was all I could do to keep from turning and/or running. The gentleman with me took the briefcase from me and gave it to the clerk behind the counter.

"We'll just keep this in our safe for you until you need it," he said smiling.

I could only manage a nod.

Our next stop was the bell desk where we retrieved the duffel bag. The trip across the lobby gave me a chance to look around, but I didn't see a sign of Martin or Bob. My escort, who was acting like my best friend, asked if he could show me to my room. I knew I didn't have a choice so I said yes as calmly as I could. We went up the elevator to the fourteenth floor of the tower and exited in a hallway that only had four sets of double doors along its length. We went to 143 and the overly helpful casino employee opened the door for me. It was by far the most luxurious and largest hotel room I'd ever seen. Actually it was a suite of rooms with a balcony running the length of the living room and bedroom that had a spectacular view of the city.

"I hope you enjoy your stay and if there is anything you need, just call the front desk and it will be arranged," said my companion as he exited.

He did leave the key to the room on a table in the entry area so I wasn't quite a prisoner but I figured that if I tried to leave some intensely polite hotel employee would offer to take me back to my room.

I sat in a chair and said, "Oh shit."

I couldn't think of anything more eloquent or more fitting. The bar in this suite was not mini. There was a fifth of Glenfiddich on the shelf behind the bar along with a wide selection of other bottles I did not recognize, a full-size refrigerator with an icemaker and a long row of cut crystal glasses. I put three ice cubes in an eight-ounce glass and poured in the Scotch until they floated. Swirling and sipping this was delightful and I needed something to make myself stop shaking.

I sat in a chair and said, "Oh shit."

I still couldn't think of anything else to say. My brain was sort of stuck on those two words.

There was a loud knock on the door. I opened it and Bob stood there in mostly black clothing. He basically pulled me into the hall and pointed me in the direction of Martin who was standing at the end of the hall holding a sheet of white paper over his head with a wire that looked like a straightened out coat hanger. Behind me Bob quietly but authoritatively said, "Run!"

I ran to where Martin was and he motioned me through a door in a small alcove that lead to stairs. Bob came in behind me and then Martin pulled the paper down and entered the stair well also. Bob had grabbed my duffel bag before he left the room and had it in his right hand. He shoved it into my arms almost spilling the Scotch I was still kind of stupidly holding.

"You carry the bag. Martin and I will need our hands free," he said.

As the door closed I saw a video camera where Martin had been holding his paper shield. Bob pointed down while Martin took the glass of Scotch out of my hand and placed in on a step of the ascending flight. We went down. I missed my Scotch. I was still shaking a little and I didn't think things were going to get more relaxing for a while.

We got to the second floor. There were no video cameras visible here and we went to the southeast corner of the building and then took a long hall that ran the length of the back of the casino to the southwest corner. In the hall we passed a covered walkway leading farther south to several two-story buildings that housed the cheaper rooms that the majority of tourists stayed in. When we got to the corner, there was another set of stairs. We hadn't passed anybody so far. We went down one flight to the main floor and the stair well opened out into a hall running north. Directly across from the stairs were roll-up doors used for loading and unloading trucks so I assumed the loading docks were just outside. All of the large doors were closed, fortunately there weren't many deliveries at one AM. There was a fire door at the corner with a sign that said, *Alarm will sound if opened.*

Bob looked around and then quietly said, "Security is trying to find us. We're going to make a distraction by opening this fire door and then we're going to run back up to the second floor."

I asked the obvious question, "Why don't we just exit the exit and get the hell out of here?" I got the answer I didn't want to hear.

"Because we've got to go get our money," Bob said, straining not to reach out and swat me.

"Oh shit," was the only response I could come up with, pretty limited vocabulary for a smart guy.

Bob tried the door. It was locked, which was against the law I pointed out. Bob looked at me like I was an idiot, and at that particular moment I was. He led me back to the stairs as Martin moved out into the hall. He stood about ten feet from the door and exploded into motion. He moved toward the door while executing a 360-degree spin, which he came out of in mid-air with his legs up under him. As he flew rapidly toward the door his right leg shot out and the entire momentum of his leg and body struck the door near the latch mechanism. The door blew open and stayed open because it was bent pretty significantly from the power of Martin's kick. Martin landed lightly on his feet and was barreling towards us before I even had time to turn and run up the stairs. He went past sort of like a freight train and Bob and I followed. A loud ringing noise began and seemed to be omnipresent in the building.

We waited at the second-floor stairwell door for a moment. Bob cracked it and looked out. "All clear," he whispered. We moved out into the hall and moved north toward the front of the building.

When we got to the end of the hall we entered yet another stairwell. On the landing Bob whispered, "We should be just above the west end of the check-in desk where the safe is. When we get down to the first floor there will be two doors immediately to our left. The first one goes into the office where the safe is and will be locked. The second door goes into the lobby just in front of the desk. We have to go through that door, get to and over the counter without being seen and quietly take out the night man behind the counter. There should only be one guy and he's probably armed. His job is really to stay at this end of the counter and make sure no one tries to mess with the safe."

"Boy, I'm glad we have a simple and effective plan," I said. "Are you guys crazy?"

Martin and Bob just looked at me for a minute then Martin said, "Yes, let's go."

We went down the stairs. Bob checked the hall. On the first floor it ended after the side door to the lobby. I was afraid it would run the length of the west side of the building like the one above us, which would mean we'd be looking down the long hall toward the loading docks and at our distraction. Hopefully all of the security people were down there trying to find us.

We moved into the hall and to the second door. After a peek, Bob opened it wide and Martin went through. I heard a quiet thud or two and then Bob motioned me through and made an up and over movement with his hand. I think I knew what he meant and made a dash for the counter, turned my back to it and jumped. My butt landed on the counter and I spun on it as my momentum slid me across the smooth surface. I came off the counter, landed on my feet and ended in a crouch behind it.

This was the most coordinated thing I had ever done and I was starting to feel proud of myself when Bob came over in a forward dive. He did a beautiful tuck and roll and ended up standing in the doorway to an office area behind the counter where Martin stood watching. My pride melted. Bob waved me over and I sort of crawled and shuffled over to the door and into the small room.

"All clear," Bob said.

That's when I noticed the unconscious guy on the floor. Martin had dragged him into the room. I saw his chest rise and fall so Martin must have given him just a little tap. I assumed it was the "sleeping" man's gun that Martin had tucked in his belt.

I couldn't believe we made it without being seen! There were only a few people in the lobby area but all of them were turning away from our end of the desk and moving toward the casino.

Martin went over to the safe. It was tucked snuggly into a space in the wall at about the height of an average man's chest. It was a little lower than Martin's. The safe had a stainless steel wheel on the front a bit smaller than a steering wheel on a car. Martin grabbed the wheel, tensed and with a monumental effort, slid the safe out of its cranny and tried to set it on the floor. It must have weighed 300 pounds or more and even Martin had trouble lowering it slowly. It made a fair amount of noise as it hit the floor and plaster and paint chips also scattered everywhere. At that moment, the alarm was turned off. The quiet was actually scarier than the noise but the ringing had lasted long enough to cover the noise we were making.

The safe had landed on its back with the wheel facing up. Bob opened a door in the back of the room that led to a small break area with a table, some chairs and a counter with a coffeepot and a sink on it, a small fridge below.

Across from the door were tinted windows running the length of the room. They extended from the ceiling down about three feet so I couldn't see out of them. What I did see was Martin bracing himself with his knees bent and his hands on the wheel of the safe. I would not have believed it if I hadn't seen it. He lifted the safe a hair above the carpeted floor and shuffled with it into the break room. The safe dragged on the floor a bit when he got it into the room but he had actually lifted the thing for several feet. He stood up slowly. I closed my mouth.

Bob was grabbing handfuls of plaster and paint and using them to make scraping marks on the floor leading through the locked door and into the hall. He held the door open and tossed plaster along the hall toward the stairwell door. He then closed and locked the hall door and came back into the break room, closing and locking that door also.

I stood there with a blank mind. I didn't have the slightest idea what was going on or what to do next. I thought for a moment that Martin would just plunged his fist through the side of the safe and rip it open. I don't think I would have been surprised.

Instead Bob put his ear down on the door and began turning the combination dial. I started to ask what the plan was now but Martin made a move toward me that scared me into silence and he let me know I better stay that way with his look and the finger placed over his lips.

Bob kept turning the little dial. He seemed to be getting a bit frustrated. Suddenly his hand stopped and his eyebrows went up. He then began slowly turning the dial in the opposite direction. I didn't hear a sound but Bob's hand stopped again. There were actually beads of sweat forming on the guy's forehead. For him the concentration seemed to be as much an effort as carrying the safe had been for Martin. He was turning the wheel again and stopped once more, stood up and got out of the way. Martin grabbed the large wheel again and turned it. He grunted a bit as he swung the heavy door up and to the side. Bob grabbed my bag and began emptying everything in the safe into the duffel. I naively figured we would just take our money, but while we were there, it suddenly seemed reasonable to take it all.

Martin had picked up one of the metal-framed chairs. He stepped back and swung the chair by its back so that the front of the seat and the front legs hit the window just above his head level. Nothing happened. He swung again and a crack formed in the glass, which I could then see was thick and probably bulletproof. He swung again and the glass shattered like a car windshield. It didn't fall out, it just fragmented into cubes and sat there. I thought Martin was going to hit the window with the chair again but instead he stood on the chair and with blows from his fist, knocked the glass out of its frame. He moved the chair out of the way and Bob pushed the table under the window and climbed up.

"Watch, and do what I do," he said softly.

He turned his back to the window, arched it and put his arms and head outside. Grasping something above the window frame he pulled himself up to where he was sitting on the windowsill with his legs dangling inside. He then reached up to an overhang that extended about a foot away from the outside wall. Holding this he lifted his legs out of the window and hung there. I expected him to drop to the ground but instead he did a sort of chin up while he swung one leg up and out, catching it on the ledge above. Using his arms and leg for leverage, he pulled himself up onto the roof. I had gotten up onto the table with the duffel bag and passed it out to Bob's dangling hand. I looked at Martin who made a head movement that told me to get the hell out the window. The guy had great non-verbal communication skills.

I tried to mimic Bob and did fine until I was dangling from the ledge. I tried the pull-up, leg-swing thing but could not get my chin or my leg high enough to do the roll up onto the roof move. Finally Bob reached down and grabbed my foot as I swung it up and with him pulling I was able to slide up and over. I lay there panting for a moment and then got clumsily to my feet. Martin was beside me when I got up. I neither saw or heard the graceful ballet-like move he used to get onto the roof, he probably just dove head first up and out of the window, did a flip in the air, reversed direction and landed on his feet on the roof. Again it wouldn't have surprised me much if he had, but I assume he used some more conventional technique.

We were out.

EIGHTEEN

Well, we were sort of out. We were on a graveled roof that only covered an area about the size of the two rooms below us. Blank walls surrounded this area on three sides. Martin motioned us to a corner of the space. He made a foot hold with his hands and Bob stepped into it and between his jump and Martin's toss, Bob made it up onto the second-floor roof pretty neatly. Martin took the bag from me, threw it up to Bob and made the foot hold with his hands again. We looked at each other for a second or two and then he started to bare his teeth and hiss. I took this to mean I better get my ass in gear. I took a couple of quick steps, placed my right foot into his hands and jumped. I was propelled onto the roof above. I didn't have to grab at the edge of the roof and pull myself or anything. I just landed painfully on my face and belly on the gravel with my legs hanging off. It was easy to swing them up onto the roof once I got over the injury to my mouth, stomach and pride.

I stood up and felt the damage at the corner of my mouth with my hand. A little blood, a split lip. My stomach had a "roof burn" on it, which hurt like mad but wasn't really of any consequence. When I looked up, Martin was standing beside me. Shit, I had missed it again. How in the hell had the guy gotten up there so fast and quietly? I had an image of him stepping into his own hands with one foot and throwing himself up. Probably what happened.

We were now on the roof of the half-block-sized rectangular building. The tower portion of the hotel rose above us and the two-story portion of the roof ran all the way around the smaller but taller structure. Bob handed me the bag and we trotted south to the far edge of the roof. We came to where the covered walkway to the adjacent buildings connected. There was a wall here that we hid behind.

I heard a noise like a metal door slamming open and then footsteps running on the gravel roof. The door had been on the west side of the tower, facing away from us and whoever had exited through it ran away from us

150

toward the front of the building where the huge casino light display offered many hiding places. This gave us the opportunity to jog in a crouch across the roof of the walkway to the wall of the building behind the main casino.

The wall went up about six feet and extended about twenty feet in each direction. The building must have had a central hallway with rooms on either side. Each room had a covered balcony looking over a garden or pool area depending on which side of the building you were on.

The roof of the overhang for the balcony was on our level and Martin immediately grabbed the top of the wall in front of us and started pulling himself toward the overhang, dangling and swinging like a pendulum. When he got there, with seeming minimal effort, he motioned for the bag. I was about to toss it over to him when Bob caught my arm and took the duffel from me. He then threw it deftly to Martin who caught it by the handle with one hand. I felt a little slighted but they had done the right thing.

Bob motioned me to follow Martin and he hung from the wall right beside me as I clumsily made my way toward Martin and hopefully safety. I only slipped once and was able to get my hand right back up to the wall. The shot of adrenaline associated with this near fall got me over to where Martin could grab me and pull me onto the flat roof over the balcony of the room below us. Bob effortlessly made it onto the surface without help. I was beginning to feel like a burden to these guys.

We were now pretty well protected from view from the main building by the wall that extended above the overhang. We stayed low and moved quickly along the building to the southern end. Here it connected to the next identical building, which angled off at 90 degrees. We went to the south side of this building and ran along the top of its overhang to the extreme southeastern corner of the hotel complex. Two stories below us a parking lot extended to the south and east to the roads that ran behind and beside the casino property. The lot was about three-quarters full. How to get down? I didn't really want to know.

We climbed down the metal corner supports for the overhang onto the second-floor balcony and then onto the ground. Not bad at all. Bob even let me be the one to throw the duffel down to Martin. I guess he figured even I could hold a bag out and let go of it.

We were in the shadows at the side of the hotel building. Some palms shielded us from view. We had to cross the lighted parking lot. I fell back on "Oh shit," again.

Martin and Bob nonchalantly moved out into the light, Martin with the bag in one hand and his other arm over Bob's shoulders. They strolled and laughed quietly as if they hadn't a care in the world. Meanwhile I was being left behind. I issued another soft, "Oh shit."

I ran, sort of weaving, up to my friends and crashed into them, splitting them apart and putting my arms around both of their shoulders, although with Martin it was a stretch. I then went halfway limp and let them kind of support me while I stumbled along and made slurred speech sounds. Two buddies with a drunken friend leaving the hotel after a night of gambling. Inspired acting I thought.

We got to the street and crossed it, moving east. We then moved into the shadows of the building next door and into a dark alcove where a back door into the building was set in place. It was locked.

I stepped back expecting Martin to make some incredible kung fu move on the door. Instead Bob pulled a little gun-like device with wires for a barrel out of his pocket. He stuck the wires into the lock, torqued the handle of the device a little and started pulling the trigger rapidly. It made a scratching, rattling sound and it seemed to be taking it a while to do whatever it was supposed to do.

Martin said, "Come on, come on, there are people coming."

Bob was pulling that trigger as fast as he could when the device suddenly twisted clockwise and the door swung open.

We got inside and closed the door, locking it again. We were in some kind of storage building or warehouse. It took up most of the block and contained rows of slot machines, roulette wheels, tables of various kinds and a bunch of large structures that looked like pieces of sets from stage shows. It was pretty dark in the huge room and we moved along the back wall to the opposite back corner.

There was no door here but there was a window set high in the wall. This one wasn't thick and bulletproof though. It was made up of about twelve glass louvers about four inches wide. I figured Martin would bust it but instead he reached up and removed each piece of glass from its aluminum holder and sat them quietly on the floor. Bob and I wrestled a large Double Diamonds slot machine over to the window. As we did this we heard movement at the front of the building and rows of lights started to come on. Martin climbed up onto the slot machine as best he could and wiggled out of the window. Instead of dropping down he disappeared up. These guys were always doing the opposite of what I expected, which I guess is why we were still alive.

It turns out that the building next door was only about two feet across an unusable alley from us. Both ends of the alley were closed off and the space was full of trash. It wouldn't have surprised me to see a couple of bodies rotting away down there. I pulled myself out of the window and it was easy even for me to get up onto the roof of the adjacent building. Bob pushed the duffel up ahead of him and joined us but he slipped and twisted his ankle a bit. The last bank of fluorescent lights at the back of the building came on just as we started to run along the roof of the building, again moving east.

The Vega was parked on the next street over I suddenly recalled. There was a method to our movements after all. Hope!

I was carrying the duffel and was just about to the far end of the roof. When I arrived I crouched down in preparation for dropping to the ground. There were a fair number of small trees and bushes along this side of the building and then a sidewalk with a frontage area of dead grass and then the next and last street we would have to cross. I looked back for Martin and Bob.

They were about three-fourths of the way to me. I guess Bob's ankle injury was worse than I had thought and Martin was holding him up as he limped along not able to bear weight on his right leg. I caught some movement at the other end of the building. The back-lit head, shoulders and arms of a man rose from the far wall. Apparently he was standing on the window ledge we had exited through and was leaning against the wall of the building we were on now. The worst thing about this scene was the glint of metal in the man's hand.

Everything went into slow motion. Bob was to the right of Martin, closest to the edge of the roof. I saw a flash from the gun on the opposite end of the building. It seemed like I heard the sound much later, about the time that I noticed the right side of Bob's forehead fragmenting as a bullet passed through from back to front. Bob's probably already dead body spun from the impact and got loose from Martin's grip. The body twisted over the edge of the roof and fell to the pavement below.

Martin had spun also and in one fluid motion continued the turn, drew the revolver from his belt and ended in a squat as he pulled the trigger. I saw the bullet hit dead center in the other man's face and he dropped like a rock into the narrow filthy space between the buildings.

By now my legs were over the edge and I dropped the duffel to the ground behind me but kept my gaze fixed on Martin. I wanted to yell to him to come on but just couldn't make any noise. Martin moved to the back of the building and jumped at about the place where Bob had gone over. At the same time I slid backward on my stomach scraping the scrape that was already there and letting the weight of my legs carry me over the edge. I didn't even register this pain as I crumpled onto the ground behind the bushes. The bag broke my fall a bit but it didn't prevent the branches of the shrubs from impaling me in several places, none fatal fortunately.

I wiggled to where I could see around the corner of the building. The bushes extended around the back of the building for several feet so I had good cover. I was on my belly with the duffel bag under my chest. I had my head on the ground with my face turned to the side so I could see. I wish I hadn't seen that which I will now never stop seeing.

Martin had dropped his gun and was kneeling next to the body of Bob. He was facing me but didn't see me. His face was contorted into a mask of grief I could hardly recognize and he wailed at the sky. He lifted Bob's head and upper body to his chest, cradling his head in one massive palm. Blood and brain dribbled between his finger as he looked down on what was left of Bob's face.

"I'm so sorry, Robert. I'm so sorry. I love you so much, man. I loved you, Bob. God don't ever forget how much I loved you." There were only sobs from Martin after this.

While this was unfolding before my stunned unblinking eyes, people were approaching Martin. They all carried guns and they all had them pointed at his head or massive chest. Cars came screeching around the corners from both directions, some with flashing lights, some without. Martin gently placed Bob back on the ground and put his arms behind him. He continued to stare blankly down at Bob and I could see his lips moving but couldn't hear any sounds. The closest of the armed men kicked Martin's gun well out of reach where another guy, this one in uniform, picked it up. The first man then very slowly and carefully put handcuffs on Martin like he was a sedated wild beast who could spring back into deadly action at any moment, a reasonable assessment.

I pulled my head back around the edge of the wall and lay there with my head on the duffel bag. All I could see was Martin's face and all I could think was that I was never going to allow myself to be hurt that badly.

I'm not really sure what happened after that. I must have passed out or gone into some kind of trance. I dreamt the most awful possible dream. I flew up from the bushes where I was hidden and passed through the walls of several buildings, rising and accelerating. I approached a large official-looking building from the air and passed through its walls and floors slowing and coming to a stop just as my head emerged through the wall of a basement room with a door of iron bars.

In the center of the room, facing me, was Martin. His hands were cuffed behind him and he was on his knees with his ankles shackled. Three other men were in the room with nightsticks in their hands. They took turns clubbing Martin in the head with their batons. Blood was streaming down his face. He sat back with his butt resting on his manacled feet as the blows continued. I couldn't hear any sounds, just the vision of this horror.

Martin looked up at me. Right at me as if he could see me. His eyes were slits with blood flowing around them and just a small spark of life was visible in those eyes. Those eyes seemed to lock on mine as that dim light faded and his mouth moved.

I could tell what he was saying, and I could hear his words even though I couldn't hear the cracks of the wooden clubs on his scull. The words weren't clear, they weren't sounds that my ears picked up, they were a hiss inside my head, a death rattle.

"Get away."

NINETEEN

The next thing I knew I was waking up in the bushes with my head resting on the duffel bag and my face near the red brick of the building beside me. I didn't know how much time had passed but it was still dark. My body slowly came into my awareness and there was no part of it that didn't hurt.

I had apparently thrown up, and the slimy drying contents of my stomach had run down the bag that was my pillow, onto the ground. My mouth burned and tasted terrible. That's when I noticed the urine. I had peed my pants at some point and the cold wet stickiness extended from my belt to my mid-thighs. What a fucking mess. All those jokes about having the piss scared out of you, they weren't funny anymore.

I edged forward and looked around the corner. There was nothing there but a large dark stain on the pavement and I thought I could see some chalk marks, perhaps in the shape of a sprawled human body.

I rolled up into a sitting position and looked through the branches to the building across the street to the east. It was actually two buildings with a narrow alley between them that opened onto the street where the Vega was parked under a street light that Bob had taken out with a rock.

I crawled through the bushes dragging the duffel bag behind me. When I got to the sidewalk I stood up but almost fell right down again. I leaned back into the bushes for support and looked up and down the street. Nothing.

I walked across the street and entered the alley. I couldn't really move that fast and I didn't really care if I got caught, so it didn't matter. I made it anyway.

I had to weave along the alley to avoid piles of trash, trashcans, small dumpsters and other assorted junk. It seemed like a monumental obstacle course to me. I was keeping an eye on the ground and didn't see the ladder of a fire escape hanging at head level.

I had just started to turn to avoid a particularly large pile of trash bags when my head hit the metal leg of the ladder.

Searing pain and I fell. The trash bags broke my fall as I smashed down onto them barely conscious. Didn't quite pass out. The duffel bag ended up on my legs behind me. I lifted my head just in time to see the front of a police car slowly moving across the entrance to the alley. I dropped my head as the central portion of the car passed and a searchlight lingered in the alley looking for something like me. Fortunately I was hidden among the bags, more trash in a world of trash. The cop car passed on.

I got back to my feet and noticed the blood running down my face. Scalp lacerations tended to bleed like a son of a bitch. I kept pressure over the wound with my left hand even though it hurt like hell. I unzipped the duffel with my right hand and reached in. I pulled out a wad of $100 bills and crumpled them into a ball. I passed the ball to my left hand and pressed the bills onto the bleeding cut. The world's most expensive bandage.

I zipped up the duffel and made it to the end of the alley. Looking up and down the street, I saw nothing moving, and to the south, about ten yards away was my car. Sweet holy Jesus, just let me make it to my car.

I got there and opened the driver's side door. I shoved the duffel onto the driver's seat and sort of sat next to it with my feet still on the pavement. I was then able to shove the blood- and puke-stained bag over onto the passenger seat. I swung my legs in, fumbled around under the mat, located the keys, thanked God I had purchased an automatic and started the engine.

I had to keep my left hand firmly on my head and drove with my right hand. I stuck to back roads and made my way around the city toward the interstate. I finally saw a sign that said *To I-15* and followed it. I went up the on ramp slowly picking up speed, heading north as the eastern sky showed the first signs of lightening.

I got off at the next exit. Two miles, good progress. Actually I was finally starting to think again and thought I better stop while it was still pretty dark and try to clean up. I pulled as close to a gas station bathroom door as I could. When the coast was clear I made a dash and was fortunate enough to find the door unlocked.

Inside I leaned on the porcelain sink bolted to the wall. I figured I must look like death warmed over. I checked it out in the mirror. I just looked like death, not even warmed over. I pulled the blood-soaked bills away from my scalp and noticed with satisfaction that the bleeding had stopped. I got down on my knees and hung my head into the sink and began splashing water onto my face. For some reason I couldn't stop. Long after the water had stopped being red I kept splashing. Handfuls of water up into my face, handfuls plus a few drops back into the sink. I had never wept before.

I finally stood and dried my face. Still looked like death, only with a clean face and red eyes. I inspected the scalp wound more closely. I knew if I messed with it, it would start bleeding again. I got a great idea. I pulled up clumps of hair on either side of the inch-and-a-half-long laceration. They were stiff and sticky with re-wetted dried blood, perfect. I arranged two rows of five bundles on either side of the cut and starting at the front, tied each opposing pair together. When I was finished I had five neat little "stitches" holding the skin margins together. The knots would hold well because of the glue of my precious blood on them.

I smoothed the rest of my hair away from my face and would wear a baseball cap I'd seen in the car. It was one Bob had worn on occasion. I stripped down to naked and splashed water all over my self, especially around my soiled crotch. I then rinsed my underwear in the sink several times, wringing them as dry as possible. I then did the same with my expensive wool pants and after a while they began smelling less like stale urine and more like wet wool. Sort of a toss up to my nose as to which was worse.

It took a while but I held my underwear and the wet part of my pants under the air blowing hand dryer, pushing the button numerous times. The clothing never got actually dry, but it was close enough. I smoothed everything out as best I could and put the garments back on.

Still looked like shit, but that was a step up.

The bathroom was a disaster and I thought about doing something about it. Then I noticed the blood-soaked bills on the floor unfolding in a puddle of reddened water. I figured that was enough of a tip for whoever had to clean up and left.

Not quite full daylight as I headed back onto the interstate.

Back past all the landmarks until I got to the I-70 turn off. I stayed on I-15 though, made a few bathroom stops and pulled off the freeway in the southern end of the Great Salt Lake valley. I drove west to an area that was under populated and yet rundown at the same time. I finally spotted a for rent sign on a dingy house and wrote the number down. My next stop was a cheap motel by the interstate. I took some cash out of the duffel bag and carried it into the office. The manager, if that's what he was, looked at me and shook his head.

"You look like you been to war, mister. Is there anything I can do to help ya out?" he asked with genuine concern.

"No, I'm OK. I just got mugged in Mesquite last night. I got checked out and wasn't really hurt too bad, just looked bad. All I really need is a room," I explained.

"Well, you come to the right place for that," he said while pushing a little registration card over to me. As I filled it out he began to expound on the evils of gambling and had known many a man who had lost it all in satanic places like Mesquite. He concluded that I was lucky to get out of there alive. He had no idea how right he was.

I handed him a hundred and he scrambled around to find enough for change. Finally he handed me the key to a room and enough cash to make up the sizable difference between a $100 and the cost of one of his rooms.

"Could you do me a big favor?" I asked, knowing that the old guy would probably say yes to a chance to be a Good Samaritan. "I need some clothes. If I give you a couple of hundred dollars could you round up a few pairs of jeans, thirty-six waist, thirty-two length, some medium shirts and a few pairs of underwear?"

"There's a store just down the road that I can get those things from and I'll be happy to send my grandson over to pick them up," he replied with a smile.

I handed over two more bills and headed for my room. Not exactly a high-roller suite in Vegas. I again stripped and this time threw my stiff and smelly clothes into the trash. The shower was one of the best I ever had. I was even able to rinse most of the blood out of my hair, being careful around the hopefully healing wound. My stomach looked like someone had passed a belt sander with coarse paper over it a time or two. It stung like crazy in the shower, but I just stretched the skin into the spray of the shower and felt the burn. It was still nothing compared to what I'd seen Martin go through.

I wondered about the dream. It seemed too real. I wondered if Martin had joined Bob on the other side or if I'd run into him again someday, assuming he was alive and ever got out of prison. The knock on the door broke into my morbid thoughts. A kid with a couple of big bags was at the door, which I answered with a towel barely wrapped around my waist. No complimentary terry cloth robe here. The kid's eyes widened when he saw the abrasion covering my abdomen.

"Thanks," I said as I took the bags from him. "How much was it?"

He finally tore his eyes away from my traumatized gut and said, "Um, about two hundred dollars."

I got the drift of this and let it go. "OK, well thanks again." I closed the door on his exploring eyes.

I called the number from the for rent sign and asked to get together with the landlord and firm up a deal. He said he'd meet me at the house. Dressed and walking straight for the first time in what seemed to be a long time, straight in terms of standing and in terms of a line, I felt almost human. I got into the car and drove out to the house.

A few minutes later a pickup truck pulled into the dirt driveway and a man in cowboy boots got out. He was wearing a cowboy hat too and had one of the most tortured bow-legged walks I had ever seen. He looked to be in his mid-50s but could have been anywhere from 45 to 65. He looked me right in the eye as he held out his hand.

"Paul Liddle, with Ds," he said.

I took his hand and gave him a name but without any spelling hints and tried to hold the eye contact. It was the manly thing to do. His hand felt like it was made of tortured wood. He could probably actually "hand" finish a piece of furniture with his callused paw. Decent grip and I picked up the smell of manure, so the cowboy accoutrements were not just for show.

We chatted for a while and I tried to put on a convincing good old boy act. I think it was my yellow Caterpillar hat that really sold him though.

"The place is clean and everything works," he said.

We walked to the front door and he opened it with a key from a sizable ring connected to his belt by a chain.

"The basement ain't finished but there're washer-dryer hook ups down there. There's no furniture but we could round you up some if you don't have any of your own, cost a little more. The kitchen has a good fridge and stove, oven works and I think there are a few pots and pans in the drawer underneath it."

He kept this drawling narrative up as we walked from room to room. "Nice view of the pasture land out the back windows," he concluded as we headed for the stairs. Nice view if you like scrubby vegetation interrupted by occasional piles of dirt, I thought to myself.

The house was a rectangular prefab. A shallow basement had been dug and concrete poured to make up the foundation on which concrete blocks had been layered to make up the walls. These rose about three feet above the ground level and had small windows looking out onto the non-existent lawn. The top story was probably trucked in, in two pieces, mounted onto the foundation and nailed together. A little siding, a little roofing and violà, instant house. It was everything I needed. The basement was perfect. A wide-open unfinished rectangle of cement, plumbed on one end and with red-

160

painted steel supports running down the centerline.

"I could probably lay my hands on a washer and dryer for you too if you'd like, add a little to the rent of course," Paul said. We just stood at the bottom of the stairs. There was no need to walk around, everything that could be seen could be seen from right there.

I told him that I would be having my own things delivered. "Speaking of the rent," I tried to drawl a bit, "what exactly are we talkin'."

He mentioned a figure I thought was very reasonable, having been used to rents in the Boston area.

"Good enough," I said and held out my hand to seal the deal. "I'll get you a few months in advance and pay ahead so you won't have to worry about collectin'."

He asked, "Do you ride horse much?"

I said I hadn't but sure did like the idea, to which he offered, "Well, Martha and I will have to have you over after you get settled in and I'll teach ya the basics."

"Great," I told him trying to sound convincing, "when can I start movin' in?" I was getting into the swing of leaving the Gs off of my verbs.

"Soon as ya want. Don't make no difference to me, place is just sittin' here," he replied.

We went up and out onto the front yard such as it was. I went to the car and discretely took the first three months' rent out of the duffel while he struggled with getting the house key off his ring. He had powerful hands, but between the calluses and the apparent arthritis, he had trouble with small things. He finally got the key off while I tried to pretend like I didn't notice his difficulty. He handed over the key and I handed over the cash. He counted it out carefully. I had managed to get bills not stained or too foul smelling.

"You sure you can afford to pay this much up front?" Paul asked.

"Yea, it shouldn't be a problem."

"Well OK then. We got a deal." He smiled and held out his hand one more time. His teeth left a lot to be desired and as he swayed over to his pickup he spat a fair volume of thick brown liquid onto the dirt. To each his own, I thought. He was a basic, good man, kind of the epitome of a western independent sort. Secure as a brick with himself and his world.

I went back to the motel. I wasn't going to be able to do much more today. I needed rest. When I got back I asked the clerk for a good restaurant and about where I could buy some good Scotch. He gave me the name of a steakhouse on State Street and directions to a state liquor store.

"You better hurry though, they close at seven," he said as I went out the door.

Weird.

I made it to the liquor store on time and learned that they only took cash, which was fine because that's all I had. The bottle of Glenlivit would have to do. They didn't carry any other single malts.

The restaurant was pretty good homecooking style food. It felt great to eat a leisurely meal and get my stomach a little more than comfortably full. I even had the apple pie à la mode.

In the motel, I poured Scotch into a paper cup and sipped. I wondered if it was illegal to drink after seven PM or if that rule just applied to the purchase of alcohol.

I hit the sack, I had a lot to do tomorrow.

I couldn't sleep. In the dark, even with the Scotch, images from the last two days flashed with fury in front of my eyes. The destroyed faces of Bob and Martin over and over again. I just couldn't figure out what had happened. Why did I get away?

It was years later that I found out. Indeed, Martin had died in custody, an unfortunate accident of some kind. Right. Apparently the Mafia-controlled casino employees and the Mafia-owned police had been trying to track down just Martin and Bob. They knew about me but thought I was still in my room so Martin's little paper over the camera for a few seconds trick had actually worked. During "gentle questioning," Martin had told his captors that he and Bob had hidden the cash in the warehouse where they could come back for it later.

Soon after that everything in that warehouse was removed and dismantled. No money was found but this took up a lot of time. Martin had already suffered his fatal "accident," so the authorities could not get any new information from him.

They connected me with the scheme but didn't think I was involved with the safe robbery. When I was not present in my room when they checked the next morning, they figured I had left town and lost interest in me.

How had it all gone down?

The pickpocket. When he, Larry Coleman, a.k.a. "Larry the Pigpocket," had given me back my wallet and winked, it wasn't out of professional respect. He later sold the three of us out to the casino bosses for a fee. The bosses knew I was a front and really wanted Martin and Bob. Again, their interest in me was minimal. I'm sure they would have arranged an accident for me if they had come across me, but I wasn't worth a nationwide manhunt.

One of the best things I did in the months after was spend a large sum of money to have Larry the Pigpocket taken care of. The size of the payment and my instructions about making sure there was adequate suffering ensured my satisfaction.

I heard that Larry was staked out in a dry lake bed in the middle of the desert. His genitals were removed with a dull knife and he was left there for the interest of the ground and air scavengers that would be attracted by his blood. Some weeks later someone gathered up his sun-baked bones and buried them. There will never be a trace.

TWENTY

Early the next morning I carried the duffel into my new home and went into the bathroom. I opened the bag and dumped everything onto the vinyl floor then sat on the edge of the tub and started counting. A few hours later I had came up with the figure $2,147, 720. I doubt if that was exact, but it didn't matter. It was a hell of a lot of money, more than I could spend in a lifetime, especially since my lifetime might be pretty short. Quite a few of the bills went into the tub which I filled with hot water and some dish soap I found in the kitchen. I stirred this around for a while with a pot I got from under the stove and the mess slowly turned dirty red in color. I let it soak.

I took the Vega to the most disreputable used car dealership I could find on south State Street. I had plenty of choices. I told the sleazy salesman who smelled of cheap booze and cigarettes that I wanted to trade the Vega in on a pickup truck.

"Four-wheel drive?" he asked.

"Sure."

He looked at the Vega and looked back at me in my new clothes and figured he had spotted a sucker from the east, which is just what I wanted him to figure.

"I can't give you much for your old car. There's not much call for Vegas in this part of the country. Most people want a truck or something with four-wheel drive. That's why four-wheel drive trucks are in such demand here and carry a premium price you understand."

This wasn't really a question, it was a statement of "fact" you understand, I said to myself.

Verbally I said, "Yes, I understand that, I just need a reliable truck to get me around on dirt roads. It doesn't have to be pretty, it just has to work."

"I know just what you mean," the salesman replied, and I knew he would have said this no matter what I had said, even if it were in French. "I've got just the thing over here. It's a 1976 Ford Camper Special with two gas tanks and trailer brakes already installed. It has about, well, a lot of mileage on it, but the engine is only a few years old. It was replaced when the original burned out. A four hundred-cubic-inch monster in there that runs like mad." He pronounced hundred like hunert.

He got some papers out of the glove box, which seemed to indicate that the engine had indeed been replaced. They even looked genuine. He opened the hood to let me see the massive power plant he was trying to sell me, probably thinking that I knew nothing about such things.

I could tell the engine probably was only three years old or so but it had been driven hard. It didn't look like anyone had been under the hood for a while to check on the belts and fluid levels. I asked about this.

"Oh, we do a careful inspection of everything and we make sure all the fluid levels are topped off. This is the kind of truck you can't go wrong with, the parts are easy to get and just about anybody can work on 'em," he said in a reassuring voice.

I asked the price since there was no price on the vehicle as far as I could see. He pulled one off the top of his head that was about $1,000 higher than the truck was worth even if it didn't have all the rust.

He added, "Now that's the full price, for you and with your trade-in and all, I'll take three hunert dollars off that price, and that's a pretty good deal."

It sure was, for him. I couldn't stand it so I haggled him down to within about $200 of what the thing was worth. He still came out ahead, but he acted like I was bankrupting him by making him sell so low.

We did the paperwork and traded keys. I climbed up into the cab and turned the ignition switch. The engine practically exploded to life and roared. The salesman stood beside the open door with a smile on his face.

"Headers," he yelled, "I told you that engine was strong!"

I nodded and smiled stupidly back, closed the door and waved back at him as I drove the truck off the lot. I started to notice that about half the vehicles on the road were rusted-out four-wheel drive pickups. Perfect. I wanted to blend in as if I were invisible.

My next stop was a Sears store. I pulled a young acned salesman aside and told him I needed to order a whole bunch of furniture and appliances and I'd really appreciate it if he would stick with me and help me make sure I got everything on my list. I'll be paying cash, I said, and let him see one of the wads of hundreds (or 'hunerts' I thought to myself) I had on me.

His eyes got appropriately wide and he became very cooperative.

King-sized bed and matching dresser, the "Sears Best" model. Washer and dryer also "Best." Living room furniture and TV/stereo, the best they had. Dishes, cookware, silverware, small dining room table and chairs. I bought a tool box on wheels and enough automotive-related tools to fill it up. I wanted to be able to work on the truck. Most of this junk I couldn't care less about but I needed some of it. I really just wanted to generate enough enthusiasm in the sales clerk to get him to push for delivery the next day. It was a struggle, but he managed to arrange it. I forked over the bills under the wide eyes of the sales clerk and the wary eyes of his supervisor. Done deal. The clerk even helped me load the tools and other smaller items into the back of my truck.

Next stop, school supply. I bought a case of dustless white chalk and looked through a catalog of blackboards. I ordered ten of the best quality slate boards, all four feet by twelve feet. The amazed clerk took the order and told me that they could not be delivered for at least ten days but that she would try to hurry the delivery up. When she naturally asked, I made up some story about donating them to a local school, which she actually seemed to buy. People will accept just about anything if it makes them feel good.

Last stop for the day. A computer store. I went in and paid cash for a state-of-the-art Apple IIe with dual external 5.25-inch floppies. Made another friend for life in the salesman. It helped that I bought a large desk designed just for the computer as well as the latest printer, an Epson 1500LQ, wide carriage, with a 24 pin print head, very high resolution, almost as good as a real typewriter I was assured.

A bunch of software and boxes of fan-folded perforated track drive paper and I was ready to rock and roll. We had to rearrange things in the truck to get the boxes into the back. The desk would be delivered in a few days I was told.

Back to the house. Unloaded everything. This took the better part of an hour and I didn't even bother to unpack most of the stuff.

I stayed at the motel another night and drank more Scotch, even after 7:00. I again was kept from sleep by images of Bob and Martin. I had to do something to get control of this or I might not ever sleep again. As long as I was active, I didn't think about them. My plan was to stay active and force the painful memories from my brain.

The next day my Sears furniture came. The delivery guys were great. They set everything up and hauled away all the packing, even the boxes from the computer stuff, which hadn't even come from Sears. There are a few nice people around I guess.

I stayed at home most of the day and tried to get everything organized. My thoughts were not particularly well regimented so this wasn't easy. By evening I had everything just about where I wanted it, threw the empty pizza box I had delivered out and drove to the liquor store. I wanted to stock up on some things, I told the clerk. She told me to go to the special state wine Store where they had more high-end wines, beers and distilled beverages.

I found the place almost downtown and bought several fifths of Glenfiddich, some Usquebach in a maroon felt box just for fun, some 1966 Dow's Port which I had heard Martin talk about once, a 1963 Mouton Rothchild cabernet ("the last bottle in the state"), and a bottle of cognac that was over $1,000 because I had heard Bob talk about it and because it cost over $1,000, and because I could. The state of Utah had a revenue surplus that year; I think it was because of me. The clerk at the liquor store tried not to be stunned by my purchases but the beautiful young woman behind me in line didn't try to hide her interest.

"Where's the party?" she asked while brushing up against me.

"No party, don't drink, just collect," I said coolly and left.

The next place I went was a grocery store. Again the tab was extraordinary because I stocked up on dry goods like paper towels, soap, laundry detergent and other staples. I also bought a lot of food that was quick and easy to prepare. With three carts and the help of a bag boy, I got everything into the back of my truck.

"Cool truck," the bag boy said as I handed him a five. I assumed he had a fondness for rust.

Back at home. Putting stuff away. Slept in my new bed. Well tossed and turned in my new bed. I had to get up several times to splash water on my face repeatedly, something of a nighttime ritual now. Shit, it hurt.

I had to get all the soggy money out of the tub the next morning and put it all into my Lady Kenmore. It came out of the dryer later looking like new but badly wrinkled. I wasn't about to iron them all so I just stuffed them into a pillowcase and put them on a shelf in my closet. I had plenty of others that were smooth and flat to spend before I would need those.

Mostly I sat and thought in my comfortable new recliner and sipped on exotic liqueurs. I decided I liked the Glenfiddich and the port the best, but the port seemed to give me more of a hangover. The cognac was great but not $1,000 great. I made sure the empty bottle broke when I threw it into the can outside the back door. No neighbors around to hear. This was pretty much my life for two weeks while the various things I had ordered arrived.

The big day finally came. The blackboards.

I had the delivery guys take them all downstairs. This was not an easy task. Each board weighed about as much as I did and they were bulky. The delivery guys had to carry them around the back of the house and in through the back door to get a fairly straight shot at the stairs to the basement. Once down the stairs, with a minimal of cussing, I had them line them up along the walls. Three along one long wall then a space for the furnace, two along the shorter wall, four along the long front wall even though they would partially cover the windows, and one on the wall where the washer and dryer took up a fair amount of space. The deliverymen were sweating like pigs, but the $100 I slid into each of their hands got them back into pretty good moods.

I scanned my domain. A desk with the computer and related paraphernalia in the center, black boards all around and a whole case of chalk. What more could I ask?

Well, I could have asked the delivery guys to help me hang the damn boards. I about killed myself putting in anchor bolts and lifting one end of each board up onto a hook and then going to the other end and struggling to get it up to its hook. I almost dropped two of them. They would have shattered impressively onto the floor. All the while I thought about Martin. He wouldn't have even broken into a sweat putting these things up. Shit, it hurt.

Before hanging the ones along the front wall, I put foil over the windows. I didn't want any eyes seeing my work. I didn't think anyone would comprehend what I was writing on the boards but I was pretty sure they would think I was crazy. I didn't want to do anything that would call attention to myself.

I started working.

I went to the left edge of the first blackboard on the back wall, opened a box of chalk, took out a stick and started writing. This was not English, it was math. I began with relativity and worked it into quantum physics and went from there through equations recruited from chaos theory. I then went back, modifying the equations based on differing assumptions about the nature of the universe, matter and energy. I had filled all three boards on that wall. It had taken seven hours and eleven pieces of chalk. I climbed the stairs and slept for the first time without images of Bob or Martin. Instead, symbols and equations and galaxies and universes cavorted in my head. I dedicated myself to this intellectual pursuit and was able to wall off the emotions. Never again would I feel passion or compassion, love or even hatred. Logic and knowledge became my gods and I wanted to pursue nothing else.

I woke at an hour when it was light and returned to the basement. I reviewed the information on the first three boards and took up where I had left off. The fresh chalk in my hand was cool and smooth and the soft noise it made as it met with the slate and left particles of itself there in patterns that my mind dictated was like music to me. After several hours and two more blackboards, my stomach got my attention. I went to the kitchen and made some canned food and ate it just to quiet my gut so I could concentrate. I carried my new coffee maker down to the basement with all the stuff I would need for coffee, plugged it in, started it up and went back to the boards. Along the front wall I had four of them, all virgins. It was almost sexual to be the first to place chalk upon these black surfaces. They would never again be quite as black.

I decided to start the same sets of equations over and make a different assumption about the mass of neutrinos. It was supposed to be zero but this didn't fit with what we knew of reality. They had to have some infinitesimal mass in order for the universe to behave as it does. There just wasn't enough material in the universe unless neutrinos weighed something.

I got to the end of my pot of coffee and to the end of that wall of boards. It was dark but seemed to be getting lighter. I went to my bed and slept, dreams of the cosmos floating through my mind. The irregular distribution of matter and energy in the universe having come from a uniform singularity. Something missing in this explanation, but I couldn't see what in my dream.

I woke up while it was light. It seemed about noon from the sun. I went down to the basement, started a new pot of coffee and stared at my boards. I liked the flow of equations on the front wall better than the back wall so I took a moist towel and cleaned the three boards there. I went to the single board next to the washer and dryer and wrote an assumption: *Neutrinos have mass*.

This seemed to lead to a more elegant set of solutions in my equations that were now hybrids of standard quantum physics and chaos calculus. I drank coffee and started again on the back wall.

Days went by like this. I'd sleep when I felt I must, I ate when my stomach complained and I showered when I smelled myself.

I did go out. I bought a cot and a small refrigerator for the basement so I could nap and get at some food without having to go upstairs. I also entered data into my computer, the information that seemed to make sense from my calculations and condensed theories and ideas I had about various aspects of space and time. I hadn't written any new assumptions on my one board by the washer yet.

169

Paul came to the door one day and invited me over for horseback riding and dinner. I begged off saying I was a writer and was in the middle of my next book and couldn't tear myself away. I gave him six additional months' rent while he was there.

On another day I had a large safe brought to the house and installed in the corner of the basement. Even Martin could not have moved this one. I put all the money in it and back-up disks of my work on the computer.

On another excursion I went to the computer store and purchased a modem. I hooked my computer to the phone line and thus hooked myself into a web of computers all over the country. I had to pretend an academic affiliation with MIT to get access but this wasn't difficult. I could now get my hands on information from campuses and government facilities all over America, and I had a feeling this was just the start of what might become available on the phone line.

I worked on the truck. The engine proved to be in good shape but all the fluids had to be drained and replaced. There seemed to be a small leak in the automatic transmission somewhere but I couldn't find it. I'd just have to remember to check it and add fluid from time to time. I got the engine tuned and upgraded with top-notch high-performance components. I might need a vehicle to escape in and it needed to be in good shape mechanically, have as much horsepower as I could get out of it and be able to go about anywhere. I also bolted a massive steel push bar and a winch on the front.

But mostly I played with chalk. After hours of writing on the boards I would stop, having lost all sense of the passage of time. I would have chalk dust up to my shoulder and over my chest. The fine powder was in my nose and was visible when I blew it. The taste of it was always in my mouth. I was in love with chalk.

Each fresh stick was like a new lover, but by the time it was half worn, it was also warm and a bit moist from the sweat of my fingers. It would be tossed onto the floor behind me and a new cylindrical piece would be drawn from the box in my pocket as if it were a pack of cigarettes.

I found myself standing for hours in one place in front of one board or another turning a piece of chalk in my hands. I would be contemplating a calculation or the variations in a calculation based on different assumptions about the initial character of the universe.

I would sleep and eat and pee and shower, but mostly I would hold chalk in my hand.

When I would sleep I would dream about having chalk in my hand and found that I couldn't think if I wasn't holding some. I then started keeping a piece in my hand when I went to bed. It seemed to help the dreams become more organized. Sometimes I would wake from a dream with a new insight and would rush to a place on the boards where that area was described in the language of math. Sometimes these insights dead-ended, sometimes they opened a door just a crack more so I could see the true nature of the universe.

Sometimes the dreams would make no sense, parabolas of space time with metal grids forming their outer surface. Time and the hands on clocks would turn the wrong way. The hands like little arrows would fly off the clock and all point in one direction and that direction would be aligned with the long axis of a parabolic reflector. They would rush to the flat circular expanding mouth of the three-dimensional curve and reflect off, moving back in the exact path they had traveled before. Somehow this was significant but I didn't know how. It may have been sleep deprivation, it may have been chalk toxicity!

One day I was standing near the end of one of the boards on the back wall. These I erased frequently. On the front wall I kept concepts that seemed to have value and erased them only when new data or calculations clarified or simplified the equations. The single board on the far wall still had only the one radical assumption on it. I was working with some math having to do with quantum tunneling. I absently started pushing the chalk in my hand around on the slate surface, holding the chalk about perpendicular to the plane of the board.

The chalk suddenly started vibrating in my hand and I was startled out of my reverie to see a dotted line instead of a solid line on the board. I played around with the angle and grip until I could get the chalk to do its little dance along the board. It made a pleasing rapid tapping. If I moved fast, the dots would be farther apart and I could swirl the dotted lines around and around in beautiful patterns. I stopped the silly game and then suddenly realized what the chalk was trying to tell me.

From the perspective of the blackboard the chalk was rhythmically coming into and leaving its two-dimensional world. This was quantum tunneling! For our three-dimensional world, electrons and photons and theoretically any matter could disappear from one place and reappear in another. We could not fathom where the particles were when they weren't "here," just as the blackboard could not comprehend where the chalk goes between dots from the board's two-dimensional perspective.

In and out of the physical universe. In flow and out flow. Tides of energy,

171

tides of matter. An equilibrium with a place outside. Where was the missing matter, what form did it take? Perhaps at any given time, a significant fraction of the matter and energy in the universe was outside of the universe. We could not account for it because we had no ability to see into that place beyond our universe where it existed in some incomprehensible state.

Black holes were places where this happened. Gravitational power so vast that it drew in all known forms of matter and energy. What did they give back? What flowed in to balance all that flowed out? What power did they have that exerted itself in our physical universe?

Gravity.

Could gravity be another form of matter/energy that could be converted back and forth? The substance of the universe could exist in a gravitational state unrecognizable to us and account for all the "missing matter."

On the board by the washer I wrote, *Gravity is another form of matter and energy*.

I started reworking all the equations with an assumption that "gravitons" had mass and could therefore account for the missing matter. This was blatantly false but it served a purpose.

On and on this went. Few and far between were the forward steps. I would spend days on the growing network of academic computers. I would upgrade my computer whenever something faster or more powerful came out. I switched to IBM compatible devices because I could buy a wider array of components for them and dismantle and rebuild them easier. My computer would go for years without its cover on while I fiddled. Chalk dust was a constant problem, but I loved it too much to try to eliminate the source. My chalk and my blackboards had never hurt me, never let me down.

Around and around my ring of slate I went depositing pounds of chalk upon the surface. Erasing pounds. Shoveling pounds of chalk pieces off the floor when they had served their purpose.

And I finally got there. It boiled down to this. We had fundamentally misconstrued time. Time was a vector force, a substance we had not learned to measure yet in a physical sense, only as it pertained arbitrarily to the movements of the Earth, moon, sun and other planets.

This was not what time was. Time was independent of movement. Time was the cause of movement, for time and gravity were one and the same force and propelled matter into motion. And it became clear to me why physics could only account for half of the material in the universe that had to be there in order to explain everything. The missing half was time and this meant that time could be converted into matter or energy and vice versa.

In fact, my calculations indicated that matter and energy were being converted into gravitation/time at the event horizon of black holes. The matter and energy were going into the black hole in a one-to-one ratio and when these proportions met at the event horizon they were converted into gravitational energy which flowed back into our universe. There were other places where gravitational/time energy flowed out and matter and energy flowed in.

There was a grand equilibrium between the universe we perceived and the place beyond it. A timeless place of another form of existence that could compress itself into singularities with infinitesimal irregularities that would then explode to form balanced and opposite parabolic universes, one arbitrarily designated as matter, one as anti-matter, just as electrons are arbitrarily assigned a minus charge and protons a positive.

There is no such thing as innate positivety or negativity. They are just conventions we agreed on in the past that now limit our view of how things really are. Thus have we assigned names to all things. Names that have no meaning and yet their meaning to us misleads us. The nature of the universes and the spaces in between are wordless, can't be put into words, can't be described with an equation. There are none of sufficient beauty and brevity to encompass reality.

Einstein had really come closer than he knew. To illustrate this, solve his equation for time.

$E = mc_2$; $c_2 = E/m$ $c = 3.0 \times 10$ 8 meters/second $= E/m$

Keep going and you find that one second equals 3.0 times ten to the eighth meters divided by the square root of Energy over mass. The numerical constant 3.0 is actually arbitrary, it just happens to be the distance a photon can go in one second. This speed limit for photons does not necessarily apply in a realm without time. What stands out is that when equivalent parts of matter and energy are forced to leave this universe, time/gravity is produced. You say that the solution is simply unity, one. But one what?

One time, one moment, one century—it didn't matter.

A second is simply an artificial construct based on how long it takes the Earth to make one rotation on its axis. This has nothing to do with the force or state of material, gravity/time. Time is not a second or a minute. Time is the amount of gravitational force produced when you convert equal parts of matter and photons into it. Conversely, you can convert gravitational energy into equal parts of matter and energy.

If you took all the gravitation/time and all the energy detectable as photons and converted everything to matter only, then you would have the mass of the universe.

The mass of the universe will always be twice the sum of the detectable matter and energy. It's like the little drawing:

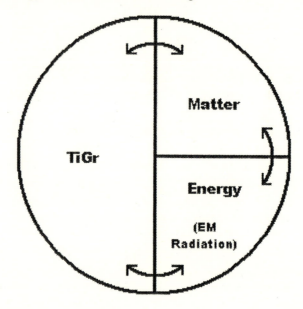

We know too well that matter and energy can be interchanged. We do not yet know how to make the jump outside the physical universe to tap into the power of gravity/time. But I think I knew somebody that did.

I got to my GUT through years of work, but had no idea how to practically apply it. But on the Internet, I heard about a guy right here in Salt Lake City who had conceptualized and was supposedly building just such a device, to capture and control time/gravitational energy. If there was even the slightest probability that this was true, I had to find that guy. I got into my now nearly antique pickup truck and roared up into the "Avenues" section of town. I pulled up in front of a nondescript house at 1582 D Street. The door had just closed as I bound up the stairs and knocked on it.

TIME
FOUR

TWENTY-ONE

I can see my birth as if I had been a dislocated spirit hovering near my mother while she pushed my scrawny body out into the world. Upon delivery my disembodied self moved over to my tiny-bodied self and took up residence near my wet and deformed head. The next thing I remember was being a child and seeing from within this newborn body. The whole thing may have been my imagination or it may have been a prelude to the spiritual calling I would follow in my later life.

My mother told me that I was a quiet and observant child but that I didn't speak until I was almost three and a half years old. I remember this. It's not that I couldn't talk, it was more that I was gathering data and had not really found anything that I felt I could talk about intelligently.

My first words were on a Sunday evening when I asked my mother, "So who is this God you pray to in your church?" I figured she was the best person to ask because to me she seemed to embody the traits that were talked about in church and thought of as saintly. So she should know. She was a bit too stunned to answer the question at first and the attempt she made was woefully inadequate and relied upon the dogma of her church's beliefs rather than relying on independent thought for the purpose of arriving at Truth. I was disappointed to say the least. I had seen in her eyes the love and wisdom that I thought would give her the insight needed to see reality, and maybe it was there but she simply couldn't express it or even retrieve it from within her.

Even at that young age I knew that my spiritual journey would be my own, that it would be an internal struggle rather than coming from without. I spoke very little and continued to observe. I observed good and I observed bad, in my mother, in my father and in my siblings. The other people we would visit or who would visit us were often of interest, but only temporarily. Their spiritual strengths and weaknesses would become apparent within a few minutes or a few hours of observation. It wasn't always their words that told me this and it wasn't even their outward behavior. It was subtleties in the movements of their eyes and eyelids, the corners of their mouths, their nostrils and many other aspects of their almost imperceptible body language. I learned that most people were absolutely unaware of this data and would rely only on the words spoken for understanding. This I saw led to a great deal of confusion and misunderstanding.

In addition there was this sense I had about most people, a kind of feeling that the person I was with was basically "good" and honest, or basically dishonest and therefore "bad." Most people were somewhere in between. A few were truly "good" either because of discipline and the genuine search for Truth or simply because of innocence, as could be seen in many children and interestingly, most people with Down's syndrome. People who had been through tremendous ordeals or who had lived with horrible pain for many years also seemed to be survivors simply because of some innate "goodness" they had, usually related to faith.

At the other extreme there seemed to be people with an innate evil within them. They had no conscience, no sense of the value of life in general, much less human life. They were the con-men and self-indulgent pleasure seekers in addition to many who had fortunes handed to them without the need to work for it. Some of these people were so expert at passing themselves off as "good," they were actually able to control their body language to a degree that fooled even me sometimes. But there was still that other sense that gave them away, the feeling when they were close that there was some dark force within them.

Being quiet and observant taught me a lot about the value of silence and of concise communication. The vast majority of words spoken were meaningless at best or wasted on topics like sports or celebrities. It also isolated me from my age-related peers and even most adults.

I did get enmeshed in the material world at times. In the fifth grade I had a crush on a girl named Kathy who had dark hair and dark eyes and often wore a pink dress that would irresistibly bring out the glowing pink of her cheeks. My love and lust for her brought me crashing into the "real" world of kid love where my mind could not stray from thoughts of her. It was irrational to the point where I finally talked myself into fighting another suitor for her everlasting and undying love.

I went to the dirt road near her house and waited for Tommy to show up. As he walked down the road toward me I could sense his confidence and lack of fear and I was pretty sure he could sense just the opposite from me. He also looked bigger than I remembered, well muscled and well coordinated and again I'm sure I looked, and in fact was, just the opposite.

I remained silent trying to summon up some spiritual strength or mystic intimidation. As he approached I began to talk about love and what Kathy meant to me.

He beat the shit out of me.

Kathy screamed at him and ran to me, comforting me as I lay moaning on the ground. She cared! She told Tommy to get lost and helped me up, took me into her house and let me wash up a little. It seemed that by losing the battle I had won the war.

The next day, she was with Tommy, hanging on his arm and staring at his face with intense affection and interest as if he were some kind of religious icon worthy of adoration and worship. I about puked my guts out.

Women were obviously fickle and two-faced and I wanted nothing more to do with them or the pain that they could inflict. They were merely a distraction on the road to enlightenment and I understood then why monks and priests from various religions remained celibate. With a woman around you had too much to worry about to concentrate on heaven.

Other childish fears had bothered me early in my life like fear of the dark and fear of falling. These things came from early childhood experiences. I had sublimated these fears just as I had sublimated lust. One early childhood event was particularly memorable however. I had gone down into the basement of our big old house in Orlando. This was some years before the Kathy event and I was busy in the basement tearing things apart and putting them back together again or building things from junk that I could give away to people who needed them. Intense curiosity drove me, a burden I and my parents had to bear.

On this particular trip, it was after sunset and I had to lift the heavy door to the basement and pass down into the darkness. Once down there the darkness was pretty complete and I'd have to walk to a memorized place in the center of the floor and reach up to pull the string that turned on the lights. Turn just slightly to the right from the last step and go four and a half steps straight ahead. The string would then be within grasping range and you wouldn't get far enough to run into the post it hung near.

This time I stopped in my tracks before I even made any.

Floating just above the floor and moving slowly to the right was a softly glowing orb. I was drawn to it and got down on my knees to look at it. It was translucent yet had form. I couldn't focus on it, couldn't see detail within it.

It was like a dim picture of a distant galaxy I had seen on TV once.

I scooped the object or substance into my hands. It floated and rotated there. I held it close to my face and could suddenly see everything within it. Millions of galaxies twirling within universes, rivers of energy flowing in and out of these universes that looked like little bow ties to me, all spinning in a timeless void that I somehow felt as love. My brother had come in quietly and turned on the light, which scared the crap out of me. I flung my hands up and stood, turning to face him. I then remembered my little blob and looked at my hands, I looked at the floor, I reached up and turned off the light.

There was no trace. I looked at my brother, whom I blamed for making me lose this treasure of infinite value. But I said nothing, even though he was having a hearty laugh at my expense. I left the basement and went to bed where I could contemplate what I had seen.

It was mystical, it was spiritual, it was a sign that this was where my life should be focused. Not on material things, not even on knowledge, but on the understanding of the spiritual nature of the universe.

I had to finish school first and become independent of my parents before I could really start my search. In the meanwhile, in addition to my mandatory studies, I read great works of literature. The philosophers, the psychologists, the futurists. I read the great religious works of the planet, but found them wanting. I read poetry and found in this condensed language of thought and emotion that divine ideas could almost be clothed in words, but nothing could reach clarity, all was still open to interpretation.

Each man's interpretation differed, each group's interpretation was considered by the insiders to be the Truth. For many the Truth was believed to come from God and in so doing, was infallible. If you were not an insider of that group, then whatever you believed came not from God. Anything not from God could not be Truth and must therefore be False, and this was usually interpreted to mean evil. It therefore became rational to destroy those who believed in evil, all of those outside the group. In fact it became a duty and an honor to destroy those who must be enemies of God because they would not adhere to God's word.

In this way so many were tortured and killed. Uncountable bodies mangled in agony then their spirits sent free. That almost all of these groups claimed that love and tolerance, forgiveness and charity were their highest ideals was the epitome of hypocrisy.

I spent years hating mankind for this until I realized that I had made myself a group of one and was condemning those who did not see as I saw. My own hypocrisy was greater than theirs. I had to learn to forgive or I would be sucked into the same fanatic behavior that the people and groups I despised displayed.

I had rebelled against my own species and did not know how to rejoin them, much less rise above them spiritually. I searched for ways through drugs to no avail and finally gave up on their empty and in fact misleading promises of altered states and expanding consciousness. All they offered was addiction at best with physical and mental damage in between and death at worst.

I was isolated from my peers and even from my family. My parents had adopted the narrow view of the so-called born-again Christians whose goal had become like all the other groups, to spread their beliefs to every man on Earth.

How could they be so blind? With hundreds of groups throughout the world holding the same desire, there could be nothing but conflict and harm. And what if one group succeeded? What kind of horrifying world would exist? No further learning, because the Truth was already known. The language of the sacred texts would be the word of God and thus perfected. No new words could be added to the language, much less new ideas.

People with new ideas would be killed or the fear of being killed would forever seal their mouths.

"What fools these mortals be."

I progressed through school with reasonable grades and learned of math and science and the view of the universe these "religions" held. Man's knowledge was so incomplete as to be laughable and yet they theorized grand schemes concerning the nature of the universe. It was like blindly taking one grain of sand off the beach of this planet and thus concluding that the entire orb must be pure silicon.

I could hardly stand to be human.

It was the knife, the razor, the accidental cut through the jugular while shaving as Herman Hesse discussed in *Steppenwolf,* that I was sure awaited me. I could not live with my people or with myself.

The logic that controlled my thoughts became paramount. I wished to expel all emotion from my soul. I thought, I continued to read. I learned to meditate, but learned nothing from meditation. I was sinking into despair. I defined hell as a timeless place without hope, and this is how my life seemed. Hell.

It was in my seventeenth year that this changed.

I was again thinking of divinity and how pathetic the concept was that there could be something like a caring or planning God. If it were true then why would life be one day of soul-torturing confusion after another. The all-loving God of heaven could not exist unless the Earth was the place called hell and we were the already condemned, living through countless lives and deaths in view of paradise but without hope of ever reaching it.

Yet I could not bring about my own death. As desperate as I sometimes felt, I could not end it. Destroying life just had to be one of the truly "wrong" things to do, and even my life, as barren as it was, could not be taken.

I decided to try again to see if I could make the assumption of a holy creator fit with the seemingly unholy reality in which I lived. I kept still and thought of how the universe would be if I assumed there was a plan, and thus a planner.

I don't know how long I contemplated this. There was either a plan for the universe, or there was not. If there were not, then living life in its current horrid state would be irrational. Trying to do "good" would be irrational. There would be no consequences to behaviors and therefore any behaviors could be undertaken. Mass murder, rape, robbery, all of these "crimes" would be as acceptable as healing, loving and giving. If the culture in which you lived condemned you for your acts and elected to destroy you, so what? Without a plan or a life after life, there could be no consequences, therefore you could live your life as you wished, hedonist, professor or self-proclaimed enlightened soul.

But to adhere to a moral code that was self imposed and denied pleasure in a world without consequences was irrational.

So what if there was a Plan?

This immediately implied a Planner. It implied that there must be some reason for our being that fit into this Plan, some ultimate goal that the Planner had in mind for us, if indeed we were its creation. If there was a Goal then there must be roads leading to it and there must be a choice as to which road one took. There must be consequences for choosing the right road versus the wrong, or choosing a road that moves you toward the Goal rather than away.

If you assumed or in some way knew innately that there must be a Plan, and you chose to ignore this and take a path away from whatever your Goal might be, then it was your choice to abandon the Plan and thus the Planner. If you chose routes that took you closer to the Goal, then you were fulfilling the Plan and by doing so there was a reasonable expectation of reward. This would imply that by *not* choosing to cooperate with the Plan, there could be a reasonable expectation of punishment. The paths and the choices, even like a child's board game, had to follow rules. Faced with a choice, there had to be a method to making that choice that would ultimately depend on the nature of the Plan.

Rules. An absolute or externally imposed set of guidelines designed to assist us in reaching the Goal and thus contributing to the fulfillment of the Plan. Guidelines to suggest "yes, this is the path that will lead in the direction that will fulfill the plan," or "no, this is not the road that will lead to your goal." These guidelines must be what humans universally accept as "moral" behavior. The Ten Commandments, the golden rule and many other embodiments of "do good, don't do bad."

Good and bad. Could such concepts exist independent of the mind of man, an innate property of the universe in some way? And if so, are our choices in life based on the relative "goodness" or "badness" of every decision we make? In the end, are we judged or do we simply see the errors in our choices and thus judge ourselves like "OK, you were right and I was wrong, I deserve what I get?"

I had no idea what the answers were. I simply forged ahead in this line of thought, concentrating harder and harder on the logical consequences of assuming the existence of a Plan.

I can't remember where my thoughts went from there. I may have slept. I may have dreamt. I may have found the answers.

TWENTY-TWO

I became aware that I could not move. It was a gradual process. I think I emerged from a truly unconscious state and gradually became aware again, but my perspective was from a location within my head looking, or in some other way, sensing my body stretched out below "me." Although I could sense it, I could not control it. I had a feeling that my consciousness had just withdrawn from the rest of me and was concentrated entirely in my cranium.

Then my perception rotated and I began a short journey out through the top of my head. A feeling and sound almost like static electricity accompanied this movement, and was also associated with a vibration in my head that was almost painful.

I found myself hovering in the room just above and to the left of my bed. I didn't have to turn to look around but I could sense the world around me in all directions at once. I could focus my concentration on one area or another, but I didn't actually have to turn my head to do it. I'm not even sure I had a head to turn or that the concept of "turning" had any meaning where I was.

I was simply aware. Aware of all the substance around me and beyond the walls and ceiling of my room which I had once thought of as solid. I could perceive two beings as life forms in a room that corresponded to my parents'. These beings were my parents, I somehow knew, but they appeared to be patterns of light rather than flesh and bone. I assumed that this is what I looked like also. There was no top or bottom, no head or tail. There just was. This accounted for my spherical perceptual abilities.

What I could not perceive was the passage of time. In describing this experience as a sequence of events, it gives the impression that some of these experiences preceded others. This gives the false impression that time existed where I was. It did not. Everything that happened, happened simultaneously. This included "looking" down.

I saw a being on my bed that was not a pattern of light. It was a body without light, a body without life. It was my body.

Intense fear. I did not want to be dead. I don't know if I willed this or if fear drove it, but I was sucked back into my body and again was a physical person but was still stuck in my head. It took tremendous effort to move. A faint vibration of my right big toe, and I was "normal." I was sweating, I was panting and my heart was racing but I was back.

I decided I didn't want to be back if I could leave again, now secure in the knowledge that I could return. I moved no other muscle other than the one that wiggled my toe. Sure enough, the process started again.

This time I became more aware of the sky. There was something up there or out there. It could be described as a light, it could be said to be at the end of a tunnel, but these were terms that had meaning only in the physical realm. Where I was, so was this something. It radiated peace, it radiated what I could only describe as love. It was the fount of all wisdom, and everything I ever wanted to know, I knew.

I was moving toward this thing. Although movement again implies time and the events outside my body weren't hindered by time. It was all a simultaneous event that I have only words to describe, only words cannot describe it.

Somehow my perception was drawn back through the transparent pastel-colored roof of my house and to the bed on which I usually slept. I was there, or the solid part of me that allowed me to interface with the physical world was there. Again, the overwhelming fear. It seemed irrational to want to go back but I couldn't seem to control it.

I was in my body. I waited. I was out of my body. I was "moving" more quickly now away from my bed and my house and my planet. As I seemed to get closer to whatever it is that was out there, I learned the great secret of the universe. I learned why the universe existed. I saw clearly the reason for man's existence. I saw the purpose and beauty of all things. I saw that this purpose was simplicity itself, made so complicated by men as to be invisible to us. And in this I saw the humor. What funny beings we were to put so much importance on ourselves and on our things. We were trivial specks, and yet it was true that the universe revolved around each and every one of us individually.

We were infinitely small, but infinitely important. Utterly weak, but all-powerful. I remember laughing, or the equivalent of laughing in that reality. Without humor, it seems we lose sight of the light, the reason for being. It was even a part of our speech, to be in a "dark mood." With acceptance of our state, free of judgement and full of forgiveness for our near blindness, we could finally love one another. All the flaws were laughable compared to the perfect beauty of our being. Thus was the connection between humor and love, laughter and forgiveness, childishness and acceptance of others.

Even from what seemed to be a million miles away, my body drew my attention. I wanted to stay and be forever a part of this joy, but I could not. The trip back through the "tunnel." The jolt of arriving back into my physical form. The panting and sweating, the feel of my damp sheets and even the ability to control my body, suddenly returned.

I had taken as much as I could. I was physically, intellectually and spiritually drained. All I knew was that I had received a gift so great that it could not even be described in this reality. I had been given the gift of the sure knowledge that there was a Plan and that there was a Planner. What others had to take on faith, I knew as surely as I knew my name.

I couldn't stay where I was. Finishing school, keeping a job, having a career, these things were meaningless now. I got up, put on a T-shirt and a pair of jeans, some thick wool socks and some hiking boots and left the house. I didn't even look back at my bed to make sure I was physically leaving this time and I didn't take anything else with me. I knew that all would be provided.

The darkness that surrounded me was gone. Thoughts about the despicable nature of man were banished. Thoughts of my own death at my own hands were unthinkable now. I longed for death. I could not wait to die because I would be back in that out-of-body place, but I knew I could not hasten this event. I had a purpose, I fit into the Plan, I had to continue as I was until that Plan called for my death in order to fulfill itself.

I was on Earth, but my heart was in heaven.

Unfortunately, it didn't stay there.

I was soon to learn that this enlightened state could not be maintained in the material world. The cold hard physical reality drove its relentless fingers into your being as if it were crushing an overripe tomato. The spiritual juices ran out and you were left with the shell, your body and its needs. Needs to eat, needs to be warm, needs to be with somebody, needs to do all of the things that the society within which you lived expected of you. Even though I was sure I had known all the answers, these answers could not be voiced in our everyday reality. Just as a three-dimensional object could not be conceived of or fit into a two-dimensional world, what exists and is obvious in the world beyond cannot exist here and can only be poorly described at best.

But as long as I could laugh, I could tolerate. This became the theme behind one of the two legs of my underlying philosophy. It had to do with losing your sense of humor. Not entirely necessarily, but your sense of humor about yourself. If you began to take yourself or your beliefs too seriously, then you lost the ability to laugh at yourself. By taking your physical self and the material things around you so seriously, you lost sight of the big picture. You became a slave to your physical goals like accumulating wealth, experiencing ever-greater pleasures or assuming great power over others.

You became a fanatic, so driven by your desires that even the lives of others became subservient to your beliefs and material endeavors. If anyone dared get in your way, or laughed at you for your deluded self-importance, you could, without conscience, destroy them.

You could be a fanatic Republican or Democrat. You could be a fanatic Christian or Hindu or Moslem. You could be a fanatic stamp collector. It's all the same. Once you put your life and your needs above the lives and needs of others, you were lost. Once you lost the ability to see the humor in the sharp contrast between how seriously we take ourselves and how silly we really are, you were lost. Once you had chosen to follow your own path instead of the path that you were meant to take, you were working against the Plan, working against the Planner, and you were lost. Once you got to the end of your life and you found out what you were supposed to be doing and what you chose to do instead, you were lost for eternity and you couldn't even complain. It was all of your own choosing.

The correct choices were made obvious but by ignoring them time and time again, they became less clear until you were eventually blinded by your own actions and could no longer even tell the difference between the correct and incorrect paths. Eventually you become stuck in a pattern of choosing the wrong road and you run out of time to backtrack and start again. You are lost.

Never become a fanatic. Never become so fixed in you beliefs that you can justify hurting others or that others can hurt you by pointing out the humor in how seriously you take yourself.

Thus Voltaire became a hero of mine. He signed his personal letters with the phrase in French that in English is best translated as "flee fanaticism." He knew from experience and insight that fanaticism is, in fact, the only form of evil.

TWENTY-THREE

After leaving home I walked until daylight and then hitchhiked north to the relatively small college town of Gainesville, the seat of the University of Florida. I figured that on a college campus I could find people who shared my view of the universe and could help me refine that view.

I made it to the Plaza of the Americas at the center of the university campus and knew I had come to the right place. There were groups of students standing and sitting, walking and lying all over the grassy park-like area. The members of one of the groups wore orange robes, had bald heads, except for a lock of hair in the back, and more importantly, they were serving free food. It was now about noon and I was hungry.

The vegetarian fare suited me fine and the discussion, although superficial and both spiritually and intellectually naïve, had promise. I listened but did not participate. I explored the campus.

What an exciting place! People everywhere, mostly young people. Always something going on. There was a vibrancy, a vigor to the very atmosphere, and the air seemed permeated with knowledge and learning. I walked through the library and found everything I could ask for in terms of references and literature related to spirituality and religion. I knew the library would be a place where I would be spending a lot of time.

In fact I had spent hours just getting to know the building. It was getting dark on this mid-spring day, which meant it was fairly late and I was feeling the needs of my stomach again. On the plaza, there were no robed people serving food. I continued west and ended up in a smaller plaza with the wonderful smell of pizza wafting from one of the surrounding buildings. I studied the scene from the sidelines. This seemed like a place I knew. There was a building to my right with an ornate archway leading to another small open area. The archway had an adjacent tower and then a long row of what had to be dorm rooms. Directly across from this was the origin of the smell of food. A sign on the front of the building said *Rathskeller*.

I was starting to walk toward the entrance when the door burst open and 30 or so people came rushing out and began running around the plaza screaming and laughing. What distinguished them however was not their boisterousness, it was their total lack of clothing. Some of these people were even female and I had not until then even seen the female body uncovered. Some of those bodies were at least as appealing as the smell of the food. Temptation, an ever-present danger.

I followed the crowd back into the restaurant-beer hall. As everyone else put clothing back on I reconnoitered. My nose was first to be assaulted. Beer spilled upon wooden floors over many years produced an aroma that was far from pleasant.

The people were pleasant in terms of their generosity. Someone asked me if I had any pot to sell. I told them no but they invited me to their table anyway and, being high and in high spirits, offered to share their food. By that time the group of young men were more interested in the young women and the beer than in their half-eaten large pizza, I ate the other half. No one seemed to notice or care. I left the tavern bloated and content.

I returned to the library. In the old library building were some areas that had undergone reconstruction and this produced some architecturally interesting results. Some of the "stacks" where little used reference materials were stored were offset from the main floors by half a story. There were some very low doors and some half-high stairs that led up and down to these older sections. I almost had to crawl to get into some of these spaces and I found a niche behind a bookshelf where I could probably sleep undetected. My hiding place was covered with dust that had that distinctive, nothing's-been-disturbed-here-for-many-years smell.

Even the bookshelves and floor outside my little space looked as if it had been months if not years since anyone had been back there. I slept.

I woke to noises in the building and to what little daylight had penetrated my space. I crawled out of my hiding place and after dusting myself off as much as possible, grabbed a random book off a nearby shelf and began paging through it as I walked out of the stacks. This gave the impression that I had just been back there to find this obscure reference. I couldn't check the book out however so I sat for a few minutes scanning the worthless drivel of someone's doctoral thesis as if it were of interest. I did learn that people could be granted a Ph.D. for just about anything. This one was apparently rewarded for a study on how blackjack related to chaos theory, by some guy named

Wertmeyer. No wonder this stuff was kept in the dungeon-like realm that was now my bedroom. What a crock of crap. Oh well, I had to try to be non-judgmental and forgiving.

I left the library and went out onto the Plaza of the Americas. It was a beautiful morning and there were crowds of people moving around, some even with apparent purpose. There was a small gathering around one individual on a short platform, a soapbox if you will. I joined this crowd to listen in.

"The end times are fast approaching. The Jews now have their own secure homeland, the Bear from the north is making ready to wage war and the great harlot, America, is building up arms to meet that foe on the battle field of Armageddon." The speaker was enthusiastic but not quite charismatic. He continued his lopsided interpretation of the book of Revelations. Obviously he had not had any revelations about its true meaning himself.

"You know these things are true, you can see them on the evening news. Already Israel has plans in place to rebuild the temple and that will be the final step on the road to cataclysm. Now is the time to repent, now is the time to come to the Savior Jesus and be among his flock who will be spared from the coming holocaust. Come and join this joyful group, share with us the paradise freely offered. Come to the Church of Christ just across from the north end of the campus and fellowship with us."

He stepped down from his platform and mingled with the crowd. As he approached me I was able to ask when he thought the second coming might be. He pulled me aside a bit and spoke softly and conspiratorially.

"We've been studying the scriptures in English and in Greek and we've been looking at the early data from the Dead Sea scrolls. Our research has turned up a pretty accurate date. Don't be spreading this around but it looks like January of 1975, about a year and a half from now. You should come down to the church and join us, it could be your salvation."

I thanked him for his time. He was obviously full of shit. Anyone who thinks they know the time of the second coming can be instantly labeled as a charlatan. Not that I believed in a second coming, to me this was yet another human concept believed to be of divine origin that was open to interpretation.

Throughout time there had been movements that speculated on the end times. In the time of Jesus and ever since, the end was felt by someone somewhere to be near. Groups small and large would give away all their possessions and wander into the wilderness or hide in caves to await the coming of the Lord. He never came. The foolish people and their amazingly unhumbled leaders would go back to their futile calculations and announce a new date in the near future while apologizing for the error they made the first time around. It was amazing, but the movement would usually survive and there would still be plenty of followers for these fools. The gullibility of man was nearly infinite it seemed, something quite characteristic of our species.

The fact that he mentioned the Dead Sea scrolls was impressive to the uninformed. Not many people had read what little had been translated thus far, so it was a safe bet that no one would be able to contradict the claim that they somehow shed light on the rapture and that it was all part of God's plan that the scrolls had surfaced at this time.

I had read them. They were copies of non-prophetic Old Testament books and had nothing to do with the end times. People, such as this preacher on the plaza, would act as if they had secret information from the scrolls that had not yet been translated or released to the public. This was an absurdity because the scrolls were jealously guarded by a very small group of scholars who would rather die than release information prematurely.

I actually went to the Church of Christ and found out that this particular group had formed what was essentially a doomsday cult. Their recruiting techniques were in the finest tradition of brainwashing psychology and it became clear that what they really wanted were the financial resources of their members. I had visions of the church leaders being "raptured" up to "paradise" by way of a jet to Brazil. The church in question was called a Church of Christ but it turned out that they were so malignant that they had been cut off from the worldwide organization of the Churches of Christ. Even this relatively obnoxious religious denomination could not tolerate the absurdity of the Church of Christ in Gainesville.

As noon approached on the plaza, the robed ones returned with their free fare. I ate gratefully and listened to them chat and chant. I learned that that night there would be a holy man from India speaking at their shrine. This sounded like a good opportunity to listen to someone steeped in the wisdom of Hinduism. From the "Hare Krishna's," as the members of the Krishna Consciousness Movement were called, I got the sense that this holy man was right up there with God.

I went that evening, as much for more free food as anything else. Then the great man spoke. He spoke with a wonderful and innocent accent. He spoke the usual Hindu influenced cliches and parables. He spoke of the people on the moon that we failed to see in spite of being there, because they had bodies of rock.

OK, I'd heard enough. There was more pseudo-relativity, pseudo-Hindu, pseudo-intellectual rubbish that the uninformed ate up like manna but I didn't stay to hear it all. Con-artists come from all countries and all walks of life. Americans it seemed were particularly susceptible to those that claimed to be Hindu or Buddhist.

I crawled into my hideaway in the library and slept. At least I wasn't hungry.

The next morning I was, and headed across campus to see what I could find. I found Bob. Bob was someone I had known from high school who had graduated two years ahead of me, that is if I had stayed around to graduate. He had been one of the overachievers like myself, majoring in hard sciences. He also had long hair and a tendency to use drugs at that time and in fact he and some of his friends were the first to "turn me on" to marijuana.

He seemed pleased but not surprised to see me. I asked him why this was so. He said that everything that happened was exactly what happened and that being surprised by it was illogical and a waste of energy. I thought this was a pretty good answer so I stayed and talked for a while. It turned out that he lived with some other people from our high school that I knew and one was a woman I had spent a fair amount of time with, although not romantically. He invited me to the house.

My arrival was of sufficient import to justify a celebration of food and pot smoking. I held off on the weed but looked forward to the food. I was soon to learn that just about anything prompted a celebration involving food and drugs in this group, so my appearance was on a par with say, getting the sink to drain or noticing a new leaf on a house plant. The food was vegetarian, wonderful and homemade by the house mom, my old friend Brenda.

I stayed with them for three months at which point the quarter changed and members of the household moved in or out as dictated by their class schedules. I was one who moved out, not because of classes, I wasn't enrolled, but because paying renters took priority and my space could now generate income for the group. My presence had been tolerated because the room I used was vacant anyway and I was, after all, an old friend.

While at the house I learned about a vegetarian restaurant called the New Harvest, which was directly north of the oldest part of the campus. I was able to get work there first as a bus boy and then as a waiter. This gave me numerous opportunities to interact with spiritual and pseudo-spiritual people in the community. The frauds were frequent and easy to spot, the truly spiritual were also easy to spot but far less numerous. One was named

Jonathan, but went by the name Jonny. He was the closest person yet I had seen who embodied devotion to the acceptance of others with love and without judgement. I learned that he had his own ashram north of the city in a large wooded area adjacent to some horse pastures. I decided I would travel to his place and visit with him and his "followers."

This plan was interrupted by my need to find a new place to live. I hid out in the library for a few nights but on one of my days off from the restaurant I decided to go to Jonny's. It was a long walk but I viewed it as a pilgrimage.

When I arrived there was no one home so I sat on the porch and waited. After several hours, as the hazy dusk was arriving, I heard my name being called. Jonny walked up to the house and somehow knew I was present even though I had told no one I was coming and, as far as I knew, had never told Jonny my name. I took it as a sign.

He invited me in and served me simple food. His ashram was a beautiful place of pale wood and glass, large open rooms and a loft that was his bedroom. That night we talked of superficialities and I slept on the floor downstairs with pillows and blankets for a mattress. The next morning was a meeting day, Sunday.

A crowd of about 40 showed up, which was about the capacity of the room, particularly since there were no chairs. Everyone brought pillows to sit upon in the lotus position or a close approximation.

While living in my old friend's house I had spent my spare time studying yoga and my spare money on books about religion, philosophy and cults. At night I would practice meditation techniques that allowed me to master the out-of-body experience. Ever since the night I left home I kept having similar occurrences but lacking the power and beauty of the first. Over the months I had learned to control and explore each phase of the process but not the environment outside. This was still a frightening place sometimes and I had encounters with beings that seemed, for lack of a better term, "evil," but also unreal.

That morning as I sat in the back listening to a guest speaker tell the blind men and the elephant parable, I went through my routine and ascended from my body to hover in the room. My perspective was upward so I did not "see" the other people in the room. If I had turned my attention downward I would have seen constellations, patterns of light that represented each person. I had not yet learned how to interpret the various hues and colors much less the complex forms. The other thing I would have seen is one person who was not a pattern of light. Me. My body would be the only thing that would appear as

193

if I were seeing it in physical reality and this still freaked me out a bit, so I kept my perspective away from the crowd.

This experience was fairly neutral. I was staring into the sky which slowly turned inky blue-black and stars emerged, although there were not many. Two stars began to move. They traveled together side by side and as they approached they took on a blue glow. The two lights, which I knew to be conscious or sentient beings, stopped in front of me, about two feet from my face it seemed. They were what I would call about four inches in diameter if such description had meaning. I regarded them calmly. They regarded me calmly. There was a sense of mutual acceptance and a feeling that the three of us were "OK," and that we communicated this by what could be interpreted as a nod of recognition, although there were no heads to bob.

I don't know how they perceived me. I might have been a pattern to them or they may have come to visit because I was a blue orb also and thus we felt the camaraderie. Most of these events really make no sense in language but these words attempt to describe wordless things.

I returned to my body at a point near the end of the discussion. Time in the real world continues even while the spirit is in a timeless state. Many people around me were staring at me and one woman, in tears, asked me how I achieved such bliss and glowed faintly blue as I had. I had no idea what she was talking about and said something along the lines of "beats me," only with slightly more eloquence.

Thus began my career as a reluctant guru.

I spoke, I taught, I continued to work at the restaurant and live at the ashram. As I taught I learned. I learned that my words were hopelessly inadequate and that very few people got the message I was trying to convey. I sometimes heard myself and sounded much like the quasi-religious metaphysical types that spoke on campus that clearly were in the business of spiritualism for fun and profit, freeloaders. I therefore took a vow of silence.

Even at the restaurant this worked. I would walk up to the table and bow a greeting. The regulars knew me and of my vow and would order without expecting to be asked anything or greeted verbally. Smiles were all that were needed. New patrons were a little confused but most were expecting an odd experience at this hang out for long-haired mystics.

For six months this went on. I would speak only to Jonny when we were alone at the ashram. The discussions were minimal because we both knew where we were and what we were experiencing. Jonny had had more experience in the astral realm but knew he could not tell me about it. His trips out were unique to him and couldn't be of help to me. I had to find my own way. I would have thoughts about the interpretation of events or observations and would express them. He would confirm or reject my ideas based on his perceptions, but what he thought made no difference because his perspective was different from mine. He bounced his thoughts off me also and I let him know whether or not my experience could support his concepts. Acceptance or rejection did not carry positive or negative connotations; however, there were no arguments, there were just thoughts.

Our conversations usually consisted of short phrases cut off prematurely because the other would grasp the idea before the need for completion of the words and respond, to be likewise cut off. This does not to imply impolite interruptions, but as we spoke we would recognize in the other's eyes that the message had been transmitted and stop speaking because it was unnecessary, and would await the response. Sometimes the response would be immediate, sometimes it would be days later, it didn't matter. If I made a statement and Jonny said nothing, I knew he was just processing and would eventually reply even if it were only with a shrug of a shoulder.

It was exceptionally efficient communication and was surprisingly hard work. It took what I came to call "paying attention." This involved focusing entirely on the task at hand regardless of whether it was communication or washing dishes. In each activity the concentration was such that the early stages of the out-of-body process would occur, so everything done became a meditation rather than a chore, and in every action there was joy.

Jonny and I became known for walking around town and becoming suddenly stationary as we were "blissed out" as people would call it.

I began to draw more attention than I wanted. Privacy was becoming an issue and even the fact that I didn't speak did not prevent people from wanting to be in my presence.

It was on a rainy Tuesday that I decided I needed to leave. I was walking across the Plaza of the Americas once again, on my way to illegally sit in on a physics class that interested me. I carried with me a canvas bag slung over my shoulder. I had sewn it myself and it contained papers, books, a T-shirt and my shoes. I had decided that I would be at peace with the rain rather than at odds with it and enjoy the liquid falling upon me. The rain and I were one as I walked wearing only a pair of cut-off jeans.

As it turned out, this oneness resulted in my staying completely dry as I walked along the paths of the plaza in the gentle rain. This became apparent to the people I passed and they began shouting and pointing.

"He's not getting wet! He's not even getting wet!"

The notoriety was more than I could handle. My concentration was immediately broken and I immediately got drenched. I had to leave Gainesville. I asked Jonny about it.

"Solitary…" I stopped because he gave me a barely perceptible look of agreement.

"India."

His face told me that eventually this would be true, but that I should be alone for a time first. I knew he meant I had to go on my own journey inward before setting off on an outward journey to be with others like me. He knew I agreed with his assessment because I said no more and turned to pack.

TWENTY-FOUR

I took what money I had saved and purchased supplies. The largest Kelty backpack, freeze-dried food, excellent hiking boots by Vasque, a sleeping bag and pad and a small but very expensive North Face tent. I also purchased a tiny one-burner cook stove and fuel along with basic "kitchen" supplies.

In addition I reserved a seat on a flight to India three months hence and began walking north. I hitchhiked at times and took a Greyhound bus part of the way but eventually ended up at Amicalola Falls State Park in the extreme north of Georgia. I camped at the foot of a trail to the top of Springer Mountain, the southern terminus of the Appalachian Trail.

It was very early spring and there was a little frost on the ground that morning as I broke camp and walked into the woods. I had no preparation, no conditioning, brand-new boots and a pack that weighed 55 pounds. This contained enough food for two weeks. By then I had to be at a point on the trail where it intersected a road that I could use to hitchhike into a nearby town and pick up fresh supplies. I had repackaged two weeks of supplies into plastic bags and packed these bags into larger bags that went into a box. I then mailed the boxes to myself at post offices in towns near the trail. I could re-supply at these locations with the minimum of trouble. Take the big bag out of the box, put it into the top of my pack where the empty old bag had been and presto, instant readiness for another two weeks.

It was slow going at first. The trail in this part of Georgia was not well graded or maintained and had not yet been cleared for the summer camping season. The trail conditions were a minor problem compared to my inability to walk more than ten steps uphill without stopping to pant for breath. It was I, not the environment, that slowed me down.

I made it to the lean-to on the top of Springer Mountain in the late afternoon. It felt fantastic to remove my pack. I sequentially cooked a variety of food in my one little cook pot, ate it all and went to bed on a wire mesh bunk in the 55-year-old mouse-infested wooden structure. I was warm and comfortable wrapped in my sleeping bag with all my clothes on over my Duofold long underwear.

I was up with the sun and ate breakfast, such as it was. I refilled my canteens and headed up the trail in solitude. Very few people would be on this section of the trail at this time of year so I would hike alone and in silence for the weeks ahead, which suited me fine. Those that were hiking were in excellent condition and had set a goal of reaching the northern terminus of the trail at Mount Katahdin, Maine, over two thousand miles away. Needless to say they raced past me with barely a nod, never to be encountered again.

I had a vague schedule in mind but didn't really feel any need to stick to it. Some days I would hike close to 20 miles, others just a few. I eventually got into excellent condition going from a flabby 175 pounds to a lean and mean 135.

If I came upon a particularly pleasant location, I would stop, set up camp and use the rest of the day to contemplate nature. It was these contemplative times, the isolation and the silence that helped me grow.

On the third day of my trip I had only walked two miles and came into a peaceful saddle filled with new spring growth in countless shades of pale green. I stopped immediately and found a place to sit with a view of this tiny paradise. I began to meditate. I left my body and flew above the trees and over the nearby mountains. The elevated vantage point, and the nature of the out-of-body state made this one of the most glorious experiences. Every living thing was glowing, their life exuberant in the warming spring air. The life energy from plants leapt into the air to greet the light energy from the sun. Patterns of light, some large some small, indicating mobile life forms from insects to black bears. So many interconnections between these life forms, some glowing yellow between related species and mating pairs, red stings glowing between predator and prey.

There were lines from all these life forms to me in a variety of shades and intensities, most of these were grays and blacks. There were moods. Between the hunter and the hunted there was respect, understanding and care. It seemed that the destruction of life for the greater purpose of the promotion of life was an accepted process.

The feeling associated with the darker lines leading to my "chest" was fear. I was a member of the only species that destroyed life for no reason and was the only species in the woods with these dark lines radiating to and from me. I didn't like this at all. I was almost overwhelmed with remorse for the fear I brought to this wild place. Waves of contrition moved out from me along with love and a request for forgiveness. The connecting bands from me to many of the other animals and plants began to take on a blue hue and some faded into green toward yellow. I felt a sense of mild camaraderie and at least acceptance.

The lines from one group to me were yellow-white and glowing though. These concentrated around my supplies. The mice were overjoyed to find my granola and nuts. Uh-oh.

I shot back into my body and walked over to my pack. There was a hole through the thick tough nylon shell and through three layers of plastic directly into the small plastic bags that contained my supply of trail mix and mixed nuts! The sharp-toothed rodents knew exactly where to chew to find the ideal food for them. I saw no mice of course. They had scattered with my approach. I let out a laugh and tried to radiate understanding into the surrounding ground cover. Then I set out to patch my pack with my sewing kit, a peaceful and gentle activity.

The next morning I walked nearly 16 miles, the first of many very long hikes. This was through rough terrain with steep grades so I was proud of myself for making it to my CCC lean-to destination. It was already getting dark as I made my way into the site and I was exhausted but exuberant. I cooked my series of foods on my miniature stove finishing with broth and then Tang. These two liquid portions were last because they cleaned all the solid food particles out of my cook pot, which then only needed a brief rinse in the nearby spring to be clean and ready for morning.

Before I climbed into my bunk, I suspended my pack from the rafters of the shelter and midway between the ceiling and the pack I placed an inverted metal pie pan I had found nearby. The rope went through the center of the pan to act as a deterrent for the mice I knew were abundant in the old structure.

In my sleeping bag, I was too comfortable and too tired to meditate and went very quickly to sleep. I was awakened in the night by thumping sounds from the floor of the shelter. Fear unnecessarily jolted me awake. I grabbed for my flashlight and produced a round spot of visibility on the dirt floor. At that moment several mice landed there as if falling from the sky. They made a significant plop as they hit but seemed no worse for wear. I directed the light upward. Ten or twelve mice were on the rafters above my pack and several were attempting to descend the rope to my coveted food stores but when they hit the pie pan, their weight tipped it and they could not get purchase on the smooth surface. Plop.

I laughed at my own and my companions' ingenuity. It was nice to know I could at least outsmart the tiny-brained mice. I shone my light along the length of my bag. There was one brown mouse sitting on my bag, nestled into a warm spot between my legs. He or she yawned and stared into the light, which had disturbed its nap. It then looked directly at me, curled up and went back to sleep. I did the same thing, trying not to disturb my comfortable little friend.

The next morning I ate my simple breakfast and sat for a few moments to think about the day. It was only seven miles to the next campsite so I had a little extra time to watch the world around me wake up. I found myself out of my body once again. The connections between all of the living things, including myself, seemed in harmony today. It was a rush to feel included in the web with less fear. I found myself drawn to the north and hovered over a lean-to probably three or four days ahead on the trail. Beside the log structure was a spring with a massive fallen tree alongside of it. It was obvious that many people knelt or sat on this log while accessing the spring for various purposes. It created an overhang above the small pool of water.

I was suddenly sucked back into my body. Upon arrival I was restored to normal consciousness and immediately turned my attention to a good-sized wild pig or boar that was standing near me. There was no fear in the animal's eyes. There was curiosity and belligerence, more of the latter than the former. It had some pretty impressive tusk-like teeth extending from its snout and I had heard about the ability of these animals to tear into things with these sharp dental appendages. Things like human flesh.

I smiled and rose. The smaller animal showed brief fear and then resignation as it turned and pranced away. I think he or she had hoped to scare me as some sort of animal test of will. I never saw another boar so I never got to ask.

I hiked to the next shelter. The log and stone lean-tos were strong structures built in the 1930s by workers in the Civilian Conservation Corp. This was a Great Depression-era, make-work program that produced such sturdy buildings, that they were still usable and in good shape to this day. They had a sense of history about them. Some of the history was carved into the wood in the form of names and occasional obscenities or racially motivated phrases of hate. I was happy to be alone. The mice made better company than most people.

That evening I flew again. The world of the Appalachians at night was just as amazing as the day. Different creatures, different activities, still with all the connections. It was the same timeless state however, hovering between light and dark. The absence of the sun was apparent somehow but it did not alter perception.

I witnessed death.

A tremor in the web. A raccoon had captured a fish in a stream flowing down one of the many lush valleys. There was fear, there was pain, there was acceptance, there was a loss of one source of light in the giant web of light around me. There was gratitude, there was rejoicing, there was the elimination of hunger in the furry-faced mammal that carefully washed his meal before eating it and then carefully washed his face and paws.

I had decided to return to my body and think about this but was drawn north once more and found myself looking down on the log and the spring again. It was a peaceful scene but there was an ominous feel to the place. I went back inside my physical being and got ready for bed. I was now a little worried about the location I was to camp the night after next. Why I had been drawn to that place I was not sure but there was something about it that made me feel uncomfortable.

In the morning I ate and hiked. I ended the day on top of Blood Mountain where a two-room shelter had been built with glassless windows and a doorless door. I read that this place was called Blood Mountain because of the number of men killed here during the Civil War. Not particularly comforting. I had filled my canteens from a spring near the last saddle I had been through. There was no water at the peak of this rounded granite mountain. I cooked, I ate and I set up camp although it was still light. I was readying myself for a little meditation before darkness set in when I heard the unmistakable sounds of humans approaching.

It was Friday evening, a fact of which I had lost awareness. A group of about seven adults trooped into the shelter and unloaded their gear. These were the first people into which I had run. I assumed they were the dreaded "weekenders." Books on the Appalachian Trail had made note of this phenomenon. On weekends, large numbers of people would pack up food and supplies and hike into the mountains to enjoy nature for two nights. The implication was that these boisterous groups usually did more destroying than enjoying.

No matter, all was as it should be. I greeted several of the people with a nod. They asked me a few questions but I pointed to my neck and indicated that I could not speak. They expressed their condolences for my terrible plight. I felt a little bad about misleading them but I wanted to maintain the wonderful silence of which I had grown accustom.

I was about to walk into the woods and meditate in privacy but one of the weekend outdoorsmen asked me to stay for dinner.

Food! It seemed like a good idea to partake. The weekenders were not so concerned with weight as the through hikers were. My food supply was generally cardboard-tasting and freeze-dried. Resurrecting this pre-prepared fare with water and heat did very little to make it more appetizing. The weekend hikers however carried in fresh food. In fact, it was usually very good food in large quantities and often was accompanied by wine or other spirits.

My stomach won. I stayed.

Corn on the cob with real butter. Chicken and steaks. Rolls, blueberry muffins and Scotch. I partook heartily. Even with my extra mouth there was plenty left over. I had no qualms about eating meat. I knew that this was natural for humans. I did remember to send out a thank you to whatever anonymous cow and fowl had given its life to sustain mine. I also didn't mind the Scotch but due to the fact that I had not consumed alcohol to any great extent, a little went a long way and the owner of the bottle was a very generous man. I started to think that I might look forward to weekends.

Everyone got ready to turn in. There was a great deal of happy banter and good spirits but fatigue from the day's hike slowly settled in and quiet descended upon Blood Mountain.

My sleeping bag was on the floor next to the wall of the cabin just under one of the windows. The rest of the people were arranged parallel to me and extended over to the other wall that had the door in it which led to the second room. We were evenly divided between the rooms, four in each.

I was fairly high from the liquor but managed to stay still and concentrate. I left my body and learned for the first time that drugs not only work on the physical brain, but also on the disembodied mind of the user. I was now an out-of-body drunk and the world was a very different place.

There were ghosts. Wisps of beings fluttering around. It was somehow darker than ever before. All of the light patterns of the life forms were dimmer and there were very few around the cabin except for the seven bright ones inside. There was malevolence in the air. There were currents flowing back and forth, creating turbulence in the substance of the astral world.

I was confused. I had no sense of direction. I was very sorry to be drunk because I could not control myself or my environment. I was swept to the north by a dark wind, a breeze of bad tidings. The mountains below were barren, scorched as if there had been a great forest fire. The dimly lit life forms were isolated. There were no connections between them. We were all cut off from one another as if death had severed our ties. Every living thing seemed to be alone, suffering, frightened and lost.

I was at the lean-to next to the spring that I was supposed to be staying at the next night. There was a howling as a dark beast came up a side trail to the lean-to. The beast was a pattern of black on black, a web of negative energy that was the opposite of the white glowing patterns of people full of grace. Someone pale like this was with the beast and was full of innocence. The black form led the white, the white form could not see the black as such, but saw a man and no threat. I saw the threat, I felt the threat, the whole world around us felt the threat, the Earth itself was parched and darkened by the threat.

The black form, stinking of evil, thick with it, pulled the white to where the log ran over the spring. I tried to rush back to my body, I tried not to be aware. I only managed to move back a little, but this didn't help.

Red sparks began forming on the black web of energy, sparks of foul intent. The white form turned silver gray and contracted in size. The beast turned upon it and it was as if it fed. The white form contracted more and there was terror in the air. Streaks and sparks of white light flew out from the white form, tentacles reaching out into the night for help. Those arms of energy found nothing to grasp onto, nothing to give comfort.

I managed to pull back a bit more but still could see and feel too much. The black form now glowed in ultraviolet and rage exuded from it. The white form sent out spikes of red energy like bolts of lightning and these were felt as pain. The pain grew until the air around me roared with it and roared with the delight of the evil. There was a crescendo of movement and force as the black form moved over the white and devoured it. As the white form writhed and twisted, its once beautiful pattern now torn and broken, its light suddenly blinked out.

A moment of eerie silence then the jubilation of the black form sounded like thunder, the force of which drove me even higher above the trees. Every living thing shuddered, the sky turned darker and bands of red raced across it. There was despair so deep that death itself would be relief from it.

For the man below me had not just raped and killed the woman with his bare hands. He had taken pleasure in it and fed not only off her body, but much worse, he had extinguished and devoured her soul.

The black pattern looked to where I was and gave no damn to see me there.

There was a coldness in that brief attention that I never wanted to feel again. The evil one moved off into the night and the space around me grew brighter slowly as the black form moved away.

I was sucked back to my body and into it where I felt a sudden fear. Something was hitting against my leg and had awakened me from sleep. I smashed back against this thing through the material of my sleeping bag. I finally reached a state of awareness that allowed me to stop the pounding and investigate the disturbance. Standing between my leg within the bag and the log wall was a skunk.

I was glad I had stopped pounding! The skunk finally went up the wall and out the window. Several other people in the room had been awakened by the disturbance and two flashlights illuminated the long-haired black and white creature as it slipped into the night.

We had not been sprayed. Everyone laughed with relief and returned to their slumbers shortly. I could not. Something about the black and white coloration of the skunk bothered me. There was something strange in the air, something I should remember, something that was eating at me from deep inside somewhere, something involving black and white. I couldn't identify it so I chalked it up to the scare from the skunk. Grateful that I had no out-of-body experiences that night, I rolled within my bag as best I could and returned to sleep.

TWENTY-FIVE

The next morning I waved to my seven overnight companions and headed into the woods. It was a typical spring day but it was odd. I felt almost sad and this mood made the woods seem less friendly. I noticed more trash, more flaws, more decay and less new life. I'm sure that there were no differences in the environment, it was more a difference in perception. I walked in quiet contemplation. I knew that whatever mood this was, it would pass as the day went on.

This didn't happen. If anything the day and my internal feelings grew darker. The day changed because clouds rolled in and a gentle rain began to fall. I took a break at noon and stripped down to my shorts and boots putting a waterproof cover over my pack only. I could not manage the state where I was at peace with the rain and by so doing stay dry, but the rain did not disturb me. It did bother me that I could not feel the closeness with nature that I had come to enjoy and even expect. I couldn't feel the connections, and felt that the animals were shrinking from me, that the fear of man had once again overwhelmed them for some reason and they would not open themselves to me.

The rain stopped as I arrived at the lean-to. It was just as I had envisioned it with the fallen tree and the spring. I was a little surprised by this. In my travels outside my body, I never really knew what was real and what might be only a spiritual experience simulating reality. Apparently I had in spirit visited this place.

I didn't like it. The shelter was not a well-built structure of logs and stone full of proud craftsmanship. It was a dark and foreboding, full of the detritus of men and wind, infested with creatures to which I no longer felt akin. It's as if I had lost a good friend. The mice had always been my welcome companions, but here I did not feel that. They were hidden and they were frightened and I even felt a fear of them, chewing on my belongings and

205

potentially on myself. It was bizarre and irrational but I couldn't shake it. I had never felt ill at ease in the woods before, but I did now.

I went to the spring to replenish my canteens. Indeed the fallen trunk made an excellent place to kneel while dipping the containers under the deepest portion of the tiny pond fed by the clear cold water from beneath the ground. This water had the typical floaters in it, bugs and debris from the forest. This usually didn't bother me. It was part of the outdoor experience and I expected to have to chew my water now and then. Today it bugged me. I tried to keep the contaminants from being sucked into my canteens but couldn't. I kept emptying the plastic jugs and trying to refill them with uncontaminated water. I kept doing this over and over until I left the empty canteens on the log and walked away from the spring to think.

I couldn't believe my almost obsessive-compulsive determination to try to obtain perfectly clear and uncontaminated water. I paced around for a while and finally returned quickly to the spring, filled the canteens without even looking to see how many organic and inorganic particles entered them. I capped them and went back to the lean-to.

I sat and calmed myself and went through my evening meal preparation routine. The food didn't even taste as good as it usually did, which wasn't that great anyway. I expected to see a crowd of people on this Saturday night because this shelter was pretty easily accessible by a side trail, but no one showed up. Perhaps the rain kept them away. I would have enjoyed a little human company and the food that company would have brought. I wished I had some of the Scotch from the previous night to quiet my nerves.

I went to bed early, as soon as darkness set in. It felt much colder than on previous nights and even my down-filled sleeping bag wasn't keeping me entirely warm. I tossed and turned to the extent that my mummy-type bag would permit. For long periods I would hold still and listen. I heard no scurrying little feet, I felt no small bodies treading over my bag, no fuzzy friend curled up in the folds of the feather-filled nylon. I hadn't even hung my pack up with the usual pie pan and still no mice ventured out to tear at my pack and steal my food.

It was a long and eerie night. What little sleep I had was fraught with nightmares of spider webs of black silk which I had to avoid at all cost and yet seemed to surround me at times. I would wake suddenly and look about. For some reason I would shine my light around the lean-to certain that I would see the black and white form of a skunk. Again, irrational thoughts and fears.

It was such a relief to see the sky lighten. I got up from my uncomfortable bed and packed everything up. I skipped breakfast and moved up the trail. I wanted to be away from this place. The farther I got from the shelter, the better I felt and the brighter the day became. After about two miles I came to a small trickle of water coming from beneath the rocks beside the trail. I got out of my pack as quickly as I could and poured all the water out of all of my containers and refilled them from this little spring. I even dumped this water out to rinse any residue of the other water away and filled the canteens again. I could barely fathom my behavior, but I couldn't stop myself from doing it.

Once I had my water restocked I sat by the miniature stream and filled my steel cup with water, emptying it into my mouth with huge gulps. I had not consumed any of the water from the lean-to except for what I had used to cook the night before. I wasn't all that thirsty but this water tasted so pure and clean. I must have downed ten cups of it as if it would somehow rinse away my dark mood, cleanse me.

Thanking the surrounding hills for the water, I stood and started back up the trail. Things were looking and feeling a little better. As I rounded a bend I saw another hiker approaching from the north. We stopped, as is polite on the trail, and I broke my vow of silence to have a brief discussion with this person.

"Howdy," he said and held out a hand.

"Hello."

"Where are you hiking from?"

"Springer Mountain," I answered, knowing that this would indicate to the man that I was a determined through hiker and not a weekender.

He nodded in understanding. "Where did you camp last night?" His question was a bit tentative as if he feared the answer.

"The Rocky Knob lean-to."

He looked a bit pale. "You didn't hear about it then?"

I thought about this and what I might have heard about Rocky Knob but couldn't come up with anything. "What was I supposed to hear?" was my next question, and now I was feeling a little apprehensive.

The hiker looked off into the woods as if to make sure that there was no one around or as a means to delay the answer he had for me.

"Night before last some bastard on a motorcycle brought a young lady up to the shelter and raped and killed her. They found her body stuffed under the log that sits over the little spring there. It was a real bad scene, a lot of blood and the body was pretty badly mutilated."

I listened in silence and shivered.

All I could say was something like, "Well it was quiet there last night," and I moved around the man to continue hiking. I had to keep moving. His story had filled me with a sense of dread that threatened to panic me. I had to walk. The man said good-bye as I almost jogged away and I responded with a wave of my hand without even looking back.

My brow was aching from being furrowed with worry. My eyes kept to the ground immediately in front of me. I walked as if in a trance, the rhythm of my breathing in synchrony with my steps. Something was wrong, something was very wrong.

I heard a noise off the side of the trail and stopped abruptly. At first I couldn't see what it was that had distracted me from my morbid marching. Then a skunk poked its long nose out from the thick ground cover and walked across the trail actually stepping on the toes of my boots. The animal did not seem frightened and did not threaten to hose me down with its foul secretions. All I could do was stand still. It wasn't from fear of the skunk, it was from the black and white coloring.

It all came back to me. The dark and the light. The dark snuffing out the light, the dark feeding on the light. I began to hear a loud wailing scream and as it grew in volume I realized it was my own throat that was producing this savage horrified sound. I ran into the trees, smashing my fists into the trunks of larger trees as I passed them. I fell and rolled down a small steep incline, pack and all, and landed in a tangle of nylon straps and vines. And still the scream continued. I screamed until my voice no longer issued sound and continued silently with my mouth wide open. And I wept.

I had witnessed such evil and now railed upon a reality that would let such evil exist. All my experience had been with loving and caring, oneness with the life around me. I could not tolerate the agony of knowing that evil, as powerful and as plentiful as good, existed in the realm of my body and the realm beyond.

It was perhaps an hour before I moved. I made my way back to the trail and sat on a stump. The tears had dried and I had no more to spend. I felt inside like the freeze-dried food I carried. I needed to be re-hydrated in order to go on or exist in my previous form.

The skunk came back and looked at me. The black and white fur glistened in the light from the sun, which had sprung from behind a moving cloud. The light sparkled off the fur and refracted producing thousands of tiny spectra of color. The black and white fur became difficult to differentiate one from the other. They blended into each other as the growing bright colors grew upon the animal's coat. There was harmony and balance in the black and the white. There was a division but a necessity for both. The skunk could neither be white or black, but man could chose to be. The choice had to be there so the black and the white had to exist and be real. The choice of which path to follow had to have consequences. The darkness was eternal not because of some judgmental plan to punish, but because men, all men, at one point or another, consciously chose it to be so.

The skunk moved off into the bushes as a cloud once again moved between the sun and the Earth. Lesson over, I walked on in silence feeling hollow. My breath, moving in and out in rhythm to my steps, entered and exited a desert within me and functioned only to move the dry sand of my soul around in hot gusts.

I was not only without speech by choice but it seemed that I had no thoughts or feelings, not by choice, but as if these things had been paralyzed by the horror I had witnessed. I got to my next camp site, went through my routine and into my sleeping bag without having a thought about anything other than the task at hand and no feeling whatsoever. Morning came without new experiences without my body. I felt rested. I felt. I felt as if I should rise and start the new day. As I went out of the lean-to and saw the sunlight filtering through the spring green trees, I felt the infinite beauty of the universe and everything in it. I felt.

I walked and as I did so the desert within me was filled by the beauty around me. I felt peace and I smiled, and in realizing my smile, I realized joy once again. I felt at peace, I felt happy, I felt!

That day went by with my senses simply attuned to the woods around me and I could feel the connection with the surrounding life returning. At one point I rested on a rock beside the trail. As I sat there perfectly still, I tried to be simply a part of the scene, something that belonged rather than an intrusion. I wanted to be invisible to anything that might come by, just like millions of small plants, flowers and insects were invisible to me as I walked along.

A mule deer came into the clear area by my rock and I sat as if part of that rock. It didn't work. The deer looked at me, knew I was there, but didn't seem to care. At least it was not fearful of me. Suddenly it sprang away as if my thoughts about the animal not being afraid were to be proved untrue. Maybe it was afraid of me....no, there was something else happening. I heard footsteps on the trail. Two people rounded a bend in the trail and were walking directly toward me. They were into the rhythm of their walking but were glancing about from time to time to take in the scene evolving around them. They walked up to me, then past me, almost brushing against me, looking right at me….they did not see me.

The animals knew of my presence in a way that was beyond vision, but in this state of oneness with nature I was invisible to my own kind. It seemed people had no capacity to sense a presence beyond their senses. Wherever I was, was beyond detection by eyes and ears and nose.

After an hour or so I returned to walking. It was during that afternoon that I discovered ramps.

Two elderly women had stopped at a clearing beside the trail. I was startled to come upon them and had to stop to speak to them in spite of my desire to be speechless.

One was on her hands and knees crawling around a level spot where they were going to pitch their tent. She was going about on all fours picking up every small twig and stone in the area in order to get it perfectly smooth prior to putting up their high-tech nylon shelter.

"Hello," was all I could come up with to say.

The lady cleaning the campsite said hello and got up from her task slowly and not without difficulty, but smiled the entire time nonetheless.

"You want to know why these two old ladies are out here in the middle of nowhere, don't you?" she asked.

"Of course," I chuckled back at her.

The other woman had been digging at the edge of the clearing and rose to join us. She was holding several small onion-shaped bulbs covered with dirt, these I assumed she had been digging up.

"I'm Kathleen and this is Gena," she said as she approached.

I introduced myself and took my pack off and stretched.

"Gena was about to tell me why you two are out here, but I think I know why. I'm more interested in how?" My question amused them.

Gena said, "Well, I guess it is obvious why we're here, and you're right, how we got here is more of a mystery."

"We are from California and we have seldom been out of that state," Gena continued. "I had just recently turned seventy and had read about the great Appalachian Trail for many years. It became a dream of mine to hike the trail, or at least as much of it as I could but I had a few things to take care of first."

Kathleen started laughing as Gena continued the story. "I had to get my gallbladder out, even though it wasn't giving me problems. I knew I had some stones, so I had it removed to make sure I didn't have any problems with it while hiking. While I was in the hospital, I met this old lady who had just had her knee replaced. We chatted because we were both old ladies and old ladies tend to stick together, so this was only natural. Well, it turned out that the other old lady was named Kathleen and that she had always dreamed of hiking on the trail also."

Kathleen took over the story at this point feigning dismay at having been called an old lady. "My doctor told me I would never be able to do something like this with my artificial knee, but I met this old lady," she hooked her thumb toward Gena, "and she convinced me otherwise, said it was a matter of determination and willpower. I agreed with her and set out to prove my doctor wrong."

"After I had my first surgery, my gallbladder surgery," Gena again took over, "I had to have my cataracts done. So while I was doing that, Kathleen kept on working on her knee to get in shape for our hike."

Kathleen chimed in, "I bought some good hiking boots and started walking. After I got to where I could walk five miles I started carrying a back pack, empty at first but I'd keep adding weight to it and got to where I was in good enough shape to give this hike a try. This took most of the winter and by then Gena was over her operations and had gotten herself into shape too, so at the start of summer we took off to Georgia and started hiking."

"You started at Springer Mountain?" I asked quite surprised that they had begun around the time that I had and were keeping just ahead of me.

"Yes, we did," Gena stated proudly, "but that was last year. We took six days to go from the State Park to Neal's Gap and had a real struggle. So for the last year we've been working out and came back this year to start from highway 19 at Neal's Gap and continue north so we've already hiked ten more miles than we did last year and we're feelin' pretty good."

Kathleen continued, "We hope to make it to Wallace Gap and we may even go farther if we're still feeling well enough. You see, we only cover three to five miles a day, that's as much as we can handle, so it takes us a long time to cover seventy miles."

I was amazed at their perseverance, inspired in fact. I didn't tell them this because it was obvious. Instead, I asked about the roots.

"These are ramps," Kathleen explained. "They're kind of a cross between an onion and a garlic."

She led me over to the woods and pointed out the plant that was associated with the roots. I also tasted one of the ramps she had already dug. Indeed it was a delicious taste. I asked about other edible plants and they pointed out the fiddleheads that were just getting beyond the right stage for eating. They identified the blue violets that grew everywhere and they showed me a white trillium that was edible. They told me that farther north and at higher elevations I would be able to find sassafras trees and from the roots of the seedlings I could make wonderful tea.

I thanked them for their hospitality and time, but I had to make it to the next lean-to about three more miles ahead. They waved as I got back on the trail. I don't think they stopped smiling the whole time I was there. Based on the pattern of the wrinkles in their faces, I got the impression that they had been smiling most of their lives.

Gena called to me just after I had walked a few steps so I turned to face her. She had a serious look on her face that was uncharacteristic. "You must remember that no matter what adversity you face, you must persevere," were her final words.

For the next hour and a half I thought about what I might be doing when I was in my 70s. I certainly hoped it was something as vigorous and invigorating as Gena and Kathleen.

The very next morning I made a large salad with blue violets and trillium, very attractive to see as well as to eat. It was at Bly Gap, which is a shallow saddle through which the state line between Georgia and North Carolina runs, where I developed the runs myself.

This is not a good thing. The diarrhea was copious and almost fluorescent green from the foliage I'd consumed. The stops where I would have to throw off my pack and rush into the bushes were not at all enjoyable and I ran out of toilet paper in the process. It was very difficult to clean my hairy buttocks effectively with T paper, but with leaves, it was nearly impossible. At one point my underwear were so soiled I simply left them off and buried them in the shallow grave I had dug for my liquid stool.

As I approached the next lean-to, I prayed to find something to wash myself with when I got there.

As I walked up to the shelter, a wash cloth hung on a nail in a log near the fireplace. My prayers were answered. I went into the woods with all my canteens, stripped down and took a sponge bath. While walking back to the lean-to, feeling much better, I noticed the ramps growing in the area and began digging them up. When I got back I cut the ramps up, sautéed them in a little oil I had with me and then added them to boiling water to make a delicious "onion" soup. It was warm and wonderful and seemed to settle my stomach. I slept well that night.

TWENTY-SIX

The next morning I continued the trek north. These days and nights were fairly uneventful as I simply enjoyed being with nature. I had no further encounters with evil. In fact I had managed to not leave my body for several days. The hike through the Nantahalas was particularly strenuous and included a large drop in altitude to the Nantahala River at Wesser and then a steep resumption in altitude on the other side. It was one step, breath in, next step breath out, the whole way up. Plodding.

There were also no further encounters with people. This steep unimproved section of trail was rarely used and the trail and surrounding woods were immaculate. I rejoiced in the solitude and in the aching in my muscles. Some days I would stop and stare at the misty mountains stretching out around me. The images were to my eyes like cool clear water to a thirsty throat. I hiked one morning only two miles when I came upon an overlook from a rocky bald. I sat and absorbed this scene and rested. When I got the urge to march onward it was near dusk and all I could do was hurry downhill to the next source of water and make camp. It was not meditation. It was not quite an out-of-body experience. I'm not sure what occupied my mind during those hours of staring out across the green mountains. I knew I had read about it in *Walden; or, Life in the Woods* though. It was just another source of joy.

I made it into Fontana Village early one afternoon. This was my first mail drop and I picked up the box I had addressed to myself from the post office there. I also spent the night in a real cabin in a real bed after taking a real shower. The small room had a carpeted floor. After being in boots or on rocky soil for so many days it was amazing how extraordinarily good it felt to rub my bare feet on this soft pile. It was almost sexual.

The fresh supplies were also welcome. I had been running low and was subsisting on nuts and trail mix for the most part. I had run out of all my "good" food two days before hitting Fontana. Two other monumental events

213

occurred. I washed all my clothes at a laundromat and ate "real" food in a restaurant. These simple things were heavenly to me and I found myself giving thanks frequently and liberally. It seemed at times that saying thank you to the universe was all we really needed to be doing.

The next morning I made the short hike to and over Fontana Dam, which obstructed the flow of the Little Tennessee River. I was now in the Great Smokey Mountain National Park where people were frequent and bears were not fearful of them. This usually produced several unfortunate encounters every year. The high traffic volume also meant that the trail was a one- to two-foot-deep rut eroded into the ground by thousands of footfalls over the years.

There were people constantly moving past. Some would be sitting and I would pass them with a nod, some would pass me while I sat and nod at me. Some would pass from the north and inevitably ask how far it was to the next landmark. I would answer, I couldn't bring myself to be falsely mute.

Some would pass me even while I hiked, in a hurry to get to Maine no doubt. One of these I stopped.

"Did you come from Springer?" I'd ask.

The reply would usually be yes and include an explanation of how much farther they needed to go that day and they would attempt to press onward. I stopped them just long enough to inquire about the two ladies, Kathleen and Gena.

I asked several through hikers, but no one had ever seen or heard of them.

I walked at my pace and in my rhythm, which is as individual as fingerprints. It was difficult for people on a long distance trip to walk together. One would inevitable end up ahead of the other due to a difference in leg length, stride or speed of muscle contraction. Everyone converged however on the lean-tos. It was very dangerous to sleep in the open in the Great Smokeys. People had even crawled into sleeping bags with food in their pockets only to be awakened in the night by a bear that would badly injure the person in an attempt to get at the food. Bears aren't particularly dexterous, and an attempt to get a strip of beef jerky out of a camper's pocket while that camper is zipped up in a sleeping bag is a messy process involving remarkably long, sharp claws and teeth.

The vast majority stayed in the lean-tos, which in the park were enclosed across the front with chain link fence with a door that securely latched. The bears would frequently wander around the lean-tos at night and would stand and lean against the fencing. They would then begin shaking the fence, which produced a fair amount of noise and a fair amount of people waking in abject terror. It was a delight to watch it all.

I kept to myself and spoke as little as possible but attempted to radiate warmth. Generally the only thing most of us radiated was intense body odor, but this was forgiven.

The second morning in the park I stopped at a spring near the trail to freshen my water. I drank numerous gulps of water from the metal cup I kept clipped to my belt just for this purpose. Every time I came upon fresh water I would drink as much as I wanted and save what was in my canteens for cooking.

At mid-day I arrived at a lean-to and stopped for lunch. This would be a cold lunch of dried fruit, nuts and granola washed down with Tang and water. As I reached for my cup, my hand closed upon air and I had a simultaneous vision of my cup on a rock next to the spring I had stopped at earlier.

This was a serious blow because that cup served as my cooking pot most of the time. It was what I ate out of as well as what I used to drink. I drank from my canteens and got back on the trail a bit disconcerted. As I walked I became aware of a sense that I was being cared for. The fact that I had had no serious accidents or injuries, not even any blisters from my new boots, was not an accident. I suddenly became thankful again for all the wonders I had enjoyed and the beauty around me. I felt myself becoming "blissed out."

In this state I have to stop whatever I'm doing and be still, relaxed except for a silly grin on my face. All attention is drawn to this sense of belonging, of being one with the world and being in tune with everything around me. I opened my eyes and beheld a metal cup. It was on a stump beside me. It's not too unusual to see cups like these, everyone carried similar utensils. This one happened to be the same brand and model as the one I had left behind but I was fairly certain that the pattern of scratches on it was different. I picked it up and clipped it to my belt. The universe was a majestic place.

The next campsite had two lean-tos. They faced each other across about 20 yards of packed earth. I claimed a bunk in one by spreading my mat and bag on it. As I ate and gave thanks to the world in general for supplying me with another cup, a troop of Boy Scouts descended on the camp. I was content to watch this human activity as I ate but became annoyed at the noise level after only a few minutes. I had been so used to the peace and silence that twelve or so pre-teens overwhelmed my tolerance pretty quickly and I had to retreat into the woods.

I meditated in a quiet place well away from the trail as the darkness fell. I slipped out of my body but did not get far. I was in a thick white fog,

215

essentially zero visibility. A clearing space began forming just in front of me and a face slowly emerged from the mist. It was a familiar face. It was the face of Kathleen or Gena or perhaps some combination of their two faces. The creases locked into time-carved lines of joy. The eyes seemed to overflow with love.

I reentered my body. It was not by choice, it just happened. I got up and carefully walked back to the lean-tos. I knew my way back but the lack of light made each step a little risky. I heard the camp before I saw it. The scouts had built a fire and were noisily roasting marshmallows. Most of the soft little snacks became flaming torches that dropped into the fire or were hurriedly removed and blown out occasionally causing some mild bodily harm to the roaster. I could not even force myself to feel sympathy. For long-distance hikers, nightfall was bedtime. For the young scouts it was a time to burn off energy by being physically and verbally as active as possible.

Finally at around nine PM, the scoutmaster took the little troop on a nocturnal excursion to look at the stars. Quiet descended on the lean-tos. The other adults at the site sighed with relief and hoped to get to sleep before the children returned.

I couldn't help myself. I grabbed my bag of nuts and ran across to the other lean-to. Quickly I moved from bunk to bunk tossing two or three nuts into each sleeping bag. I ran back to my bunk, got into my comfortable nut-free bag and waited.

Soon the young outdoorsmen returned and with only a half-hour or so of mayhem got quieted down for the night.

The screams started about an hour later. The first one got everyone pretty excited and the scout master had to quiet things down again and reassure the youngster involved that the mice would not likely try to get in his sleeping bag again.

Fifteen minutes of quiet, more yelling, two more kids had been panicked by the presence of furry creatures in their space. There was a great deal of jumping up and down and shaking of bags. I had to hope no one else heard me giggling. All night long the scoutmaster and his charges were mysteriously harassed by tiny rodents. I didn't get much sleep, but I rested and besides it was worth it.

In the morning it was a group of very quiet, tired and sullen scouts that readied themselves for their day's hike. I bounded up to them full of energy and asked them how they had slept. Several of them launched into the story of the night of the living mice. I feigned astonishment and told them that none of the people in my lean-to had even seen or heard a mouse.

I am an evil man.

Years later I would still laugh however. Humor seemed to be important somehow.

I hiked in the opposite direction of the scouts, continuing north. I smiled at the many people I passed and was basically too distracted by the comparative crowds to accomplish much. Every lean-to was crowded. The trail was over used. I had come to the trail hoping for isolation but it was not until I passed the last lean-to within the Great Smokey Mountains. That's when strange things started to happen.

It's not like plenty of strange events weren't already occurring, it's just that different types of oddities began.

I think it had to do with karma. I'm not sure that karma actually exists or is a real force in the universe, but it is one way of looking at things that I thought was useful. You see, I seemed to be running out, at least of "bad" karma.

Everything started to happen in a very palpably cyclical fashion. If I needed water, there would be a spring around the next bend in the trail, even in places where there weren't supposed to be springs according to the guidebooks.

On a day when I was low on food and a bit concerned about it, a large rattlesnake slithered onto the trail ahead of me. I knew and the snake somehow knew what was to happen. I killed the snake, felt sorrow for it and thanked it for nourishing me. I skinned and cleaned it and that evening built a small fire and roasted the snake meat. It was one of the most delicious meals I can recall.

This might seem to some to be a enviable condition to be in, where all of your needs are met soon after they are realized, but this is not always so. If I had a "need" for a million dollars, I'm pretty sure it wouldn't appear on the trail. If I had a need for sex, which of course being a young male, I did, I'm certain that a beautiful female would not suddenly appear. I'm sure about this because I frequently thought about a woman's company, but no woman ever came hiking along to be that company.

I would think of glorious things and the beauty of nature, and as I rounded a curve, a field of wild flowers would be there to grace my eyes. I began to see this cycle so clearly that I was getting fairly instantaneous feedback about my karmic state. If I were doing "well," I would see the effect of my thoughts, actions or desires within minutes. If I backslid and allowed myself to be

217

drawn into the material world, the time between the causal act and the effect would lengthen. The causality that became apparent as I hiked also became annoying.

It reached a climax on the day before I left the trail. I had stopped to look at the intricate spiral of an uncoiling fiddlehead fern. A small bird landed nearby and I turned my head to see it. I saw it and I saw a thousand future birds because by startling the bird I sent it flying to a spot where it met a mate and the result of that mating was uncounted bird generations.

I inhaled, and a million gnats that would have been would no longer be because of the one I had inadvertently sucked into my mouth with my breath. I exhaled and a small sprout caught the breeze from this and had just a tiny bit more carbon dioxide than its competitors and thus grew into a tree instead of being choked out by the surrounding growth.

I became paralyzed. I couldn't move without becoming aware of all of the good and bad consequences. I couldn't even breath without the burden of my action being known to me. It was an intolerable state that I assumed would lead to enlightenment or insanity, but I didn't feel ready for either one. I was losing my sense of humor about life, I was becoming fearful about into what I might be evolving.

I swore.

The cycle lengthened.

I stood in anger and let loose with a string of explicatives probably never heard before in these woods.

The cycle lengthened. The more I ranted and raved about how rotten things had become, the less I was able to see the immediate consequences of my actions, and thus I eventually arrived at peace again.

That night I contemplated this and of course left my body in this meditative state. I went up above the surrounding mountains and was pulled rapidly eastward. I rose to where I could see the Atlantic and began to cross it. I rose and traveled until I could see the coast of Europe and beyond the subcontinent of India. The face of an old man rose from there and smiled at me, inviting me. I wanted to join him, but I did not want to leave my body back in North Carolina. I was torn, I was fearful, I was instantly back in my body.

In the morning I began walking. I was nervous, out of touch with my surroundings somehow. I stopped to dig a little sassafras root and make some tea, but found my knife was no longer in its sheath and nowhere to be found along the trail, at least not as far back as I went to try to locate it.

I stopped for fresh water and my steel cup had fallen from my belt. It began to rain and I plodded on in a darkening mood and for the first time, my boots got wet and I felt blisters forming on my feet.

It was time to leave the trail.

I hiked into Hot Springs that afternoon and caught a bus heading south.

TWENTY-SEVEN

I eventually arrived back at the ashram in Gainesville. I was able to exchange my ticket to India for one that left at an earlier time and waited the several days before my new departure date in quiet contemplation.

It was bizarre to think about how apparently close to enlightenment I had been and yet I was obviously not ready to be there. For me it seemed like traveling into the astral realms was like taking a first grade child and putting him or her in charge of a space shuttle flight. I was in a little over my head.

I landed in Delhi and the first thing that struck me was the smell. It was not a good smell or a bad smell. It was different and it was strong to the point of being urgent. It was the smell of spices, the smell of people, the smell of waste. It was a complex mix of good and bad smells that ended up being neither good or bad, but rather, characteristic. As I traveled north from Delhi I would learn that each place had a characteristic olfactory identity that was as clear as any geographic landmark.

I really didn't know where I was going, I simply knew I had to meet up with the old man/woman I had seen in that white foggy place in the Appalachians and again in my out-of-body trip to India. I felt that my meeting with this person was inevitable. All I needed to do was head north and keep my senses open.

I walked, I traveled by crowded train, I got rides on the backs of dangerously overloaded trucks and in ridiculously overcrowded busses. I finally came to a place where there were no more roads. There were trails and there were pilgrims of a variety of types walking and crawling along them. Since I couldn't speak the language I was unable to communicate, which was fine with me. I walked in solitude in spite of the crowds.

It was during this time that I started seeing patterns. People began to take on a dual appearance: one was their physical form and one was, I think, a representation of the pattern of light that might be seen from the out-of-body perspective. I had traversed this part of India in silence and during those days of travel I gradually developed this ability. I'm not really sure I should call it an ability. It might have been a delusion or illusion, a figment of my imagination. Because of this uncertainty I simply observed what I saw and tried to attach no importance to it.

In relation to both ways of looking at people they were all unique individuals. I didn't have the language skills to determine if what I saw in the patterns was associated with particular characteristics of the personalities of each person, but I suspected as much.

There were people with darker patterns or dark areas within them that harkened back to the man who had killed the woman at the Rocky Knob lean-to. I avoided these people. There were also people with very yellow to white patterns and some of these were quite intricate, complex and very bright. Most people were composed of a variety of intermediate colors and variable complexity. Some of the patterns were simple and symmetric, particularly those of young children.

Most were not symmetric and there were places within each pattern where knots had formed. The knots were points where the colors would darken, where energy seemed to be restricted in its flow. Adults who were in a hurry, seemed distressed or seemed even outwardly neurotic had more knots than most. Well-dressed businessmen often had darker patterns with numerous tangles. The one thing that was apparent in all of them was that they tied the knots themselves.

Once in a while I would see someone who looked at me the same way I looked at them. I assumed that they saw some type of pattern associated with me but I could not detect my own, even in a mirror. These people could either be very dark with large patterns or very brightly white, yellow or pale blue. In either case there were fewer knots, more symmetry and more complexity in their patterns. The people who were lighter and brighter seemed to pay me deference or at least acknowledge me with acceptance. The darker forms would seem to emanate hatred or even fear. This was very reassuring to me. If it had been the other way around I would have been pretty worried.

I took all this in while trying to remain non-judgmental. Since I could not be sure that what I was seeing was real or true, I tried not to let it affect how I interacted with people. There were quite a few who obviously thought of themselves in quite a different way than the pattern they radiated would suggest. Some gave the outward appearance of being "good" and giving, while their "aura," for lack of a better term, was a tangle of choked dark lines.

I somehow got the feeling from some of these that even the persons themselves were not aware of their true nature.

I journeyed mostly without care for how I perceived people. Seeing them in some sort of spiritual form made no difference. They were all still people dealing with mysterious lives in a mysterious universe. There were very few who could be blamed for the knots in their patterns or the darker shades. The only time I took my odd perceptual skill seriously was when I encountered those who were dark and gave the distinct impression that they had chosen to be dark and in fact were working just as hard to perfect their darkness as those who were the brightest white labored to perfect theirs. These people were too frightening to ignore even though outwardly they might appear benevolent or even saintly. I avoided them and thankfully they seemed to want to avoid me also.

I made it to a temple in the mountains where it seemed few pilgrims stopped. A small side trail next to a large rounded rock led to it and in spite of its beauty and appeal, few if any took this trail. All those whom I observed, walked past without seeming to pay attention to the palatial house of worship. I wondered about this as I walked toward the gate.

I rang a large gong, which hung within the wall next to an elaborately carved wooden door. I waited for a time I judged to be reasonable and gonged again. Still there was no answer. I sat and waited for what might have been two hours. No one entered, no one exited, no one approached, there were no noises from within. The gong still went unanswered when I banged it one last time.

I walked back to the main trail. I found a woman who was clearly European (blonde hair, blue eyes) and asked if she spoke English. She did but knew nothing about the temple I had seen and told me she had never noticed it even though she had walked that trail frequently. She was an attractive woman, Swedish, named Karin, and she had been in the area for several months searching for something. She apparently had not seen many other people of northern European extraction and she said she would like to spend some time with me. I felt the old hormone-related physiologic response, something that hadn't happened in quite some time.

I walked with her to the nearby village and to a small building where food could be purchased. She made it clear during the meal that her hormones were also more active than usual. Quite a predicament. I saw that her pattern was smaller, kind of a dusty light gray with brighter areas of white and yellow. There were only a few knots. All in all my internal senses were telling me to avoid this physically desirable female. In typical male fashion I did not.

We went to a room available in the same little boarding house, the proprietor grinning at us knowingly. It was a room he would let us use by the hour. Even though there had been no alcohol available with the food, he produced a bottle of Glenfiddich that was about one-third full and apparently not watered down.

My judgement told me to flee, my testicles begged me to stay. I stayed. The young lady and I began kissing and tugging at each other's clothing. Her taste, her smell and the feel of her body were even more intoxicating than the Scotch we shared. I was being sucked into a world of pure physical pleasure without regard for consequences; pure hedonism.

Without regard for consequences.

We had not yet removed all our clothing. One glimpse of her pale, smooth, round breast and I was inflamed with lust. That's all I got to see. There was a loud knocking at the door and the proprietor burst in and made motions that we were to leave immediately. He actually seemed quite panicked and the harangue in Hindi, although incomprehensible, got the message across nonetheless that we were to leave through the window and take the Scotch with us.

We restored enough order to our clothes to be presentable and climbed out into a dusty and worse than usual smelling alley. We then walked in a way I hoped was nonchalant to the street where we had a view of the front of the building. There were police present and they were in the process of dragging the owner out along with several females who were obviously of "ill repute."

We walked away, at least I thought we did. When I looked around for Karin, she had disappeared. To add to the injury she had taken the Scotch with her. I was a bit confused and shook my head to try to clear it of the confusion and the heady mix of alcohol and lust. As I looked around I noticed that the auras I had been seeing superimposed on the people around me were no longer visible. I wasn't surprised I guess, but I was dismayed.

Another lesson. Humans were weak. Here I was, a supposedly enlightened being on my way to meet a great guru of some kind, and yet I had yielded to the temptation of the flesh. Amazing. It seemed that no matter how far we progressed on the road to the Buddha, we could always be dragged back, always capable of ignoring our inner compass and doing what our senses desired. The choice was always there, and always had to be there in fact.

I decided to make the walk back up to the ashram I had been to earlier to see if I could get someone to answer the door. It was late afternoon before I got to the turn off. I missed it on my way up, deep in thought about the consequences of my lust for Karin I suppose. I backtracked to where the trail was supposed to be and could not find it. I walked back and forth over the quarter mile or so area where the trail and the temple had been, yet I found no trace of either. I found the rounded rock beside which I thought the trail should be, but it was not. I also could not find anyone who could speak English to ask about it.

I gave up looking and would make the several mile hike back to the village to spend the night. After walking a hundred or so yards I saw a trail leading to the left. At the end of the trail was the building I had seen before. It was a little spooky because I was sure I had walked past this spot several times and had not seen the footpath. Indeed, there was the rounded rock squatting next to the trail, as if to let me know that I knew so very little.

At the door I banged the gong. I stood listening to the deep vibration for some time. It seemed to continue for much longer than I thought possible. In fact when it abruptly stopped it was dark. It was also cold. It was windy. In addition there was no path where I was. There was also no temple and no door and no gong.

"Oh shit," was about the best I could muster. All these transcendental experiences, you'd think I'd be used to weird things happening to me, but I was not. Now where was I? Now what was I supposed to do? Now what lesson was I to learn?

I rotated 360 degrees. I was on a rocky mountainside with very poor visibility due to blowing fog and darkness. There were no visible stars or moon so I assumed the clouds were thick enough to block the night sky out. Either that or I wasn't even on Earth and instead was in some strange place that had no stars or moon. It was a toss up. As far as I knew I could be resting quietly in the ashram in Gainesville or even at my parents' home in bed continuing an extremely long and detailed dream. I was really starting to lose coherence and was questioning everything now. What was real and what was not had become extremely subjective and I actually felt my mind retreating into a place where it would cease to function rather than attempt to deal with what might be cold hard reality or what might be hallucination. I had no way of knowing with which I was dealing.

The cold hard reality is what really got my attention however. The air was cold and the rock was hard. I was in danger.

If I stayed where I was I would freeze to death. If I moved I might fall or might move in the wrong direction and die of exposure anyway. I made two assumptions that were based on nothing. One was moving was the correct thing to do because I might be able to generate some body heat or I might actually find some temporary shelter. The other assumption was that it would be warmer at lower elevations. These were arbitrary because I had no way of knowing whether moving would really help and no way of knowing whether or not if, in this strange place, up might be warmer and down colder.

I guess I had to believe I was on Earth, on a mountainside where I was unable to detect even trees around me. If this was true then I should be able to walk down to a tree line and find shelter or fuel for a fire and perhaps a path back to civilization.

Time again to step out in faith.

The footing was not the best. Even where there seemed to be flat spots for my boots, there were loose rocks that threatened to make me slide with them down the mountain or at least force me to twist my ankle, a minor injury but under these circumstances fatal. This was not the Appalachian Trail!

I had gone perhaps a hundred yards angling downward in no particular direction. I was frozen in my tracks by a not distant enough growl. I switched back and continued downward at a little steeper angle than was probably safe. There was a roar of some kind. It made my hair stand up, it made my heart race and it tried to make my feet race but this would be death as sure as encountering whatever was making that noise.

It reminded me of the roaring sound of that evil person who murdered next to a spring in Georgia. I would feel better if I thought it were a tiger or bear or even Big Foot, but I had a feeling it was none of these things.

A growl again, assessing the wind, questioning, lower in tone and closer. I switch backed again and started moving faster but at a shallower angle to try to put distance between myself and what was probably tracking me, even though it would mean staying at a higher elevation. Hell, I would go back up if it meant I could get away from the "thing."

I could see no more than twenty to sometimes fifty yards around me, depending on the density of the shifting mist. I would dash across an open space if I could get a good enough glimpse of what the terrain was like but I would have to slow down at other times and pick my way along.

A snort now. Very close, sniffing, smelling and feeling its way closer to me. This animal (?) was getting closer and was in its natural environment. I was definitely out of mine and getting colder in spite of my fear and activity. I wondered what would get me first.

Another inquisitive sniff. I could hear the damn thing sniffing! I ran at a slightly upward pitch just praying that my feet would find purchase and that the "thing" would continue to move downhill for some reason. I was shaking almost out of control. The combination of shivering from the cold and shivering from fear was threatening to blow me apart. I would glance back but would see nothing.

Even when I heard the crunch of feet or paws on the loose stone, I could not see what was pursuing me. I was running as fast as I could now without regard for footing. Blind or not, I couldn't slow down even if it meant running off a cliff.

Heavy breathing from behind, couldn't, wouldn't look back, running.

Sniffing, breath now upon my neck, the feel of it was foul and then the smell of that breath became detectable. I had visions of a huge mouth lined with teeth beginning to close on my neck. I had no choice. My eyes were choked with freezing tears. I could not see anyway.

I turned straight downhill, took three long strides down the slope and then launched myself into space. I planned to land and leap over and over regardless of the pain or even death. I had to get away.

My flight stopped abruptly as my feet came back in contact with the rock. One step, pain in that ankle, second step jumped as far as possible. Was that warm moist breath at the back of my neck as I lifted off?

I came down again on my injured ankle. I knew what was going to happen. The joint refused to bear weight and as it collapsed I had no time to get my other foot under me. I pitched forward and tried to tuck and did in fact roll. I also slid, leaving enough skin from my abdomen on the rock to serve as a small meal for any carnivores in the area. My head struck against the rock once, then twice then perhaps a third time but I couldn't be sure for I was unconscious. The last things I remember as the pain and cold finally released me into coma where red glowing eyes, bright white teeth and a dangling tongue just above me.

TWENTY-EIGHT

I was hovering above a rocky slope. Below me was also a twisted body. My twisted body. Between my body and myself was web of black silk so intricate and symmetric that it was beautiful to behold. It moved toward my body as if it would posses it, steal it from its proper owner.

I was that owner and I suppose I should have felt some trepidation about this black entity moving toward my organic form. But it was just my body, badly damaged at that. Why should I care? I directed my attention to my right. There was a pattern there that I perceived as a face, a face of an old woman that morphed into the face of an old man. The words came to me.

"No matter what adversity you face, you must persevere."

I attended to my body again. I moved to posses it, I moved to defend it, I moved to battle with the darkness just above it.

I came down upon my own physical back but was immediately held from behind by what felt like numerous short stout arms. They were peeling me back away from my body and they caused a burning pain that flowed through me, the pain of hate. I twisted in my astral form and faced my attacker.

Every face of every evil and frightening thing possible glared down at me. Blood red sparks shimmered along the black velvety lines of this form. I saw a bright white tentacle move upward and push against those awful faces. It was my tentacle. I could at last perceive myself in this out-of-body form and I could see the pain my touch inflicted on my adversary. It was the pain of love.

Everywhere I touched the blackness would fade a little, a patch of dark gray would remain and the astral equivalent of a raging scream would emerge from that black web.

Ropes of darkness wrapped around me, trying to get to the center of my being and there crush the light that illuminated my pattern. I could see the black heart of the beast with which I wrestled. It was an endless dark space, a black hole in the universe of light that extended into infinity and into a place without hope.

I began to move my lines of light toward that heart, to try to fill that dark space, but was blocked at every attempt by a long digit of black. It was like disembodied martial arts—punch, block, kick, block—only there were many arms and legs, as many as you could envision it seemed, with which to attack and counter.

I became aware of a high-pitched sound, like the wailing of a flute amplified beyond reason. The sound was coming from me. It was a result of the agony. Each time the blackness touched me there would be pain and a sense of hopelessness. Each time it touched me I would lose some resolve, some strength. I would doubt my ability to continue. Each time I would touch the beast it would soften, its driving force, its hatred weakened.

As I struggled I learned. Learned to block his moves toward my core and avoid his obstructing efforts as I moved toward his. I had a part of my "chest" into the chest of my body and forced it to take a rattling breath. The black one had an "arm" in my arm and slapped at me with it, tried to pick up rocks and strike them against my physical head and cause irreparable damage.

I continued to writhe with the black form, was pulled out of my chest, but got into my legs and forced them to push against the rock making my physical form roll several yards down hill. The blackness and I were both disconnected now and I concentrated on blocking movements that would deprive the dark one from entering and controlling any part of my body.

One white tentacle inched toward his black heart; one black tentacle was dangerously close to my heart. Like two tumbleweeds tangled and rolling in a Texas windstorm, the two of us fought.

Weakness, pain, tears of blue-white light falling from me. From the thing, weakness, pain and reddish-black tears of hatred diluted, fell to the ground and scorched it. I moved over my supine physical form and moved into it to a degree to allow a ragged breath, a few beats of the heart. As blood coursed through my body, a bit of strength coursed through me. I pushed like a desperate killer with a stiletto at the heart of my opponent. Could I through sheer force of will drive my astral arm into its heart? I put everything behind that movement, every bit of strength, every bit of concentration and mental energy. I was at the threshold of that darkest place but could not penetrate. I felt a pressure in my spiritual chest like a crushing of my physical heart might feel if I were in my body. I was dangerously close to being spiritually killed.

Love versus hate, good versus evil, white versus black. I realized I was struggling to convert this black form to white. Where I touched it was gray, where I touched hard it almost turned white, but that with which I touched became darker and where the thing touched me I lost intensity and color. How could this be? How could I win? We could only extinguish each other like equal parts of matter and anti-matter.

There had to be a different way, a way around. I thought of electrons moving from energy level to energy level through quantum tunnels in another dimension. I could not fathom where these thoughts were coming from. Tunneling, a way around, a different approach. An approach beyond hatred's ability to comprehend.

I forgave.

I opened myself up into my full flat glorious pattern of bruised whiteness and I forgave the hatred, I loved the hatred, I invited the hatred in. And in it came. With evil intent it formed one blunt black extremity and plunged it toward my center. It struck there and moved into it. I felt no pain because I offered no resistance. The momentum of the black thing's thrust carried it forward and a significant portion of its energy was absorbed into this limitless place at my center.

It was startled, it was suddenly frightened, something it was not used to feeling. It tried to draw back but could not, that which had passed through me was forever gone, absorbed into an infinite ocean of white-colored caring.

With this caring, with this love, with this forgiveness, I drew the black form into me. The web of darkness unraveled as I somehow passed the string of its form through me to what was beyond me but connected to me, a place from where I could draw infinite power if I desired it.

The last bit of black thread slipped through with a whimper.

I moved to where my body was stretched out on the rocks. I moved into it and forced a contraction of my too long still heart. I forced a contraction of the muscles of my diaphragm, which sucked cold air into my lungs. I had to concentrate, like doing CPR. Contract heart, contract heart, contract heart, breath, contract heart, contract heart, breath. How long I did this I could not say but in time the contractions and the breaths became automatic and I was able to turn my attention to pain, sharp stabbing pain in my ankle. Aching burning pain in my fingers and toes half frozen. Searing pain from the deep abrasions on my stomach. A painful stiffness in every joint I tried to move.

Moving, I was moving, but not through the power of my muscles. The temperature warmed. I was flying through a space I could not see or feel. I was arriving. My destination was forming around me rather than me moving into it; although, as the place around me formed I seemed to decelerate. I sensed a cessation of motion as the room around me turned seemingly completely solid.

It was a theater, darkened, warm and comfortable. I was warm and comfortable. No pain, no apparent injuries. There were theatergoers around me though none were in my row, which was at the very front. I looked back but could not really make out any faces. The people were eating popcorn and carrying large drinks. It was festive as if everyone were looking forward to a showing of a particularly good film.

The curtain opened and the lights grew even dimmer.

A male human appeared on the screen. He was nude, disheveled and obviously confused. The audience laughed the way people would laugh at a baby trying so hard to sit up for the first time.

The man walked although there was no particular scenery around him in which he walked. He would occasionally bump into things that were not visible to him and bounce off moving in a different direction. Sometimes he would come upon things that he could see, walls, and he would push against them to try to continue his trajectory but to no avail. The crowd would laugh at these antics also.

The man would finally be bounced randomly and moved to some extent by walls he could not move or pass through, in a particular direction. At times he would change direction himself although the reasons for this were rarely apparent. At times he smiled, at times he cried, at times the audience would become subdued and tense as the man moved in a direction that was apparently dangerous; although, again the danger was not always apparent.

Finally the man came to two hallways leading off at different angles. He puzzled over this. He tried to turn around and retrace his steps but an immovable wall had formed behind him. He was forced to choose. One hall led in a direction that would result in some mild harm, one led in a direction that was neutral. The man seemed to choose arbitrarily, without thought. The audience moaned as he walked down the path toward harm. As he walked along he stepped upon a piece of glass and cut his foot. Immediately before him formed two halls. He clutched his foot and hopped ridiculously down the wrong hall.

The audience groaned again. I looked around but could still not see recognizable faces, just shadowy forms shaped like bodies scattered in the rows of seats behind me. I returned to the screen where the action was accelerating. The man was moving faster now. Apparently the cut on his foot had healed but he had several other scars and open wounds.

He ran with a limp toward hallway after hallway, careening down one and then another. He seemed at times to be in control of his mad dash and would occasionally turn down what was obviously, to me, the correct path. It certainly wasn't always obvious to him.

There was acceleration. It became like a game where the man had to make split-second decisions over and over again. The ever-branching hallways began moving by at a frightening rate, and indeed there were times the man was frightened and times when he was not.

The man's path took on an almost organic form, as if he were a lone blood cell being propelled down lonely arteries. He began to develop some skill. This was surprising to the crowd. He began surfing the hallways and flowing in the proper direction, at times seeming to be in harmony with his surroundings. Still he would make wrong turns and some would result in near fatal traumas, but he persisted.

His skill improved and the audience in the theater became entranced by his performance, hopeful for his success. He moved down the tunnels with incredible speed veering this way and that, making one good choice after another. The wrong turns were getting less frequent. It seemed his speed would reach infinite as he began making the correct choices repeatedly as if he could now see clearly where he needed to go.

He stopped. He was the same man, nude but not disheveled. Not confused but stumped.

All his wounds had healed. There were scars to be certain and his form and posture were far from perfect, but he was whole. He stood before a mirror that made up one wall of a tiny room just big enough for him. In the mirror was a man in an identical tiny room. They reached out to each other as mirrored images do. Their fingers met at the plane of the glass.

But there was no glass. Their fingers met. They were both suddenly in a tiny room where there was really only room for one. They embraced in combat. They attempted to harm and even kill each other, but were evenly matched and one could not get an advantage over the other.

As they wrestled, the room around them changed slowly to a windy scene on a rocky slope where they attempted to impale each other with sharp rocks. They drew blood from each other and tried in vain to strike a blow deep into the heart of the other. The fighting became frantic and I lost track of which man was which, I could no longer tell them apart but I had desperately wanted the man who I had watched traverse the hallways to win. The audience also wanted this and could apparently tell the two apart some how. Everyone was on their feet cheering, screaming for the man to find a tactic that would work.

Suddenly he did. He embraced the other man, held his face in his hands and looked lovingly into his eyes. He dropped all his defenses and as he did so there appeared behind him an army of similar men. The other man, who I could now in some way tell was the man in the mirror, lashed out in anger, pushing his hand directly into the chest of the original character in the film. His hand and arm passed through and the triumphant look of hatred mixed with a sense of victory turned into a look of fear and shock.

The people behind the original man grasped at the arm of the second man and pulled. Dozens, then hundreds then thousands of hands in some way held onto the arm of the second man and pulled him through the chest of the original as if that man's heart was a portal into this place of infinitely numerous people who were therefore infinitely powerful.

This task completed, the man stood alone and naked on a barren mountainside. At peace.

The crowd in the theater was joyous with applause and laughter. They stood and clapped and whistled.

The scene on the screen slowly shifted to a wooded mountainside beside a temple of some sort with a carved wooden door. Beside the door, mounted into the wall, was a gong that was sounding a long low note. I stood and turned toward the crowd. It was me they were applauding, not the film, and with intense humility I watched as the crowd faded, the sound of the gong grew louder and the space before me became filled with the carvings of a door into a temple beside which the gong chimed.

The door opened.

TWENTY-NINE

He was there. The old man, the confluence of the faces of Kathleen and Gena, looked out at me. His face still seemed illusory, as if it were in a constant state of flux which made it difficult to focus on him and difficult to describe him in detail. One thing was clear, he was smiling.

He motioned me into the courtyard. There were numerous interesting details about the experience of entering this temple for the first time. The lighting shifted. It was a golden glowing light from the same sun that was outside, but seemed warmer, kinder, without glare. I got the feeling that from this place I could stare directly into the sun without harm to my eyes.

The smell was delightful, not sweet, not flowery, not anything I could specifically describe but my olfactory bulbs were pleased, just as my eyes had been pleased with the lighting.

There was a sound, as indescribable as the smell, delightful to the ears but in no way obscured the sounds of our footsteps.

I had an almost overwhelming sense of wellness. This was particularly dramatic because I had been so recently traumatized. I felt no pain or injury, as if everything had healed completely.

At this point the old man turned and ran his index finger across my abdomen eliciting fairly intense pain. I raised the front of my shirt and looked. My abdomen was covered with parallel excoriations as if I had been dragged across sharp rocks. I had, as I far too clearly recalled.

The courtyard was packed dirt of a light brown color, enough to be indistinguishable from cement and yet had a soft feel to it. The interior walls were whitewashed and plain. In the center of the space was a tree about ten feet tall, very well cared for, no lesions on the trunk, no brown or diseased leaves. It bore no fruit but seemed to me to be the epitome of what a tree should be.

We walked past the tree and into a door opposite the entrance gate. Inside

233

it was cooler, a bit dimmer and the atmosphere was imbued with extreme peacefulness. The walls were whitewashed and seemed blank and yet when I looked closely there seemed to be images, shifting pale pastels not willing or able to be brought into focus. There were no windows, only the open doorway and the light spilling in from the door could not account for the lighting in the room. There were no lamps or candles.

We passed through another door opposite the first, moving deeper into the complex. This room was like the first but had doors in all four walls. We went through the one on the right. We took the door on the left in the next room, which had a large wooden table with chairs around it, all very neat and clean. The next room was larger than the others and was ringed with pillows in a variety of bright colors and patterns. We moved through several more rooms, sparsely furnished at best and all seemingly little used.

Finally we stopped in a room that had no exits other than the door we entered through. A large pillow-like mattress covered with blankets, eight feet long and six feet wide, perhaps two feet thick, covered most of the floor. This was all that the room contained.

The old man spoke his first words. "Here you will sleep. If you need food you will find it in the room with the large table we passed through. To relieve yourself go through the door to the left in the room outside this one."

He left before I could even ask him any questions. I had about a million it seemed and they were jumbled, tangled together and I couldn't separate any one question out quickly enough to give it voice before the old man left. I went to the door of my room hoping to catch him but was too late. I didn't even know which of the three doors he had gone through. The room just outside mine was completely bare.

I went back into my room and looked at the bed. The fatigue hit so fast and so hard I was afraid I wouldn't even make it to the bed before falling asleep. I fell forward onto the bed and rolled to my side. I could not tell if the light in the room dimmed or if my rapid slide into sleep deprived me of the perception of light. Either way it became dark and I became unaware.

As I became aware again, the lighting in the room brightened. I had no way of knowing what time it was or how long I had been asleep. It was clear that I had not moved since getting onto the bed and I felt a little stiff as I rose and stretched. The stretching activated the pain receptors on my stomach and I remembered I was wounded. This was a constant reminder, I supposed, of the reality of the experience I had gone through on the mountainside, although why nothing else hurt I could not fathom.

My bladder got my attention. I went out of my room and through the door on the left as I had been instructed. I entered a very pleasant bathroom with beautifully done tilework, a flushing toilet, two sinks and a good-sized shower. This was so incongruous with the rest of the temple that I thought I had been transported to a luxury hotel in the U.S.

I not only emptied my bladder, I took advantage of the shower also. The water stung my healing skin but otherwise felt as wonderful as any shower could. I felt at peace, content, almost joyous as I put on a wonderful lined silk robe that I found on a hook outside the shower. I hadn't noticed it there before. I also hadn't seen the slippers on the floor below the robe. My filthy, blood-stained clothes were gone.

I went out and stood in the room outside mine and looked around. There was absolutely nothing to see. I could see into my room and see the mattress on the floor, but I could not see clearly into the other two rooms off this one. I walked through the door directly across from the one to my bedroom. It was empty and blank walled just like the one I had been in. It had three additional doors leading out but I really couldn't discern the contents of those rooms. I had a feeling that I could go through any door and find an empty room and continue going from room to room indefinitely.

I went back the way I had come but instead of being in another empty room with a bathroom to one side, I was in my bedroom. Home.

I sat on my large cushion-like bed and thought. In this place, thought and meditation came easily. I rose from my body and through the ceiling on an arching beam of bright white light, which remained connected to my body below me. I could see my body on the bed, see the connection and realized that I need not fear losing contact. I shot back into my body nonetheless because the rest of what I saw stunned me.

The huge temple complex consisted only of my room, the courtyard, the tree and the gate to the outside world. It was where it was supposed to be, on a side trail off a path from the village to other holy places farther up the mountain.

I got off of my bed and ran into what should have been the courtyard, and it was. There was the tree, the inside of the main door, the blank walls. I turned back through the door I had run through. It was my room. I ran back out into the courtyard and through the door to my left. It was my room. I dashed across the courtyard, veering around the tree and through the opposite portal. It was my room.

I had a sudden need to find the old man but had no idea how to find him.

I ran back into the courtyard, but it was the room lined with pillows, many of which were occupied by men and women in robes like mine and in the center of the one doorless wall was the old man.

Everyone turned to me and smiled, although their faces were indistinct. I felt welcome and in fact the old man said, "You are welcome. You are late. Take your seat and try to pay attention to this day's lesson."

I sat on the nearest pillow. Everyone stared at me. I felt very uncomfortable until I noticed a pillow near mine that had the same coloring and patterns as my bed. I quickly scooted over to that pillow and instantly felt at ease, as did the rest of the room. The lesson began.

I sat and listened attentively but no one spoke. I looked around and everyone was sitting comfortably with their eyes closed. I shifted position and tried to close my eyes but couldn't. I was too nervous about this place, these people and this voiceless lesson.

I was startled by the old man's words.

"Would you care to join us?" he asked kindly.

I just nodded. I had foolishly thought I was already there.

He stared at me for a few moments, seemingly expecting something. When whatever he expected happened or didn't happen he made a quick upward movement with his hand.

I was out of my body floating above the ashram, connected to my body by a silver thread. All around me were patterns of light hooked to bodies below us by similar ties. The ashram was a courtyard with a tree in it and a single room where our bodies quietly sat.

I began drifting upward and felt the need to stop this and return to the group but did not know how. A few others were drifting around in poor control of themselves. A message came to me from a particularly bright and symmetric pattern that I knew somehow was the teacher. "Spin."

I tried to perceive myself and found that I could, a sort of visual proprioception. I was a glowing white pattern, but not so bright, not so symmetric, a few knots here and there. It was a humbling sight. The others around me were fairly similar for the most part. I tried to think about spinning. I looked at my numerous extremities and turned them all tangent to my outer curve. I tried to radiate energy from the ends of these by concentrating hard and imagining the outflow like little jets.

I spun so fast counterclockwise that my perception of the world was just a blur. I moved rapidly downward in fact and apparently imbedded myself deep in the Earth. I was surrounded by rock, and yet not crushed by it. I could see it, but see through it to an extent. I fortunately saw the humor in this and chuckled. I reversed the direction of my "thrusters" and forced energy out of them just as I had before.

Zip. I rose into the air, overshot a bit and stopped about three miles above the surface. I could barely discern the life forms below me. I reversed thrusters again and spun very slowly, very gently and by doing so I moved in a controlled manner back to the group below. I learned to orient myself so I could hover. I felt exhausted from my energy expenditures and seemed dimmer overall.

We were all in bodies again. Mine sort of ached all over and I wanted badly to sleep, but this was overridden by intense hunger.

The old man was there, everyone else had left. He said, "You must conserve your energy at first. You will harm yourself. I thought I would have to dig you out from the Earth or perhaps just leave you there and place a nice stone marker for you."

The old geezer was actually being sarcastic. Unfortunately I could not think of any quick come back. All I could come up with was, "I'm very hungry."

"As well you should be, you burned many calories on your little journey. Most humans learn to move around where they can see before venturing into what appears solid. It takes another type of vision you have not yet learned to see through the Earth." The old man said this as he pointed to the door on his right.

I got up and weakly went through.

The old man was sitting at the table and one place was set with a bowl of what appeared to be a mixture of several types of grains with lentils and split peas. It smelled outrageously good and tasted even better as I wolfed down several large spoonfuls.

"You know," the old one said, "that will do you far more good if you chew it carefully. I'm afraid that later you will see the exact same mixture in your toilet if you do not crush the husks of the grains between your teeth."

I stopped shoveling and looked at the old guy. Now that I knew he could be sarcastic, I had a more comfortable rapport with him. I felt no need to be worshipful as was my first impulse.

I took a bite and chewed long and slow, savoring the taste and making sure that every kernel was crushed before swallowing the mush. The old man smiled a little more and nodded. He said nothing more. I continued to eat and noticed that no matter how many spoonfuls I removed from the bowl, the level never dropped. It also never cooled as I ate. The glass of cold water beside my plate also refilled itself after each swallow and refused to warm up to room temperature. This was a very strange place, but I already loved it here. It was a school, and I knew I had a lot to learn.

"The black form on the mountain that I fought?"

"That was only the darkness inside yourself."

"Is it gone?" I asked hopefully.

"No."

"Will I have to fight it again?" I started to get a little worried.

"Perhaps."

"What can I do to keep from having to fight it again?"

"Accept yourself as you are, both the good and the bad, and love your whole being as the beautiful creation it is."

"So the blackness is still inside me?"

"It's still inside us all. We only fight with it when we refuse to acknowledge that it is a part of us."

I was full and I understood what the old man was saying. I needed sleep now but had no idea how to get to my room. The old man motioned toward the door I had entered through and vanished. After getting over the surprise of seeing him disappear, I walked through the door back into the "classroom," but it was my room. Home.

I slept.

I woke.

I had to pee and move my bowels somewhat urgently. I went out of my room to the empty one beyond and through the door to the left just in time to get onto the toilet seat before having fairly explosive diarrhea. Sure enough, in the bowl were numerous undigested grains of barley, wheat, wild rice and a few others. The old man was going to hear about this in detail I thought. I thought I'd get into a lengthy discussion of the odor also.

I showered and put on my robe and slippers. I was now hungry again and my stomach rumbled as I walked into the empty room outside of my sleeping place. It was the dining room, and the old man was sitting in the same chair. The same bowl of food and glass of water were sitting where they had been also.

I sat and looked at the grain mixture.

"What is good for you at one meal is good for you at another," he said.

I thought about the detailed description of my stool that I was going to use to gross him out. The smell of it instantly filled my nostrils and I saw it in my bowl instead of the freshly cooked meal that had been there. This resulted in my dropping my spoon and I stood up to retrieve it.

When I sat down, my food was food again.

"Childish one, do you think that I do not know what shit looks and smells like?"

I blushed. What a jerk I was!

The old one continued, "You are a newborn in this world and have so much to learn. You will be here for many decades I fear, and even then I have little hope of you finishing before your body gives out on you." He was shaking his head slowly.

"Decades?" I asked incredulous.

"You've just started pre-school, my friend, and you failed your first lesson miserably. Do you now expect to graduate with honors tomorrow?"

"Pre-school?"

"You must learn to be. How long this takes will be up to the seriousness with which you take your lessons. You should have learned that every action, every decision, every thought has a consequence. You bounce around like a baby in a crib without thought for what each movement means. You will fall and hit your head on the bars of your crib if you are not more careful. I would not like to have to hold the courtyard door open for you so you can exit."

"I do not want to exit." I said this hurriedly.

"Then pay attention. You have no idea what paying attention is all about, but it is the first thing you must master."

"May I go now?" I asked. I was falling asleep again as I sat there.

"You may always go and you may always come."

I went through the closest door expecting my bedroom to be beyond it regardless of which door I chose. It was.

I sat rather than going to sleep. I thought about being here for decades. I thought about how much there must be to learn if it was to take decades to learn it. I thought about the darkness inside me, where I knew not. I thought about decades of meals of the same grain mixture, the same bed, the same bathroom. The only thing that gave me hope was that there would also be the same old man there to help me. I thought deeply about these things and soon left my body.

The old man was there, but he was very different. I could tell it was him but he was a monumental web of blackness the likes of which I had never seen or even imagined possible. He moved over to me and enveloped me in black tentacles against which I seemed to have no defense.

It was excruciating. I had not known that such pain could exist. All of my energy was being drained and I could feel and see myself becoming a hollow shell, a mere shadow of my former form.

A blinding light removed all vision, all senses in fact. Suddenly I felt as if I had been pulled through a narrow opening, like what it must be like to pass through a mother's birth canal.

I was sitting on my bed and the old man was standing before me breathing heavily. He was actually angry, an emotion which I had not expected him to be capable.

"This room is for sleep. When you wish to travel outside you must do so with a guide."

Several other people entered, real people I had not seen before. They helped me stand and I was surprised to learn that I actually needed the help. When we exited my room, we were in the dining room and there was a bowl of gruel on the table with a large glass of water. The food was the same but had been essentially liquefied for me so I would not have to chew and in fact I was not sure that I could.

I ate until I could no longer and was carried back to my room where I slept. For the next several days this is all I did.

When I was able to move on my own I went into the dining room on my own and found an old man. This was not the same old man.

"Where is the other old man?" I asked.

"He is here, but he is busy elsewhere," was the reply.

I ate a little. "Will he be back?" I asked between bites.

"Perhaps."

"Who will I learn from?"

"From who you are with."

I felt adrift. I had assumed that the old man in my numerous visions was somehow to be my personal guru. The one who would guide me through "decades" of discovery.

"When you assume you will not see," the old one before me stated.

The original old guy came in. "We do not know how long you will be with us. It could be years, it could be many years, but you must trust us, take small steps. Do not think a thought without thinking about the consequences of that thought first. When you can do this you will be ready to leave.

"Your destiny is to the west. Your talents will be desperately needed. You cannot know the importance of what you will be asked to do. This is not a game, a voluntary schooling that you have begun by chance."

He moved closer to me, almost threatening.

"You must take each movement of your physical and spiritual mind and body very seriously."

He was right in my face now and I began to see the darkness within him, the darkness that had almost killed me. I was sweating with fear, wanting to scream. He pushed his face impossibly into mine, our flesh actually merging with terrible pain. He said, "Study. Concentrate. You must not fail."

THIRTY

Some time had passed, how much I do not know. It was many years but I do not think decades. The workings of this school were now as familiar to me as my home when I was a child. It was a thing of beauty. If you walked through a door with an objective in mind, the room you entered would have that objective. It was a temple of many rooms, infinite in fact.

All these rooms were not necessary now. My needs were few. Food, sleep, elimination and learning. I thought of the old man and food. I walked through the door from my room and he was there, a steaming bowl of grains across from him.

"You did well with the eleven-year students today," the old one said.

"Their first trip into the anti-matter universe was as enjoyable as you said it would be. The fear on the patterns of the students was a sight to see." I smiled as I finished this statement.

"Your pattern was the funniest of all I've seen," was the response.

"This universe we call ours, so many think it is not unique. So many think that the life on this very planet is not unique and that there are billions of similar planets in this universe with similar conditions and with life."

"When they are ready to learn, they will learn."

"Is this part of what I am to bring to them?"

"Perhaps."

I smiled. I wondered how many times I had heard that response. I knew immediately of course.

"Walk with me," the old one said.

I had never heard any elder make such a request.

We walked into the classroom and sat on our respective pillows. We leapt into the universe. The old master's form outshone the brightest stars and his pattern nearly filled the tiny container of this hemi-universe. It was breathtaking. My own pattern was barely 100 light years in width and I trailed

242

behind my master like an insignificant flake of snow.

We move to an event horizon and began passing through. This was not a portal to the matching anti-mater hemi-universe, it went beyond this. We emerged into the timeless essence.

The essence stretched forever, and now both of us were specks within it. Around us were a trillion universes, each like two birdcages fixed together apex to apex, spinning and rolling, exploding into existence and imploding into non.

All of the universes were seen in their timeless state. The birth and fate of all were visible. Some ended after nanoseconds of existence from their perspective. Some existed for billions of years, some would expand into infinity, but there was one, only one, with what might be a stable destiny.

We fixed our attention to our own paired universe and in one half, in one small corner, there was one small but bright light. No others had this light. It was the light of sentient life.

The essence had, in billions of places, condensed into what the humans considered a singularity, but of course their concept was naïve. Every universe started with a flaw, a different almost infinitely imperceptible asymmetry that allowed each to explode in a slightly different manner.

In trillions of variations in this initial state, trillions of universes were created. Hundreds of billions quickly faded. Billions persisted in a time state that allowed them to evolve. Of these billions, most evolved into poorly organized chaos. Millions evolved into organized clumps of matter and energy but few to the degree where anything subtler than subatomic particles were formed, a few atoms at best, temporary, fleeting.

Several thousand had elements, stable enough to exist for eons, but these remained in a boiling state, millions of degrees, and reached only five to six protons in size.

A few hundred had expanded and cooled which allowed heavier elements to form. Most of these had their matter spread as dust fairly uniformly through their allotted space.

Some were energy only with little or no matter, some were huge clumps of subatomic particles that could not move due to the lack of energy to give them motion. Every ratio of matter and energy existed in those universes stable enough to have both.

There were many where matter had formed stable heavy elements. Fewer still where matter was scattered in a way that would allow it to form masses that would rotate and gravitate in just the right way to form stable relationships with the matter and energy around them.

There were several where matter existed in such a rare state that compounds would form. A handful where these compounds were simple organic structures.

But there was one and only one universe whose matter to energy ratio was one. One and only one where matter swirled in giant wheel-like structures. And in all these billions of stable structures only one had the subtle interactions that would allow for the development of more complex organic molecules that would be able to self-replicate. In one and only one galaxy, one and only one solar system, one and only one planet, would these molecules replicate and duplicate and grow in complexity. Only one where there was stability and just the right mix of elements and temperature to allow these molecules to form structures that could respond and adapt to their environment.

One place where these structures became complex enough to look up into the sky and wonder what the sky was. There was one place where the essence had succeeded in producing a container in a time state place where that essence could be held and exist in time. Exist in a state where all was not known, a state with a past and a future, and most importantly, a future that could not be seen because of the choices these organic vessels that came to call themselves man could make.

Even the most complex universal structure was predictable based upon its initial characteristics. The key was to arrive at a state where unpredictability could evolve. And this one universe had it. There was no way to predict, even with every variable known, what choice a man would make.

There was a dark place where even the essence could not go. That place was the future of this one universe as it evolved in time. Only as it expanded and the life upon that one planet grew would its future unfold. All was seen, all was known, all was timeless until one sentient being made a choice that made no sense.

The future of this one place disappeared and would only continue at the pace dictated by the time/gravitational-matter-energy state. And the behaviors and decisions of man.

One place. One place so precious, one place that could save the essence from infinite instantaneousness. The simple being in all places at all times at once where nothing could ever change.

One place to be nurtured, cared for. One place where the essence could exist within each man and NOT KNOW.

Only if this place continued would there be an unknown future. After trillions of attempts, the essence had succeeded. Too well. The creatures that had evolved as a receptacle of the essence had too much choice. They had come to a point where they could choose to destroy themselves.

The essence shuddered at the possibility of the unknown future that might once again imprison it in a timeless all-knowing state. What care had to be taken.

Some people had lifted their own essence out of their bodies, but the trials and tribulations of these beings were massive and often fatal. Some had succeeded. Some had finally found the pathway out of the universe and back to the essence outside of time. Some had had an influence on those they left behind that gave the essence hope, something it could not have in timelessness.

To the essence, the absence of hope was hell.

Some tiny fragments of human essence would escape completely, grow to where they would no longer fit in the universe in which they formed. They would exit that universe and merge back into the infinite essence from which they came. And this would give the essence strength. The strength to keep caring, to keep the experiment going, to wait and see what man would do with his infinite power. To see if man could make decisions to a point where they could all reunite and with that power and knowledge form a single being in a time state place that could grow and evolve itself.

This merging into the essence was a rare event. Very few had made the trip. My master was one and it was his time.

I was not ready, not even close, and I might not ever reach that stage, but it was an honor to be here to see my master go. I hovered off to one side near a universe composed entirely of very cold hydrogen gas and watched.

Time came into timelessness. My master's pattern expanded and grew, stretched in every direction in this infinite direction place until he faded into the essence.

Merged.

And the essence was filled with hope because one more man had made it.

And I was filled with hope because I could feel my master everywhere now. Surely I would someday find my way back to him.

I returned to my little universe and to my tiny galaxy and to my minuscule solar system, where on a nearly invisible planet, men lived and without even knowing it, held the existence of all things in their grubby hands.

You just had to love these people.

I was back in the dining room. I ate a little. I was "blissed out" frequently and for long periods of time. I longed to be one with my master.

I went to the classroom. I sat upon my pillow. I left my body and hovered a few thousand feet above the one-room, one-courtyard ashram. I felt nothing, I thought nothing, I moved nothing. I was suddenly in the courtyard and so was my master.

"You would not understand," he said as he waved his hand at me in a sign that meant "don't even ask." He pointed to the tree. "Why is this tree here?" he asked.

"Because if it were not this universe would cease to exist," I replied.

"Explain."

"This tree is the very center around which this universe revolves."

"Go on."

"If the tree, once here, ceased to be here, everything would cease to be here."

"And if I cut down this tree?" the wise old man asked.

"The universe would continue as if nothing had happened."

"Because?"

"It was a choice."

"And what of the tree you climbed beside your house in Orlando?"

"It is the same for that tree for it is the very center around which this universe revolves. It is the same for every atom in this universe, every particle and every human. Each is the very center around which all else exists. Any that cease, destroy this universe and all other universes. They are here, therefore they must be. If any were to not be, all would not be."

I continued on with my discourse hoping to be moving in the right direction. "Only the free choice of a human allows for the alteration of this reality and that alteration can be destructive or nurturing. It can bring humans closer to annihilation or closer to reunion. Each human and each decision each human makes is of nearly infinite importance and yet we move through life with such abandon, such disregard, that it can be nothing less than humorous. One must be able to laugh, or every breath of every being would have to be fretted over. Only with humor can hope exist, and only with humor can we have faith in ourselves, and only with humor can the very essence have hope and faith in a future."

The old man and I flew within our physical form, him holding my hand, in an experience I had not had before. We flew west, over Europe, over the Atlantic, over most of North America to a bowl-like depression adjacent to a large salty lake. We flew into this valley, into a city, into a neighborhood and onto a sidewalk on a street called D in front of a house numbered 1582.

The old man motioned me to the door and vanished.

I walked up the short flight of stairs and knocked.

TIME
ONE
AGAIN

THIRTY-ONE

I got up to answer the door, miffed at being disturbed. I opened it and looked out upon an older, paler, sicker-looking version of myself. My head started to hurt a little as his eyes grew wide and his mouth fell open. I let him in and he walked in slowly. We couldn't take our eyes off each other. Everything seemed to be moving in slow motion. Just as I had turned from the door another knock sounded.

I ignored it for a second, staring at the ill man in front of me staring back at me. The knock came again and this time I slowly turned and gripped the knob, turning it and pulling open the door as if in a trance. I was there, with a fine coating of chalk dust on the sleeve of my right arm fading onto my upper chest. The chalky person's jaw dropped and my head began to hurt a little more. He opened the screen and entered. I did nothing to prevent this and the three of us turned to face each other in a small circle in my living room.

I think I heard a knock. We kept looking back and forth at each other. No thoughts or words could form in my brain and apparently this was true of the others. I think I heard a knock again and the others turned their heads to stare at the door instead of me or each other. I didn't think I could move, but when the knock came for the third time, I turned and opened the door. I had a feeling I would be there once again.

This man looked more weathered, but wise. In fact there was a love that shown out of his face, a love for me. As he moved past me into the living room I could see that same love extending out to the other two also.

We stood and stared. They all stared at me. My head was hurting more. We migrated to places to sit and stared some more.

"Well," I said with uncertain inflection so that even I couldn't tell whether it was a statement or a question. That word, forced from my mouth opened the mouths of the others and suddenly the slow-motion spell was broken.

Everyone started talking at once except for the last guy. The rest of us stopped talking and looked at him.

"All is as it should be," he said quietly and smiled.

We waited, but he said no more.

The man who had come in second asked me, "I heard you were building a machine that could harness gravitational energy, is that true?"

I looked at him suspiciously. I had talked to a few people on the Net about such a device but in theoretical terms only, or so I had thought. Events were so strange at this point that I answered truthfully. "Yes."

"How far along have you gotten?" he asked excitedly.

I cleared my throat and asked in return, "Don't you think it's a bit odd that we all look just about identical and have all come together here? Who are you people and why have you come to my house?" I was getting a bit agitated, as in about to completely freak out.

The second man looked at the others and said something about a strong resemblance but that he was here because he had completed the calculations that clearly showed that such an energy source could be built, but had no idea how to go about it. This got my attention, but before I could form my next question the first and sickly appearing man spoke.

"I'm here for the same reason. I got info off the Net that you were building some kind of power unit that would even outdo fusion, which is what I've been working on for years. I just think I was going in the wrong direction, bigger instead of smaller, and it was costing me billions of dollars to do."

I looked at the third guy expecting to hear something about the power supply from him. He seemed sublimely at peace.

"All is as it should be," he repeated.

The second guy chimed in with, "Tell me how far you've gotten? Do you have a working model?"

I was shaking my head. This was all too weird. I asked the first guy if I could get him anything and asked if he was OK.

"I could use some water," he said. "I've got colon cancer and it has spread to my liver. I only have a short time to live." He left out the part about the HIV.

I got him a glass of water but I also brought in a triangular bottle of Glenfiddich.

Seeing the bottle, the second and third men both said, "Pour me enough to float three ice cubes."

We all stared at each other. I had returned with three glasses, each with three cubes of ice, and poured enough to get the ice cubes to lift off the bottom of the glass.

I had assumed that the first guy wouldn't want any due to his poor liver function. He looked longingly at the bottle and said, "What the hell, I'll have some too. It's my favorite brand."

I handed the third guy his drink and looked at him a little quizzically. He laughed softly and took a sip, seeming to enjoy it immensely. He was the strangest one of all I decided. He nodded at me and winked as if he had heard my thought and agreed. I went to get the fourth glass and handed it to the first man.

We sipped in silence for a few minutes and stared at each other.

I finally broke the silence. "I have built the damn machine but I'm stuck. I don't have the money to buy some of the materials I need and I still haven't solved a couple of key equations that I need to finalize some of the specifications."

The first guy said, "I still have a few billion bucks around that you can use."

He said this in a way that made it seem like "a few billion bucks" was trivial and yet he was somehow believable. I shook my head anyway.

The second guy wanted to see the device.

I led them all down into the basement. I stopped for a minute beside a wall with some tools hanging on it. They looked at me a bit confused. I shrugged my shoulders and pushed on one of the bricks, which allowed me to swing open the wall and enter the hidden basement.

The sick man was apparently impressed by this. "Wow, I had a set-up just like this in an apartment in LA one time. Remind me to tell you that story. I just about got killed."

He was getting a bit tipsy from the Scotch. Between the fact that he hadn't had any in a while and the fact that his liver couldn't detoxify the ethanol, he was probably going to get pretty looped.

We stood around the machine. The first guy looked at it but couldn't relate to it. He thought it would be a torus of some kind. My machine looked a bit like a tall upside-down birdcage with wires running all through it.

The second guy kept saying "Yes, yes" over and over as he traced the outlines of the machine and the wiring. He then noticed a couple of black boards I had mounted on the walls with my scrawled equations on them. He practically ran over me to get to them, pulled a piece of chalk out of a box he had in his shirt pocket, that I had figured were cigarettes, and began furiously rolling the chalk in his hand while looking over my work. He also kept up the annoying "Yes, yes" chant.

He began erasing and I started to protest but he said that I had made excellent progress and that he could show me where I had gone wrong and how to fix my calculations. I could see from his figures that he did know what he was doing even though I wasn't quite sure what his assumptions were. He seemed to think that neutrinos had mass.

The third man walked to the board and asked what an unusual symbol meant. The second man stopped and looked at it also, but stated he had not seen the symbol before. The third guy's attitude made me feel like he knew something about it, but wasn't going to say.

"That's the symbol I use for gravitational/time energy. You see, they really are the same thing and I use this capital T with a tail on it to mean Tigr, Tee Eye double Guh Er, Time-Gravity, Ti-Gr you see."

The third guy was doubled up with laughter. The second man was mildly amused but guy three was going crazy. What a weirdo.

The sick man asked the obvious question. "Will it work?"

The second guy and I answered together, "Yes."

Man two with the mathematical mind stopped writing and we all moved back upstairs to think and talk and think and drink some more. We took up our previous places and looked at each other again.

"Where did you grow up?" I asked the third man.

"Well, my father was in the Air Force so we moved around a bit. I was born in Japan in 1955..."

"Wait a minute I was born there too!" the second guy blurted, but we were all saying this in one way or another.

"OK, OK, so we've established that we were all born on an Air Force base in Tachikawa on February 15, 1955. What else?"

"Our maid's name was Tomiko," the first man said.

We all exploded again into explicatives and exclamations about this, verifying that the same was true for all of us. We had all then moved to Germany, then to Georgia and finally to the same address in Orlando.

I was getting a headache. The third guy kept chuckling in apparent amazement. The first guy slumped in his seat and seemed ready to pass out. The second guy kept shaking his head as if he were confused and couldn't think straight or as if logic were failing him.

"Where did you all go to high school?" I asked hesitantly.

"Eau Gallie High," three similar voices said in unison.

It was too much. My head began hurting so much I felt nauseated. The second guy was holding his head. The first guy did pass out and even the third guy looked a little distressed. He and I helped the first guy into the spare bedroom and onto the bed, spreading a blanket over him and making sure he was breathing OK.

The second guy had stretched out on the couch, still holding his head. I got him a softer pillow and a blanket also. I looked at the third man.

He said, "Do not worry. It is very confusing but I think this will work out. We all need some sleep. I'll be fine here on the recliner."

The guy was so caring. I felt like he actually loved me. I just nodded and went into my bedroom. I took three ibuprofen with the last sip of my now watery Scotch and got into my waterbed.

My head was spinning. I still felt queasy. I couldn't imagine sleeping, but I guess I did.

THIRTY-TWO

I woke up with a bit of a headache and a bit of confusion. With a sudden rush it all came to me though, and I do mean all. It was excruciating. I rolled out of bed holding my head and ran into the living room. The couch had only a rumpled blanket and a pillow on it. The recliner was reclined but empty. Into the spare bedroom. The bed was mussed but there was no jaundiced man in it. Back to the living room still holding my head. The front door was locked from the inside.

Inside. That's where they all were. During the night's tortured sleep we had recombined, and my brain was in the process of assimilating three additional lifetimes. I had no idea how this had happened and was having difficulty separating my memories from the others. Flashes of wild sexual activity, flashes of blackboards filled with figures, flashes of men I apparently cared about but had never seen before dying before my eyes, flashes of barren mountain retreats and the face of a wise old man. I wanted to pass out. I wanted to go back to sleep, or if this were as nightmarish as it seemed, I wanted to wake up.

Instead I sat. For quite some time I sat holding my head. My cat wouldn't come up on my lap as if she sensed I was not myself, or was more than myself. It hurt to even think about it. It was like being forced to watch three lives unfold on a video set to fast forward, all three intermeshed as if being shown simultaneously on the same screen. And I had to make sense of it.

I'm not sure how long I sat there. It was dark again when I was able to pull my hands away from the sides of my head. They were stiff and my head felt wooden and heavy. But I was whole.

I could see now. I could see the solutions to the equations I had been unable to solve. They were beautiful in their simplicity and symmetry. I also knew where vast sums of money could be found so I could afford to purchase the equipment and materials needed to complete the construction of my power supply and the Vehicle that would use it. I also knew I had the moral strength to use this power wisely.

The last thing I knew was that it had worked and that I had succeeded in building the Vehicle and had won control of time. I knew because that was how I was going to send my consciousness back in time to alter my development along three divergent paths so that those three beings and my "original" self could come together at this time and at this place.

In no one lifetime could any one man gather the wealth needed to build my device while at the same time gaining the knowledge needed to solve the complex mathematics and yet also develop the spiritual strength to make it work to serve a greater cause.

In my not too distant future I had found a solution to this problem, a solution which required the use of the machine that no one man could ever build, but as three whole men in one, I now could. I held the universes in my hands.

Printed in the United States
22394LVS00006B/1-51